At seven o'clock the next morning, Angel left the house, not closing the door completely for fear someone upstairs would hear and come down. She ran all the way home, her eyes red and puffy from crying and lack of sleep, her mind in a turmoil. Who could she tell? Not Mona, that was for sure. She'd say she brought it on herself, then put it round the parish. Nor could she tell her mother, who'd be up to the house and cause a scene. Either way poor Mrs Gorman would be made a show of. And it wasn't Angel's fault. But maybe it was, she thought as she neared home. Maybe it's true what Mona says about me. Maybe I ask for trouble. In case I've committed a sin I'll go to confession. You can trust a priest. No one except him knows what you tell in confession.

'What in the name of God brings you home at this hour of the morning?' Aggie cried when Angel got home. 'You dragged me out of my sleep. Don't stand there, come in, child, come in. You look queer. Your eyes are like burnt holes in a blanket.'

'I was up and down during the night, running to the lav. It must have been the rhubarb,' Angel lied.

Aggie, getting the fire going, said over her shoulder, 'Rhubarb never agrees with you. Get into bed, you look jaded. I'll wet a sup of tea and make a bit of cornflour to bind you.'

'Don't let me sleep too long. Call me before eleven – I'm going to confession.'

'Lie down now,' said Aggie. 'I'll slip a hot jar in at your feet and call you at eleven. You'll be in plenty of time for confession.'

Elaine Crowley was born in Dublin, and has also lived in England, Egypt and Germany. She has had a variety of occupations, including apprentice tailor, a stint in the ATS, Avon lady and in the personnel department of British Steel. In addition to numerous articles, she has written six successful novels and a collection of short stories. Elaine Crowley is married and lives in Port Talbot.

By Elaine Crowley

Man Made to Measure
Waves Upon the Shore
Dreams of Other Days
The Petunia Coloured Coat and Other Stories
The Ways of Women
A Family Cursed
Wayward Angel
The Young Wives

WAYWARD ANGEL

Elaine Crowley

ORION

An Orion paperback
First published in Great Britain by Orion in 1999
This paperback edition published in 2000 by
Orion Books Ltd,
Orion House, 5 Upper St Martin's Lane,
London WC2H 9EA

Third impression 2002

A CIP catalogue record for this book
is available from the British Library.

ISBN 0 75283 420 7

Typeset in Great Britain by
Deltatype Ltd, Birkenhead, Merseyside
Printed and bound in Great Britain by
Clays Ltd, St Ives plc

Chapter One

Lizzie, the handy woman who delivered babies, washed and laid out the dead, bent over the woman on the bed, the heel of her hand on the woman's belly. 'One more push and it'll be all over,' she said. Wrapped in a towel and a piece of blanket, tightly swaddled, its head turning searching for the breast, the baby lay on the sofa. 'Push now,' Lizzie commanded, and pressed down with her hand. The afterbirth was expelled on to a doubled sheet of newspaper. Looking closely at the substance, which resembled a couple of pounds of liver, Lizzie smiled. 'Grand, every bit of it there, thank God. That's the boy that could finish you off. Leave a bit inside you and you'd be poisoned, not get it out and you'd be a goner. Bleed to death like a stuck pig before hand or help could come to your aid.'

She wrapped the placenta in the paper and then in several more sheets that were by the bed. She would take it away later for burning. On the hob a big iron kettle sang. Lizzie poured some of the hot water into a basin then added cold from a jug. She tested the heat until it was tepid, then put the bowl on a bedside table and began to tidy Aggie. She sponged her face and hands and in between her legs. 'There, now, don't you feel a new woman?'

'I do. I'm grand. Wasn't as bad as I expected. When can I have a hold of her?'

1

'In a minute, after I've fixed the bed. Lift up your bum and I'll give you a clean drawsheet. That's the girl. And now the pins.' She undid the rows of safety-pins from the back and front of Aggie's nightdress which had kept it from being soiled during her labour and delivery.

'There y'are, all clean and tidy,' she said, arranging the bedclothes. 'You can have her now. Put her to the breast, but only for a couple of minutes.'

Aggie gazed in delighted wonderment at the little face, kissed the soft downy scalp and stroked the little one's cheeks. The baby clamped her lips greedily around the nipple and suckled.

'That's long enough. Put her down now.'

Aggie laid the child beside her, and Lizzie opened two bottles of stout then poured them with a practised hand until a creamy top collared each glass. Handing one to Aggie, she said, 'Get that down you. Better for your milk than all the cups of tea,' sat by the bed and drank from hers. Froth coated her top lip which she wiped away with the back of her hand before she spoke. 'God bless and spare her, she's the loveliest child I've ever brought into the world. Not a crease or crumple. Neither red nor purple in the face. As fair as a primrose.'

Aggie glowed with pleasure, and again touched the velvet-textured skin of her little daughter. Between mouthfuls of stout Lizzie continued to talk. 'D'ye know what she reminds me of? An angel. She's the spitten image of an angel.'

'I thought,' replied Aggie, 'that angels were boys, little fellas or men – ye know, like Michael and Gabriel.'

'Well, aren't you the terrible serious woman? How would I know what's under their robes? It's their faces I'm on about. You know the ones I mean, the little ones you see flying round in holy pictures. She's the spitten image of one of them. What are you going to christen her?'

'Katherine, after my mother, Lord have mercy on her.'

'Well, to me that saw her first, she'll always be Angel. Mark my words, she'll grow into a raving beauty.'

Father Clancy, the parish priest, a distant cousin of Aggie's, used the pet name, as did everyone in the village, except the nuns in school and Miss Heffernan, the infant school headmistress.

Angel grew into the beauty Lizzie had foreseen: her hair was like golden floss, her eyes blue and, in a certain light, with a hint of violet. Few praised her to her face: it wasn't lucky to do so – you didn't want to tempt the ill-wishers, them with the evil eye or fairies, jealous of a mortal child, who in a fit of spite could mar a lovely face or maim a limb. Not everyone was aware of their reasons for withholding compliments – they were too deeply buried in the pagan past. Instead they found other ways to praise her, telling her what a good girl she was, how kind and obedient, never cheeky or answering back. They laid hands on her silky hair, touched her cheek, asked her to say a prayer for them before giving her pennies for sweets.

As she grew older she asked questions about her father. 'Why haven't I got a daddy?'

Time and time again her mother told her, 'Before you were born, before I even knew God was sending you to me, your daddy went to the potato-picking in Scotland and never came back.'

'Did he go to heaven?'

'That I couldn't tell you. The same thing happened

with my own father. He went to America and was never seen again. I think it was with us not having the "wiles and ways"! Your granny was a beauty, and in my young days I wasn't bad to look at. But neither of us had them. And beauty on its own won't get you far.'

'What are they, them things?'

Aggie promised to tell Angel when she was older.

The village was three miles from Dublin. The local men worked in the quarry on the outskirts, and in the tram depot, where preference was given to men who came from rural Ireland. For the women there was only domestic service.

There were two streets, and in the longest lived the working men and their families in small houses, some of which were owned by the tram company. These had four small rooms, two up and two down. Cold water was laid on to the kitchen, where meals were prepared and eaten. Children did their homework on the kitchen table, women cut out dresses and caring fathers mounted their lasts to mend the shoes and boots. The ironing was done on it, too, and in enamel basins the delph washed.

More industrious men, or those with forceful wives, had built lean-to sheds against the kitchen walls – outhouses where women had clothes-boilers, mangles and stored odds and ends. In the street there were a few one-storey cottages; some had half-doors, one a thatched roof, cold-water pipes in the minuscule back yards, and there were two communal lavatories to share by the cottagers. The cottages predated the tram company. They were believed to be two hundred years old. Some were whitewashed regularly, others neglected. In one of the neglected ones Angel lived with Aggie, who intended every summer to get a bucket of lime and give inside and out a lick of white.

Across the street, down a fairly steep slope, ran the river, hardly more than a stream, not deep enough to be feared when the children played there but with enough water for pinkeens to swim and be caught in ha'penny gauze nets fixed to the ends of canes. They were carried home triumphantly in jam jars, well stuffed with water weed, which was supposed to keep the fish alive. It didn't and they died. Cats ate them, or sometimes the children gave them a fine funeral.

Aggie often wished she hadn't been an only child. It would be grand to have a brother who would do a turn for you – whitewash the cottage, mend a leak in the roof – or a sister to confide in. But she could tell Lizzie her troubles. Lizzie was the only one she had been close to since her mother died. But Lizzie was getting on, and worn out with bringing babies into the world at all hours of the day and night. Sometimes you'd be talking to her and in the middle of it Lizzie's chin would drop on to her chest and she'd fall fast asleep. It's a friend of my own age I'd like, Aggie would think, but Mammy put paid to that. Never letting me bring anyone to the house, never letting me go into anyone else's home. Lord have mercy on her, I thought she was being hard on me then. I could play with the children in the street, walk to school and home again with them but never set foot inside their homes nor they in mine. And everyone else did that, were given cuts of bread and jam, pieces of blackberry tart or apple. I used to be so jealous and hated my mother for what she deprived me of. And she'd go on and on about their mothers. I can still hear her voice . . .

My poor mother, I didn't understand her then, didn't know what it was to be a deserted wife. And she so proud and having to go on parish relief, live in a house that was falling asunder, never able to buy a new bit of oilcloth for the floor or a bit of stuff to run up a pair of curtains, dressing me in the off-falls of clothes belonging to the children of women she cleaned for. Not that I minded the second-hand clothes. Sure most of them in school were dressed like that. But they had fathers who if they were off the drink sometimes handed over money, and when they did there'd be a big splash. Especially at Christmas or Easter.

By the time I was ready to leave school the girls no longer invited me home and seldom knocked on our door. They'd found their bosom pals, walked arm in arm together and told each other their secrets. They'd talk to me in the street, pass the time of day outside the chapel, as was the custom in the village. And if we met in the shops or outside Mass they'd nod and smile and comment on the weather.

But Mammy knew what was said behind her back: 'Couldn't hold on to her man . . . It takes two to make a marriage. How does anyone know what goes on between man and wife?' So whenever possible she shunned them, knowing their feelings for her were pity and derision. And once Aggie was old enough to understand, her mother drummed the same suspicions into her.

Being young, Aggie ignored most of what her mother said, but she was not bold enough to ignore the ban on going to people's homes or inviting them to theirs. 'Nosing that's all they'd be. And as for coming here, wouldn't that satisfy them? Seeing the dilapidated state of the cottage. "The price of her," they'd say. "Well,

6

pride goes before a fall, and she the one who thought herself a beauty."' And they'd feel smug that their men, drunkards though they might be, whose blows they often felt, were still by their sides.

Gradually, as Aggie grew older, she came to appreciate her mother's position: the real or imagined scorn, pity and backbiting must have crucified her. She experienced it herself, a dig here and there, a reference to women who couldn't hold their men. Eventually she had less and less to do with the others she worked with in the laundry and, without being vain, understood that had she been ugly or plain her lot might have been easier.

Then she met Larry and fell madly in love with him. They married and she was in heaven until he, too, deserted her. Then, at last, she could fully sympathise with her mother. Not only that, but she determined when Angel was born to instill in her what her mother had imprinted on her mind. And so that Angel, too, grew up with few close friends – except for Mona. Mona was like a leech. Aggie didn't like her: for all her family was generous, they were a sneering, jeering crowd, self-satisfied in the midst of their big family. Lucky too, there was always someone earning.

Aggie didn't envy them. She didn't envy anyone. While her mother was alive she had her for company and her mother's friend, Lizzie, the midwife, and there was her cousin and confessor too, Father Clancy, a second cousin once removed, but a blood relation all the same.

Behind the street, on a low rise, were other houses where the few professionals, the managers of the quarry and the tram company, lived, and a quarter of a mile from the village, in a large detached house, the doctor and his family. To support herself and Angel, Aggie cleaned some of their homes and drew parish relief. It scalded her heart that Angel couldn't have many things other than the bare necessities so she scrimped and saved to buy her a pretty frock occasionally or take her into Dublin for a treat.

If she was aware of being deprived, Angel never complained, never made comparisons between herself and other girls, never showed envy of her best friend, Mona. Every night Aggie prayed that something wonderful would happen to change their circumstances. Maybe one day her long-lost husband would turn up, loaded with money, and they'd live happily ever after. They could open a shop. Lots of women had shops in their front rooms. But she didn't have a front room, except the one used for everything, and a little scullery. In any case, she consoled herself, those who had shops didn't seem to make much.

To make money from a shop you'd want one like Danny Connolly's. That was a shop and a half, 'Connolly and Son, Provision Merchant' painted in gold letters over it. His father had added 'and Son' when Danny was born.

Aggie wondered if Danny would ever marry, ever have a son? He wasn't bad-looking. Quite takish, if you didn't mind his gammy leg and the high boot. And many a woman wouldn't. But he seemed in no hurry to get married. And sure why would he? Didn't he have all the comfort in the world? Even with his parents gone to their long rest, wasn't he waited on hand and foot by his housekeeper? And, unlike a woman, he had years before him. A man in his forties was in his prime whereas a woman of that age was 'an oul wan'.

When Danny was forty, Angel'd be old enough for

marrying, Aggie thought. Wouldn't it be the grand thing if there was a match there? Mrs Connolly, no less, on a par with the doctor's and solicitor's wives, living in the lap of luxury. And, the best thing of all, she'd have a good man who'd cherish and respect her. Always, after indulging in these fantasies, she'd smile in the darkness of the room – dark except for the dying fire and the little red lamp burning below the picture of the Sacred Heart – and remind herself that Angel, sleeping beside her, was still only a child with years in front of her. Then she'd kiss her daughter's forehead or cheek and settle down for the night.

When Angel was twelve years old, she had the flower-like face of a child and the body of a woman. The changes that had come upon her frightened her, not so much the breasts for all grown-up girls and women had those, but the hair that grew under her arms and between her legs. Sometimes she imagined it might grow to cover all of her body. She brooded about it, remembering a story her mother had told her of a woman in the city whose face was covered with hair. She had turned a beggarwoman away from the door, telling her to take herself and her monkey-like children off out of that. The beggarwoman had cursed her and said, 'For all you know it's a monkey you might be carrying.'

One day, when she could bear her fears no longer, Angel told Mona about the hair and how she was sure she was getting like the hairy woman in Dublin. 'You're the greatest eejit I ever met in my life. Everyone gets that – even fellas,' Mona said scornfully.

'Honest to God?'

'As true as I'm standing here.'

Angel was relieved, until she remembered how in the

summer she and Mona had gone into the river where a pool formed deep enough to swim. Angel had kept on her vest and knickers but Mona had stripped to her skin and there was hair only on her head. Angel reminded her friend of this and said, 'You're an awful liar, Mona, so you are.'

'I am not. It wasn't there in the summer but now it's growing. And in any case haven't I seen my sister's? And she says when the hair grows it means you're turning into a woman. And another thing that happens is you get the others!'

'The others? What's them?'

'Angel,' Mona's voice sounded exasperated, 'I told you before, millions of times. You're in gores of blood from down there. That's when you get babies.'

'But how d'ye get babies?' asked Angel, her face screwed up with worry.

Mona shrugged her thin shoulders. 'How would I know? My sister won't tell *me*. Not till I'm grown up. But the blood's got something to do with it.'

Angel felt sick and frightened. Gores of blood. She wanted to know all the secrets Mona got from her sister but at the same time hated her for the telling. When she talked about them she reminded Angel of a monkey. She'd seen a monkey in the zoo, with black hair like Mona's and little brown eyes, grinning the way Mona did too.

She'd seen a black panther in the zoo, too, but that was beautiful. Black, smooth hair, big green eyes and muscles that rippled. It reminded her of Johnny Quinn. She'd love to have put her hand through the cage and touched the beast. She imagined its hair would be soft and silky. But she was afraid. She'd love to touch Johnny, stroke his black hair, get the smell of him. Sometimes, if you were close enough, you got a whiff. It wasn't hair oil, nothing like that, just a smell that no one else had. But you wouldn't touch him any more than the panther. Johnny could take the head off you with just a look.

Boys got queer when they grew up. Johnny hadn't always been horrible. When they were small, he used to play with her in a gang of boys and girls, fishing for pinkeens, chasing each other in the woods, building dens and, in the dark evenings, knocking on doors and running away, hiding to watch people open up and wave their fists. But that all changed when they were ten or eleven. Just about the time when Angel began to notice Johnny's lovely smell.

Since he turned fourteen and went to work in the bike shop, he had been worse. When he had a bike upside down on the path to mend a puncture and you had to squeeze by him, he'd let on not to see you. She wondered if he'd change back, would be nice to her again one day.

She confided in Mona, who had no time for Johnny. 'All the Quinns are piggish in their manner. Me ma says it's after their oul fella they take. She'd kill me sister if she ever went out with one of them. Me ma says they'll finish up drunkards like their da and knock their wives about. Did ye never see the shiners he gives her? She does be black and blue all over, never mind her eyes. And in any case Johnny has his heart set on being a boxer and getting outta here.'

Angel was flabbergasted. 'Where do you get all your information?' she asked, in a sarcastic tone to conceal her shock.

'From my brothers,' replied Mona, 'so you're wasting your time fancying him.'

After leaving Mona, while Angel was walking home she remembered 'the wiles and ways'. Her mother had never explained properly what they were, something about helping you to get a fella. She'd ask Aggie when she got in.

Aggie had been soaking her feet and was now paring a corn on her little toe with a cut-throat razor – the only thing her husband had left behind when he went, apart from the newly conceived Angel. Angel kissed her mother's cheek and asked if she'd like a cup of tea. 'I'm that thirsty I'd drink one off a sore leg. Were you with Mona?'

'I was. We were talking.'

'Sometimes I think that young wan's too knowing. I hope she doesn't be telling you things, filling your head with notions. They're a flighty lot, Mona and her sisters. Thanks, love.' Aggie poured some of her tea into the saucer to cool it.

'D'ye know, Ma, I was just thinking about them wiles and ways. Is it true if you've got them you could marry anyone you fancied?'

'Oh, indeed it is. Them that's got them has been known to marry kings and lords. And one was an orange-seller in the street.'

'In our street, Ma?' Angel was all agog.

'Ah, no, it was in London in the olden days.'

'But she became a queen?'

'Well, no, because the King was already married. Maybe if he'd lived longer he might have married her. But her name was the last word on his lips before he

12

died. And many's the one that did marry lords and gentlemen and lived happily ever after.'

'What are they, these wiles and ways? You never said.'

'To tell you the truth, I'm not sure. Like, it's ways of doing things. The way you walk. Making eyes. All sorts of things.' Aggie put down her cup and saucer on the fender and spread out her hands in a helpless gesture. 'I don't know for sure, except that I haven't and never did have them.'

'Have I got them?'

'Ah, sure, darlin', you're only a child still. Maybe when you grow up. And if you're lucky to be blessed with them you can have any man you choose. Anyone in the whole world. Certainly anyone in the village.'

Angel thought about Johnny Quinn and hoped he was the one she'd get.

'Take, for instance, Danny. Now there'd be a grand husband. A little gentleman.'

Angel said nothing. As far as she was concerned, Danny was an old man. A nice old man, but old all the same.

Poor foolish Aggie went back to paring her corns and relating the news she'd heard in the village. There was talk of a strike. 'Everyone in the city will be idle. If it comes off I could lose my bit of work.' Angel, her thoughts still centred on Johnny, wasn't interested in strikes or whether her mother was in or out of work. In her mind's eye, she was walking past the bike shop having learned the wiles and ways. Johnny had noticed her, stopped her, and was pleading with her to go for a walk with him. Her mother's voice cut in on her dreams. 'Would you ever empty the basin and then brush my

13

hair? I've one of my headaches and the brushing always does the trick.'

Angel carried the basin to the half-door, looked to make sure no one was in the way, and threw the soapy water on to the pavement.

Aggie took down her hair. Thin and wispy it had once been the colour of Angel's, but now little of the gold remained among the ashy grey strands.

While Angel brushed it gently, Aggie talked. 'Father Clancy says he'll put in a word for you with Mrs Gorman. She's looking for a general and you're nearly thirteen.'

'Ah, but, Ma, I wanted to stay in school. Mother Imelda said I could be a monitor.'

'I know that, love, and wouldn't I have been the proud woman? But if this strike comes to a head and I lose the bit of work, how would we manage? But I'll tell you what, as a treat before you start work, we'll go to Dublin for the day. A special treat. We'll have our tea out and I'll take you to see the waxworks. That'll cheer you up.'

Chapter Two

'Thank God, isn't it a lovely day? It was like this the day you were born, thirteen years ago. The time does go that quick. Lizzie, God be good to her, said you were as fair as a primrose. It was her that put the nickname on you. She said you were like an angel.' Aggie continued talking as she and Angel made their way to catch the tram into

Dublin. She wanted to distract her daughter from brooding over starting work the following week. She was not aware that Angel's mind was occupied with Johnny Quinn, the fair that would come in September, and the boxing booth where he'd try his luck. She was imagining him being beaten to a pulp or, worse still, winning and going out of her life for ever.

On the day that Aggie and Angel went to see the waxworks, Danny Connolly whistled as he went about the shop. His friend, Brian Nolan, was coming to visit later in the evening.

They'd been in Gormanstown and had seen little of each other since their schooldays but for an occasional meeting in town where they talked about old times, or whether the Home Rule Bill would ever see the light of day. Brian was a Redmond man and believed the Bill would settle the Irish question. Danny was a nationalist and didn't agree. Their arguments were lively but never left any bad feelings.

Tonight, Danny thought, they'd have one of the liveliest with the strike brewing. If it came off, he'd be in for supplying his customers with credit: they were decent, honest people and he wouldn't see them short. He doubted that the strike would last long – between most of the clergy who, in the name of religion, would side with the employers, and William Martin Murphy, the biggest blood-sucking employer of them all, the strikers would get nowhere.

He blessed the day his father had opened the shop. He had left the tram company and, with a little money inherited from his parents and some land in the country left to his wife, they'd taken the plunge and opened the shop. Many a time he'd heard his father talk of the struggle it had been to begin with, the never knowing from week to week if you could make ends meet. 'But we did. It was hard work, but with God's help and a bit of luck we made it. I'm beholden to no one and I'm my own master. That's the great thing, Danny, always remember that.'

Aggie and Angel took the tram as far as Leonard's Corner. 'It'll be a nice walk from here. Plenty to see,' said Aggie, when they'd dismounted. 'Down there there's lots of Jews living, over from a foreign country. Some of them don't speak a word of English. And another thing, a lot of the women wear wigs.'

'Wigs,' repeated Angel, her attention captured for the moment. 'Are they baldy?'

'Not really. After they get married their heads are shaved, so I believe. I knew a woman who used to work for them. She told me. They've quare ways – don't lift a hand of a Saturday because Saturday to them is like our Sunday.'

'But we do plenty of a Sunday.'

'We don't sew or iron or anything that can wait till through the week.'

They turned on to the South Circular Road, and Aggie pointed out the Cock Church. 'I suppose it's got a real name,' she said, 'but that's what it goes by.'

Angel's thoughts had returned again to Johnny. She was wishing it was with him she was walking instead of her mother, holding his hand, looking at the big red-brick houses, picking out the one they'd live in when they got married.

'Are you tired, love? Maybe we should have gone on

16

to the Green, only this way we saved twopence on the fare. You can have it for the penny bazaar. And Harcourt Street's nice.'

They turned into it. The houses here were bigger than the ones on the South Circular Road – and Angel decided this was where they'd live.

'Over there's the railway station. You can go from there to Bray. It's a seaside place. I knew a woman who went there for a day and never stopped talking about it. The most beautiful place, she said it was.'

'When I grow up and am rich I'll take you,' Angel said, catching hold of her mother's hand.

They began their walk down Grafton Street. From previous walks there, Angel identified shops and smells. 'That's the coffee being ground in Bewley's,' she said. 'And there's the smell of the flowers from the dealer's baskets and the perfume and powder that the rich women passing by are wearing. This must be the most wonderful street in the whole world. A magic street.'

Sauntering on, Aggie drew Angel's attention to Trinity College – 'That's where all the rich Protestants go, and over there's the Bank of Ireland.'

They walked down Westmoreland Street, crossed the road and stood on the bridge. The tide was in, and for a few minutes they watched Guinness's barges going down the Liffey. Angel asked what was in the barrels. 'Porter going over to England,' Aggie replied. 'It's the best in the world. Ireland's famous for a lot of things. Sackville Street's the widest street in the world and the Phoenix Park the biggest. Maybe for our next treat we'll go there again, and to the zoo. You loved the zoo. I couldn't get you away from that cage with the black beast in it. What was its name?'

'A panther.'

'So it was. A queer name, that, for an animal. Still, I suppose it's because it's foreign. The penny bazaar's not far now. And we'll go to the waxworks too, of course.'

A military band crossed Carlisle Bridge, the music, loud, rousing. A crowd of young boys followed it. 'Some of them'll join up. That's how Tommy Maguire took the King's shilling. His poor mother was broken-hearted. You never know where you'll finish up when you join the Army. But sure maybe he did the right thing. He'd never had a day's work in his life. You have to be landed into a job – someone belonging to you in the know. Thank God you've got the bit of work with Mrs Gorman. They're a good family and the doctor's a gentleman. It's not far now. You must be jaded. I know a little place off Henry Street – we'll stop there first and have a cup of tea.'

Angel had listened to barely a quarter of what her mother had been saying, her thoughts still focused on Johnny. She was wishing she lived in Dublin, had lovely dresses and big hats decked with flowers, ribbons and feathers. Then Johnny might notice her. Arm in arm they'd walk down Grafton Street. She'd be looking up into his face and he smiling at her so the whole world would know they were sweethearts.

On the way to the eating-house, they passed through narrow alleys and streets of enormous tenement houses. Aggie said that once the gentry had lived in them. Then most of them had gone back to England because of a thing called the Union and the poor people had moved in.

Women were sitting on the tenement steps, laughing and joking, jeering some of the passers-by. They had

18

babies at the breast and small children playing round their feet. Older children swung from ropes slung round the lamp-posts while others climbed over the tall railings around the basement area. Their mothers screamed, 'Mikey or Paddy, Bridie or Mary get down before you fall and break your shaggin' neck.' On corners their fathers leant, smoking, coughing, hawking, spitting and laughing.

From out of the open tenement doors, foul smells drifted on to the summer air. Angel covered her nose with the piece of rag she used as a handkerchief, and pretended not to hear the remarks called after her by the boys: 'Are ye looking for a ride? You've got the makin's of a fine pair of diddies.'

After their meal of vinegar-soaked cold peas, tea and bread and butter, Angel and Aggie went to the penny bazaar. Angel was mesmerised by the sights inside: never in her life had she seen so many beautiful things, so many brilliant colours: gold and silver rings, bangles and beads, hanging from hooks on the wall; bunches of feathers, purple, pink, silver, blue, black, emerald and lavender; bunches of balloons, as many-coloured as the feathers; papier-mâché birds, trays, vases; celluloid windmills; spangled snoods, imitation tortoiseshell combs, ribbons and hair-slides; cameo brooches. All sorts of everything, and everything sparkling with fake jewels or glittery paint. 'Are they all only a penny, Ma?'

'Some's a bit more but not much.'

Angel bought three rings for a penny each, set with a ruby, an emerald and a sapphire stone. Aggie treated herself to a silver-coloured mesh snood, then counted the money left in her purse, took out twopence and gave it to Angel. 'Take this,' she said, 'I've still got enough for the waxworks and our tram fare.'

She bought a tiny box with butterflies on the lid and sides. 'D'ye like it, Ma?'

'It's lovely. It'll be great for keeping your rings in.'

They left the bazaar and crossed Henry Street to where the waxworks was. Aggie wasn't interested in kings or queens: she had come to see the murderers. 'Look at that fella! You wouldn't think butter'd melt in his mouth. Oul Crippen. Not the size of a naggin' bottle. Oul Specksy Four Eyes. Poisoned his poor wife, poor Belle Elmore. She used to sing in the music halls. I read every word about it in the *News of the World*. And he buried her in the coal cellar. Being a doctor he knew how to do her in. Mind you, I felt sorry for Miss Le Neve.'

'Who was she?' asked Angel, who'd been studying the figure of the little man with pop eyes and a straggly moustache.

'His fancy woman. I was glad she wasn't hanged. I don't think she had hand or part in it. And, to give him his due, he never said she did. He was mad about her. She was his secretary. Nothing to look at. When he knew the police were on to him he dressed Miss La Neve up as a boy and they set sail for Canada on a big ship, the *Melrose* – no the *Montrose*. Crippen let on he was his son but they got caught. Word was sent out from England by telegraph and that settled his hash.'

Interrupting her mother Angel asked, 'What's a telegraph?'

'I'm not sure, love, only that it was the first time it was used from land to a ship. I read every word about the trial. Sir Bernard Spilsbury nailed him to the floor.'

Angel shifted from one foot to the other, wanting to

pee, wanting to get out of this horrible place full of murderers who looked so real she could imagine one of them pouncing on her. But Aggie took her time seeking out men and women who'd murdered then been hanged, all the while giving Angel a detailed account of the gruesome methods used by the killers. It wasn't until her bunions hurt, pressured by cast-off shoes too tight for her, that she said, 'My feet are killing me, love. I know you're enjoying it but we'll have to make a move.'

As Aggie made her pronouncement, Angel's fear overcame her and she fainted. When she came to, an attendant was holding a glass of water to her lips and assuring her mother she'd be all right in a minute. 'Right as rain. Happens all the time to some young girls. It's their age.' And in a few minutes, although with wobbly legs, she did feel better. Once out of the place in the fresh air, she recovered completely.

'Only across to the Pillar for the tram,' said Aggie, 'and no saving on the fare. We'll go all the way home on it.'

Danny's housekeeper had left supper for him. She had boiled a tongue for hours, peeled away the rough skin and pressed it overnight. She had packed it into a bowl that barely fitted it, placed a tea-plate inside the rim and weighted it with two heavy stones. When she had turned it out, it had taken the shape of the bowl and jelly had filled in any empty spaces. There was another dish of pink, succulent Roscrea ham, its fat toasted with golden breadcrumbs, some beetroot and scallions. The cut-glass celery vase was packed with the whitest of stalks.

Brian and Danny ate, drank cups of strong sweet tea and talked, mainly about the threatened strike. 'Bad for business,' Brian said, buttering a slice of home-made brown bread.

'Aye,' agreed Danny, 'but I'll survive. There'll be plenty of scabs and the Protestant gentry. They buy most of their provisions from Findlater's but still give me a fair bit of custom. It's the other poor unfortunates I worry about, the ones who'll strike, who believe this time they'll get justice.'

'Nothing short of a revolution will bring that. D'ye know I was over the north side today – I wanted a few things from Eason's. Then I had time to kill and rambled up as far as Gardiner Street. You wouldn't believe the poverty. I was reading somewhere that Dublin has worse slums than Calcutta and the highest infant mortality rate in Europe. I can well believe it, too.'

'It's a place I seldom if ever go – the north side.'

'It's the same with me. Only, as I said, there were a few things I wanted from Eason's, books and a new pen. They sell grand pens.'

Danny brought a bottle of Jameson's from the sideboard and a jug of water. Then he and Brian reminisced about their schooldays.

'D'ye remember when you thought you had a vocation?' asked Danny.

Brian laughed. 'Indeed I do. I was terrified I might have. Though now and then I think being a priest would have been a better life than that of a school inspector.'

'What about Moira? Aren't you doing a strong line there?'

'I was, or thought I was, until she met the farmer from West Meath. She broke it off.'

'God, I'm sorry to hear that. I thought that was almost a certainty.'

'So did I. What about yourself? Anything doing?'

'I'm a confirmed bachelor. Forsook women as well as drink the day the Bishop confirmed me.'

'So what's that you're knocking back there?'

Danny held up his whiskey tumbler. 'For medicinal purposes, Brian.'

'You'll be forgiven for that, so.' Brian yawned. 'I'm jaded,' he said, getting up from the chair. 'I think I'll go up. The usual room?'

'The usual. I'll see you in the morning.'

They bade each other goodnight. Brian was almost at the door when he turned and said, 'There was something I was going to ask you the minute I arrived, and then it went straight out of my head.'

'What was that?'

'There was a woman and a little girl on the tram coming out. A mother and daughter, I'd say, the woman thirtyish, maybe. You wouldn't give her a second glance but I've never seen such a beautiful child. They got off the tram two stops down the road. I was wondering who they were.'

'Angel and Aggie. Poor unfortunate creature, her husband skipped it a few months after they got married. Never saw the face of his child.'

'And what a face. Not one you'd forget in a hurry,' said Brian, before bidding Danny goodnight again.

Before he fell asleep, Brian wondered what Danny would say if he knew the truth of why he'd gone over to the north side, how any time he came up to Dublin he always went there to the streets known as Monto of which Gardiner Street wasn't one.

There was a street called Montgomery Street from which the area took its name, so he'd heard tell. He'd also heard tell that Monto was the largest brothel area in the world. In the dark he smiled and thought of the girl he'd had that afternoon. He usually asked for the same one. A lovely girl, for all she was a whore. He was a new man after leaving her. Confession at the weekend, and he'd be back in God's grace. After all, he wasn't an adulterer – not that he'd enquired if his partner was married, but he truly believed she wasn't so he didn't consider intercourse with her a grievous sin. And his confessor was lenient and not curious, never went into details as some priests did, so he'd been told.

He wondered about Danny. Was he still a virgin? More than likely. A few trips to Monto would make a new man of him. Now, to another fella you could broach such a subject but not to Danny. He never talked smut, not even at the age when almost every boy in the class did. Maybe *he* should have been a priest. While pondering the question, Brian fell asleep.

Out of consideration for his housekeeper, Danny piled dishes and glasses on to a tray, took it to the kitchen then came back and sat for a while before going to bed. He'd enjoyed Brian's company. Evenings could be a lonely oul time. His mother used to irritate him with her constant talking even when he was reading a book but nowadays he sometimes longed for the sound of her voice.

He wondered would the strike come off, and if it did how would the men fare? Then he wondered what sort of a day it would be tomorrow. When the evenings were fine, he'd sometimes go for a ramble, walk until he came to where the river widened and deepened, where the serious fishermen were. He knew them all. He'd stop and chat. It was a grand way to kill time. He should get a dog. Then he'd have to go out every night, not only when the fancy took him. It would be grand company. You could talk to a dog and no one would think you were mad.

And now Brian was in the same position as himself, a bachelor living on his own, coming into an empty house, not a soul to throw you the time of day. In fact, Brian was worse off: he had no shop to go down into where he could fiddle with shelves, arranging and rearranging them, thinking up new ways to display the goods. He supposed there were reports to write up on the schools he visited and the teachers he observed.

Until tonight he'd envied his friend, thinking of him and Moira settling down, having a family. Brian might have asked him to be his best man and godfather to his first child. He'd have liked that. He must try and get him to visit more regularly.

He had deliberately kept Angel from his mind, and might have succeeded if Brian hadn't remarked on how beautiful she was. These days, Angel had a disturbing effect on him. Among the many children who came to the shop, she had always shone like a bright star, a quiet dreamy little girl, unaware of the radiance she shed about her, a good child, who never pushed her way to the counter. She was never cheeky or answered back.

Then one day, it must have been a year, maybe eighteen months ago, he had seen the change in her: Angel was no longer a child. When he handed her the paper cone of toffee, their hands touched, as they had many times before but until that day he had never been aware of the contact. Now he was conscious of a frisson of pleasure, excitement; his heart beat faster and he felt blood rush to his face. Angel had grown into a woman. She had breasts, their shape discernible through her thin, washed-out summer frock. She was a woman with a child's face. And her eyes were different, with a sleepy look in them. Sleepy was the only word he could think of to describe it. Sleepy . . . but something else. Then he realised what it was: for the first time since she'd been coming into the shop, Angel wasn't seeing him only as Danny the shopkeeper but as a man – though he felt certain it wasn't a conscious recognition. She wasn't being forward. Nothing like that. It was like a bud flowering. A happening in nature. It was definitely beyond her control. For, apart from her innocence, what girl or woman would ever regard him as a man in that sense? Only the fly, loose ones. A few of that kind bought in the shop, sometimes on score, and now and then gave him the eye when they were short of funds. He'd heard tell they wouldn't be slow in granting favours in return for a clean slate.

From that day he had tried to avoid serving her. He felt it was sinful to feel such attraction to the sleepy, dreamy eyes, budding breasts and rounding hips. For, when all was said and done, Angel *was* still a child. And unchaste thoughts were a sin, at any age. Night and morning when he said his prayers, he prayed for them to be banished and consoled himself that there was more to his feelings than lust. He wanted to cherish Angel, protect her, guard her.

He got up from the fire and went to bed, where he lay praying, still wishing that Brian hadn't mentioned Angel. For now she'd be in his mind until he fell asleep.

Chapter Three

The following week Angel started working for Mrs Gorman. There were four children and the doctor. Tim, the eldest boy, boarded at school during the week. Angel thought he was very handsome, but not as handsome as Johnny, nor as well built. He was pleasant and friendly, too, and had a chat with her when he came home on Friday evening before she finished for the weekend.

His sisters, Esther and Teresa, were twins, big girls for nine years, and the baby, Rory, was nearly two. Angel loved Rory and could have played with him all day, hugging, kissing and making him laugh when she tickled him. But, although Mrs Gorman wasn't a slave-driver, there wasn't much time for playing with the baby. The steps had to be scrubbed, the brass on the door polished – the doctor's plate was the hardest: the Brasso went in round the letters on it until Mrs Gorman bought a little brush and told her to use that. The vegetables had to be washed and peeled, the clothes laundered, the whites boiled and blued, and the shirts starched. After inspecting Angel's first attempts to iron shirts Mrs Gorman said, 'Angel, one of these days when I've time I'll show you how to do it. There's a knack to ironing shirts. For the time being I'll do them myself.'

Angel liked her. She was kind and good-humoured, told Angel she was a pretty girl and gave her clothes for her mother that still had plenty of wear in them. In cold weather, when the creases in her fingers and palms of her hands cracked, Mrs Gorman blamed it on the washing-soda and told her to dry her hands thoroughly before hanging out the lines and bought her Zambuk to rub into the sore places.

At Mass on Sundays Angel would look admiringly at the Gorman family, walking up the aisle to the sixpenny place where the solicitors, managers, Danny Connolly and the likes heard Mass. She thought Mrs Gorman looked gorgeous, wearing her musquash coat and velvet tam. The fur was in big panels, soft and glossy, and Mrs Gorman's face was soft too, and powdered. She told herself that when she was old and married to Johnny, she'd have a musquash coat and sit in the sixpenny place.

Now and then Mrs Gorman would tidy her jewellery box. She let Angel help her, telling her what was valuable and what wasn't. 'The girls bought me those earrings as a keepsake after our holiday in Tramore. I've so many bits and pieces, rubbish mostly, but I wouldn't hurt their feelings by throwing them out. Tim bought me that pendant. It's glass but he saved his pocket money to get it.' Then there was the valuable stuff: cameos that had belonged to her mother and aunts; the gold watch, cross and chain the doctor had given her, her engagement ring and bracelets; memorial brooches framed in gold, glass-fronted and lying on red velvet, locks of hair cut from her mother's and little children she had buried. 'One of these days I'll buy another box; one for the good stuff and another for the children's presents.'

Angel told her about the penny bazaar and the grand boxes you could buy there for next to nothing. 'If I go there again I'll get you one,' she promised.

One day Mrs Gorman gave her a string of blue glass beads. 'Oh,' Angel exclaimed, 'they're beautiful – but sure I couldn't take them,' she said, holding them up to her face.

'You can, so,' Mrs Gorman replied. 'They're the colour of your eyes.' She slipped them over Angel's head. 'My first sweetheart gave them to me.' A sad, dreamy look came into her eyes. 'We were sixteen. I loved him. We said we'd get married when we were eighteen, but my parents put between us. They were making a match for me with the doctor. He was more suitable, they said. They are for you. Well may you wear them. But in the house slip them inside your frock. The doctor's a jealous man.' Angel cherished them and wore them on special occasions.

When the doctor finished seeing patients in one of the front rooms, which was his surgery, or came home after his calls, he always had a smile for Angel. He told her she was 'a fine girl', always to eat her porridge and wear a scarf in cold weather. 'A scarf is as good as a heavy coat any day. It keeps the chest warm.' When he talked about chests, Angel noticed that his eyes would fix on hers. He was a fleshy man and had a big belly. Once, when he and Angel were passing in a narrow passage, close to each other – so close that their bodies touched – he slipped an arm round her waist and gave it a little squeeze. For an instant his fingers tickled her and she laughed, for she was very ticklish. But for all that she laughed and couldn't say she disliked the doctor, she often felt uneasy when they were alone.

'Sure you're asking for something to happen to you,' Mona said, when she heard what Angel had to say. 'You've changed since you went to work there.'

'How d'ye mean I've changed?'

'You're full of yourself. Lowering your eyes, fluttering your eyelashes and sticking out your diddies.'

'I am not. You're a terrible liar so you are, Mona.'

'If you don't believe me ask anyone. I think you have a yen for that Tim. That's why you're making calf's eyes. What a hope you've got! They wouldn't let Tim walk you home – not if Jack the Ripper was outside the door – never mind start walking you out.'

'I'm never going to tell you anything again, so I'm not.' Angel started to cry. 'You know it's not true. You know it's Johnny I love.'

'Another lost cause,' retorted Mona. 'Ah, look, I'm sorry.' She linked her arm through Angel's. 'You're my best friend in the whole world. Maybe you can't help it. Maybe it's being in a house with men for the first time in your life. Not like me, always in a houseful of fellas. Anyway, let's forget about it. Come on, I'll buy you a single.' Arm in arm, they walked to the chip shop.

After they'd parted and Angel was walking home, she thought about what Mona had said and into her mind came her mother's tales of 'wiles and ways'. Maybe she was getting them. Maybe you got them without knowing you were, for as true as she was walking home, she had never knowingly fluttered her eyelashes or made eyes at anyone. But wouldn't it be wonderful if she was getting them? Her mother had told her that if you had them any man was yours for the taking. That meant Johnny would be hers.

On her next Saturday off she walked past the bike shop. As usual Johnny was bent over a bike. Above the smell of grease, glue and rubber, she caught his scent and, emboldened by the belief that now she could charm him, she cleared her throat and said, 'Isn't it a grand day? I bet you'd rather be off for a spin on the bike than fixing an oul puncture.' He grunted something she couldn't understand, left the bike upended on the path and went into the shop.

She walked away thinking, That Mona's a terrible liar, so she is. Letting me make an eejit of myself. Wiles and Ways, how are you? There was no wrapping him round my finger. All I want him to do is say hello, smile, anything so long as he recognises me.

Johnny sat in the lavatory, not that he needed to go but it was the only place where Smullen, his boss, left him alone for five minutes. He shook one of his last two Woodbines from the green paper packet, lit it, drew the smoke far down into his lungs and thought about Angel. She was the most beautiful creature he had ever seen. From the time he had first noticed her running in the playground next to the boys' school he had thought that, and had fallen in love with her.

He chose her to play on his side in games, caught pinkeens for her, fixed the twine round the neck of her jam jar so she could carry it, reached for the fattest, juiciest blackberries and loved catching her in chasing games, holding her tight, feeling her hair against his face. Then everything had changed. Earlier for him than a lot of the fellas, he became one of the big boys, and too big to play with girls any more. No one had laid down this law. It just was. At a certain time, boys stuck to boys and girls to girls.

Now he was sixteen and the time had come when fellas and girls could begin trickin'. He could walk out with a girl, could get married, but he wanted nothing to do with girls – and certainly not Angel. He wouldn't trust himself with her. He didn't want to finish up like his oul fella, married at sixteen, ten children before he was

31

twenty-five, the talk of the village for all the Quinns were 'raggedy-arsed'. The oul fella beat Johnny's mother black and blue and they were looked down on by everyone. Well, he'd show them. He'd make something of himself. One day he'd win the Lonsdale Belt. One day he'd be the heavyweight champion of the world.

'Have you got the scutters?' The bike-shop owner had run out of patience. 'Cramps,' Johnny shouted back. 'I'll be out in a minute. You wouldn't want me shiting all over the path.'

'Oh, isn't that lovely language? But sure what more could you expect from one of the Quinns? I must have been outta my mind ever takin' on the likes of you. Hurry up and get back to that bike. I won't tell you again.'

For two pins I'd go out there and smather you, paste you on the wall, Johnny thought, and lit his last Woodbine. But I won't because I need the job – a few bob for my mother and a few for myself, for the magazines that keep me up to date with the boxing world.

One day I'll come back here and show them and if Angel hasn't already been snatched up I'll deck her in diamonds, throw the oul fella out and give me ma a bit of comfort and peace in her old age.

Early in the following week Mrs Gorman came to the kitchen where Angel was peeling vegetables for the Irish stew the family including herself would have for dinner. 'I was wondering, Angel, if you'd do me a favour. I know it's short notice and I won't be offended if you say no.'

Angel dropped the carrot she'd been scraping back into the basin, wiped her hands down the sides of her pinny and looked at the woman she had come to love almost as much as Aggie. Her gingery hair was never tidy, her face always had a flushed look, but no matter how harassed she was – and she was that, Angel thought, doing the doctor's books, kept talking by arriving and departing patients – she was always kind and thoughtful. Mrs Gorman was always at her husband's beck and call, or helping Teresa and Esther with their exercise books, sitting beside them as they wrote in them whatever homework the nuns had set. And then there was Rory, still cutting his back teeth: sometimes she'd be up half the night walking the floor with him – Angel often wondered why the doctor couldn't give him medicine to make him sleep. But there she'd be in the morning with a smile for everyone.

'Of course I'll do you a favour,' she assured Mrs Gorman.

'Well, you know Friday is my whist night and how much I look forward to it? It's great getting out of the house for a few hours – the cards and the chat and no rush on me, for whether the doctor's in or out Tim's home for the weekend and minds the children. Only tonight his father wants him to go to a smoker in the Antient Rooms. A concert and a bit of a social. He says it's time Tim got out a bit more into adult company. So that's cheerio to my night out, my one and only I might add.'

'And you're wondering if I'd stay on to mind the children. Well, of course I will.'

'You'd have to sleep in. Sometimes I'm late getting back.'

'That's no bother. I'll let me ma know not to expect me until Saturday morning.'

'The twins will be no trouble. They'll go to bed when you tell them. I'll get Rory off before I go and leave a bottle for him.'

'He'll be grand. Sure if he wakes I'll nurse him, sing to him – he likes that.'

'Are you sure you won't mind?'

'Of course I am.'

'I'll make it up to you.'

Angel knew Mrs Gorman was promising her money and wouldn't take no for an answer, so she didn't argue. 'I'd do anything for you. You're that good to me. I love coming here.'

'And I love having you. I don't know how I'd ever manage without you.' She gave Angel a hug before leaving the kitchen and said, 'Maybe you'll stay until you get married. Wouldn't that be grand?' They both laughed.

At seven o'clock the next morning, Angel left the house, not closing the door completely for fear someone upstairs would hear and come down. She ran all the way home, her eyes red and puffy from crying and lack of sleep, her mind in a turmoil. Who could she tell? Not Mona, that was for sure. She'd say she brought it on herself, then put it round the parish. Nor could she tell her mother, who'd be up to the house and cause a scene. Either way poor Mrs Gorman would be made a show of. And it wasn't Angel's fault. But maybe it was, she thought as she neared home. Maybe it's true what Mona says about me. Maybe I ask for trouble. In case I've committed a sin I'll go to confession. You can trust a priest. No one except him knows what you tell in confession.

'What in the name of God brings you home at this hour of the morning?' Aggie cried when Angel got home. 'You dragged me out of my sleep. Don't stand there, come in, child, come in. You look queer. Your eyes are like burnt holes in a blanket.'

'I was up and down during the night, running to the lav. It must have been the rhubarb,' Angel lied.

Aggie, getting the fire going, said over her shoulder, 'Rhubarb never agrees with you. Get into bed, you look jaded. I'll wet a sup of tea and make a bit of cornflour to bind you.'

'Don't let me sleep too long. Call me before eleven – I'm going to confession.'

'I suppose the baby wanted nursing. God bless him, he's a dote but a ton weight.'

'He had the back dragged out of me,' Angel lied again, as she waited for the tea and cornflour, which reminded her of wall-paper paste, but to keep up the pretence she forced herself to swallow it.

'Lie down now,' said Aggie. 'I'll slip a hot jar in at your feet and call you at eleven. You'll be in plenty of time for confession.'

'Bless me, Father, for I have sinned. It's two weeks since my last confession.' Angel began to cry.

Father Clancy recognised her voice. 'Stop the crying or I won't be able to hear you. Take a deep breath, now, like a good girl.'

Angel controlled herself and began to speak, lowering her voice so that those kneeling outside in the pew couldn't hear what she said. 'Something terrible nearly happened to me last night.'

'And what was that?'

'Well, you know, Father, that I work for the Gormans.'

'Didn't I get you the job? Go on, then, tell me what this terrible thing was. Take your time now.'

'I go home every Friday night, only last night they were all going out. Mrs Gorman asked me if I'd do her an obligement and stop over. D'ye see, Friday's her night for the whist. The doctor does be out of a Friday night but Tim's home from school and he minds the children only last night his father was taking him to a concert. So that's how I stayed.' She paused and the priest heard a shuddering sigh. 'Take your time, child, and go on when you're ready.'

'I'd just finished saying my prayers and got into bed. Then the door opened and the doctor came into the room. I thought maybe he was looking for something or going to ask if the children had been all right. Ask, like, while he was still standing by the door. But he shut the door and came right up to the bed. I could smell the whiskey on him. And then he touched my hair. Well, I didn't mind that only then his hand was on my face and I got frightened. I wanted to say something but couldn't think of anything. I was trying to get down under the bedclothes, like, bury myself. Only he kept pulling at them. He kissed my neck and was saying awful things and trying to pull down the quilt.'

'What sort of things?'

'I couldn't repeat them, Father. They were dirty things.'

'You're in the confessional. In here you can say anything. So tell me.'

Angel coughed and cleared her throat. '"Diddies, let's see your diddies," that's what he kept saying, and trying to strip off the clothes. I was praying to Our Lady all the time. Asking her to protect me. He'd got the clothes down a bit. Then I said if he didn't stop I'd scream. He left me alone then. And he said he was sorry, that he didn't know what had come over him. He took money from his pocket, a handful of silver, and wanted me to take it. I wouldn't. He tried coaxing me. "Go on take it. Buy something nice for yourself." I wouldn't. Then he got angry and told me if I mentioned it to Mrs Gorman I'd be sacked, I'd never get work anywhere in the village. "Who'd believe you in any case?" he said. Then he went. I was shaking with fright and thinking how if I fell asleep he might come back.

'So I stayed awake until I heard Mrs Gorman come home. I was safe then. I wanted to get up and run all the way home. Only she'd have heard me and I might have blurted it all out, and I'd have put the heart crossways in my mother coming in at that hour of the night.'

'You would indeed. What ails you now? Don't start crying again. Is there something you haven't told me?'

'I think, Father, it may have been my fault – you know, what happened.'

'How is that so?'

Angel sniffed a few times. 'It might have been my "wiles and ways". Mona says I'm full of myself these days. But I don't know that I am.'

'What in the name of God are "wiles and ways"?'

'Things my mother told me about. I'm not really sure. I think you have to make eyes, give certain looks, I don't really know. But Mona says I'm full of affectation so maybe I was to blame.'

'Now, you listen to me. Listen carefully and remember it always. You did nothing wrong. Forget about the wiles

37

and ways. That was just your mother talking nonsense. You're just a little girl that a scoundrel tried to take advantage of. And there's nothing I can do about it for you told me under the seal of the confessional. But you'll work there no more. Let on to your mother your back is bad. The work's too heavy. Any excuse. Your mother's a kind, loving soul, who won't force you to go back. Tell no one about it for very few would believe you. The doctor's word would be taken every time, although your poor mother wouldn't doubt you. You're a credit to her. God knows what Aggie might do. I wouldn't put it past her to attack that man and I can't say I'd blame her. But she'd be the loser, maybe get herself arrested. Promise me now you'll breathe a word to no one.'

Angel gave her promise. Then Father Clancy told her to make an act of contrition, gave her absolution and three Hail Marys for her penance.

On Sunday morning Angel complained that her back was killing her. Aggie sympathised and said she'd give her a rub of Sloane's liniment. 'Don't stir out of the bed. God'll forgive you for missing Mass. That job's too heavy for you. All that scrubbing and pulling and hauling and lifting that child. You're not going back to it. I'll have a word with Mrs Gorman. She's very understanding.'

She arranged the pillows behind Angel's head. 'We won't starve for the loss of half a crown. I'll ask Father Clancy to keep an eye out for something more suitable.' The chapel bells pealed. 'If I don't go now I'll be late. You've got everything to hand. Don't let the tea get cold.' Aggie kissed the top of her daughter's golden head, took her rosary beads from the table and left.

Though the room was dark because the two windows

were deep set and small, when her mother opened the door Angel saw that it was a fine day. The lads would be playing football after dinner. If she wasn't letting on to be sick she'd have gone to watch the match Johnny'd be playing. He was the best in the team, scored all the goals. He was taller than the others, broader. His muscles stood out on his legs – there were whorls of black hair on them that she dreamed about stroking. He'd have put a stop to Gorman's gallop. When they were married she'd tell him. She lay day-dreaming about Johnny and marriage, how she'd coax him not to go in for the boxing. He'd get a job on the trams and the company would give them a house. She'd have a lovely wedding-dress and go to Bray for the day. Bray, her mother had said, was beautiful. The sea was there. She'd never seen the sea. They'd be happy for the rest of their lives.

Her mother came home from Mass, and while she was making the breakfast told Angel all the news. Mrs Gorman had been very understanding. 'She's sorry to lose you but, as she said, your health comes first and any time you're passing you're to drop in. And Father Clancy thinks he'll be able to find you an opening. He'll let you know through the week.' She basted the eggs with bacon fat. Angel's mouth was watering with the smell.

'I was talking to Mrs Maguire for a minute. Remember, I told you about Tommy joining the Army. Well, next year he'll be off to India. The poor unfortunate woman and him her only child. She was telling me he may be gone for ten years.'

'I don't know him.'

'You'd have seen him about. A nice fella, good to his mother. You probably wouldn't have noticed him – he's years older than you. But, as his mother said, maybe he's better off in the Army. I don't think he's the full shilling. A gobshite, anyone could fool him up to the two eyes. But his mother's right, if this strike comes off there'll be no work. September, that's when it's supposed to start. Miss Heffernan was outside the chapel with her cronies. She never bids me the time of day. Always a miserable oul puss on her.' She wet the tea, laid an old tin tray and gave Angel her breakfast, then sat on the side of the bed with her own plate on her lap. 'She's terrible plain-looking – she always was, and age doesn't improve any woman.'

'I don't like her either,' said Angel. 'She was never nice, not a day in her life. I tried to be good but she was always picking on me. She used to pull my hair, blame me for everything when I'd done nothing.'

Aggie wiped a piece of bread round her plate, mopping up the bacon fat and spilled egg yolk before saying any more. Then, 'You know why that was?' she said. 'Because you resemble your father. She was mad about him. From the first night I walked out with him she stopped recognising me. As if he'd have looked twice at her! Apart from her ugly puss she was years older than him.'

'I thought I was the image of you and me granny.'

'So you are but there's a resemblance to him all the same. It's the way you smile sometimes. It must have crucified her every time she looked at you. Though, when all's said and done, oul Heffernan didn't miss much when he passed her over.' She took Angel's plate from her and laid it further down the bed. 'You enjoyed that. Will I pour you another cup of tea?'

'It was gorgeous, thanks, and I'd love another sup of tea.'

Aggie sucked the fat from her bacon rind, carried the two plates to the kitchen table and said over her shoulder, 'The other thing I heard was that the fair's coming in September. Mrs Maguire mentioned it.'

Angel's stomach turned over. Johnny was having a go at the boxing booth, she knew. He could be killed, disfigured, left like the men you saw with noses splattered all over their faces and cauliflower ears or, worse still, simple in the head. Every day, from now until the fair came, she'd say an extra decade of the rosary that he wouldn't enter the contest, and that if he did God and His Holy Mother would protect him.

Chapter Four

One morning the following week Father Clancy went to see Danny in the shop, beckoned him to one side and said he had a favour to ask him.

'We'll go into the room,' Danny said, lifting a section of the counter to admit the priest. 'You'll have a cup of tea.'

'I will,' replied Father Clancy, and sat down. The elderly housekeeper said the tea wouldn't take a minute, and after she'd brought it in told Danny she had to slip to the post office.

'That,' said Danny, 'is to let us know she won't be earwiggin'. So what's the favour you want, Father?'

'A job for Angel.'

'I thought she was above in the Gormans.'

'She was. But sure it was slavery.'

41

'The poor child, she was never meant to be a skivvy. The unfortunate thing is that just before you dropped in I'd promised to give Mona a start. But I'll take Angel from now until Christmas. See then how things go. I'm sure Martin Murphy will break the back of the strikers and that there'll be scabs in droves, but you never know. Larkin's a powerful man. Has great sway. And I've heard tell he can count on the support of workers over the other side.'

'I've heard the same thing. And wouldn't it be the great thing if the working man got a fair crack of the whip? But I have my doubts. I feel sorry for the men, but it's their poor wives my heart goes out to, struggling to make ends meet, with children, God bless them, like steps of stairs. How they'll manage on strike pay God alone knows.'

'Will you have a glass, Father?'

'I'd love to but I won't. It'd be just my luck to run into Miss Heffernan with her bloodhound nose and she'd have me on the Market Cross as an alcoholic. I'll drop in one evening and we'll have a few jars and at the same time put the world to rights.'

That night Danny couldn't sleep. Angel in the shop all day! His adored Angel. He said a few prayers hoping they'd lull him to sleep. They didn't. The pillow became lumpy, the bed too hot. His body itched and his bad leg ached. He got up and in the dark, went down to the kitchen and made tea. Sitting by the dying fire he drank it and thought about her and his love for her, remembering her as a little girl coming in with her ha'penny for taffy or sweets. The noisy children shoved each other, pushing, jostling, taking longer to decide on their choice than a woman buying a hat, but never her: she behaved as an angel would, smiling, friendly, saying please and thank you. A well-behaved, beautiful child, who he welcomed in the shop. Until the day he had seen the woman in the child. Now she'd be in the shop from nine till six, in the confined space behind the counter, where you couldn't pass without touching each other. It would be torture for him. He'd have to pray all the more fervently.

'I love the job, Ma,' she told her mother, 'I can't believe I'm being paid for it. Honest to God, it's like being in heaven after the way I slaved in the Gormans'. And it's great Mona being there. The gas we have. Some of the oul wans would drive you mad – 'Cut my rashers thick', 'Cut mine thin', changing their minds every five minutes, feeling the loaves and turnovers, taking ages to choose their biscuits. If you could see the faces me and Mona make behind their backs you'd die laughing.'

'I hope Danny doesn't catch the pair of you at it. Don't forget every customer means a lot to him. How's he treating you?'

'You know him. He wouldn't say boo to a goose. He's grand, really. And I'll get five bob a week. Of course, it might only be till Christmas.'

'Twice as much as the Gormans. We're quids in. I'll get you a new skirt for Christmas. God's good, and Danny may find an opening for you in the New Year.'

Workers belonging to the union were locked out by the hundreds, dockers, biscuit-makers, foundry-workers, tram drivers and conductors, men and women. Jim Larkin called meetings of strikers and those locked out. Small employers feared their businesses would be ruined.

The majority of the clergy sided with the employers. Martin Murphy, the biggest employer with interests in newspapers, in almost all places of employment, wouldn't budge an inch. Workers had no right in a say as to what they earned. He was a good, practising Catholic.

Many of the other big bosses were good-living Protestants and Quakers. And although they followed in different religions they were united in their belief that the working class deserved not a penny more than they earned already. There were mass meetings, angry scenes, baton charges by the police, who were reputedly fuelled and refuelled with drink to keep up the strength of their baton-wielding arms. Innocent bystanders were injured and two of the protestors, James Byrne and James Nolan, were killed, Nolan clubbed to death and Byrne dying of head injuries.

Because of the riots it had been decided that the fair would miss Dublin that year. Mona brought the news in to work.

'God answered my prayers. Now Johnny'll be safe,' Angel said.

'Feck you and Johnny Quinn. I was really looking forward to the fair.'

'Angel, come here for a minute,' Danny called, from where he was cleaning the bacon-slicer.

'Listen,' he said, when she was close to him. 'It's about your hair. Would you ever tie it back? Only Miss Heffernan complained that she found hairs on her butter. I like it as it is, but you know what she's like. Before you know it, every one of the women's Sodality will be finding your hair in their butter and rashers. You don't mind me mentioning it?'

'Of course I don't.' She was so happy that Johnny

wouldn't be trying the boxing she wouldn't have cared if Danny had sacked her on the spot. She was thinking all the while about Johnny's lucky escape and how by the following year he might have given up the idea of boxing altogether.

Chapter Five

Danny suffered torment when he saw men watching Angel in the shop. He had kept her on after Christmas, even though trade had slackened because of the striking men and those locked out. The scabs' wives bought their usual amount of food, and they were in the majority, but the women handling only strike pay and those whose husbands were locked out, purchased just the bare necessities. For, although Danny would let them buy on score, a time would come when the debts had to be settled, even if it was only at a shilling a week.

He'd keep Angel in the shop, no matter how bad business was, and endure his torment and jealousy as he watched the men and boys who came to buy cigarettes, which they could have bought close to home. He knew they came to feast their eyes on her. They smiled at her. Sometimes their fingers touched her as she handed them change. The older men cracked jokes, inoffensive funny ones, that sent her into kinks of laughter. But the younger awkward ones blushed when they mumbled what they wanted, stuttering and fumbling for coins, dropping them, every man jack affected by her looks, her presence. Everyone except surly Johnny Quinn, who was too wrapped up in himself and that body of his, yet who turned the head of every young girl in the village with his showing off on the football and hurling field. Now rumour had it he was interested in boxing, would have had a go in the booth if the fair hadn't been cancelled, hoping, so Danny had heard, to make it into the big time. It scalded his heart to know that any one of them, except those near their dotage or married, had more chance of captivating Angel than he had or ever would.

And so the spring and summer passed. Angel had her fourteenth birthday. Through the shop window she saw the children going with their jars and cans to pick blackberries. And Johnny Quinn still ignored her when she passed him outside the bike shop. He was aware always of her, wished he had an ease about him so that he could at least say, 'How's it going, Angel? Will'ye be going to the fair? Keep your fingers crossed for me.' But he daren't. Look her in the face, look into her eyes, and he'd be doomed. Doomed, as his father had been. Though love her he might, she'd be a stone round his neck that would drag him into the depths of poverty and degradation. He wouldn't let that happen. First he would make it as a boxer, secure his place in the world. Nothing would stand in his way.

Each time Johnny rebuffed her Angel consoled herself. He wasn't surly. Shy, that's what he was.

'That fella shy?' Mona said scornfully. 'He doesn't know the meaning of the word. Only nice, kind, gentle people are shy. I think you're mad wasting your time on him.'

'It's easy for you to talk. You're not in love with him. I dream about him, all sorts of gorgeous dreams. He's kissing me and stroking my hair and whispering in my ear that he loves me. Sometimes I dream we've just been married and there's a wedding breakfast and then we go to Bray. And have this lovely big bedroom, like the one the Gormans have. And he takes off my veil.' Angel sighed.

Mona was carried along with the tale, her expression dreamy. 'Go on. What happens next?'

'That's always when me ma shakes me and tells me it's time to get up.'

'Oh, you,' said Mona. 'You spoiled it now. And in any case you wouldn't still have your veil on. Not if you went away. Not if you had a proper wedding. You'd have changed your clothes. And how could your mother afford a wedding breakfast?'

'I told you it was only a dream,' said Angel, and her eyes filled with tears.

'I'm sorry, honest to God I am. You're too romantic, that's your trouble. I wasn't trying to hurt you. And for all I know maybe Johnny does like you. Maybe he *is* shy. D'ye know what my sister says is the best way to get a fella that might be soft on you to come to his senses?'

'What?' asked Angel.

'Make him jealous. Get another fella and let on you're mad about him. That usually works.'

'But I don't want to make him jealous. I wouldn't hurt him for the world.'

'Then suit yourself. Commere, this'll cheer you up. The fair's definitely coming this September. We'll have great gas at that. And do you know who I saw yesterday? Tommy Maguire. He's on embarkation leave. The uniform suits him down to the ground. I wouldn't have looked twice at him before but now I could take a shine to him.'

'I suppose he'll be going to the war.'

'No, he told me it's still India. He's a howl. There's always wars in India, that's what he said. I only hope my brothers don't join up. All them oul Protestant women done up in their Moygashel summer frocks and straw hats. Fecky-looking oul hats you wouldn't be seen dead in going round encouraging the young fellas to join up for King and Country. As me da says it's not our King and Country. Did you ever notice how the Protestant oul wans are nearly all skinny? Skinny oul shanks on them and no diddies.'

'They're not all like that,' said Angel. 'I like serving them. They smell nice.'

'I think they look all dried up. Not much of a hoult on them. Anyway, come down after your tea and we'll plan what we'll wear to go to the fair.'

Angel confided to her mother how she felt about Johnny. 'I'm mad about him. Don't you think he's gorgeous?'

Aggie looked at her daughter, who in her eyes was still a child. I do forget she's fourteen, she thought, and remembered herself at the age. 'You'll be mad about many a one, so you will. But that fella Quinn, put him out of your mind. There's bad blood in him. He's the sort that would take advantage of a girl then leave her in the lurch. His father was the same. There's many a child in the village calling the wrong man Father. Quinn wasn't fussy, married or single made no difference to him. The married women were able to palm off their bastards as their husband's. It was the unfortunate single girls I felt sorry for. Few of their families let them stay at home. They never showed their face in the village till after the child was born, put out to nurse or got rid of.'

'How d'ye mean got rid of?'

'There's time enough for you to learn about them things.' And to herself Aggie said a quick prayer to Our Blessed Lady to protect her child from ever being in a predicament where she needed to know about the women with crochet hooks, knitting needles and carbolic douches. God forbid such a thing should happen to Angel. So long as she was alive there'd be no reneging on her child. No packing her into a home run by the nuns for fallen women, either. And let the village put her on the Market Cross! She'd stand by her and the child she'd have, rear it and love it. Wouldn't it be her own flesh and blood? But it was all very well to think like that. Some girls didn't always confide in their mothers when they were in trouble: out of fear or shame they left home. The fear would usually be of their fathers. Thank God Angel wouldn't have that to contend with.

'Ma, you're not listening to a word I'm saying.'

'Sorry, love, I was wool-gathering. What was it you said?'

'I was telling you about the fair. It starts tomorrow night. Can I go?'

'So long as you come home at a reasonable time. And no tricking or laughing with fellas from the fair. Here today and gone tomorrow, fair people, a dangerous lot. Are you going with Mona?'

'Who else?'

'I was only wondering. She's terrible flighty. Don't let her lead you astray.'

'Can I wash my hair?'

'You'll do no such thing, not while you're unwell. You

could get a chill and go into consumption. Give it a good rub with a damp cloth and I'll brush it before you go to bed.'

Angel sat behind the lace hangings watching Mona fiddle with a long feather on the brim of her hat. 'It's gorgeous – where did you get it?'

'That oul wan me ma irons for. It was a garden-party hat,' replied Mona. 'The feather was broken, drooping, but I fixed it with a bit of gum paper. Yours is lovely. That blue suits you.'

'Goes with my eyes.' Angel laughed. 'Two little girls in blue.' She hummed a few bars of the song. 'That's us. It's nearly seven. Johnny should be passing any minute now.' She turned to look through the window of Mona's parlour and continued talking. 'I was awake nearly all night praying he won't get hurt and when I wasn't praying for that I was praying for him to win. That's only because I never want anything to go against him. But winning might be the cause of him going away.'

'You're not right in the head,' said Mona. 'He never even looks at you. Never opens his mouth.'

'He doesn't talk much to anyone.'

'So you keep telling me. My father was in the shop getting his bike mended and he said getting a word out of your man was like trying to get blood out of a stone.' Mona put on her hat.

'I think it's because of his family. He's ashamed of them.'

'So he should be. But what's that got to do with not having a word to throw to a dog? How do I look?' asked Mona, twirling round.

'Gorgeous. Whisht for a minute, someone's coming,'

Angel said, and peeped through the lace curtains. 'I thought it was him – Tommy Maguire all done up in his uniform.'

Mona joined her by the curtains. 'Now he's a nice fella. Not gabby, but he will salute you and always says please and thanks in the shop.'

'You can have him. He's ancient and, in any case, he's going to India. It's only Johnny I'm interested in.'

'Thanks very much. You're very generous. All the same, Tommy's not bad-looking and not that old. There's someone else coming. It's Johnny. Will you look at him? The walk of him. Anyone would think he owned the place.'

'Give him a few minutes and then we'll follow him,' said Angel, her heart racing like a hunted hare.

Dressed in their assortment of clothes, second-hand, borrowed or run up by Mona's sister, they waited the time then set out after Johnny. Angel wore a three-quarter-length dark blue coat over a lighter blue almost ankle-length skirt with a frothy white camisole, one Mona had lent her, with a daringly low neckline. Afraid of her mother's disapproval, she had worn a blouse over it until she arrived at Mona's. Whispering and giggling, they hurried to come abreast of Johnny. 'I'll say hello and wish him luck.'

'You'll never get sense,' said Mona, and complained that her sister's boots were killing her.

'I thought it was you,' Angel said, as they drew alongside him. 'Isn't it a grand evening for the fair?' She hadn't intended to say more but her nerves got the better of her and she gabbled on, 'I've been praying you won't be hurt. And praying you win. Is it right that there's going to be a man, you know, like, a man on the lookout for fellas that show promise?'

Johnny looked through her, increased his pace almost to a run and left the girls behind.

'I told you, didn't I?' said Mona. 'I don't know how you could make so little of yourself. I wouldn't do that for any fella.'

'You're delighted, aren't you? It's written all over your face. But I don't care. I love him, so I do. And I'll get him, so I will.'

'I hope it keeps fine for you.'

'It will. You'll see. It will.'

They walked the rest of the way in silence. Before they went into the fair, Angel said, 'I'm sorry for what I said. I shouldn't have bit the nose off of you but I was heartbroken. I'll die if I don't get him, honest to God I will.'

From the distance they could hear the merry-go-round organ and saw Johnny climb the incline in the road, then disappear from their view as he descended the other side.

Johnny was talking silently to himself. I might have said hello to Angel if monkey-faced Mona wasn't with her. Always grinning and giggling. A sneering jeer, that's what she is. I hate her and all belonging to her. One of the village clique that looks down on us. Thinks the Quinns are dirt. But I'll show them – them and my oul fella as well. I'd love to do him in! God, I hate him. I hate him for what he's done to my mother. You'd never think she used to be good-looking until he got his hands on her. Got her up the pole and left her till the last minute before marrying her. Any minute now he'll get the sack. More complaints from passengers about his language and being stocious. And me being codded up to the two eyes when I was a kid, believing every word he said. 'You're my son,' he used to say. 'I'll walk you into a job. That's how it goes, father to son.' Like a gobshite I was landed. A tram-driver. Set for life I thought, swaying through the city in my tram, like sailing a big ship. But I soon got sense, realised it was the drink talking. On his recommendation I'd have been on my arse. But I'll make it through the boxing. I'm good at that. I know that in my heart. Handy with my mitts. Quick on my feet, enough aggression and plenty of ambition. I'll come back here when I've made it. I'll show monkey Mona and her family. Money in my pocket. All the gear. Suits, shoes, overcoats. Someone to be reckoned with. Someone that that oul Heffernan and the craw thumpers from her Sodality won't be able to treat like dirt.

He swaggered into the fairground. The fella down from Dublin'll spot me, bound to. Not anyone as good as me'll be competing. Then it'll be time up in Dublin, training in a gym. They work you hard, watch how you're shaping up. Show promise and they keep you on, arrange fights – small ones to start off with. Slack off and you're out on your ear. I'll be good, battle my way to the top. And maybe then there'll be a place for Angel. Any fella'd be proud to have her on his arm. 'Angel, my wife,' I'll say, in England and America, and see the envy in their eyes.

'I love the hobby-horses, the colours of them and the way they go up and down. I could ride them all night. And the music, it makes me feel so happy.'

'I love riding them, too,' said Angel, 'but I hate their

53

faces. Horrible, wicked, cruel-looking faces. I'm glad they're not real.'

'Of course they're not real. Wooden things all painted, that's all they are. You come out with the queerest things. That's the boxing booth. And there's Tommy Maguire. I wonder if he'll have a go. I wouldn't mind having a court with him. And Danny's just gone into that tent where the fella does the card tricks. I wouldn't have thought he'd be the sort to come to fairs. Probably a gambler. I bet he looks a sight without his boot and in his coms. Fancy being married to *him*!'

'I can't see Johnny anywhere,' Angel said, craning her neck to look round. 'Maybe he went on somewhere else.'

'I bet you he came. The place is packed. He'll show up at the last minute. Draw attention to himself. Eh, look, Tommy's heading our way. Don't you let on that I fancy him. I'll kill you if you do.'

'I won't open my mouth. I hope he won't hang round us all night. If Johnny shows up and goes his rounds he might be in a good humour. He might even walk us home.'

'That fella walk you home! Sure he won't recognise you so why all of a sudden would he walk you home? Talk about living in hopes.'

Tommy approached them hesitantly, 'A grand evening for the fair. Have you been here long?' he asked.

'Not long, and yourself?' Mona enquired.

'The same as me then. Would you like taffy apples or a bag of monkey-nuts? There's a stall over there.'

'In a minute, maybe,' replied Mona, giving him an excuse to linger. 'I believe you're off to India.'

'In a week or so.'

Mona kept firing questions at him, but his eyes turned to Angel.

'How about a ride on the hobby-horses or the swinging boats?' he said.

'Great,' Mona said. 'Come on, Angel.'

Angel made an excuse that it was too soon after her tea. 'My stomach would get upset. I'll wait here till you get back.'

Mona gave her a look that said, 'You're afraid to stir in case you miss Johnny. But thanks all the same. I've been dying to get Tommy to myself.'

Round and round and up and down went the hobby-horses in time to Weber's 'Gold and Silver Waltz'. Ribbons and scarves from the girls' hats streamed behind them and their laughter floated on the air. An attendant moved from horse to horse checking tickets, collecting money from young men who had jumped on to the platform after the ride began – showing off, trying to impress the girls.

The naphtha flares were lit. More people arrived, swelling the throng. Enviously Angel watched boys and girls clicking. Outside the boxing booth, which was a large tent, two men were erecting a platform. People, mostly men, were gathering round it. Still there was no sign of Johnny.

Chapter Six

Tommy and Mona came back from the swinging boats, she carrying taffy apples, his hands filled with paper cones of monkey-nuts, unshelled. 'Did he show up?' Mona asked, after the nuts and apples were shared. Tommy excused himself and walked away to the edge of the field.

'Not a glimpse of him. Where's he off to?'

'To do something you can't do for him.'

'Did you enjoy the boats?'

'I might have done if I'd been with someone who wanted my company. I might as well have been on my own. It was you he wanted with him. That fella's mad about you.'

'Me?' exclaimed Angel.

'Yeah, you, and don't act the innocent.'

'I'm not. I never knew he fancied me, honest to God.'

'You get on my nerves sometimes. Every time a fella comes into the shop your ribbon slips its bow so you're fiddling with your curls, or making eyes or pouting. Anything to draw attention to yourself. Danny'll give you the sack one of these days.'

'I don't know I'm doing those things, and in any case they get me nowhere. Did Tommy say anything about me when you were in the boats?'

'He didn't need to. It was as plain as the nose on your face it wasn't me he was interested in – he couldn't wait for the ride to stop. He never even touched me. And when we got off he said, "Poor Angel, we shouldn't have left her on her own." Anyone would think we'd deserted you in Timbuktu.'

A man with a battered face came on to the platform in front of the boxing booth.

'Jaysus!' exclaimed Mona. 'Isn't he an awful-looking ticket? I wouldn't want to meet him in a dark alley.'

Tommy came back. 'An old fighter,' he said. 'Clapped out. He'll be asking for challengers any minute now.'

'Will you take him up on it?'

'Indeed I won't.'

'And you a soldier. I thought soldiers were afraid of nothing,' Mona said, needling him.

'I'd be afraid of the bruisers the fair puts on. Anyhow I've never hit anyone in my life. Eh, look, there's Johnny.'

'I told you, didn't I? I said he'd wait till the last minute to show up,' Mona said smugly.

Angel's heart skipped a beat. Please, God, don't let him be hurt. In a hoarse, flat Dublin accent the barker addressed the crowd, who were still mostly men and boys. Shabby men and boys. Boys wondering if they would take up the challenge. Men desperate for money, who'd been blackballed by their former employers for taking part in the strike, who might never again get permanent work. And then there was Johnny, eager to take a challenge, eager to be recognised as someone with talent.

'Here's your chance, lads, to challenge a three-times winner of the Lonsdale Belt. Three times Paddy Gaffney won it. Now it's his for keeps. Any one of youse who goes the time with him gets two quid. Knock him out and the price doubles. Do five rounds for a pound. You can't ask fairer than that.'

No one rushed to volunteer. 'What ails the lotta you? Fine big men. What about you there in the front? Sure you're like Finn McCool. A giant with hands as big as shovels. A dig from one of them and the champ'll see stars for a month of Sundays. And another thing, you could be spotted. There's a fella down from Dublin looking for talent. There's a great future.' The barker lit a cigarette to replace the one almost burned down to his bottom lip, dragged on it deeply then shouted through the flap of the booth, 'Here, Paddy, let them see the opposition.'

Paddy came out, stood on the platform, clasped his gloved hands above his head and waved them in the air. He had a well-muscled body, hairy, and tattoos on his arms. There was a shifting of feet in the crowd, a clearing of throats. Paddy danced on the spot and shadow-boxed.

'Sixpence admission. No ladies.'

Two youths and a skinny man, who looked as if the wind could blow him out, went up on the makeshift platform and shook hands with the barker, who said, 'Grand, Paddy's a welterweight.' The crowd gave a half-hearted cheer. The boxer and his hopeful challengers went into the booth.

Then the barker started his spiel all over again. This time he wanted big strong fellas. Their opponent was in the heavyweight class. 'A great fighter, went ten rounds with the world champion. Only lost on points.' The cigarette was clamped in the corner of his mouth and one eye watched the trickle of spectators begin heading towards the booth. He was an expert at counting heads. Another ten minutes and he'd have taken what he reckoned on.

The heavyweight champion came on to the little platform, and Johnny began pushing his way through the crowd. The crowd shouted encouragement. 'Good man yourself, Quinn. Show him what you're made of. Kick the shite outta him.' Others called, 'Big-headed Quinn, fancies his chance. He'll be carried out on a stretcher.'

Angel whispered prayers. 'Holy, Mary, Mother of God, don't let him do it. Blessed Mother of Jesus, protect him from that fella who looks like a gorilla.' Tears poured down her face.

Now the crowd was fighting to get into the tent. Angel couldn't bear to watch Johnny be introduced to the fighter. She turned and walked away, thinking, he'll be killed or his lovely face destroyed, disfigured for life.

Mona found her, grabbed hold of her. 'You shaggin' eejit, you've been crying. Sure Johnny'll dance rings round that fella. Make mincemeat of him. World champion, me arse. That's all lies. Everyone knows that. It's a cod to get people into the booth. Johnny'll smather that oul fella.'

'D'ye really think so?'

'Course I do. Isn't me father always talking about the tricksters in the fair? Biggest liars under the sun. Come on back. Them bouts last no time – one or the other gets knocked out. Johnny'll be the winner. They'll bring him on to the platform. See, sometimes an ordinary fella has to win – they fix it. Well, if they didn't, nobody'd volunteer so no one would spend sixpence to go in. People want to see one of their own winning. All tricks, all lies, but great gas. We'll wait up the front. Get a look at Johnny when he comes out.'

Mona pushed and shoved her way through those who hadn't gone in to see the fight, dragging Angel behind her. They heard the roaring, cheering, Johnny's name being yelled. The sound of a bell. Then a tremendous cheer. And voices saying, 'He's knocked him out. Johnny Quinn knocked him out.'

And then he was on the platform. The barker holding his gloved hand aloft. 'The winner, Johnny Quinn. Had to stop the fight before he killed my man. Keep your eye on this one, he's going places.'

Angel's eyes had never left his face. She saw him scan the crowd, saw him see her and his gaze pass on, ignoring her smile, her wave. He was deliberately ignoring her. She thought her heart would break. Then anger surged through her as she remembered her fear for his safety, her prayers for him. Well, it was time he was taken down a peg or two. She'd take Mona's advice and try making him jealous. And who better with than Tommy? She linked her arm through Tommy's, smiled up at him, pouted, lowered her eyes, fluttered her lashes. She ignored Mona's glare and devoted all her attention to Tommy, hanging on every word he said as if he was the only man in the world. Tommy thought he'd died, gone to heaven and woken to find an angel looking at him adoringly. Then, realising he wasn't dead and it was the real Angel gazing at him, he grabbed the bull by the horns and said, 'Come on, girls, I'll walk you home.'

Mona fumed inwardly because they'd come to her house first. She'd get her own back tomorrow, so she would. She'd never talk to Angel, the sleeveen, again. And she'd pray that never in a million years would Johnny recognise the sly, slithery one she had believed was her best friend. Look at her now! All over Tommy when she didn't give twopence for him and herself only dying for a chance to get him on his own.

After seeing Mona to her door Tommy and Angel went on their way towards her home. Already she was regretting having given him any encouragement – all the more so as she didn't think Johnny was aware of it: after his appearance on the platform the barker had hurried him inside the tent.

Outside her house Tommy asked if she'd see him the following night. She felt sorry for him: he'd been so generous, buying the monkey-nuts and taffy apples. And maybe they might bump into Johnny tomorrow night. In any case if she didn't go out with him she'd have nowhere to go and nothing to do for Mona'd give her the cold shoulder for a day or two. 'After work, Tommy. Meet me outside the shop,' she said.

Beside himself with disbelief and happiness, Tommy wanted to grab hold of Angel, kiss her and keep kissing her until she begged for breath. He controlled himself and kissed her gently on the cheek, then went away walking on air.

Johnny also walked on air as he made his way home. He'd spent the last couple of hours in the barker's caravan. The talent scout down from Dublin had been there as well. He and the barker drank whiskey and Johnny red lemonade. The Dublin man, Jackser, had outlined what lay in store for Johnny, if he kept up the promise he'd shown in the ring earlier. 'You've got the makings of a champion. Not for a few years yet, but it's there all right. You'll work harder than you've done in your life. And train until you'll never want to see another punch-bag, glove, ring, hear a bell, skip or look on another broken nose and cauliflower ear. There'll be times when you'll say, "Fuck it altogether. Why am I doing this? Wouldn't I be better off in the Army, digging ditches, heaving coal, anything rather than spending my life like this? And who's to say at the end of the day if I'll get anywhere?" That's where the belief in yourself has to come in. The ambition, the determination to be a champ.'

Jackser topped up his whiskey tumbler and continued, 'You've got all that it takes. I can see it in you. Saw it straight away. But only you can bring it out. Amn't I right, Jemmy?'

'You're right. You never spoke a truer word,' the barker replied. His voice was slurred and his eyes bleary. 'The makings of a champ, you have that, so listen to what the man says. He won't lead you astray.'

Johnny saw a glorious future ahead of him. Fame and fortune. Travel. England and America. Carnegie Hall. Another Jimmy Driscoll. But he'd mind his money and his health better than Driscoll had. He'd watch the drink and not spend his strength on women. So far he'd managed without them and another few years wouldn't kill him. When he was rich and famous he could have the pick of women. Maybe then he'd marry Angel. Maybe not. Time enough to decide that.

'I'll want you up in Dublin three nights a week. In the gym.'

'No bother.'

'There'll be no money in it for a while.'

'Yeah, that's gameball.'

Jemmy had fallen asleep, his head on the table. Jackser continued, 'If a training session goes on late so that you miss the last tram we'll find you somewhere to doss down. I'll see you next week, Wednesday. The gym's in a turn off Aungier Street, facing Whitefriars Street chapel. Up the lane and you can't miss it.' He stood, held out his hand to Johnny. 'Shake on it.'

Danny wasn't a gambler, wasn't interested in card tricks. He had gone to the fair hoping that he might meet Angel and invite her to ride in the swinging boats, on the merry-go-round or to have some refreshments. He hoped she might be alone but accepted the almost certainty that Mona would be with her. All the better, he had reasoned, for there wouldn't be anything unusual in offering a treat to two of his young assistants. A generous gesture, that's all it would appear to be.

It didn't take him long to spot the girls, dressed to the nines, giggling, looking ludicrously grown-up and yet like two little girls wearing their mothers' clothes. His nerve failed him and he slunk away, finding shelter in the tent where the three-card trick was being played.

He stayed for a long time. It was getting dark when he left. He saw Angel alone. This, he thought, was his opportunity. But then he saw Mona and Tommy Maguire approach her. Danny wandered away and moved through the crowd, stopping now and then to have a word with people he knew, meeting young men who had enlisted, sometimes brothers, sometimes fathers and sons who had responded to the thrill of the drumbeat, the young men for the excitement and adventure of going to war and the fathers in desperation after being out of work for months. They reasoned that nothing could be worse than being penniless, and having hungry children looking up in your face for food. He hoped for all their sakes that, as rumour had it, the war would be over by Christmas, and ridiculed himself for the fool he was: a cripple pursuing Angel to the fair where whole men were in abundance, men like Tommy, handsome in his uniform, Tommy who, when he came into the shop, was mesmerised by Angel. Tommy and all the others, including Johnny Quinn, like a young Adonis, whom he had spotted skulking on the outskirts of the field. Tonight Johnny was going to challenge a boxer in the booth, so he'd heard. He could well win. Often Danny had covertly watched him in the shop, his silent hostility towards Angel, and had felt instinctively it was a pose, a barrier he had erected deliberately to keep her at arm's length. The poor child had made her feelings for the Quinn fella obvious. Danny had a premonition that at some time in the future Johnny and Angel would come together and Angel be the loser. Disconsolately he began his journey home. Passers-by greeted him. He was well known not only for his honest dealing, but also for his pleasant disposition. But he had a poor image of himself. Every time he appeared in public he was mortified, believing everyone he met was aware of his short leg and the orthopaedic boot. In reality, though, people were used to his appearance and only noticed his smile and curly brown hair. They frequently commented to each other on his lovely open face.

In the house he poured himself a glass of whiskey. As the drink went down his spirits lifted. It was unlikely, but not impossible, that in years to come he might make headway with Angel. Say, in another four or five years. She'd be going on for nineteen then, and himself fortyish, not over the hill. And that fella Quinn might well have cleared off to America.

Aggie would be a great ally. Poor Aggie, a streel of a woman, coming to the shop in her trodden-down slippers, buying small quantities of his best produce, which he knew never crossed her lips. Everything was for Angel. Always when he served her, he gave extra weight – an extra slice of cooked ham, butter, a few more fancy biscuits. Aggie'd be all for a match between him and her one chick.

He poured another glass of Jameson's and dismissed Angel from his mind. He thought instead about his friend Brian, wondered why he'd never heard a word from him since his last visit. That was a year ago now. Perhaps Brian and Moira had patched things up. Maybe he should drop him a line.

Buoyed up with the drink he went to bed and slept immediately. He had a wonderful dream. He was sixteen, it was his last year in school, before he broke his thigh, before the row with his mother and father. She had wanted Danny taken down the country to a bone-setter, a man with a grand reputation. People came from all over the place to have their fractures mended. His father wouldn't hear of it. 'A bloody oul quack. He'll never lay hands on my son. It's Danny's femur that's broken and he'll have the best money can buy.' So Danny went to the orthopaedic hospital in Merrion Square and came out with one leg two inches shorter than the other. The expression on his mother's face said, 'I told you so,' but never once did she reproach his father aloud.

In Danny's dream his two legs were the same length and he'd been picked to play a game of rugby against Belvedere. Even in the dream he was amazed at the choice, for he had never been good at games, but in dreams anything was possible. Not only was he chosen but he was the best kicker in the pack. He'd never been known to miss a conversion. It was a glorious day, the trees round the pitch with gold and red and yellow leaves, the sky brilliantly blue, the first nip of autumn in the air. With his heel he marked the place for the ball, kicked, and saw it soar through the air and through the posts. His conversion had won the game for Gormanstown. The crowd went wild. He heard his name called, heard the exultation in their voices.

Then he woke. For a few seconds the dream lingered.

He opened his eyes and it was gone. He got up and walked towards the bathroom, passing the long glass, seeing in it a middle-aged man in a nightshirt, a lame man with one leg two inches shorter than the other.

Chapter Seven

For three nights Tommy asked Angel out. They went to the fair again and twice walked along the riverbank. Everywhere she went she hoped to meet Johnny, and for that reason always linked her arm in Tommy's, smiled often and talked a lot so that if Johnny passed he would think she loved Tommy and be jealous.

And Tommy, when he could get a word in, talked, though she heard little of what he said. She nodded and made what she hoped were appropriate noises in the right places, and all the while her thoughts were of Johnny, willing him to turn a corner and appear. She imagined him coming up to them, catching hold of Tommy, asking, 'What's your game, Maguire? What are you doing with my girl?' and punching Tommy on the nose, telling him to clear off before he got seriously hurt. She saw herself crying, pleading with Johnny to stop, explaining that she and Tommy were only going for a walk, begging his forgiveness. Promising she'd never, ever in her whole life even look at another man. In her mind's eyes she saw Tommy cowed, slinking off, then Johnny shaking her roughly and threatening that he'd kill her if she ever made so little of him again.

What she didn't know was that for the last three nights

after finishing work Johnny had taken the tram into Dublin, travelled on to Leonard's Corner, then walked through back lanes to Aungier Street. He wanted no one to know his business, no one to know of his trial run at the gymnasium. He didn't believe he would fail his trial period but, just in case, he was covering his tracks. He'd have no one crow over him if he didn't make the grade. When his mother had asked where he was off to he told her, 'To play billiards.'

On the third night after their walking out had begun, Tommy said, as they stopped outside Angel's door, 'I was just wondering . . .' Then he went silent and lit a cigarette.

'Wondering what?' asked Angel, not bothering to hide her impatience. He'd worn her out with the walk. Her feet were tired and she wanted to go in. Then, out of the corner of her eye, she saw someone walking towards them. Convinced it was Johnny, she put her arms round Tommy's neck and nestled close to him, almost making him faint with delight and giving him the confidence to tell her what it was he was wondering. 'What I was going to say was . . .' The figure wasn't Johnny. She could have screamed, pushed Tommy away and shouted, 'Leave me alone! I never want to see you again.' But Tommy now had a firm hold of her and said confidently, 'I was going to ask if you'd get engaged to me. You know I'm going to India and it'd be grand to get engaged before I went.'

Angel nearly fainted. Three nights they'd walked out. Their lips had only lightly touched each other's. It was all she allowed, and Tommy wasn't the insistent type. He was a dope – nice enough, but a dope all the same. She'd rather die an old maid than marry someone like him. Then she had other thoughts. Supposing she did agree to get engaged, a ring would surely bring Johnny to his senses. Engagement rings meant serious business. Johnny'd be bound to show his hand. He wouldn't want her walking round flashing Maguire's ring. And as for Tommy – he'd be gone. Off to India for ten years. No punch-ups with Johnny. Dope and all as he was, she wouldn't want Johnny hurting him. All she had to do was tell Johnny she'd only done it to make him jealous. They'd make it up. Then she'd write and tell Tommy how sorry she was for leading him on and send him back his ring. It was all so simple. So she said yes to Tommy.

He was thrilled, and hugged her so tight she thought he'd break her ribs. 'For God's sake, let go of me, you're squashing the life out of me and you'll destroy my coat. Throw that butt away.'

Tommy obeyed her commands, then nervously said, 'There's only one hitch. I've no money to buy a ring but I'll send you a beauty from India, honest to God.'

She was right, he was a dope. Fancy asking anyone to get engaged and not having the money for a ring! Sure anyone could say they were engaged, but without a ring there was no way to make Johnny jealous. She was about to send Tommy about his business when she had an idea: the rings she'd bought in the penny bazaar. Apart from the gentry and people like Mrs Gorman, no one in the village would be able to tell the difference. The blue one that matched her beads, she'd have that for her engagement ring.

'I've got a ring, a joking one. I could wear that until you send me the real thing. Come in and I'll show you so you'll know what to buy.'

'What about your mother?' Tommy asked.

'She's gone to a wake. She'll be there all night.' She

opened the door and he followed her in. As usual the kettle sang on the hob and the little red lamp burned before the Sacred Heart. Mice skittered across the floor and found refuge in the holes around the skirting-boards.

Angel got her jewellery box and took out the ring. 'Take a good look and then measure my finger.'

'What for?'

'So you'll know the size to buy. And don't forget the colour – it's called sapphire blue.'

'I'd better write all that down. Have you got a pencil and paper? And I'll have to have a bit of twine.'

'What d'ye want twine for?'

'To measure for the size of the ring.'

She brought the pencil and paper and searched a drawer of odds and ends for twine.

'Is it one or two Fs in sapphire?'

'I don't know, but sure as long as you can say it it doesn't matter. And don't forget the colour's blue. Write that down too. Here's the twine.'

'I'll want a knife or scissors to cut it.'

Angel brought the string and a knife . . . Tommy looped a biggish piece of twine round her finger. 'The scissors might be safer.'

'The knife'll do. Hurry up.'

'I have to get it right,' he said, bringing the ends of the twine to overlap on her finger. He fiddled with it until satisfied he had a good measurement, cut the ends and put the twine wrapped inside the paper with the description of the ring into a black leatherette wallet in his breast pocket.

Angel put the ring on her finger and forgot about it. 'You might as well have a cup of tea before you go.'

'I wouldn't say no,' Tommy replied, not sure if all this was happening or if he was dreaming. Angel cut and buttered soda bread, and Tommy, in a state of euphoria that blew caution to the wind, said, 'I was wondering if we could get married in the next few days. Then you could sail to India with me.'

Angel got such a fright she almost sliced her thumb in half. 'Married!' she exclaimed, and put her thumb in her mouth to staunch the blood. 'Are you losing your mind? Three days I've known you and five minutes we've been engaged and you're talking about marriage.' Her voice conveyed nothing of the fear she felt. What had she landed herself into? 'You're a caution, honest to God,' she said, trying to make light of what she feared. She knew nothing about Tommy Maguire. He might not be the full shilling. He could turn nasty. She remembered all the murderers she'd seen in the waxworks. Nearly all the victims had known their killers – wives, husbands, sweethearts, hardly a stranger among them. Oh, God, what have I let myself in for? And the carving knife's beside his hand. It was long with a yellow bone handle, sharp, very pointed from Aggie's years of honing it on the window-sill. It could pierce her heart in a second.

'It's just that I'll be gone for such a long time. We'll miss each other. And India's supposed to be a grand place.'

Angel looked at his pleasant face. Poor Tommy, she thought. There isn't an ounce of harm in you. I've fooled you up to the two eyes, God forgive me. But he'll be gone in a few days and forget all about me. There's no real harm done. So she laughed and said, 'If you didn't have the money for a ring, where would you get money to get married on?'

'My mother has a few bob put by for her funeral. She'd let me have a loan of it. We could have a quiet wedding. Our mothers, Mona, and maybe Mr Connolly.'

Angel was recalling girls, not many, who'd been pregnant and married. Not one she could recall had got married in a few days. The priest wouldn't allow such a thing, or maybe it was the Bishop. Someone, anyway. 'You'd have to talk to Father Clancy,' she said. 'He'd be able to tell you whether we could. Go and see him in the morning.' She knew that the priest was off to Maynooth after first Mass the next day. She'd heard him say so to Danny in the shop.

'I suppose you're right. And I suppose I'd better be off home.' She saw him to the door where he kissed her lightly. And she thought, Poor, kind, decent Tommy, not a bit free-making. I'm terrible so I am, making an eejit of him, taking him from Mona who's mad about him.

When he'd left she tidied the table, rinsed the cups, swept the crumbs with one hand into the other and threw them into the fire. She thought about lighting the lamp but decided not to. There was a knack to levelling the wick and she didn't have it. The flame could flare and black sooty smoke pour out, covering everywhere with smuts. So she sat, with only the light of the Sacred Heart lamp's glow, regretting what she'd done in getting engaged to make Johnny jealous. It might have worked if he ever got to know about it. But how would he? She couldn't wear the ring. Not because it was a penny one but because of her mother and Mona and Mrs Maguire. It would break Mona's heart – and Mona knew who Angel loved and that it wasn't Tommy. She and Mona could never be friends again. And after her mother and Johnny she loved Mona better than anyone else in the world. She took the ring off her finger and put it back in the box.

Her mother would be broken-hearted as well, and disappointed. Broken-hearted that she hadn't confided in her, asked her advice. And when she'd explain it was all a cod, done for a laugh, her disappointment would show. That'd be hard to bear. For her mother wouldn't rant and rave, wouldn't hit her. She'd sit with her head bowed and ask, How could a daughter of hers play such a terrible trick on poor Tommy? She hadn't reared her to be dishonest, or cruel to someone who'd never done her an ounce of harm, a poor unfortunate off to foreign parts with his heart full of high hopes. And then there was Tommy's mother. She was supposed to be a quiet, God-fearing woman and Tommy was her only son. Wouldn't she feel she had the right to be told, asked, even, about them getting engaged?

Round and round in her mind twirled her thoughts, like scraps of paper in a whirlwind. She couldn't distinguish one from another. Couldn't remember if she and Tommy had agreed to keep the engagement secret.

'If only Ma hadn't gone to the wake it wouldn't have happened,' she said, talking to herself. 'What'll I do? How will I get out of it? I'd run away if I could. But where could I go? And maybe there are times when the priest or bishop lets you marry in a hurry. In a couple of days. Oh, sweet Jesus, I'm destroyed altogether. I could be his wife in no time and off to India before I knew it.'

Sitting before the spent fire in semi-darkness, she cried herself to sleep.

She didn't wake until her mother came home as daylight was breaking.

'Ah, darlin', why aren't you in your bed? You look jaded.'

'I got frightened. I started thinking about Mrs Dignum. I wish I hadn't gone to see her. I hate looking at dead people. And yesterday she was grand, in the shop buying rashers. And today in her coffin and the little dead baby lying at her feet. Me and Mona went to see her on the way home from work.'

'They're in heaven in the arms of God and His Blessed Mother. Poor Maggie'd have come through her confinement but for the strike. Starvation killed her. A terrible proud woman – wouldn't ask for anything on score, though Danny would have obliged her.'

Aggie took off her coat, hung it behind the door and continued talking as she set about making a pot of tea. 'Starved herself to give to him and the children. Destroyed her constitution to feed her family. And I wouldn't mind, only the people of Liverpool and other places are willing to take the Irish children and feed them till things improve. The boats are waiting at the North Wall and good Catholics preventing them going. May God forgive them. You look terrible. Strip off and get into bed. I'll tell Danny you won't be in today.'

In the comfort of the bed Angel felt safe. Her mother would protect her. Her mother always did.

'Father Clancy made an early start for Maynooth. I saw him leaving the presbytery as I was passing.' Angel felt safer still. Maybe by tomorrow it would all have blown over. Tommy'd realise he'd been hasty, tell her engagements and marriages shouldn't be rushed into. But they'd agree to write to each other. She'd like that, getting a letter from foreign parts. She'd never had a letter from anywhere.

She nestled further down in the old soft bed, listening to what else her mother had to relate about the wake.

'Mrs Quinn never showed her face. It's seldom or ever she misses a wake but I suppose she's demented not knowing where that bowsie's gone.'

'Who are you talking about? Who's gone where?' Angel sat up, alert now that the Quinns' name had been mentioned.

'Johnny, the one that wants to be a boxer. He's vanished. Some fella from Dublin was filling his head with ideas. Anyway, so I heard tell the night after the fair, Johnny went off without his tea, left word he was going into Dublin for a game of billiards down around Leonard's Corner. He didn't come home that night nor show up in work the next day and hasn't been back since. The Quinns think it's something to do with the boxing. For all that he had his queer ways, Johnny was the one who stood up for his mother. Saved her from many a puck from the oul fella. An oul get, if ever there was one.'

Johnny's gone, Angel kept thinking, but where? He'd have little or no money. He couldn't have gone far. She'd comb the city until she found him. Mona would help – her brothers knew everything that went on in the village. They drank in the pubs. Someone would let something drop. She'd find him.

Her mother yawned. 'I'm jaded. I think I'll throw myself down for a minute. I'll only doze. Then I'll get to the pawn before the rush.'

'What have you left to pawn?'

'I'll make up a bundle. There's a couple of frocks Mrs

Devereaux gave me. Terrible yokes – I'd say she's had them since Adam was in the Highlanders – but the stuff's good and there's not a brack on them. If Tom's in good humour he'll give me two bob, maybe half a crown on them. It'll see me in for a couple of days.'

She took off her shoes and slipped in beside Angel, who put an arm round her. 'I love you, Ma. You're that kind. One day I'll make it all up to you.'

'Sure don't I know that, love. Try and have a little sleep, there's a good girl.' Cuddling up to each other they both slept.

'He's away for the day, gone to Maynooth. You'll catch him in the morning after ten Mass.'

Tommy thanked the priest's housekeeper and went looking for Angel in Connolly's.

Mona told him she wasn't in. 'She must have a cold or something. I expect her ma'll be in later on to tell us.' She looked at him with adoring eyes. The more often she saw him the more she fancied him. 'Could I give her a message, like tell her ma you were looking for her?'

'No, it was nothing really. I'll see her again.'

'You're looking all spruced up,' said Mona. 'The uniform's very becoming. You keep it lovely.'

He smiled. 'I gave it a good bang of the iron last night. It's not always this smart.'

'Were you going somewhere special today, then?'

He almost blurted out about the priest but stopped himself in time and told a white lie. 'Nowhere. I just thought I'd better get back in practice with spit and polish. I'll soon be finished the leave and then back to barracks.'

'And then,' said Mona, almost on the verge of tears, 'off to India.'

'Aye, in a few days.'

She leant across the counter, gazing earnestly at him. 'Would you do me a favour, Tommy? I'd never tell a soul. Would you ever drop me a line from out there? Would you do that, Tommy?'

Once again, because he wasn't in the habit of telling lies, he nearly said, 'But I'm engaged to Angel. We might even get married before I sail, so I couldn't write to you. It wouldn't be the right thing to do.' But in time he remembered that he wasn't sure if Angel wanted everything kept secret for the time being. He told another little lie. 'I will. I'll do that. Only don't expect a letter in a hurry. They take ages to come from there.'

And he thought, Where's the harm in it? Mona'll forget I promised. And Angel'll never know that I did.

And Mona thought, That Angel, fooling him up to the two eyes, letting on she likes him, all to make Johnny jealous. He'll get no letters from her, and I might be in with a chance. Though ten years is a long time. Still, I'm only fourteen. If we keep writing, and God spares us both, I'd be the right age to marry when he comes home. In any case, there's no harm in trying.

Tommy went to the ten o'clock funeral Mass. Maggie Dignum's coffin was in the centre aisle, close to the altar, her husband and her many small children filling a pew. The ten Mass was popular: it gave the women time to wash up, make the beds, put a stew on to simmer, hear Mass and buy their messages on the way home. The church was almost full.

Tommy looked at the cheap coffin. No wreaths rested

on the lid, only a bunch of wild flowers – picked by Maggie's older children he guessed – bound with a piece of twine, the ends straggling down. He remembered Maggie from school. She had been one of the big girls when he was in the high babies. Everyone used the same playground. One day he fell, or was pushed over, and grazed his knees. Gravel was embedded in them and he cried from the pain but mostly from seeing the blood. Maggie came and picked him up and told him Sister Imelda would clean his knees, put lovely ointment on them and bandages.

He supposed she had left school shortly afterwards and gone out to work. He couldn't recall seeing her again for a long time, not until he was grown-up. When he saw her then she had a child by each hand and was expecting another. She smiled at him but he let on not to see her. He felt awkward and embarrassed. Pregnant women had that effect on him.

Kneeling, watching the priest, followed by an altar boy, come down the altar steps and approach the coffin, he realised Maggie would have been eleven going on twelve when she carried him to Sister Imelda, seven maybe eight years older than him. The same age difference as between him and Angel. Poor Maggie, he thought, your time was short.

The altar boy handed the holy-water bucket to the priest. It wasn't very big, made of brass with a feathery brush in it. Saying prayers, Father Clancy sprinkled the coffin with the water. The church doors were opened wide and, the priest leading the way, the coffin was shouldered out. After the congregation left, Tommy knelt again, bowed his head and prayed for all to go well between him and Angel.

The graveyard was at the back of the chapel. The burial wouldn't take long. He continued praying until he could tell by the silence that everyone had gone home. He waited for at least another ten minutes before leaving for the presbytery.

The housekeeper showed him into the parlour, a dark room that smelt of furniture polish, incense, and holiness, Tommy supposed. 'Sit down there at the table. I'll tell Father you're here. It's not the most convenient of times and him just coming in after the funeral. But wait anyway.'

The alb and stole had been removed and Father Clancy wore his black suit and clerical collar. 'Hello, Tommy. Were you at the funeral?'

'I didn't go to the graveside. I was in the chapel.'

'D'ye know something? No matter what sort of a day it is – the sun could be splitting the trees – I always feel cold after a burial.' He sat facing Tommy. 'And I always want a cup of scalding strong tea so I asked Mrs Lynham to bring in two. So now tell me what brings you here.'

After the tea came and the woman left, he told hesitantly of the engagement and wanting to marry Angel.

'You're off to India, so your mother was telling me. Ten years. That'll be a long engagement.'

'No, Father. D'ye see, I was wondering about marrying before I sailed.'

Sometimes down the years Father Clancy had wondered if there was a want in Tommy. He looked normal enough and, though no great scholar, was average at the spelling, sums and reading, though very good at the catechism and religious knowledge. A great memory. But, all the same, you always felt there was something

78

missing. Or maybe it was just that he'd never left his childhood innocence behind him, never got into scraps or trouble of any sort. Father Clancy had never had a complaint about Tommy from anyone. But now his doubts were reinforced. Tommy wanted to marry a child.

'Don't let the tea go cold.' The priest drank some of his own before speaking again. 'I know there's a madness taking hold of the young men and women, a fever of marriages – it's the war. But so far I've not heard of a fourteen-year-old bride.'

'But girls can marry at fourteen. They can at twelve, Father.'

'How d'ye know that?' Father Clancy asked.

'From school. The catechism. It's canon law.'

'You're right, it is. I bet there's not another boy who went to school remembers that. But that law wasn't meant for the hoi-polloi. It was for royalty, when they wanted the right princess for their son and heir. Some of the unfortunate children were betrothed when they were infants and married as soon as they reached the allowable age, all to ensure the right connections so they could keep their power. Barbarism. The law wasn't for the benefit of a child of the poor that had been made pregnant. Bastards were ten a penny then, kept, drowned, given away. No one cared about them. There's nothing like that worrying you?'

Tommy looked baffled. But Father Clancy remembered Angel's ripeness, and Aggie's nonsense about 'wiles and ways', and persisted in probing. 'You didn't take advantage of the child?'

Tommy's face and neck went the colour of a beetroot.

Embarrassment and anger were in his eyes. 'I did no such thing, Father. I wouldn't harm a hair of her head.'

'Calm down, calm down. I had to ask, though I didn't think you had because of the hurry in which you want to marry. Anyway, it would have availed you nothing. No bishop that I know of would have sanctioned a marriage at such short notice.

'But, Tommy, there's more to it than that. It's not only a bishop you'd have to contend with. You'd be up against the British Army as well. They wouldn't give you permission to marry. You're not twenty-five. You wouldn't be on the "strength" yet. Not an extra penny to keep Angel. You'd have to pay her passage to India. And India, I've heard tell, is a hell-hole for women not of the memsahib class. Would you want your child-wife to live like that? You wouldn't. You're a decent boy. You'd die a thousand deaths seeing that lovely child suffering.'

'I love her. I want her beside me. I never loved a woman before. Is there nothing we can do, Father?'

'How long did you say you'll be away?'

'Ten years, Father.'

'I'd say there's no harm done in the engagement. Time flies. Believe me, I know. Write to each other. It could last the distance – and if it doesn't you're both honourable enough to let the other know. I wish the circumstances had been different. You'd be right for her. You'd mind and cherish her. But that's how it is. Go along now and tell her. And I'll have a word with Aggie.'

Father Clancy stood, indicating the talks were over. Tommy did, too, saying, 'Not her mother. She knew nothing about it. We weren't going to tell her mother until I'd seen you.'

'Right, so. I'll not breathe a word. Come to confession

before you embark. Go now, like a good lad.' He raised his hand and blessed Tommy before he left the parlour.

As he neared Connolly's shop the Angelus bell was ringing. It was a busy time of the day. Danny and Mona were serving the crowd of customers but there was no sign of Angel. Whatever ailed her yesterday she must still have. His poor little sweetheart, and here was he bringing her the bad news. She'd be broken-hearted with the news that the wedding was off.

Angel had pleaded that she still did not feel well, and Aggie said that another day at home would do her all the good in the world. 'Danny won't mind. And sure isn't it the only time you've been off since you started? Mrs Gorman was asking about you the other day. She said she'd never found another to match you. The girls she's had since stay no time. Four there's been since you left.' And Angel thought, The doctor's been up to his tricks again, and that it was a crying shame something couldn't be done about it. But, as Father Clancy had said, 'Who'd take the word of a young girl against the Gormans?'

'I won't be back till tea-time. If you saw the state of Mrs Fagan's place you'd faint, tea chests everywhere waiting to be packed. I told you she's moving up north. But I've left everything out for you. A lovely bit of cooked ham, and there's a head of salad and beetroot. Make sure you eat it. You have to keep your strength up.'

I'll need it, thought Angel, when her mother left, to face Tommy. What'll I do if Father Clancy says we can marry? I'll die so I will. My mother'll come home and find me stretched on the floor stone dead. Oh, God help me. Holy Mary, Mother of God, assist me. How did I let

81

myself into this? As if my heart wasn't scalded enough not knowing where Johnny is. And now this to contend with and not a soul to open my mind to. He'll come with a smile all over his face with what he'll think is good news. And I'll be destroyed for life. Be killed by one of them Indians, get a fever and die. The ship will sink. The best thing for me – better to be dead than tied to Tommy for life. No hope of ever seeing Johnny again. Johnny, my beautiful boy. Johnny who I know loves me. Sacred Heart of Jesus, help me.

Tommy approached the cottage, not knowing how to break the bad news, not knowing if Aggie was at home. If she was, could he tell Angel what he had to tell her? He decided he'd have to. It wouldn't be fair to her to do otherwise. He kept telling himself, 'I shouldn't have been so hasty. I should have been content with the engagement. My poor little love. I wouldn't hurt you for the world. And now I have to break your heart.'

He looked over the half-door. Angel was lying on the couch, a wet cloth on her forehead. She had thought of a ploy. She'd let on to be still very sick. She had had to have the doctor. And she had decided on the doctor's findings too: she was in no state to travel; complete rest was what she needed, at least a month, rest and nourishment, invalid food. She was completely run down. That would knock the wedding on the head. She'd promise to write to Tommy every week, wear his ring, and think of him every single day, do novenas, and sure the ten years would fly. The excuse was well concocted before he pushed open the door. The minute she saw his face she knew it wouldn't be needed, thanks be to God and His Blessed Mother.

He sat at the end of the couch and held her hand. For

a few minutes he said nothing and then, like a child, he cried, 'Oh, darlin', I'm so sorry. I built up your hopes. I was so sure. Certain sure. I knew the canon law. But Father Clancy put me right.' He explained to her all that the priest had told him about canon law and then he told her about the Army's part in it. 'I couldn't claim an allowance for you nor a quarter, and they wouldn't pay your passage. You wouldn't even be able to travel out with me.' He let go of her hand, clasped his head in both of his and she heard his sobs. She patted his back as you would a crying child, and said soothing words aloud while thanking God for her lucky escape.

Eventually he stopped crying and took her left hand in his, running his thumb gently across it. Then he exclaimed, 'The ring, you're not wearing it. We're still engaged, aren't we?'

The ready-made lies rolled off her tongue. 'Of course we are, only didn't I forget Mona saw the ring when I bought it? She knew how much it was and I didn't want her putting it round the place that we'd got engaged with a ring from the penny bazaar. Look, here it is.' She put her hand inside her blouse and drew out a double strand of wool on which the ring was threaded. 'I'll wear it there, next to my heart, until the real one comes.'

'I'll get it at the first chance and send it. And I'll buy other presents for you as well.'

'And I'll write you lovely long letters, tell you all the goings on. Before you know it you'll be back and everything grand between us. Maybe you ought to make a move, me ma'll be back soon.'

'Wouldn't it be better if I stayed and explained things?'

'You're forgetting. I never said I'd tell her. She'd have

given out yards. You know what mothers are like.' She sighed a long, deep sigh, as if sorrowing, which induced Tommy to hold her tight, tell her how he adored her, then kiss her for longer than he had previously and promise to come the next day.

'Ah, no, don't. It'll only upset me again, remind me of how different things might have been. By the way, did you mention anything to your mother?'

'At the last minute I lost my nerve. She's as good as gold but I'd have got a lecture about the suddenness and you being only a child.'

'Mothers,' Angel said, 'they're all the same,' and thought, He'll be gone in a few days and no one knows what I nearly let myself in for except the priest and it'll be safe with him. Mona'd have had a fit, and she fancying him.

She saw Tommy to the door, kissed his cheek before opening it then waved him goodbye, danced a few steps of a jig, took the penny bazaar ring from her neck and, after putting it back in her box, sat on the sofa making plans to find Johnny, wherever he was hiding.

In the second post Danny got a field card from Brian Nolan.

Can't write much because of the censor but you can see that I joined up, the Royal Dublin Fusiliers, and got a commission. It's a great improvement on being a school inspector. This address, so long as you always use my Army number, will find me wherever I go. Unless it's heaven or the place below. Love to hear from you.

Your old friend,
Brian.

*

A couple of months after Tommy sailed for India he sent her the sapphire ring. Pretending surprise, she showed it to her mother, who was puzzled but greatly impressed. 'That's a beauty. It looks like the real thing,' she said, trying it on one of her swollen fingers. It wouldn't go past the first joint. 'What in the name of God possessed him to do a thing like that?'

'I don't think he's right in the head. How much would that have cost him, I wonder?'

'Tom in the pawn would have an idea. Will I ask him?'

Angel took the ring from her mother. 'No, don't you dare, and don't mention it to anyone else.'

'All right, all right. Keep your hair on. Though I don't know why it has to be a secret.'

'It's his mother I'm thinking about. How d'ye think she'd feel knowing her son was spending his money on me?'

'I could make a guess. You're right, we'll say nothing about it. But for the life of me, I can't understand why he sent it. It's like an engagement ring. Sure you never even went out with the fella? Still, I suppose he could have taken a fancy to you. There wasn't anything that went on between the pair of you that I didn't know about, was there? Only, come to think of it, you've been very down in the mouth since the time he went.'

'Ma, will you give over. As if I'd have anything to do with Tommy Maguire!'

'Maybe you gave him ideas without knowing you were doing it. Nobody sends presents like that unless there was something going on.'

'Well, for your information there was nothing going

on,' Angel snapped. 'Once or twice I talked to him. One night he walked me and Mona home from the fair. She was trickin' with him. He asked us both to write. I let on I would. Now, are you satisfied?'

'I suppose he could have believed you,' Aggie said. She didn't want to have a row with Angel, though these days she was very trying: a big change had come over her. It could be her age, or maybe she was run down, needed a strengthening bottle. She'd ask the chemist tomorrow. She looked well enough but was very irritable. There'd been a coolness between her and Mona – Aggie had never got to the bottom of that – but they were bosom pals again. I suppose she's growing up, the days of telling me her secrets past. I was the same with my own mother. Please God, one day she'll change back again, when she's married and has a child of her own. Daughters come back to you then.

In a good-humoured mood Angel wrote and thanked Tommy for the ring, and lied that she wore it all the time, that everyone admired it and Mona was green with envy. After she had posted the letter she felt guilty. She was giving him the wrong impression, codding him up to the two eyes. And that wasn't right. But poor Tommy had a lack in him, he'd believe anything. Everyone thought that about him. And anyway she had to thank him – he'd probably be glad to get a letter from anyone. She only hoped he wouldn't make a regular thing of writing to her. Maybe he'd meet someone in India, a grown-up daughter of a soldier, and forget all about her. But Tommy didn't forget, still believed in their engagement, and was still writing to her in 1915. Now and then she replied.

Chapter Eight

Nineteen sixteen was a momentous year in Dublin. On Easter Monday a group of Volunteers commandeered the General Post Office, ran up the tricolour, and declared a republic. They fought against overwhelming odds but at the end of the week, to avoid more bloodshed, surrendered.

In July, in France, the battle of the Somme commenced. On the first day thousands of British troops were killed. During the following months there were few homes in England, Scotland, Wales or Ireland where telegrams didn't arrive with news of a father, son or sweetheart missing or killed in action.

One came to the Quinns. Johnny's oldest brother had died. His mother came running up the street, waving the telegram, screaming, 'My son, my son Anto's dead.'

Angel heard the screams and ran out of the shop. Seeing and hearing Mrs Quinn, she assumed it was Johnny who had been killed and fainted. She was carried into the shop where Danny had also brought Mrs Quinn. He fed them sips of brandy. As Angel came round, Mrs Quinn was lamenting her son, calling his name so that Angel realised it was Anthony not Johnny who had been shot or blown to pieces. She said, 'Lord have mercy on him,' and thanked God that it wasn't her beloved dead on a French battlefield.

Her relief from grief was only temporary for, despite all her searching, prying and probing, she had neither seen nor heard of him from the night he had boxed at the fair. For all she knew he might well be dead too, though in the depths of her heart she refused to believe this telling herself that, loving him as she did, she would have known if he had died. At the moment of his passing she would have experienced some terrible sensation; he would have appeared to her. Johnny would have said goodbye. He was alive, somewhere, and she would find him.

Johnny was touring England. On the evening two years ago when he had first gone to the gymnasium off Aungier Street he had missed the last tram home and, as Jackser the talent scout had promised, had been found somewhere to doss down.

The next morning he had decided he was packing in the bike shop. He told Jackser of his decision. Jackser approved. 'You made a great impression last night. You've got what it takes. But there's a hard road in front of you. For a start there's no money in it yet. That'll come later on but, in the meantime, you can't live on air. What else can you do besides mend bikes?'

'This and that,' replied Johnny. 'I'm strong as an ox, done plenty of labouring, all sorts of things.'

'All sorts of things is not on. It's the hands. They're precious. You want no injuries to your mitts. It's them that'll make your fortune in the future. Leave it with me. I'll sort something out. What about them at home? Will you send word?'

'No,' Johnny said. 'I want them to know nothing. I've a bastard of an oul fella. He'd be down here demanding me out of it, squaring up to me. I can do without that.'

'Right y'are. Stay in that doss-house for tonight. Tomorrow I'll find you somewhere else over the north side. I'll get you a start as well, a few hours each day so as not to interfere with the training.'

88

'Gameball,' said Johnny.

His lodgings were in a tall, narrow house on Summer Hill. And 'the start' in an undertaker's. He balked at that news. 'Jesus Christ, I couldn't handle the dead.'

'Less likely to injure you than any other bastard. In any case you won't be called on often to handle a corpse. You'll do a bit of clerical work, lend a hand now and then to get a fat oul wan or oul fella into a habit. No lifting coffins – getting them down the stairs in some of the kips of tenements could do for a hand. If you squash one between the coffin and a red raddled wall that could be the end of your career.'

Jackser lived in the same house. 'Without benefit of clergy,' he explained, after Johnny had met his woman. She was years younger than Jackser, stout and pleasant-looking. She kept a good table and took only a pittance from Johnny – which was as well for the undertaker paid him little more than that.

The majority of his time was spent in the gym where he skipped, shadow-boxed, worked on the punch-bag, always with Jackser supervising, exhorting him to punch harder, lead from the shoulder, stay light on his feet, dodge and dart.

When the time was considered right to fight another boxer, one was chosen who would put him through his paces but never injure him. Gradually he was matched against tougher opposition but still in the gymnasium. Then the time came when Jackser declared him ready to take to the road, 'But over the other side to begin with. And another thing, Johnny, you'll have a change of name.'

Johnny kicked against that. 'I want to fight in my own

name. I want people out there to know who I am, to know it's Johnny Quinn.'

'And so they will, all in good time. You'll do the fairs and booths over the other side. You'll get experience. Larry the Lad, that's who you'll be. Larry the Lad with the lethal left.'

'But I'm not a south paw.'

'You're right there. You're not. Leave it with me. I'll come up with something.'

Danny was aware of the change in Angel: her long brooding silences when she wasn't serving a customer; the preoccupied expression in her eyes. And, though never ill-tempered, never impolite or disobliging, she no longer radiated her once joyful exuberance. He thought that few of the customers would discern the change or, if they did, would assume it was to do with her age. He, having her welfare always uppermost in his mind, adoring her more as each day passed, believed he knew the reason. Angel was grieving for Johnny Quinn, who had vanished without trace.

Occasionally as he passed her and Mona gossiping during a slack period, he'd hear Johnny's name mentioned, hear Angel say, 'I've walked the feet off myself, gone to every gym on the south side, and not one knew anything about him.'

'They wouldn't tell you if they did. They'd think you were a wan he'd thrown over, maybe pregnant and chasing him. Them fellas stick close together. Though, mind you, I've asked my brothers about him, never mentioning your name, lettin' on it was just a thought that had come into my mind. They've never heard a word about him, and his mother was sayin' the same thing last week to Danny – though she's more flush with money these days. She came in one day last week with a ten-shilling note. I wonder where she got that? Not from the oul fella and that's for sure.'

Danny had also noticed that Mrs Quinn was often in funds these days and had wondered about their source. But it wasn't something you could enquire into. If Johnny was sending his mother money he'd have sworn her to secrecy, and she wouldn't want to kill the goose that laid the golden eggs. And, anyway, he didn't want to know for fear that, out of pity for Angel, to put her out of her misery, he might divulge where Johnny was. Johnny would bring more heartache into her life. What she was going through now would pass and one day in the future she'd meet another man, one who would love and cherish her as she deserved. He cursed his misfortune that the man would never be himself.

'I've gone right off that Tommy Maguire. A feckin' chancer if ever there was one. He promised to write to me before he went away and I never heard tale or tidings from him.'

'That was ages ago. He's been gone nearly two years,' Angel said, wiping the blades of the bacon slicer.

'I know that. I can count. But, all the same, I was hoping for a long time – until I met Benny. He's gorgeous. I think things are getting serious. Nowadays I never give your man a second thought. God knows what put him into my mind today.'

Angel said nothing about the letters that came regularly from Tommy, how they irritated and bored her and how difficult she found them to answer. There was one at home now waiting for a reply. After work, while walking home, she thought about Tommy's letters, the things he wrote. Pink elephants! The heat must have affected his brain. He admitted not to have seen them himself but other blokes had. Of course, they were fluthered after a night on the batter and swore they existed. He believed that when the lads were walking home as the sun was rising the elephants at the river drinking appeared pink as the sun shone on them. One bloke, when he got home, was going to open a pub and call it the Pink Elephant. He couldn't imagine that going down well in Ireland where public-houses were named after their owners.

He also wrote about the journey out, how there was a terrible storm in the Bay of Biscay although it was summer. The troop ship was packed and everyone was sick. The smell lasted for days, although the decks were scrubbed down regularly. He was glad she wasn't with him, but only then for otherwise he missed her every minute of the day. In the long run though he had to admit that Father Clancy hadn't been far out when he said it was no place to take a young girl.

But there were plenty of women there, white women. The memsahibs, they were the officers' wives, they had a cushy life, waited on hand and foot by cooks and sweepers, with ayahs to mind the babies and little boys to work the punkahs, sitting there day and night pulling the ropes of the fans. And when the English children were seven or eight they were sent back to England and boarding-school. But yet, despite all the pampering, the local graveyard was full of memsahibs. They died in childbirth, from fevers. There was a terrible lot of fevers in India. Sometimes he'd go to the graveyard, it was fairly cool there, and he'd read the tombstones and feel sorry for the poor women dead and buried so far away from home. It made him think of Maggie Dignum, but at least she was buried among her own.

The NCOs' wives got a fair crack of the whip. They had decent quarters and a few servants. And even if the heat was killing they weren't bent over a tin bath doing the washing: there were dhobis, or washermen, to do it for them for next to nothing.

Then there were the native women, some Hindus and some Muslims. And there was a caste system, which he didn't understand, although he knew the bottom layer were called Untouchables. By the time he came home he'd be an expert on India.

The women he felt most sorry for were the half-castes, whose mothers had married white railway workers. Some were black, some brown, some almost white – but some feature or their hair showed the lick of the tar-brush. The sad thing was that they had delusions of grandeur: they tried to imitate the memsahibs' voices, their ways, and considered themselves above the ordinary soldiers' wives, not realising that they were looked down on by their own people and all the whites.

But India was a beautiful country. The only thing that spoiled it was being so far away from her. But two years had nearly gone already and, please God, the other years would pass as quickly.

Angel had had ten letters since he'd gone and she never welcomed any. She'd never wanted her mother to know they had come and she'd been lucky with the first two – Aggie had already left the cottage when they arrived. But she had been there for the others. Now it was questions, questions all the time. 'Why is that fella writing to you? What's made him interested in someone that scarcely bade him the time of day? You're keeping things from me, so you are. Why? That's what I want to know.' And when the creased ten-shilling note fell out of an envelope Aggie had come closer to hitting Angel than at any time in her life. 'Men only send money to them that there's some tie with. What did you get up to that night he walked you home from the fair? I've a good mind to send for Father Clancy. Maybe he'll get the truth out of you.'

It was the first time they had ever rowed, Aggie shouting, Angel shouting, and in the long run breaking down and crying, telling her mother about the engagement, Tommy's visit to the priest wanting permission to get married, and how she'd agreed to the ring. Sobbing, she confessed she'd done it to make Johnny Quinn jealous. 'Ma, I didn't know what to do. How to get out of what I'd got myself into.'

'And why didn't you tell me? My poor child, little did I know what you were going through.' She took Angel in her arms and comforted her. 'I was that frightened that he'd taken advantage of you – destroyed you. Damaged goods, you'd have been.'

'Poor Tommy,' said Angel. 'I don't think he kissed me half a dozen times. I felt sorry for him. I wish I could have felt more but he's got something lacking – he's not all there.'

'He's a decent enough boy and everyone belonging to him. You should have been straight with him. A bit of a thick, all the more reason for not fooling about with him. And what's the money for?'

'He wants me to save up for when he comes back. When we get married.'

Aggie let go of her. 'Now, listen to me. You have to

put a stop to this. Not one more letter will you write, except one telling him the truth and sending back his ten-shilling note.'

It was agreed. But gradually they drifted back into their easy lifestyle and good intentions were put on the long finger. Tommy's letters and sums of money arrived regularly. The letters were skimmed through, thrown to one side and occasionally answered, but Aggie made Angel open a post-office savings account and checked that Tommy's money was deposited in it. 'Then,' she told Angel 'when you pluck up the courage to tell him you don't love him, never have, that it was all a mistake and he'd be better off not writing, draw his money and send it back.'

'What about the ring? Should I send that as well?'

'I wouldn't bother. Tom in the pawn had a look at it. The stone's not real. He said in foreign bazaars you can trust no one, and that he wouldn't give you a quid for it. You don't have to hurt Tommy's feelings by telling him that, though let it be known that you'll not be treating it as an engagement ring. More like a keepsake.'

After having her tea, fish because it was Friday, Angel sighed and said, 'Well, I suppose I should attempt a letter, but I don't know what to write about.'

'When are you going to tell him the truth? It's always the next letter and the next.'

'I know. I'm terrible. It's just that I feel sorry for him out there. I'll definitely tell him next time.'

'Well, for your sake and his I only hope he isn't shipped home suddenly.'

'He won't, he's another eight years to do. We could all be dead and buried before then.'

'With God's holy help we won't. D'ye want more tea?'

'Later on. I want to get the letter written. What can I write about?'

'I suppose you could tell him about the rebellion and Maggie Dignum's husband, his sister taking over the minding of the children, then finding they were too much of a burden and putting them into the orphanage all except the eldest. Poor Mag must be turning in her grave.'

And so Angel wrote to Tommy about the rebellion.

You'll never believe what happened here. On Easter Monday didn't a crowd of Volunteers take over the GPO and as bold as brass march down Middle Abbey Street, in uniform and with guns, and heave all the workers out of the post office, put up the Irish flag, stick posters on lamp-posts saying Ireland was now a republic. One of the Volunteer leaders, I think it was Patrick Pearse, came out and made a speech saying the same thing. Out in the village we knew nothing about it until trams that couldn't get into the city came back to the depot. Nearly everyone thought the Volunteers were mad taking on the British Army. A few said they were very brave. In the shop that's all the talk was about, Them with sons or anyone belonging to them in France were raging. 'Playing into the hands of the Germans, that's what the fellas in the post office were doing.' No one seemed to have much time for them. There was a lot of sneering and jeering. Bowsies and gougers and corner boys, that's what they were being called.

You wouldn't have recognised the town. Me and Mona went in one night after tea. Everywhere was blown to bits. There was even a gunboat in the Liffey firing shells. And up the top of the street near the Pillar all these gorgeous Lancers shot dead, lying on the ground, and their lovely horses dead as well. All sorts of people were killed, soldiers, people just passing in the street. Some were shot by the fellas in the post office and some by the British soldiers.

But all the same there was great gas as well, crowds of oul wans, oul fellas and even children robbing all before them. They had go-carts, hand-carts and prams. The windows in the big shops were put in. You were crunching through the broken glass. And the robbers were piling fur coats, jewellery, frocks, everything they could lay hands on in their carts. Looting, that's what the authorities called it, and said the robbers could be shot for it, though I didn't hear tell of one that was. Anyway, it went on for five days. Then on the Saturday the Volunteers gave in, to save more bloodshed, so they said. When they were being marched away the crowds gathered jeered them.

There wasn't a good word said about them. Mind you, Danny – remember Danny from the shop? – he praised them. Said they'd shown great courage. Everyone knew the leaders would be gaoled and that'd be the end of it. But didn't the English decide to execute them? No one could believe it. Said the English'd change their minds. But they didn't. In August one after the other was shot in Kilmainham Gaol. I needn't tell you that changed the minds of the people. They were raging and calling the English all sorts of names. And hundreds of people would be kneeling outside the gaol on the morning of a shooting saying the rosary. The fella, Patrick Pearse, had a brother, they were both shot and Patrick wrote a lovely poem for his poor mother before he was killed. And another very sad thing, one of the leaders was a fella named Plunkett and he married his sweetheart, the night before he was killed, in the chapel in the gaol.

But the worst thing of all was what happened to a fella called Connolly, James Connolly.

Hadn't he been wounded during the shooting? In his leg, I think. Anyway, he was very bad, had to be taken out of the Post Office on a stretcher, carried into the yard in Kilmainham Gaol and propped in a chair to be shot. Imagine that! Danny was fit to be tied. I heard him saying that the English had hammered nails into their own coffin. It was the beginning of the end for them in Ireland. I never knew they'd been over here for seven hundred years, or that Patrick's Cathedral and Christ Church had been ours years ago, did you? Fancy anyone robbing someone else's chapel. Danny says that now the people are behind the Volunteers and that Ireland's day is coming.

I can't think of any more for now so I'll say bye-bye.
Angel

Tommy finished the letter then read it aloud to half a dozen soldiers he knew were Irish who were lolling on their bunks, sweating and smoking and waving their hands about to prevent flies landing on their faces.

'And here we are,' said one of the soldiers. 'We took the King's shilling when we could have stayed at home and become heroes.'

'Sure wasn't it a bit of adventure and regular food we were looking for, nothing to do with the King?'

'Aye right enough, it was,' a man called Finbar agreed. 'I never knew what was going on at home. All the different organisations – I couldn't make head nor tail of them. Who are the Volunteers?'

Another soldier, known as the barrack-room lawyer because he was such a know-all, said if they'd have the patience to listen, he'd explain.

'So long as you don't take too long about it,' another voice said, and everyone laughed.

'Well, it was the Protestants in the North that started it when it looked as if the Home Rule Bill would go through. Carson was the instigator. Guns and that were bought from Germany, and the Ulster Volunteers said they were prepared to go up to their necks in blood if Home Rule was granted. So our fellas got arms, and started drilling and parading and preparing to meet the lot from the North if they should attack. Then there's Sinn Fein but they're after a peaceful settlement for National Unity. Poor Connolly, Lord have mercy on him, he had the Irish Citizens' Army. He was all for the workers of the world having a say in their own affairs. But he was a Nationalist as well. And then there's the Irish Republican Brotherhood. Are you with me so far?'

'Yeah, I know about them,' Finbar interrupted. 'There was a fellow from my village in them. My mother wrote and told me. I was in school with him. A fella by the name of Mick Collins. His ould fella was seventy-five when Mick was born! Would you believe it? So his house was always full of oul fellas telling stories about dead Irish heroes, half of them fairy tales about Finn and Cuchulain, but about real men as well. Mick'd get in such a lather when he'd talk about the Famine or previous risings. But he was clever at the lessons all right. He went on to the secondary school and got into the Civil Service in London. There's a hot bed of Irish Nationalists over beyond, Irish speakers, dancers, members of the Gaelic League. Well, to cut a long story short, when the war started, Home Rule was put on the long finger and Mick became a member of the I.R.B.'

'And who are they?' Tommy enquired.

'A militant group founded in Ireland and America about the same time. But Mick stayed on in London until he thought he might be conscripted. Then he hotfooted it back to Ireland.'

'I never read much about his part in the rebellion,' another soldier chimed in.

'He wasn't one of the leaders but he was there all right and arrested. He's in gaol in Wales now with hundreds of others. Making useful contacts, you can be sure. You haven't heard the last of him.'

'You never told us how the different organisations came to fight together on Easter Monday?' another of the soldiers spoke up.

'That nearly didn't come off,' the know-all soldier replied. 'Patrick Pearse, who was executed with his brother, was a poet and believed in an Ireland free from England. But he also believed that, to achieve this, blood would have to be spilled. So all the organisations came together and declared an Irish Republic and the different groups became known as the Irish Republican Army. And that's about it. Anyone got a fag?'

He was pelted with several.

The game of brag was finished, the greasy cards collected. 'Luck of the bloody Irish,' a soldier said. Tommy Maguire grinned as he gathered in his winnings. He and the soldier were mates. They had been together in India for nearly five years, putting down skirmishes when they rose, side by side bayoneting or shooting the thin, half-starved, rebellious, brown-skinned men of the sub-continent. Tommy and his mates lived cheek by jowl in a greystone barracks, forty men to a room. Some were cranky bastards, some surly, but all in all, Tommy thought, good mates, blokes you could depend on to cover your back.

During the summer months the heat was stifling. Geordie Wallace swore that if you cracked an egg on the ground it would cook. Prickly heat was a scourge. You wanted to reef your arms, legs, neck and crotch but scratches turned septic: you could get blood poisoning, be dead today and buried in the morning. That had to be: nothing kept in the heat – least of all dead flesh. The Indians were ceremoniously burnt on funeral pyres, or placed on the towers for the vultures.

Disgusting, scabrous creatures, was how one bloke with a bit of schooling had described them. 'D'ye mean like scabby?' Tommy had asked, never having heard the other word before.

'Something like that. Comes from the Latin for scabies.'

'They make me sick to look at them,' said Tommy. 'Only I've been thinking, they do a good job. Keep the place clean. Imagine, if they didn't exist the place'd be littered with rotting corpses.'

'You have a point, I suppose. But they still make my flesh crawl.'

The heartbreaking notes of the bugle playing the Last Post floated across the compound. It was sounded for lights out and at funerals. Getting ready for bed, Tommy thought it was the saddest music he had ever heard. He took off his khaki drill trousers, folded them along the crease lines and put them beneath the biscuits, hard fibre squares, three, that served as a mattress. A thin blanket covered the criss-cross wire springs. The pants went on this and the biscuits on top, otherwise the imprint of the springs would be on them and the sergeant–major would have a field day at inspection in the morning. The Tilley lamps were extinguished; the enormous moths that hovered round them went wherever they went in the dark. Mosquitoes hung like bats on the walls, next to the blood-splattered remains of their kin, who'd met their deaths beneath the swipe of hand or a fly-swat.

Cigarettes glowed like fireflies from each bed. Tommy's mate said, 'More money to send to Angel.' It was common knowledge in the barrack room that Tommy sent his winnings home to his sweetheart. 'Aye,' replied Tommy. 'Got a nice little nest egg for when we get married.'

'You should have been a padre – one of them Roman ones that can't marry or have sex. Nearly five years without a woman! I'd go mad. All the lovely little bints you could have had in that time.'

'And all the doses of clap,' replied Tommy.

'A tin of mercury ointment fixes that.'

'Maybe it cures the sores on your cock,' Tommy said, stubbing out his cigarette in an old tobacco tin on the bedside locker, 'but there's more than one sort of clap. The sort you can't see. Gets in your blood. You'd give it to your wife, to your children and destroy them.' His mate began to snore.

Tommy lay in the dark and thought of Angel. She was a woman now, still with the beautiful childlike face, but she was taller, her breasts more prominent.

He'd had to coax and coax her to have the likeness

taken. Three letters it took before she sent the photograph. And she hadn't forgotten to wear the engagement ring. That was important. He wanted his mates to see it. Half the time he didn't think they believed she was waiting for him. He couldn't understand why, for many of them had sweethearts waiting for them at home. There were even married men, whose wives weren't with them, some from choice, while others were waiting for their husbands to be twenty-five and on the Regiment's strength. Then they could apply for a passage out, a marriage allowance, and put their name down for a married quarter. Even then you could wait three, four years, maybe longer, before a place was allocated. He had never thought of himself as good-looking or as having a way with women. This might be what his mates saw in him, not that anyone said it to his face. All the same, when he was down he sensed this. Or, if he was very low, he wondered if they thought he wasn't all there. A slate missing. There were those at home in Dublin he'd overheard say such things. Maybe his mates thought he made it all up about Angel. That's why the photograph was so important. He never tired of looking at it, kissing it when no one was about. She was nineteen now. You couldn't forget her age; she was born in the first year of the century, 1900. He had sent her a silver bangle, though she never acknowledged it, or the money.

If it wasn't for his mother he'd never know what was going on in the village. She kept him up to date. For such a small place the village had lost a lot of men during the war. Poor Joe Dignum had been killed just as the war was coming to an end. His mother wrote that Maggie's eldest son, the only one not to go into an orphanage, was terrible wild. Never worked a day. Always in trouble with the police. And drinking, though only God knew where he laid hands on the money.

In her last letter she mentioned Johnny Quinn, reminding him that he was the one who wanted to be a boxer. He seemed to have vanished off the face of the earth, never a glimpse of him after he won the fight at the fair. The oul fella was still knocking his poor wife about. Wasn't it sad how things worked out? Why couldn't it have been oul Quinn who went to the war and was killed instead of poor Joe Dignum?

Tommy fell asleep thinking about Angel and the night at the fair.

Aggie and Angel rowed more frequently than they had ever done over sending back Tommy's money. 'It's too much trouble going to the post office,' Angel would say.

And Aggie would retort, 'But not too much trouble for me to put it in. I swear to God, if you don't do it soon I'll tell Tommy's mother about the whole business. She won't be long about putting her son right – maybe even dragging you to the post office to draw out the money and send it back.'

Angel ignored the threat, knowing her mother would never do anything to shame her. But not long after a recent row she made the effort to withdraw the money, register the envelope and wave the receipt in Aggie's face. She included a few lines with the money, telling Tommy she couldn't wait for him any longer. It wasn't that she was seeing anyone else but she wanted to feel free again.

She couldn't believe that five years had passed since

she'd last seen Johnny or heard anything about him. As each day passed she hoped and prayed for news. One minute she'd be buoyed up with hope, the next so despondent she wanted to bang her head against the wall and tear her hair out. Then another day would dawn and she'd convince herself that today was the day she'd get news of him. He'd come back to claim her, declare his love. They'd marry and live happily ever after. But the black days always returned. And it was at such times she longed for a true friend like Mona had been. But she had never confided in Mona about Tommy sending the ring or wanting to marry her. Or about saving the money to get a home together. Or how she had encouraged him by writing. If Mona hadn't fancied Tommy she'd have thought it was a howl. Almost everything was a howl to Mona and her family. But as the years passed she remembered her mother's words from long ago. People could be all over you, letting on sympathy and reefing you behind your back. Lately she'd often noticed how cruel Mona's comments could be. Angel still mentioned Johnny and her interest in him and asked Mona to tell her if she ever heard word of him. But not in such a way to let Mona think she'd die if one day he didn't come back. Though she believed she would.

Mona had been great when they were younger to gossip and giggle with, exchange secrets that weren't important. Mona could annoy you, make you laugh, but Mona and her family, Angel had come to realise as she grew older, were like the people her mother had warned her against when she was growing up: all right for the lend of a frock but not to be trusted. And, in any case, Mona had Benny now.

Chapter Nine

If anyone in the village, other than Angel and his mother, wondered about Johnny's disappearance, they would have assumed he was dead, killed in the war. If they pondered why his next of kin hadn't been notified, they'd have said, 'Simple. Joined up under an assumed name or let on he had no next of kin. He was always close-mouthed, surly and secretive.'

Every day of her life Angel thought about Johnny. She prayed in the morning and at night, did novenas and lit penny candles for his safety and his return to her. Never for a moment did she believe that he had died.

Recently her mother and Mona had persuaded her to go dancing at the Ancient Order of Hibernians, an American/Irish fund raising hall. 'You can come with me and Benny. We do have great nights in the Ierne and the AOH.'

'I've been telling her that this long time,' said Aggie. 'I don't want her turning into a recluse at her age. Sure it's the normal thing for girls to go to dances.'

So she went, almost every Saturday night and sometimes through the week. Benny gave her a few duty dances and then she took her place among the other hopefuls at one end of the hall being given the once-over by the crowd of men at the other. The chance of being asked up increased when the public-houses shut and the men who'd been drinking came in. They were less choosy, eager to find someone for a good court later on. And the bashful ones were full of Dutch courage.

While they waited to be chosen, the wallflowers chatted among themselves, making a laugh of any fella who differed from their standard of what made an attractive man. 'Will you look at the get-up of that fella. Like something you'd throw balls at in a fancy fair. And him with the duck's arse. Sweeping the floor with it. And your man, there, him with his hair slicked back. Thinks he's Charlie Chaplin.' And they'd laugh and giggle.

Angel made many acquaintances among the group, who waited on the whim of the men to ask them for a dance. The most beautiful girl in the dance hall, she seldom waited long. 'I hate having to wait for a fella to look me over,' the girls would say. 'You feel like a heifer up for sale. I'd love to go to one of them posh dances where you have cards and the fellas fill them in. Then you're never at a loss. Wouldn't you love that?'

Angel lied, and said that would be grand. And thought, I'm lucky. I'm not here looking for a fella, trying to find a husband. I have my fella. I don't know where he is. But someday I'll find him. He'll come back and marry me.

She enjoyed the dancing, the music, getting dressed up to go out. Several times during the evening she would ask if they'd ever heard of a boxer called Johnny Quinn. Some would answer, 'Never,' straight away. Others, mostly men, would reply, 'That name sounds familiar. A boxer, did you say? Let me think. Are you sure it was Quinn not Quinlan?' and appear to be searching their memories, eventually admitting that they'd never come across a Johnny Quinn.

Johnny was still serving his apprenticeship, moving around Scotland, England and Wales, sometimes in boxing booths, sometimes at venues in seaside towns. He won most of the fights, and as he progressed the purse was bigger. He had grown several inches, put on two stone, muscle no fat, and Jackser had found a name for him, the 'Bruiser Brennan'.

He was minding himself. Very seldom did he have a woman, and when he did it was a prostitute chosen by Jackser. 'See, Johnny,' he'd advised, 'it isn't the sex that weakens you, so long as the girl is clean and there's no strings attached. What can ruin a boxer in the making is serious attachments. A woman will make demands, nag about being left while you're touring, demand money, have kids.

'That's all right when you've made it, when you're in the big time but not yet.'

Now and then he sent his mother ten shillings, sometimes a pound note. Only once had he written, taking the risk that his father might get hold of the letter. He gave his mother the address where Jackser's common-law wife lived. There she could leave a letter but only in an emergency, otherwise he would send no more money.

She called to the house once a month. Usually there was an envelope with money inside. It was a blank envelope. And it was in a blank envelope that she enclosed a note telling him that Anto had been killed. She prayed for Anto's soul and for God to protect Johnny. She was careful how she spent the extra money, never bringing in big quantities of food which would have aroused any suspicions. Her husband would have accused her of whoring, then beaten the truth out of her, got drunk and gone to the house on the north side. She wished for him to die a long, lingering death. She wished for the courage to kill him.

Johnny thought often of Angel, wondered if she had

108

married and if so whom. In all his moving about he had never seen a girl as beautiful as her. He cherished a dream, that if she hadn't married one day he'd claim her. When he was famous she'd be his.

Danny had replied to Brian Nolan's field card, making sure he used the correct Army number, but never got an answer. He could have been killed, but Danny didn't think so, for when Brian had sent the field card it gave his rank. He'd been commissioned, and Danny had checked every newspaper list of officer casualties but never found Brian's name among them. Now that the war was over, like the bad penny, he'd show up one day.

Danny's love for Angel was as strong as ever and he hoped that one day a miraculous happening would occur and she'd declare her love for him. Yet he knew he was fantasising. However, she was less down in the mouth these days. Time was doing its work in helping her to get over Johnny Quinn – either that or she was a great actress. But nothing in her behaviour towards him suggested that Danny Connolly entered her mind other than as the man she worked for.

Sometimes he toyed with the idea of going to see a specialist, a bone man. He'd read recently that one benefit, probably the only one, to come out of the war was the advances made in medicine. You'd never know, they might include new treatments for his complaint. For days he'd imagine an operation that would add a couple of inches to his short leg, the bonfire he'd make of the high boot. He'd walk without a limp, be able to dance. Then maybe Angel would look his way. But he knew he was deluding himself. Why should she give him a second glance when she could have the pick of anyone in the village, in the city, in the country? Like many another man he'd carry his unrequited love to the grave. Would she ever marry? he often asked himself. As far as he knew, she had never done a serious line – unless you counted the letters between her and Tommy Maguire in India. Aggie had let the cat out of the bag about those, and the money Tommy sent. 'Honest to God, Danny,' she had said, 'I don't understand none of it. I've told her and told her to write and tell Tommy he's wasting his time. I'm only hoping that now she's dancing regularly she'll meet a nice fella.' 'Please God, she will,' Danny had said. 'Though the war took the best of the young men. You must have noticed all the old maids left behind. And them that are getting married have to settle for fellas years younger than themselves, widowers or men old enough to be their fathers.'

'Indeed I have,' replied Aggie, 'and I'd be the last to object if she found a good man even if he was old enough to be her father. I do worry about her being left on her own if anything happened to me.'

'You're still only a young woman, hale and hearty. With the help of God you'll be around for years yet.'

Again his hopes soared: Aggie would approve of him as a husband. And so his days passed, some when he'd convince himself that it wasn't impossible that one day he might marry Angel, and others when he faced reality.

Danny's friend, Brian, had survived the war, and attained the rank of major. In peacetime he found Army life more convivial than that of school inspector. The uniform with a crown on his shoulder epaulettes opened many doors previously closed to him. His salary was better and he enjoyed mess life. When the war finished he came on leave to Ireland. There was his parents' house to sell and furniture to auction. Schoolbooks and letters that he found while preparing for the auction reminded him of Danny, and he felt guilty for never contacting him, other than the field card. All in good time, he said to himself, assuaging his conscience. He knew that Danny was a Nationalist and wouldn't approve of his decision to become a regular soldier. And he had to admit that it could be awkward: the rebellion had ignited a spark that was smouldering and any minute might catch light. Then he would have to take up arms against his own. He'd leave the renewing of his friendship with Danny for a while. Perhaps the rumours circulating might come to nothing, and in a peaceful period they could take up again.

He still visited Monto when he wanted a woman – and discovered that in his new status he was entitled to a better class of house and girl. As an officer, and therefore considered a gentleman, he was only one step down from the gentry and aristocrats who frequented Monto, layers above the dockers and labourers and, in the brothel hierarchy, well above school inspectors, teachers and all but the most senior civil servants. In 1919 life in Dublin suited him well.

Mona and Benny were engaged and saving up. They seldom went dancing now but Angel continued to go regularly, continued to pray for Johnny and still enquired of newcomers to the dance halls if they'd ever heard tell of him.

Sometimes she missed the dances on a Saturday night to go to an all-night hooley. She was invited to them by one of the many girls she had got to know in the dance halls. The parties were held in the enormous tenements on the north side, the first of the Georgian houses to be built towards the end of the eighteenth century. The houses were let in rooms. Depending on their income, a tenant rented one, two, three and sometimes four. The four-room accommodation usually included the front and back drawing rooms, which were spacious and divided by sliding doors, which when opened provided a miniature ballroom, ideally suited to hooleys. In many of these drawing rooms the original marble fireplaces had remained. So had the beautiful almost floor-to-ceiling sash windows and exquisite plaster friezes.

The windows were now draped with cheap lace hangings. Lurid pictures of a bleeding Sacred Heart and His Mother in Virgin blue robes hung on the walls, which had once been graced by oil paintings of the gentry's ancestors.

Gone was the Hepplewhite and Chippendale, replaced now by heavy Victorian sideboards and chiffoniers, whatnots, and suites of leatherette stuffed with horsehair. As the majority of people living in these rooms had large families, there were numerous beds squeezed into drawing rooms, front and back, into downstairs parlours. The furniture was highly polished, the bedding white and starched with valances that reached the floors. Many of the rooms had closets off them. In these were kept chamber-pots for the use of girls attending the hooleys. The men had to go down many flights of beautiful shallow stairs, adorned with mahogany curved banisters, to a lavatory in the backyard.

Music and refreshments were provided. Each guest paid two shillings, which bought ham and cheese sandwiches, sweet cake, biscuits and minerals. A bottle of cheap port was available for the chaperones. Some sort of musical instrument was always available, a piano, accordion, banjo or mandoline. Many of the guests could play them. The furniture was pushed against the walls to make room for dancing, which was the main activity of the evening, though singing also featured and recitations. 'Mad Carew' was a great favourite of the men. The melodies of Tom Moore were popular and Balfe's songs from *The Bohemian Girl*. They also played Spin the Bottle: the fellow and the girl to whom the bottle pointed when it finished spinning were entitled to a few minutes alone on the landing but they knew that a few minutes was all they'd get before a granny, aunt or some other elderly woman appeared to bring them back.

The hooley lasted from eight o'clock until daybreak. Then the revellers made their way home, stopping to hear the first Mass of the day along the journey. Hooleys figured large in the life of Dublin and Aggie was always delighted when Angel went to one, knowing she'd be safe, and that there was always the chance that she might meet her intended.

But so far she hadn't and Aggie couldn't understand why. She didn't know that Angel was interested in no man except Johnny Quinn. Years ago when she had confessed her love of him to her mother, she had been hardly more than a child, not to be taken seriously. Young girls were forever falling in and out of love. But Aggie thanked God that Angel wrote no more to Tommy and had sent back his money.

While preparing a snack Aggie talked to Angel, who sat absorbed in her thoughts. As usual, they were of Johnny and how she could find him. Lately she had begun to consider England. America was out of the question, too far, too big, and although Danny might lend the fare for her and Aggie to go to England, America would involve more money than he might be willing to part with. And it wasn't only fares she'd need to borrow: there'd have to be a bit more for board and lodging until she found work. England was her best bet, Liverpool, London or Birmingham where there were thousands of Irish. Someone in one of those cities might know of Johnny's whereabouts. One minute she'd be full of the idea and the next every possible obstacle presented itself to her: finding work in a strange city; approaching strangers to make her enquiries.

Aggie had the table laid and said to Angel, 'You're not listening to a word I'm saying.'

Angel apologised. 'I was miles away.'

'Well, come back from wherever you were and let me in on your secrets. You always used to.'

Angel came to the table. 'Now listen,' she said to her mother, 'and don't jump down my throat before I finish telling you. I've been thinking of going to England.'

Aggie was so startled she let the tea she was pouring dribble over her fingers. For a few seconds she didn't feel the searing pain. Angel reached over and took the pot from her, brought a cup of cold water and made Aggie put her fingers in it. Aggie began to cry. 'Oh, but you couldn't, you wouldn't. Not go to England and desert me. I'd die so I would.'

'No, you wouldn't, because I'd take yóu with me.' Angel refilled the cup with cold water. 'The sting will go in a minute.'

The tears were running down Aggie's cheeks. 'Maybe I shouldn't but I've lived every minute of my life through you, praying and hoping that God would spare you, and me to rear you. That was my greatest fear, that I'd die

114

and with no one else belonging to you there'd be nothing but a school for you or an orphanage. And the way little children are treated in them places is a sin against God.'

'Stop it, Ma. You didn't die and I am reared. Don't work yourself up. And about going to England, it was only a thought, the chances are I'll never go. Dry your eyes and eat a bit of bread and cheese. How are your fingers?'

Aggie dried her eyes. 'A bit better.'

'You know I'd never desert you.'

'You're a good daughter, the best. But I wish you were married and settled down. Then I could die happy.'

'Give over about dying! You're as strong as a horse.'

'But we're not long livers in my family, at least not on my side.'

'So eat your bread and cheese. It's good for you.'

Aggie calmed down and began to question Angel as to what had put the idea of going beyond into her mind.

'What's here for me except cutting rashers for the next forty years?'

'But I thought you liked Danny.'

'I've nothing against Danny. I'm just fed up.'

'It'd be different if you were courting.'

'Well, I'm not,' Angel replied, rudely, and Aggie knew it was time to change the conversation. She repeated what she had heard in Danny's shop. 'Mr Bennet is letting Father Clancy have the village hall. It seems that each year there are less Protestants in the village so the hall's seldom used. There's a good few on the outskirts in the big houses but they use the other, older church and would have dances and that in their own homes. Anyway, we've got the hall. And the best thing, it's rent-free and was never used for anything religious so it doesn't have to be reconsecrated or deconsecrated, I'm not sure which.'

Angel showed no enthusiasm about the hall, so Aggie told her the other bit of news. Dr Gorman had had a massive stroke during the night. Angel thought it was the price of him and again was unresponsive, which irritated her mother who had not yet recovered from the earlier news that Angel might go to England. Letting her irritation get the better of her, she said, 'I do often wonder about the morning you came home here in a state after you'd stayed the night in Gorman's, and several times it crossed my mind that he might have tried molesting you during the night. He didn't, did he?'

Hating to be reminded of the incident, Angel turned on her mother. 'You've a terrible bad mind sometimes, Ma. Wouldn't you have been the first one I'd have told?' she lied.

She seldom thought of that night. No harm had come to her and she was always glad she had never mentioned it to anyone except Father Clancy. She still had a great affection for Mrs Gorman and the family. The twins had grown into two lovely girls, away at school. Tim was up at university in the medical school, and the baby must be going on for six or seven.

A few times she'd been tempted to tell Mona about the doctor, though she knew what her response would have been: 'You probably led him on,' the sort of flip remark Mona would make. But since Angel grew older she came to realise that Mona and her family would have spread the news round the village, not caring whether Angel was believed or not. It would just be gossip to them, but Mrs Gorman would have been hurt. And

Angel loved Mrs Gorman. Whenever she dressed up she always wore the string of blue beads Mrs Gorman had given her.

Aggie, still ratty, began to cross-hackle Angel. 'I know it can be lonely for you in the village. You haven't friends beating their way to the door, except that Mona. Maybe I shouldn't have discouraged you so much from making pals when you were growing up. I thought it was for the best. God knows, I haven't many myself and, now and then, I wish I had a friend to confide in. Poor Lizzie, Lord have mercy on her, she was the only true friend. But what about all the girls you meet in the dances and hooleys?'

'I'm not regretting not having a bosom pal. You don't miss what you never had. And as for the girls in the dances, they live on Summer Hill, Blessington Street, Buckingham Street.'

'What's wrong with that?'

'It's the north side. That's where all the dance halls are. They'll marry fellas from the north side. You might never lay eyes on them again.'

'That I find hard to believe.'

'Then tell me this, how often have you been there? Maybe once a year to Moore Street or Henry Street looking for bargains at Christmas. I'm telling you, Dublin's like two different cities.'

'Still and all, you've always got Mona, though you're not so great any more. Not that I'm sorry. I was never mad about her.'

'I won't have her for long. Herself and Benny are getting married.'

'Well, he's not from the north side.'

'No,' said Angel, 'he's from Athlone, the middle of

Ireland. That's where they're going to live. She won't be coming up that often. Who could afford the train fares?'

Months after Angel jilted him Tommy still grieved. He told no one, but his sadness showed on his face. His mates noticed and asked, 'What ails you, Pad?'

He shrugged and replied, 'Think I may have a touch of fever.'

Sometimes in bed he cried silently. He cursed the day he joined the Army, cursed the day he was posted to India. If he'd stayed in Dublin, by now Angel would have been his wife, living in his mother's house as snug as bugs in a rug. He wouldn't have had to go to the war. The British had tried hard enough to bring conscription to Ireland but hadn't succeeded. He'd have got a job. He was big and strong. He'd have done labouring, swept the streets, emptied ash bins, anything to earn a living for Angel and the family they'd have had.

When the crying stopped and he'd calmed down, he'd upbraid himself for a fool. Angel, the most beautiful girl in the village, didn't I fancy myself? Wasn't I aiming high? And the nerve of me trying to tie her to me and she only a child who didn't know how to refuse.

This line of thought stayed with him for several days. Then his spirits would rise and he would be convinced that he mustn't give up hope. Angel must have been in a bad humour when she wrote the letter. Maybe she was already regretting being so hasty. He wouldn't lose heart. He'd give her a bit of time then write again.

Chapter Ten

The village had not made much of the Armistice. Too many of the small population had been killed during the war, or returned home mutilated, blinded, their lungs destroyed by gas. And for the still able-bodied, there was no great prospect of work. Father Clancy said a Mass and prayed for the souls of all those who had lost their lives in the conflict.

In the Protestant church still in use, there was an elaborate service with a large attendance. The few Protestant ex-servicemen who were able to marched behind the Boys' Brigade band, and many of the gentry gave celebration dinners. The biggest house on the outskirts of the village had a celebratory ball. A handful of old men who'd survived the Boer War gathered in one of the local public-houses, reminiscing about their time in South Africa, and attempted to get a sing-song going but their hearts weren't in it and there wasn't enough money to get their spirits going.

Before the year was out Angel overheard Danny and Father Clancy talking about an influenza outbreak that was sweeping the world. 'God between us and all harm,' said the priest, making the sign of the Cross, 'I believe it's killing people in droves. According to the paper, twenty millions are expected to die, more than in the whole of the war.'

'So far,' Danny said, 'I haven't heard tell of a case here. Tell me, how's the new curate settling in?'

'Grand,' replied the priest, 'and I can tell you I'm glad of him. I was beginning to feel my age. But Father

Brennan's taken a heavy part of the load. It was the sick calls during the night that were taking their toll. I'll be off, so.'

Mona was making frantic signs to Angel, waving a piece of newspaper and mouthing that she wanted her to move up the counter. The shop wasn't busy so Angel went to where she was arranging weighed-up packets of tea. 'Look at that,' she said, thrusting the piece of newspaper in front of Angel. 'I'd swear it's him.'

It was a badly blurred print and only half a picture at that. Angel looked and saw half of a man's head, a side of the face missing and a hole through where an eye should have been.

'How could you tell anything from that? It's in bits. Where did you get it?'

'Where d'ye think? From the lav. Me ma tears the paper into small squares and I leaf through them. The minute I saw it I said, "That's Johnny." Can't you see the likeness?'

'It'd be hard for me to do that. Sure there isn't even half of him there.'

'Next time I'll tell my mother to cut the squares life-size. I thought you'd have been delighted. You're terrible hard to please so you are.'

'Thanks very much, Mona. It was kind of you to bring it in. But there's no writing or anything.'

'Well, feck you anyway. Maybe I should have brought you the newspaper. It's the last time I'll bother bringing anything into you.'

'I said I was sorry, didn't I? Did you want me to tell a lie? Let on it was Johnny? That could be a picture of anything. Don't get in a huff about it.'

But Mona was in a huff and didn't talk to Angel until after dinner.

The Irish people whose conciousness had been raised when the leaders of the rebellion were executed in 1916 had been further incensed in 1918 when the British government proposed passing an Act to conscript Irish citizens. Bishops, priests and political leaders were determined to resist it. An anti-conscription pledge was organised and signed in vast numbers. The Bill was dropped.

Many who had escaped execution in 1916 were still in English prisons. Many who had sneered and jeered as the Volunteers who led the rebellion were marched to gaol after surrendering now joined the organisation. And Danny, serving customers, would remind those inter-ested that he had foretold how the executions were the beginning of the end for England in Ireland. 'Wait'll you see the election results. We'll walk it.' The men and women he talked to shared his beliefs: they wanted an Ireland freed once and for all from the tyranny of England.

They worked hard during the run-up to the general election and throughout the country, as did those of like minds. Many who stood for election were still in prison. Of the 105 constituencies, 73 rejected British rule and voted for an Irish republic.

To Mona and Angel it meant nothing. They weren't interested in politics.

Mona's mind was permanently filled with plans for her wedding, the dress she would wear and whether or not to ask Angel to be her bridesmaid. 'It's you I want, only my ma says I should have my sister and relations. But she's years older than me and the others are like horses. I'll feel terrible if me ma makes me have them.'

'I won't mind a bit, honest to God,' Angel told her, every time the issue of bridesmaids came up.

One morning when they'd been discussing it, Mona changed the subject abruptly. 'I knew there was something I wanted to tell you. Remember that newspaper picture I showed you? Well, I mentioned it to my brother the other day and he says it was definitely Johnny Quinn. He saw the paper, read it in the barber's. Only the funny thing was it didn't give Johnny's real name, nor mentioned that he was Irish. The Bruiser Brennan, that's what he's called now. He boxes in England. But the brother's certain sure it's your man.'

'Nobody could be sure who it was from that picture.'

'Ah, but don't forget he saw the whole picture. Like it was in the newspaper not cut up for lavatory paper.'

Maybe it is him, Angel thought. Oh, please, God, let it be him. Please, Holy God, let it be Johnny.

Mona interrupted her prayers and thoughts. 'Christy, don't forget, was in school with him. He wouldn't forget his face.'

'Has Christy got the paper? Would he give me a lend of it?'

'Didn't I tell you he read it in the barber's? They have bundles of them there. It'd have been thrown out by now. Or maybe he brought it home with him and me ma cut it up for the lav.' She shrugged. 'If I was you I'd buy the paper from now on. You might come across something else about him.'

That day Angel told Aggie that from now on she was to get her the newspaper. 'I'll give you the money for it.'

'A newspaper, all of a sudden. What's brought that about?'

'I just fancy a read now and then.'

'Wonders'll never cease,' said Aggie.

*

Every day Angel went through the newspaper carefully, searching for a picture of Johnny or a mention of the Bruiser Brennan. Then one day, when she had decided she was throwing money away, she read a few lines describing an up-and-coming boxer, Bruiser Brennan, who in 1919 would be beginning a tour of Ireland. He was someone to be watched, the small article said. 'This young man is being tipped as the future Heavyweight Champion of the World.'

'That's him. I told you, didn't I?' Mona said, when Angel showed her the paper. 'That's about Johnny.'

'But without a photograph how can you be sure?'

'God, you're terrible hard to convince. My brother saw the photograph. The Bruiser Brennan, that's him. Keep getting the paper. There'll be plenty of pictures nearer the time of the fight, wait'll you see.'

Danny had ordered the hams for Christmas. Women whose husbands had worked throughout the year and saved weekly in Danny's ham club checked how much they'd put by. Most had enough funds for a bottle of port wine, a ham and the makings of their Christmas pudding. But in the days before Christmas they'd be possessed by a frenzy to buy nuts and sweets, fancy biscuits and small toys for children and grandchildren, saying to themselves, 'Sure God's good for tomorrow,' and having the extra goods on score.

Danny longed to be able to give Angel an expensive, personal present – a gold watch, a bracelet – to present her with a jeweller's box and watch her face when she opened it. But expensive presents were only given between sweethearts with a serious understanding. A gold watch was the forerunner of an engagement ring.

He wouldn't dream of compromising Angel with such a gift. In no time news of it would be all round the village. And nods and winks as to the favours Angel must be granting Danny. A large box of chocolates he'd settle for and one exactly the same for Mona.

It was a cold, damp November morning when Mrs Dempsey, Father Clancy's housekeeper, went out to do her shopping. She was well wrapped up, wearing a pull-on felt hat, brown, the same colour as her heavy tweed coat, a knitted scarf, woollen gloves, stockings and thick-soled flat leather shoes. Her pleasant rosy face creased into a becoming smile as she passed parishioners and stopped to speak with friends and acquaintants. Most made a comment about the weather. 'It's a raw morning,' they said, 'terrible weather for anyone chesty. But, please God, the day might pick up.' A few mentioned the increasing raids on police barracks and the amount of arms that had been stolen. One man said to Mrs Dempsey, 'D'ye know, Mary, I'd say there's trouble brewing.'

'I hope to God you're wrong,' replied Mrs Dempsey. 'Wouldn't it be the grand thing if we could live in peace? Not that I'm saying things should stay as they are. There's just cause for discontent. But if only a peaceable way could be found to settle the differences. Hasn't there been enough bloodshed all over the world in the last few years? Millions and millions of young men dead before their time.'

'Indeed, and you never said a truer word. All the same, I feel it in my bones that there's something afoot.'

'What I'm feeling in my bones is the cold.'

'Like myself, you're getting on. We shouldn't be

standing around trying to put the world to rights in this weather.'

'We should not, Billy. I've got shivers running up and down my back. I'll see you again. Tell Maisie I was asking for her. And mind yourself.'

'You, too, Mary.' Billy touched the brim of his hat and they parted.

Mrs Dempsey bought lamb chops, centre loin for Father Clancy and the curate's dinner, a gigot chop for herself, three apple turnovers and a head of cabbage. The shivers got worse, her head had begun to ache and she sneezed several times. 'I think I'm in for a cold,' she said to the greengrocer.

'I think you're right there, Mary. Nip it in the bud, that's my advice. Get home to the fire, make a strong cup of tea and don't stint on the whiskey. The best cure in the world.'

'I wanted a few other things, onions and carrots, pot-herbs. Isn't that terrible? My head's that muzzy I can't remember the other things.'

'Listen,' said the vegetable man, 'don't I know what you're in the habit of buying? You go home and I'll get the young fella to run up on the bike with them. Anything you don't want, send back.'

'You're very obliging. This is the queerest cold I've ever had. One minute I'm freezing and the next feeling like a furnace. I'll take your advice and go. Please God, I'll be myself tomorrow.'

'Please God you will.'

Two days later Mrs Dempsey died.

'Was it her heart?' a shocked and grief-stricken Father Clancy asked the doctor who had replaced Dr Gorman.

'Her heart was as sound as a bell. She died of influenza. It's being called Spanish flu. They're dying like flies all over the world with it, the frail and elderly usually. But Mrs Dempsey was a fine woman and only fifty. Still, you never know with these infections. But, as sure as God, she won't be the last in the village to succumb to it.'

Father Clancy made the sign of the Cross. 'We're all in God's hands,' he said resignedly.

After the doctor left, he made arrangements for Mrs Dempsey's funeral, she not having anyone belonging to her, and then had to find another housekeeper, a temporary one for the time being. Mrs Dempsey had been a treasure, but he knew from long experience that treasures were few and far between. He didn't want someone coming in who'd upend the house with reorganisations, nor one that would treat him and his curate as if she was their mother. But the ones he dreaded most were the dragons, and of those he'd had a few, pompous and pious, hero-worshippers of the clergy, self-appointed guardians who took it upon themselves to decide who should have access to the presbytery and the priest. Invariably those they turned from the door were the shabby, the poor, those they considered common or a nuisance, those often in desperate straits. As if the unfortunates didn't suffer enough humiliation! No, that wasn't the sort of housekeeper he wanted.

The cases of flu increased in the village and throughout the country. It was terrifying. As Aggie said to Danny one day when she was in the shop, buying two ounces of hard red cheese, 'I saw her and him one day in the whole of their health, laughing and tricking the way they always were after a couple of bottles of stout, and before the end of the week they were dead and buried. A couple that'd never been laid up in their lives.'

Angel and Mona, still in their teens and believing themselves immortal, scoffed at their mothers' warnings to wrap up well, wear their scarves, never to put on a screed that wasn't thoroughly aired and on no account go to bed if their hair was still damp. Angel skipped through her newspaper, ignoring reports of the flu and accounts of police barracks being raided for arms as she searched each page for news of the Bruiser Brennan. She was ecstatic the day she found a few lines hinting that in the New Year he'd be fighting in Dublin. 'Oh, please, God, let it be him,' she said, showing Mona the article.

'Of course it's him. You get on my nerves sometimes. Didn't Christy see his photograph?'

'Yeah, I know that but I didn't, at least not properly.'

'All right. But why you're in such a lather over someone who never gave you the time of day I don't know.'

'He will this time, if it's him. I know that in my heart. He was bashful, that's all.'

'Bashful my eye,' retorted Mona. 'But I'll say a prayer.'

Aggie went to confession and before leaving the box, having been given absolution and three Hail Marys for her penance, she whispered through the mesh screen, 'I wanted to talk to you about Angel. Would you have the time, Father?'

'How many were waiting when you came in?'

'I was the last one.'

'That's great. So tell me now what's worrying you about the child.'

'I couldn't put my finger on it exactly, but something about her has changed in the last couple of weeks. When she's not daydreaming, she's before the glass doing herself up. And she's not going across the door. Then she's trying on frocks and hats. And then for that again she'll burst into a fit of crying. D'ye think she's getting too much attention from fellas in the shop?'

'It could be,' said the priest, 'or maybe not enough from the right fella. Has she mentioned one in particular?'

'Not at all. Sure amn't I always on at her to find one? She goes dancing and to all-night hooleys but for all the good it does she might as well be an oul maid in a garret.'

'Wasn't she doing a line with Tommy Maguire? I remember something about that.'

'Poor Tommy, she was coddin' him up to the two eyes for years. The poor eejit used to send her money to save for their wedding. Letters came from India regularly. Sometimes she'd write, sometimes she wouldn't. Thank God that's all stopped. You know his poor mother's been taken bad with the flu?'

'I do. Dr Cassidy doesn't think she'll pull through.'

'D'ye think Tommy would get one of the compassionate leaves?'

'Not from India. His mother'd be long dead and buried before he even got a boat. The vagaries of youth, that's my guess as to what ails Angel. I wouldn't worry about it. She's a good girl. Now is there anything else bothering you, Aggie?'

'No, thank you, Father, you've put my mind at rest.'

'Good, then that's grand. My supper'll be on the table and Mrs Flanagan flapping like a mother hen in case it goes cold.'

Aggie rose from her knees and thanked the priest, who blessed her before she left the confessional.

He pondered the situation. Aggie was genuinely worried. Maybe Angel was losing the run of herself. She attracted too much attention in the shop. It could be flattering but not for her own good, and all the more so if it wasn't from someone she was interested in. It could account for her moods. A spell in a quiet atmosphere might be what she needed. There was no harm in trying it and he was always glad to oblige Aggie.

He'd mention it to Danny. He wrote to the Bishop, explaining that his temporary housekeeper was leaving in February and he mightn't get another in a hurry. Then he mentioned Angel, her youth, her attractiveness, the unblemished character of the girl and her mother, who was his cousin, how he had known Angel all her life, christened her and prepared her for confirmation. She would be employed on the understanding that the post wasn't permanent and she wouldn't live in.

The Bishop, who had been in the seminary with Father Clancy, wrote back to say, 'Go ahead, I trust your judgement.'

Mrs Flanagan brought in his supper, left him to eat it, and then returned with his pudding, baked rice with a golden nutmeg-flavoured crust. She lingered while he ate it, asking, 'I was wondering, Father, if you'd found anyone for when I leave?'

'I have,' he said. 'This very day.'

Dying with curiosity, Mrs Flanagan waited to see if he'd mention a name. She shifted a few plates, taking her time to stack them on the tray.

'I thought I'd have Angel in for a while.'

'Oh, Father!' A look of alarm wiped the usual good-natured smile from Mrs Flanagan's face. 'Would that be wise?'

'She'd be grand for the time being. No fear of her taking the nose off an unfortunate creature who came to the door looking for help.'

'No, indeed there wouldn't, she has a lovely manner. But, if you don't mind me saying it, she's a bit too young and very pretty. God knows, she's not flighty or free-making but it's bound to cause talk. Maybe if it was only you here, but the young priest . . . And another thing, isn't there a custom about priests' housekeepers being of a certain age? I hope you won't think bad of me talking out like this, but I know only too well many of the women in the village.'

Father Clancy got up from the table and placed a hand on Mrs Flanagan's shoulder. 'You're a good woman so you are. And you can stop worrying about certain women in the village. First of all, Angel's a blood relation, distant it's true but it grants exemption from the laws you were talking about. The next thing is it's only a temporary job and she won't be sleeping in. And, of course, the most important of all, I've got the Bishop's permission to employ her. Now, does that satisfy you? Come to think of it, that explanation and the Bishop's permission wouldn't have been needed if that daughter of yours wasn't poaching you. You'd have made the grand housekeeper.'

Angel was working herself up to fever pitch with expectations of soon hearing that Johnny would be back in Dublin, trying on hats, frocks, different hairstyles, as her mother had told the priest, one minute buoyed up with such hope, planning what she would say when she and Johnny met, then drowning in waves of despair as she remembered how never once had he given her a second glance, nor spoken a civil word to her.

Aggie was frantic, fearing for her daughter's sanity, recalling that long ago a relation on her mother's side of the family had died in the madhouse. A girl, a beauty, so her mother had said, who even in the asylum wore hats and was always titivating herself. So when Father Clancy called to talk about employing Angel after Christmas she was greatly relieved. 'May God bless you, Father. A break away from the shop is the very thing. Living in a peaceful, holy atmosphere will be the making of her.'

He was coming home. In the New Year he'd be back in Dublin, under a different name, but they'd know who he was. Word would get out. The Bruiser Brennan was Johnny Quinn – Johnny Quinn made good. Money in his pocket, dressed to the nines. Money for his mother. He'd set her up, maybe in a little shop. And as for the oul fella, if there was a way of doing him in without being detected he'd do it. But he wasn't worth hanging for. Money would buy him over, a weekly amount with the threat that if he ever laid a finger on his mother again he was finished. He knew plenty in the boxing world who'd kick the shite out of him, leave him for as good as dead, but not quite. And another thing, he'd buy the house for his mother but in his own name. Then, apart from the hiding, if his father made one false move, he'd have him evicted. Nothing for him then but the union.

He wondered about Angel, wondered if she was still single. Sometimes he dreamed of her, dreams that to begin with were beautiful, dreams in which, with arms about each other, they walked by the river. Her golden hair was loose about her shoulders and she wore a dress the colour of violets, the same colour as her eyes.

In the dream it was always a hazy summer's day. There were dog-roses in the hedge along the river. They were the palest of pink, almost white, and he wanted to pick them and put them in Angel's hair. But he remembered their small pricking thorns and how that once they were picked their petals dropped away.

The sun would break through the haze now and then, and always when he and Angel came to where the river deepened the sun went again into the hazy mist and the day grew dark and gloomy. The young boys were swimming and tricking, ducking each other under the water, their white skinny arms thrashing the water, their bundles of ragged clothes and thin greyish towels weighted by stones on the bank. They were laughing and shouting good-naturedly to each other until they caught sight of him. Then they began jeering him, chanting in chorus, 'Raggedy-arsed Quinn', as they had when he was a small boy. 'You're oul fella's mad. All the Quinns are mad and you're oul wan's the town's bike.' He felt as he had when a boy, the lump choking him. Stones were here and there beside the path; big enough to smash one of the seal-like heads. But he was afraid. He was always on his own. And they were a crowd.

Now it was different. He was holding Angel's arm. The warm, firm flesh gave him courage. And he shouted at them, 'Sticks and stones may break my bones but names will never hurt me,' the way he had wanted to shout years ago, but never had, only whispered it to himself. And Angel squeezed his arm to her side, and he said, 'Snotty-nosed kids, that's all they are. I've got you and all the world before me.' It was still dark in his dream but a little breeze blew off the water and he shivered. At the same time Angel let go of his arm and jumped into the river, among the still laughing, jeering boys. She laughed and screamed with them, her voice louder than theirs. And she screamed, 'Raggedy-arsed Quinn. You haven't got me. I wouldn't be seen dead with you. Put that in your pipe and smoke it.'

He turned away and ran stumbling along the bank, the voices and jeering laughter pursuing him and Angel's voice was the loudest of them all. And he cried as he ran. And for an instant after he woke, he thought, There is no one, no one to trust.

In the first week of December he sent money to his mother. As usual he addressed it to Jackser's common-law wife who, as usual, put it underneath a statue of the Infant of Prague on top of a sixpenny bit she kept there for luck. Before Christmas, Johnny's mother would come to collect the brown envelope.

She had begun wall-papering the kitchen when the post had come and now returned to the task, singing as she trimmed and pasted and, with a soft cloth, smoothed the wrinkles and air bubbles from the last piece she had stuck to the wall. She was in great humour for soon Jackser would be back from England and, by all accounts, home for a couple of months. The place had to be spick and span. That's how her Jackser liked it. He'd notice the new wall-paper and praise it and her for the grand woman she was. She sat down for a rest before she gave the ornaments one of their twice-yearly washes. Easter was the other time when her vast collection of jugs, plates, small and large statues were immersed in soapy suds. While washing her lustre jugs she admired their gold, brown and deep blue glaze. They had been presents from Jackser. When it was the Infant of Prague's turn she moved the brown envelope and put it in a safe place.

Danny couldn't refuse Father Clancy's request to borrow Angel for a few weeks. After Christmas things would be slack, the women regretting their extravagance and buying only what was essential while they cleared their Christmas debts. But the prospect of the shop without her depressed him. He'd miss her radiant presence, the movement of her body as she walked in front of him to the storeroom, the cloud of silky golden hair held back from her face by ribbons or slides but still cascading down her back. Most of all he'd miss the fantasy he indulged in every evening as closing-time drew near. Once the tidying up was done, the till checked, money in the safe, doors and windows secured, he'd go up to the living quarters. Already Angel would be there, in the kitchen, making his supper.

While eating it he'd gaze at her across the table, marvelling that she was his wife. They'd laugh and chat about the day's happenings. He wouldn't talk about anything too serious, nothing about the state of the country, his fears that the killings would begin again. She was still only a child on whose shoulders you shouldn't put an old head.

'Go and work in the presbytery, Ma! Me? A priest's housekeeper? Have you and Father Clancy lost your minds? You have to be ancient to be a priest's house-keeper. And, for another thing, I can't boil an egg. It'd be the end of my dancing days and all-night hooleys.'

'Indeed you can boil an egg and cook a dinner. Simple food, like ourselves, is all you'll have to do. And no heavy cleaning. There's a woman comes in twice a week for that. It's the bit of food and answering the telephone and the door that's Father Clancy's biggest want. And another thing, after the supper you can come home. 'Twouldn't be fair to keep you there in the evening. You're too young, he said, to spend your time with a pair of crusty old bachelors. You'll get six shillings a week and three meals a day.'

'I don't want to leave the shop. Mona'll make a laugh of me. I love the shop, there's always something going on.'

Too much, if you ask me, thought Aggie. The turning of your head for one thing. And I wouldn't mind if it was getting you anywhere.

'And another thing . . .' Angel said, then realised she had almost let the cat out of the bag. She said nothing of the news of Johnny, instead complained how she'd miss Mona and the news of her wedding plans.

'It seemed to me as if it was something else you were going to say,' said Aggie. 'What was it?'

'Nothing,' replied Angel. 'I'll go to work at the presbytery. But I'm telling you now I'm not making it a permanent thing.'

'It won't be, love, you've my promise. Now, there's a

few things I have to talk to you about. Listen and pay attention.'

'I am,' said Angel sulkily.

'Well, it's going to be different from the shop.'

'Who are you telling?'

'You're getting very impertinent all of a sudden.'

Angel shrugged. 'Go on, then, tell me. I'm all ears.'

'You'll have to be very modest when you're working for Father Clancy. He mightn't notice but don't forget the young priest.'

'He is gorgeous. I've never seen such beautiful eyes. Though, come to think of it, Tommy Maguire had nice eyes.'

'After nearly six years how would you know what colour his eyes were? I wish you wouldn't keep interrupting me, you've put my thoughts astray. Oh, yes, it was about young Father Brennan, the curate. Don't be laughing and tricking too much, or shaking that golden poll of yours or making them eyes. Poor Father Brennan's only a bit of a boy with a long, hard road in front of him.'

'But, Ma, I'd never trick or laugh with a priest. How could you, and them so holy? But I can't go round with a sack over my head for the time I'm in the presbytery.'

Aggie put a shovelful of coal on the fire. 'There's places in the world where women have to.'

'Where?' asked Angel.

'Out foreign somewhere. Their fathers or brothers would cut their throats if they showed their faces.'

'A sack, imagine. I'm glad I don't live there.'

'Maybe not a sack exactly, but they're covered up. Oh, and the other thing I heard was that Mrs Quinn is on her last. The flu – though, mind you, thanks be to God, they say it's petering out.'

Angel's heart was racing like a hare being chased by hounds, not giving the dying Mrs Quinn a thought. After all the years, she'd see him soon. He'd come for his mother's funeral.

But he didn't. No one in the village knew where he was. Mrs Quinn's death wasn't put in the evening paper so Jackser's common-law wife, who read the deaths in the paper every night, no matter how long the column was, didn't hear of it. She had wondered why Mrs Quinn hadn't called to collect the envelope – it was strange with Christmas just around the corner – but at the same time she was greatly relieved, for she couldn't remember where she had hidden the money. High and low she'd searched, and no sign of it. Tomorrow she'd go out and buy a brown envelope and put a pound note in it. A ten-shilling note was what Johnny usually sent. She knew because she often steamed open the envelopes. But at Easter, Christmas and for St Patrick's Day it was a pound. Mrs Quinn would be none the wiser and the other envelope was bound to turn up.

Angel pinned her hopes on the morning of the burial. He'd surely arrive for that, and afterwards she'd go up to him and say, 'I'm terrible sorry for your trouble.' From there on it'd be up to him. There wouldn't be any tea and sandwiches laid on in the Quinns.' She couldn't see his father arranging that, and the girls had long since left home. In such a case the neighbours usually stepped in and provided something, but no one would go next or near oul Quinn's place. He'd spit in their faces, accuse them of nosing around or even tell them to 'fuck off'.

Of course, that would give her the excuse to ask him home. Her mother wasn't mad about him but wouldn't refuse him a cup of tea. He was bound to open up, tell her where he'd been, when he'd be fighting in Dublin. And it could lead to something. She'd look her best in the morning. Black suited her. Luckily she had a black skirt and coat, and a black hat. There were feathers and flowers on it but they wouldn't take a minute to snip off. Her black boots wanted heeling, but by the time she got to the graveside they'd be thick with mud. No one would notice the worn-down heels. And she had a book of powder leaves. One of those would give her cheeks a bloom and a few bites of her lips have them rosy.

The burial wasn't well attended. Mr and Mrs Quinn had had few friends. Only for the regular morning Mass-goers, who after the service walked round the back of the chapel to where the cemetery was, there'd have been no one but Danny, a few of the St Vincent de Paul men, Aggie and a bitterly disappointed Angel for of Johnny there was no sign.

At about the time his mother's cheap deal coffin was being lowered into the grave and his father beating his breast and calling his wife's name, tears pouring down his stubbly cheeks, and a woman standing behind Angel whispering, 'the bloody oul hypocrite, if I was beside him I'd push him in. Beating his breast, indeed, didn't them fists of his have plenty of practise hopping off the poor unfortunate woman,' Johnny was standing naked before the mirror in his small hotel admiring his body, running his hands over his flat belly, his chest and thighs. Delighting in his well-muscled torso and his face that, so far, had never in all his bouts been damaged. Soon he'd be back in Dublin. A big fight, a big purse. After that the quarter-finals in England, then the semis, and, later on in the year, Carnegie Hall and the World Championship.

In India Tommy Maguire longed for May and the rains that would fall in solid sheets and you could breathe. The itch subsided and the dryness in your nose and throat was moistened. He'd heard a rumour that the Regiment would be going home in a couple of years, but there were always rumours of one thing or another. Wishful thinking, most of them.

Tommy hoped the one about going home was true. Then he'd find out why Angel didn't write any more. Maybe, as she'd said in the last letter he'd had from her, she'd gone to England or America. After that letter, she had sent back the money they been saving for their wedding. His tears had stopped now but he still hadn't lost hope. If she was still single and in the village perhaps he could talk her round. And if she was single and in England or America, he'd follow her. He still wrote to Angel – at least, in his mind – pleading for her to give him another chance, declaring his love.

Danny had a note from Brian Nolan, full of apologies for not getting in touch before, especially as he'd been over to Dublin for a few days, but he was up to his eyes every minute on Army affairs. Next year, which was only round the corner for sure, they'd meet up. Danny put away the card. Brian hadn't given an address. Whatever was going on wasn't his business, he was sure they'd meet again. They went back a long time.

Chapter Eleven

Many of the parishioners were outraged when it became known that Angel was to be Father Clancy's house-keeper, some widow women or spinsters, purely on the grounds that they were more in need of the employment if only for as long as it took the priest to find a suitable woman for the job. Others believed it was sinful for a girl so young and nubile to be keeping house for two priests. The leader of this group was Miss Heffernan, the retired headmistress of the Catholic school. She had great influence in many of the village women's lives, being the head prefect of the women's Sodality and a senior officer in the Legion of Mary.

She was a tall raw-boned woman, with scant ginger hair and skin that once had been fair but was now threaded with minute red and purple veins. While in her convent boarding school, she'd believed she had a vocation. The nuns encouraged her and her parents were overjoyed. Her father was the relieving officer and, while not in the league of doctors and solicitors, was consid-ered socially above the tramway men. He and his wife were devout Catholics, and the news of their daughter's vocation was an answer to their prayers. If they had had a son they'd have prayed for him to enter the priesthood, but a nun in the family was the next best thing.

Once, Miss Heffernan's scant hair had been a lustrous auburn, and her skin like thick cream, the angular face and frame clad with becoming flesh. This was her appearance when she left the convent and waited to re-enter as a postulant. In the interval she fell in love with Larry Lucas.

Larry was the handsomest man in the village, seldom sober, seldom working and with an eye for the women. He cast his eye on Miss Heffernan and caught her. They walked out for a while, at first, on her insistence, furtively, meeting after dark, choosing secluded places for their strolling. But after a while, knowing that secrecy was almost impossible in the village, they went about openly with Miss Heffernan clinging to his arm, proudly displaying her prize. Until Larry cast his eye on Aggie and jilted Miss Heffernan.

She was devastated. Her parents and the nuns were relieved that the futile affair was over and pleaded with her to resurrect her vocation. But Miss Heffernan knew now that it had only been a passing fancy, and refused. She trained instead as a teacher.

There were those in the village who believed she had never got over being jilted, 'Never looked at another man since.'

And those who'd retorted, 'Sure what man'd give her a second glance, hard, barren old bitch.'

'All the same,' the more charitable defended her, 'she softened while she courted Larry.'

'Courting – that only lasted kissing time. Pity he didn't put her up the pole. That'd've taken the starch outta her. She was stuck up even in the high babies.'

These women, who blocked the paths in groups to gossip and guffaw and drank in the snug, were anathema to Miss Heffernan. She sensed their raucous laughter was meant for her. She hated them but convinced herself their immortal souls were in danger of damnation. And that it was her duty to save them.

From time to time she broached this subject to Father Clancy, suggesting he should use his influence to have them join the Sodality. Each time his reply was the same, always couched tactfully, for Miss Heffernan was invaluable to the running of the parish. She was in charge of the altar linen with a team of expert laundresses in tow; she organised the church cleaning rota, the flower arranging, whist drives, summer fêtes, jumble sales and Christmas bazaars. At her beck and call were jam, fairy-cake and sponge makers, knitters and crochet experts, who year after year produced egg cosies, babies' booties, pincushions and knick-knacks of all kinds which sold and swelled the parish funds. For all of this he was grateful, but more grateful still that Miss Heffernan was a woman, above all others, who wouldn't apply for the house-keeper's job, considering it beneath her.

She revelled in the power and authority of the offices she held. Father Clancy believed she hadn't an ounce of charity in her. She took after her father: the priest remembered the women he'd seen crying, poor women forced to apply for relief that Mr Heffernan had means-tested; he had seen their humiliation, their dejection when their applications were turned down because their homes displayed the slightest degree of comfort or decoration, a decent quilt, an ornament, a picture. Holy pictures and religious statues weren't taken into account but all else was. They were ordered to sell or pawn the items before applying again for relief. These happenings he'd recall as he placated Miss Heffernan. 'You're a grand woman. How the parish would function without you I don't know. But these women you want to join the Sodality – I'm not so sure it would work. D'ye see, although they're good women, come to Mass and the Sacraments, they're unreliable. They'd join, all right. The first week the chapel'd be thronged with them. The next week half of them wouldn't show up. After that you could bid them goodbye. And all the work gone for nothing. The name taking and writing down. Didn't we try it a few years back after the mission when the missionary priest put the fear of God into them?'

Miss Heffernan would agree but argue that perhaps it was time to try again, and Father Clancy would say, 'I know all about their sup of porter and, believe you me, a sup is all it is. They've big families and most of them have husbands who have more than a sup of porter – knock their wives about and some of their children, too. In the morning they're heartfelt sorry. Not another drop will pass their lips. They'll take the Pledge. Come the evening and the promises have flown. But the strange thing is, I don't think I've mentioned this before, the majority of those women love their reprobates of husbands. And what keeps them going is their gathering with other women in the same circumstances. The gossiping, exchanging their woes. Hearing of men worse than their own. Taking comfort from each other. Helping each other with the lend of a shilling. Laughing and crying together. Even the jeering they do of the women you and I think respectable. And, of course, the sup of porter.'

He could always tell by Miss Heffernan's face that he hadn't convinced her. And then he'd have to pull rank. 'I know, Miss Heffernan, you have the welfare of their souls at heart and that's admirable. Pray for them and get the members of the Sodality to do the same. And the rest you'll have to leave to me.'

He smiled then, and hoped it would appear sincere, and bade her goodbye.

She thought, as she usually did after such an encounter, Men, they're all the same. All the initiative must come from them or it's dismissed. But she also thought of something he had said for the first time ever, that these women, or most of them, still loved their husbands.

And she said to herself, 'About that he's probably right, for don't I still love Larry Lucas?' And as she went on towards her home, she looked back into the past, recalling the time when she'd walked out with him. His kisses, the first kisses she had ever known. The liberties she had granted him, letting him undo the buttons on her blouse, helping him because the loops were tight and his fingers clumsy. His hands inside her bodice, cold on her warm flesh. His hands cupping her breasts, easing them out, kissing each in turn. His fingers finding her erect nipples, stroking them, transporting her into a state of rapture. A rapture she had never experienced before, not even when she received the Body and Blood of Christ. She had walked on air. All things seemed beautiful. She wanted to sing, shout, dance through the streets proclaiming that she was in love. Her courage was like that of a lion when she faced the fury of her parents after informing them that she no longer had a vocation. That she loved Larry Lucas and would marry him.

And marry they might have. But until they did even her rapturous state allowed no greater liberties. He stroked her lustrous auburn hair, her neck, her earlobes, the breasts she fumbled to push back into her bodice. Her legs trembled, all of her trembled. Silently she had prayed to the Blessed Virgin not to let her succumb to his caresses. Oh, yes, she remembered. She loved him still – an old, bitter woman in her sixties. She prayed he would not, but into her dreams he still came. Sinful dreams. Dreams she didn't understand. Dreams she could not describe but in which she was convulsed by such pleasurable sensations she knew them to be sinful.

Was that what the women Father Clancy spoke of experienced with their husbands? Was that what made them love men who were despicable? After such dreams she'd rise, kneel by her bed and say an act of contrition. But she never confessed them, reasoning that to sin was a wilful act. In dreams, your will had no command.

How she felt about Angel was a different matter. Every time she saw her, even when she had been an infant, hate surged through Miss Heffernan. Every time she looked at Angel's face, which she avoided doing if possible, she saw the face of Larry, reminding her of all she had lost. That, she knew, was a sin and she confessed it and promised to mend her ways, but knew in her heart that she never would. She longed to harm Angel, to avenge her suffering on a child who might have been hers. Perhaps an opportunity was at hand.

'It's not as bad as I thought,' Angel told Aggie, after working for a week in the presbytery. 'Not hard work at all. Father Clancy and Father Brennan are very tidy. I never have to pick up after them. They even fold the newspapers and put them in a basket. It's answering the door I do mostly. You'd be surprised the number that comes to talk to the priest. All sorts. If the priests are at home I show them into the parlour. Sometimes I'll have to make tea for them. That doesn't take a minute.'

'I hope you don't earwig outside the door.'

'Ma, what ails you? Of course I wouldn't.'

'I'm only warning you. How about the dinners and that?'

'Porridge and a fry for their breakfast, bacon and cabbage, stews, a bit of corned-beef, lamb chops, always cabbage, though sometimes yellow turnips as well. They like custard and jelly and rice puddings. The cakes are bought. Sometimes I make their tea. Boiled eggs, or cheese, and on Saturdays another fry. Then after I've washed the delft I'm finished.'

'So you don't miss the shop?'

'I do in a way. Mona, mostly. We used to have great gas.'

'But you'll see her now and again.'

'Now and again is right. She's up to her eyes with plans for the wedding. You didn't forget the paper?'

'That's right now, bury your nose in it.'

Angel did, scanning it carefully page by page, searching for news of Johnny.

'D'ye see anything of Danny these days?'

Angel sighed at the interruption. 'He was up at the presbytery yesterday, bringing prizes for the whist drive.'

'What whist drive?' asked Aggie.

There was no mention of Johnny in the paper. Angel put it down. 'Oul Heffernan's started them up again in that hut the Protestant vicar gave. Danny plays now. A few other men go. It used to be all women. I was never any good at cards. Not for the life of me could I remember what cards had gone.'

'I'd say you'd have a good head for the cards. You should go some night.'

'I wouldn't be found dead at a whist drive – only old people go to them.'

'Danny's not that old.'

'Ah, give over, Ma, he's forty at least.'

'Your man out in India's not far off that.'

'What's that got to do with me?'

Aggie decided she'd said enough, but she had put in a plug for Danny, for all the good it would do.

Miss Heffernan knew it would be of no use to tell Father Clancy the animosity felt by many women in the village at Angel being employed by him. He'd fob her off with some excuse or other, then go away smiling like Judas. She had other plans she had already aired among her cronies. She'd write a letter to the Bishop and get as many people as possible to sign it. In a couple of weeks, one night after the whist drive, she'd hold an impromptu meeting, put her point of view then pass round the petition for signing. Occasionally Father Clancy came to the drives. However, she knew he was going to Dublin in the near future for a few days. Then she would hold her meeting.

'It's fixed for Dublin, the twentieth March,' Jackser announced, coming into Johnny's hotel room in Manchester where the night before at Bellevue he had won his last big fight. 'No lying back on your laurels. The Irish bloke's good.'

'Have I ever?'

'Codding you, Johnny. I know your strength. How are you feeling this morning?'

'Gameball,' replied Johnny, stretching in the bed, displacing the covers and showing off his magnificent torso. 'Great to think I'll be in Dublin again. See me ma. A big shot, the Bruiser Brennan. Like a dream come true.'

'It's no dream, you've worked for it. You're the stuff, fists like hams, and taking the discipline. You've got it all. Listen, I'll leave you to it. We'll talk later on. Meet for a bite about one.'

Jackser didn't want to linger long. Johnny might start talking again about his mother, want to fix up sending more money to her or writing a letter. Jackser was worried about that. There was some mystery about Johnny's mother. Lily had told him how she'd never come to collect the brown envelopes. They believed she must be dead. Johnny had to be kept in the dark until after the Dublin fight. He was a great boxer but unpredictable in certain circumstances. Jackser dreaded having to tell him that the Dublin fight had to be 'thrown' but he'd make him see the sense in it. The money in it. But to discover that his mother was dead as well, God alone knew how he'd react. The news of his mother and the fixed fight had to be kept until the last minute, not a word mentioned until the publicity was out and they were in Dublin, Johnny's face on the posters. The place, the date, the time, the opponent would be plastered all over the city. Johnny was professional enough not to renege at the last minute.

By the time Miss Heffernan called her meeting, the village had taken sides in the Angel affair. The women who went to the snug called Miss Heffernan a frosty-faced oul bitch who needed a good man. The genuinely religious, although believing Angel hadn't been a wise choice, put their trust in Father Clancy and Father Brennan, and that Angel, although outstandingly allur-ing, conducted herself with decorum. Others changed their view of the situation from day to day, one day fearing the worst and the next caught up in their own business, shrugging their shoulders and saying, 'What'll happen will, if it's going to.' And then there were Miss Heffernan's followers, many of whom never suspected that anything sinful might occur but were incensed by Angel's appointment because they believed it wasn't just: Angel already had a permanent job.

However, the hard core of Miss Heffernan's cronies saw only temptation put in the way of one of God's holy anointed. They envisaged Angel as another Eve proffering the apple. At every opportunity they voiced their thoughts and inflamed feelings. Even those who didn't play whist had come along to the hut to sign Miss Heffernan's petition to the Bishop.

The tables and chairs were rearranged so that people faced the platform from which Miss Heffernan would address the meeting. She sat at a table flanked by two of her cronies. Her letter to the Bishop, attached to many sheets of paper for signing, was in front of her. There was a lot of coughing and throat clearing. When it subsided, Miss Heffernan stood up and addressed the audience. 'I think that most of you know why this meeting is being held. A young girl has been employed by Father Clancy as his temporary housekeeper. I've spoken to many of you, heard your views. They agree with my own. This job, however temporary, should never have been given to such a young woman. It is against canon law.'

She read from a notepad a Latin tag and its translation. 'It means, an elderly or mature woman, and not good-looking. Certainly nothing like Angel – such a ridiculous name, and not the one with which she was christened. I'm sure the appointment is not one of which the Bishop would approve. I have written informing his Grace of the situation, telling him how scandalised the parish is by this appointment.'

She paused to drink from a glass of water then continued. 'I know that every good Catholic man and woman here tonight will approve of my decision and will not hesitate to sign the petition, which I shall attach to the letter.'

She was about to sit down when Danny rose from his seat. 'Tell me, Miss Heffernan,' he asked, 'have you shown Father Clancy the letter you intend sending to the Bishop?'

'No,' she replied.

'Why not?'

'I didn't consider that necessary. A parishioner is entitled to write to their Bishop.' She glared at him, thinking, It's not Father Clancy you're considering but Angel. She'd seen the lascivious way Danny looked at her in the shop.

'Indeed they are. Many do, but few, I would think, write to complain about a priest's choice of housekeeper. The girl in question has an unblemished character. Is it the colour of her hair you object to or her name, which you mentioned earlier on?'

Miss Heffernan gripped the table edge with both hands. She felt slightly faint. How dare Danny Connolly question her? But she had quelled him before, before he went away to school. She had taught many of them in the hall and quelled them, ignoramuses that they were, and she'd do it again. 'My reasons for complaint I've explained. It is against canon law to employ nubile young women as priests' housekeepers.'

'Don't you think Father Clancy better versed in canon law than you, and don't you think that complaining to the Bishop about a priest who has christened many in this hall, married many of the couples, given the sacrament of extreme unction to their relatives, comforted them in bereavements is a form of disloyalty? Surely your course of action should have been to discuss the matter first with Father Clancy.'

'He's away in Dublin. Will you sit down and be quiet?' She spoke to him as if he was still in the infant school. 'This matter is no concern of yours.'

'I'm a parishioner, and it's as much my concern as yours. No one can stop you sending the letter. The petition is a different matter. It seems to me that you are attempting to browbeat people into signing it. And did you know that Angel is a blood relation of Father Clancy?' Danny continued. 'That he has written to the Bishop and obtained his permission to employ Angel on a temporary basis?'

There was a shuffling of feet, the sound of whispering. Miss Heffernan took several deep breaths to steady her nerves and then, in a voice that had never failed to restore order to her classroom, she demanded silence. When she spoke again, her voice was less assured. 'Everyone who believes that in the sending of the letter and the petition we will be doing our Christian duty put your hands up.'

No more than a dozen hands rose, and Miss Heffernan went puce in the face. Then the colour drained from it and she fainted.

Members of her clique were hovering about her as she came round, loosening her clothes, proffering a drink of water, fanning her with religious pamphlets and murmuring words condemning Danny Connolly. As she recovered, she saw that the hall was emptying and heard the buzz of talking and tittering. The letter and petition were never sent.

Father Clancy returned from his visit to Dublin. Father Brennan told about the letter, petition and Miss Heffernan's part in it. 'That woman wouldn't have her health if she wasn't trying to cause trouble,' he said resignedly to the curate.

To accommodate tram workers on the early shift Danny opened the shop at six o'clock.

Angel, on her way to make breakfast for the priests, called in for a message. He told her the gist of the previous night's meeting. She shrugged and repeated one of Father Clancy's sayings: 'There's a Miss Heffernan in every village. A cross we have to bear.'

At the first opportunity Father Clancy sought out Angel and assured her the job was hers until he found a suitable replacement. 'I must say, you're looking great. You're not upset about what happened?'

'I'm used to her,' replied Angel. 'She's been out to get me as long as I can remember. Me ma says it's because years ago she did a line with my father. Maybe it is, but there's more to it than that. It's her nature. She's a bully, and vindictive. I won't be sorry to leave the likes of her.'

'Are you planning on leaving us, then?'

'Hoping. I've hinted about it to my ma. You and her'll be the first to know when I know myself.'

'Good luck with your hopes. I hope the fulfilment of them will make you happy.'

'Oh, they will, Father. I know they will.'

He left her to carry on with her work, and she went

through the house polishing, dusting, straightening a picture, while her heart sang. In last night's *Evening Herald* she had found what she had been searching for all these weeks and months: a recognisable photograph of Johnny – a changed Johnny, but him all the same. He was older-looking now with a man's face, handsome. Better still, there had been a few lines beneath the picture stating that the Bruiser Brennan, a native of Dublin, would be fighting in his home city in the near future. The date and venue would be published shortly.

Tonight after work she'd go and tell Mona, even though she was busy with her wedding plans. She had to tell someone and there was no one else except Mona. And, besides, although she wasn't being a bridesmaid, she'd been invited to the wedding and that meant a new rig-out. She'd coax Mona to come and help her choose it. And she'd wear it when she met Johnny. How she'd arrange that she didn't know, but meet him she would.

Miss Heffernan brooded about the outcome of the meeting. Angel was still in the presbytery, flaunting herself before the priests, laughing and joking and they responding. She had her spies: her laundresses and flower arrangers, who sometimes had to call at the house. They were primed to keep a sharp lookout for anything that went beyond the bounds of decorum. So far it was only laughing and joking, with never a hand laid on anyone. Miss Heffernan conceded she needed more damning evidence. She could bide her time. One day the evidence would be there.

Grumpy, gabby but generous-hearted, Mona was delighted with Angel's news. In the parlour they sat surrounded by wedding presents, wrapped and unwrapped, and together looked at Johnny's photograph.

'God, he is gorgeous. What was it you used to say he was like?'

'A black panther I saw in the zoo.'

'You're right. Look at the hair on his chest. Mind you, I'm not sure I'd like Benny to be that hairy though he could do with a bit more on his head. He'll be baldy before he's twenty-five. What colour outfit are you going to get?'

'Blue, I think. Blue suits me best.'

'I hope you know I'm doing this as a favour. Honest to God, I haven't a minute so don't you walk the feet off me. I know what you're like – you'll search every shop in town then finish up buying the rig-out from the first one you looked in. You're terrible fussy about things, d'ye know that?'

Michael Collins, a member of the Irish Republican Brotherhood, who had taken part in the 1916 rebellion then been imprisoned in Frognach and later released, was back in Ireland and making a name for himself. In 1919, after the declaration of an Irish Republic and the establishing of Dáil Éireann, Collins began putting together a highly efficient intelligence network. He believed that the sooner fighting began and a state of disorder was created throughout the country the better it would be. Ireland was likely to gain more from such disorder than the situation as it stood. England had virtually ignored the declaration of an Irish republic and the setting up of its own parliament. Many in the Dáil opposed Collins's plan, but he went ahead. Across the country, police barracks were raided, robbed and policemen killed.

Now his name was familiar to most Irish people. By many he was regarded as heroic and, as his exploits became more daring, he was taken to their hearts. He was talked about in public-houses, on street corners, in shops and homes. His name was shortened affectionately to Mick by men and women who had never laid eyes on him and then he was nicknamed 'the Big Fella'.

Angel must have been one of the few people in Ireland who neither knew nor cared who or what he was. Her mind was focused on one thing only – when Johnny would be back in Dublin. Daily she searched the newspaper for word of him, not even glancing at reports of raided barracks, dead policemen or the exploits of Michael Collins.

Then one day she found the announcement of when and where the fight would take place. After work she ran all the way to Mona, bumping into Maggie Dignum's son as she turned a corner. She hadn't seen him for years, though now and then her mother mentioned him. 'That poor unfortunate. If Maggie was alive she'd turn in her grave. Thrown to the waves of the wind. I remember him as a little baby, Maggie's first child. He was born about the same time as you,' she'd say, and sigh heavily. 'Little do we know what's in front of our children. Maggie doted on him and look at him now.'

The first time Aggie related this, Angel said, 'I don't know who you're talking about.'

Aggie replied, ''Deed you do. He was the one not put into a school when Maggie died, the Lord have mercy on her. Her sister took him in, because he was earning, a messenger boy. But after his father was killed in the war he went a bit wild.'

'Where does he live?' asked Angel.

'That you might well ask. I told you he used to live with his aunt, a couple of doors from Mona.'

'Oh, him, yeah I do remember him. He was all right, not a bit rough. You never said where he lives now. I haven't seen him for years.'

'God only knows. Up in the mountains when the weather's fine, in hall doors in the city, on tenement stairs, no one knows and no one cares. Every so often he comes back to the village and you'll see him around for a day or two. I do think he's looking for his brothers and sisters. They'd be well left the school by now. But he's become very distant – won't open his mouth to answer you. I always slip him a few coppers. Father Clancy's tried everything. He won't talk to him either. God look down on him, the poor soul.'

'Sorry,' Angel said, after she and the young man had collided. They looked at each other. She smiled. He turned and walked away. He was dirty and unkempt. She wondered where he would sleep tonight and felt sorry for him. It was a cold bleak night. Then she dismissed him from her mind and ran on to Mona's, where she got a cool reception. Mona hesitated before inviting her in. 'Everyone's here, Benny's mother as well.'

'I won't delay you. It's this.' She held out the paper. 'The fight's on March the twentieth. God, I can't believe it. I'm that excited.'

'I hope he won't let you down again. Remember how surly he could be.'

'I know, but he's bound to have changed. Anyway,

156

listen, about the rig-out. Will Saturday be all right? Will you come with me then?'

'Only before dinner. You'll have to ask Father Clancy to let you off.'

'He will. If we go into town about ten, will that suit you?'

'It'll have to, I suppose,' replied Mona grumpily. 'I'm sorry for being so short but, honest to God, I don't know whether I'm on my head or my heels. Weddings are terrible things. Big ones anyway.'

'You're lucky,' said Angel wistfully.

'What did you say the date of the fight was again?'

'March the twentieth.'

'I'll have been married a week by then, be living down the country.'

'I'll miss you terrible. You're my best, my only friend.' Tears filled Angel's eyes, for though now she was wary of Mona, she was still fond of her.

'Don't you start or you'll have me at it. We'll see each other again, and write. I'll have to go in now. Call for me Saturday morning about quarter to ten.'

Saturday was a bright, breezy day, the sun was shining and Mona and Angel in great humour as they rode into town on the top deck of a tram. 'We'll have a look at Grafton Street first, in Brown Thomas – the window, I mean.'

'I thought you'd taken leave of your senses and were planning to go inside.'

'I'm not that much of a thick. Imagine the looks we'd get from the snotty-nosed assistants. It's the windows I want to have a dekko at. See what's the latest, especially the hats. Then we'll have coffee in Bewley's. I've never been in there. Coffee and cakes. Let on we're posh. After, we'll cut through Clarendon Street into George's Street. Kellet's and Pim's do have lovely clothes and hats, more than half the cost of Brown Thomas. But we'll have an idea what we're looking for.'

'You mean *you* will. I'm buying nothing.'

'You know what I mean,' replied Angel, her face flushed by the breeze, pleasure and excitement, her eyes sparkling.

They got down from the tram at the corner of Stephens Green, crossed the road and stepped into Grafton Street. Wafting through it was the smell of freshly ground coffee, spring flowers from the dealers' baskets, and music, the voice of a tenor singing, 'There is a flower that bloometh . . .' An occasional motor-car made slow progress down the narrow street but the majority of the traffic was horse-drawn cabs.

Every window had something to attract the eye, paintings and etchings, jewellery, baskets and jars of sweets, cakes that aroused hunger pangs. Mona and Angel became aware of how long it was since they had had breakfast.

'I'm starving. Let's go into Bewley's first,' Mona said, and Angel agreed.

Once inside, they felt shy, surrounded by well-dressed people talking loudly and laughing.

'Feck them,' said Mona defiantly. 'Our money's as good as theirs.' They drank their coffee and ate their cakes.

'I've been saving up, I've three pounds. D'ye think that'll be enough? That's got to do for everything.'

'You're not getting married, it'll be oceans. Look at

the wans smoking. Smoking's terrible common and fast. Hurry up with your coffee, I can't stay out all day.'

Brown Thomas's windows were very disappointing. 'They used to have gorgeous things,' said Angel. Mona agreed. There was nothing she fancied. Angel said, 'I suppose the war hasn't been over long enough for new fashions to be in. I thought there'd have been gorgeous things to give me ideas.'

'You couldn't have bought them anyway.'

'I know that! It was ideas I was looking for. We'll be luckier in George's Street, I hope.'

'Let's go, then,' urged Mona, conscious of the time she was sacrificing away from her wedding preparations. Linking arms, they cut through back lanes, alleys and narrow streets heading for Kellet's and Pim's, not cheap shops but more within Angel's budget.

The clothes displayed were more to their liking, more what they were accustomed to. 'That one, for instance,' said Angel, pointing to a coat and a skirt that would be above her ankles, no hobble skirt, and a three-quarter jacket that wasn't severely tailored. 'I like that. Twenty-nine and eleven, that's not bad. I'd have enough for shoes and a hat.'

'It's a pity my sister's still up to her eyes in the bridesmaids' dresses or she'd have run it up for half the price. I wish you were being one of my bridesmaids but my ma insists on only family.'

'That can't be helped. Let's go in and try it on.'

The skirt fitted perfectly. The shop assistant admired Angel's figure and said the length was all the rage, just showing the ankles. 'You could wear black lacy stockings with it and black louis-heeled shoes.'

159

Angel turned this way and that. 'Let me try on the jacket.'

It was too loose but the assistant assured her that only the buttons needed shifting. That could be done in the shop: they had their own alteration hand. Angel said she could do it herself. 'I wanted a blouse as well, a bluey mauve, more lavender than purplish.'

'I know the colour. I've the very thing, a lovely contrast with the navy coat and skirt. Amethyst, that's the shade. And the neckline's gorgeous, not too low but not choking you either.'

Angel fell in love with it. 'I'll take it if it fits.'

'It's nineteen and eleven.'

She hesitated. That would only leave ten shillings for shoes and a hat.

Mona's patience was nearing its end. 'Spend the rest of the money on a hat and I'll lend you a pair of shoes,' she said. 'We take the same size, they're louis-heeled and not a break on them.'

She had settled Angel's dilemma, and they went to the millinery section where there were hats of all colours, shapes and descriptions. Angel chose a wide-brimmed straw, trimmed with a floaty scarf. It was the wrong colour, more puce than amethyst, but there were racks of scarves and she soon discovered the colour she wanted.

They boarded the tram for home. When they were on their way Mona relaxed, complimented Angel on her purchases, then asked as the tram neared the village, 'How'll you explain to your ma what'll keep you out on the night of the fight?'

'I'll let on I'm going to a dance and maybe a hooley after.'

'Of a Monday?'

160

'I'll tell me ma that the hooley's not definite. That's in case Johnny doesn't invite me to the party, if there is one after the fight.'

'If he does, that means you'll be coming home in the middle of the night. Your ma knows hooleys last till the morning. In any case I never heard of one on a Monday. Let on you're going to a wake.'

'A girl I dance with says I can sleep in her place.'

'And the new clothes, how will you get them out without your mother seeing?'

'I know a fella in the tram office.'

'Trust you,' said Mona. 'Does he fancy you?'

'Give over. He's an old fella but very understanding. I said it was a pledge I was lending someone. But my mother would go mad if she thought I was letting my new suit go to the pawn.

'I'll get them down to him in the week when she's at the chapel and pick them up when I catch the tram.'

'God,' said Mona. 'You're a terrible liar, d'ye know that? But go on anyway.'

'I'll wear my green dress going out, then change in the girl's house where I'm staying the night. My hat's the only thing I'm worried about getting out. I'm so excited.'

'Take my advice and go for the wake.'

'Maybe you're right. I'll let on we heard in town about a girl dying suddenly, someone from the north side, someone you used to dance with. Say she always had a bad heart.'

Aggie admired the clothes, made her dress in them, turn this way and that, telling her she was a picture in them. Angel changed and hung her purchases on hooks behind the door, covering the coat, jacket and blouse with older clothes. Her mother found her a large paper bag, one supplied by pawn offices for released pledges. 'Put your hat in that so it doesn't get dusty, then it'll be safe on top of the press. I have to go out this evening, Mrs Doherty's dying. They don't think she'll last the night. You'll have to make your own tea when you come in from work.'

'That's all right, and talking about work I'd better get up to the presbytery – it's nearly their dinner-time. It's a mutton stew, I cooked it yesterday. I've only to skim off the fat and warm it up.'

'Father Clancy's taken his time about getting a replacement. D'ye think he's looking, or so satisfied he isn't bothering his head?' asked Aggie.

'He's looking, all right. Several times a week women come about the job. So far he says none have been suitable.'

'Would you fancy it as permanent?'

'Not really. He and Father Brennan are easy to work for but I miss people my own age. You get them in and out of the shop all day. And if the priests are out on call the presbytery can be lonely. I'm lucky I don't have to sleep in. I'd better be going. I'll see you tonight.'

'Have you time for a cup of tea? It won't take a minute.'

'Honest to God, I haven't and, in any case, I'm swimming in the coffee we had in town.' She kissed her mother and set off for the presbytery.

When Angel came back from work she found a note from her mother telling her Mrs Doherty was expected to die during the night. She'd stay until she did. Angel was not to wait up for her.

This pleased Angel, who had been wanting to look at her naked body.

Making sure the curtains were drawn completely and the door locked, she stripped off, stood in front of the glass and studied her reflection. She knew the feel and shape of her body, that her breasts were big and her waist narrow, but on seeing it she was surprised that it appeared beautiful. She ran her hands over her breasts, slid them down to her waist, across her slight belly and then moulded her hips with her hands. Her thighs tapered to her knees and down to her slim ankles. She said to herself, 'I have a lovely figure.' But that's vanity, she remembered, and vanity's a sin, and she recalled what a nun had said about bodies in school, 'A heap of corruption, that's all a body is. It's your immortal soul that matters.'

Quickly she put on her nightdress, said her prayers kneeling by the bed and then got in. Usually she fell asleep straight away but she couldn't tonight. There was so much going on in her mind. The fight. Her hoped-for meeting with Johnny and how she might bring it about. Her new clothes. Mona's wedding. The lies she would have to tell her mother. Round and round in circles went her thoughts, always coming back to the fight and Johnny.

She longed to touch her body in its secret places but knew that that was a sin too. She longed for Johnny to touch her secret places. That would also be a sin. She wasn't sure which would be the most sinful. But if he loves me, if we get married, it would be a sin for me to touch myself but not for Johnny. Husbands were allowed to do that. She'd surprise him after the fight. He was bound to win and be in great humour. He'd probably be with a crowd. But he'd talk to her, arrange to see her another time . . . She imagined bringing him home, them walking out together. And, after a while, getting engaged. She fell asleep wondering what sort of ring he'd buy for her.

Everyone at Mona's wedding admired Angel's outfit. 'It's a good job I'm the bride or I'd be jealous of you,' Mona hissed in Angel's ear. 'Benny's brother's mad about you and he's not bad-looking. Don't tell me, let me guess. He couldn't hold a candle to Johnny Quinn. You're not right in the head, you'll never get him so you won't.'

'Wait and see then,' said Angel.

During the day they travelled to Holyhead arriving on Friday evening. 'Better this way,' Jackser said, as the train left Euston. 'Sleep in a bed tonight, better than a bunk in a sleeper. And the hotel in Dublin's a decent place.'

Johnny nodded his agreement. They had a carriage to themselves, Jackser, Johnny, his trainer and the two men who'd tend Johnny during the fight.

Jackser was still trying to find the right moment to tell Johnny that the fight had to be thrown and of the possibility that his mother was dead. He couldn't delay much longer. The fight was in two days' time and the train had crossed the Menai Straits. They were now in Wales and soon would be sailing to Dublin. The train went on its way, whistling now and then, clouds of steam, soot and minute cinders blew in through the window.

'For Christ's sake, Jackser, will you shut the window?' the trainer said.

Jackser undid the leather strap from its stud on the door and hoisted up the window. 'There y'are,' he said. 'Choke on the cigarette smoke or be blinded by the smuts and cinders.'

'You all right, Johnny?' asked the trainer.

'Yeah,' said Johnny, not raising his head from the Wild West story he was pretending to read while he thought about the coming fight, the tactics he'd use. He'd probably knock his opponent out in the fifth round – give the spectators value for their money without inflicting or receiving too much punishment. He'd go to see his mother the following day. She'd know already about the fight. Jackser had told him his face was pasted on every lamp-post in Dublin, in every huckster's shop window and in the newspapers. She and his father would know where it was taking place, though neither of them would see it. Few, if any, women went to boxing matches, and his father wouldn't from spite apart from not having the entrance money.

Angel, he supposed, would also know about it. Well, she would if she still lived in the village. If she did he'd find her. He imagined her face, the expression of surprise replaced by admiration when she saw the change in him, his clothes, how he'd grown, filled out, lost his pimples, looked sleek, well-nourished, with not an ounce of fat. He'd swagger through the village, his arrogant demeanour silently proclaiming, 'Take a good look. Yeah, it's me, raggedy-arsed Quinn, only I'm not ragged any more. Take a good look. Your days of sneering and jeering are finished.'

They disembarked and took a horse and cab into the city. The hotel was in North Great George's Street in what had once been a gentleman's Georgian town-house.

It now looked what it was, a third-rate hotel. Coat on top of coat of paint had been applied to the slender, spear-topped railings and the elegant front door, but Jackser knew that it was warm and comfortable, served good food, frys and thick steaks, the Guinness was first class and, into the bargain, it didn't fleece you.

After a wash and brush-up, they went to the dining room where all ordered steak, onions, and fried potatoes. With food inside him and apple tart in front of him Johnny felt mellow.

Jackser made short work of the apple tart, lit a Player's, took a deep drag and said, 'Johnny, me oul son, you're not going to like what I have to tell you, but hear me out before you lose your rag.'

'Right,' said Johnny, his mouth full of tart. 'Fire away.'

'You've got to throw the fight.'

Pastry crumbs went against his breath, he gagged, coughed, spluttered and sprayed the table with them. 'I didn't hear you right, Jackser, say it again.'

Jackser did. 'You know it happens, you've seen it done.'

'Not to me it effin' well doesn't,' Johnny roared, and crashed his fist on the table making the cruet dance a jig. 'Not to me. Never. Not to me. Not to Johnny Quinn.'

'Listen, will you?' said Jackser, reaching out a hand to touch him, but Johnny pushed it away shouting, 'No, you effin' well listen to me. D'ye know what this fight means to me? D'ye know how long I was on the road? How I broke my balls training? Didn't drink, only had a woman when I could stand the strain no longer. I let no one belonging to me know where I was in case they'd interfere. And now you sit there and tell me to throw the fight.'

'In the name of Christ, will you hear me out?' Jackser's voice was raised too now. 'It's got to be done. I owe someone a favour. It's all about money, big money. You'll do well out of it. You'll get the loser's purse and a share of the bet. What that'll be depends on how much you bet against yourself. Finish up quids in and no disgrace. You'll lose, barely, on points. No disgrace in that. Are you following me?'

'Following you? Fucking strangling you is what I'd like to be doing.'

'So it's a lousy trick to pull on you. I'd be leppen' too, if I was in your shoes. Think of it as business.'

'Think of it as me coming back to Dublin, cock of the walk. Me, Johnny Quinn, come back to show the begrudgers the real me. Oh, sweet Holy Jasus, Jackser, what are you trying to do to me? I trusted you. You were my hero, my fucking saviour.' Johnny's voice had quietened, he held his head in his hands. Then, all of a sudden, he raised his head from his hands and brought them crashing down on the table. A plate fell to the floor and smashed. Full tumblers spilled their frothy stout collars.

From the doorway a young waiter looked on unconcernedly. He witnessed similar scenes often, especially at the weekends after a fight. It was that sort of hotel.

'Easy now, oul son,' Jackser said, in tones of sympathy.

In a less belligerent voice, Johnny asked, 'Why didn't you tell me sooner?'

'Couldn't take the risk of you packing in the fight – there'd have been time for a cancellation. But not now, not at the last minute. You're a professional, we banked on that. The posters are out, the venue picked, the tickets sold. We knew you wouldn't renege at this stage.

Knew you'd know the rumours that would circulate. The "Bruiser Brennan" got the wind up. White-livered. Afraid of the opposition. That'd have done more damage to you than a fight lost on points.'

Jackser watched Johnny's face. It was calmer, more resigned, but he didn't look ready to be told that it was likely his mother was dead. Somehow that news had to be silenced until after the fight. 'You look all in. Go to bed, that's my advice. We'll take it easy tomorrow, a bit of training, the same on the day of the fight. Talk about your tactics. Make sure you can throw it without raising the crowd's suspicion.'

Johnny went to his room, threw himself on the bed seething with rage, disappointment and a sense of betrayal, repeating over and over again, 'The bastards, the conniving bastards.' If he had enough principles he'd pack the whole thing in, tell Jackser what to do with his fake of a fight. But he knew himself. He didn't have high principles. He didn't care about the thousands of bets his supporters would lose out on and took comfort from the fact that he didn't stand to lose money. His biggest regret was for his mother. She'd be broken-hearted. She wouldn't understand the underhand dealing that went on in sport. He was furious that the day after the fight he wouldn't be able to swagger through the village with his head held high and his chest out.

He got up from the bed and paced the room, chest bare, muscles rippling, the whorls of black hair in which it was covered contrasting starkly against his long white drawers. All the while he was thinking about his mother. He had to see her. He'd go now. She never went to sleep until the small hours.

He dressed and went down the stairs. He heard the

sounds of carousing from the bar – Jackser and the boys. He went out, walked to the nearest hackney stand and told the driver to take him to the village. When they neared his street at half past two on the Saturday morning no one was about. Even so, he directed the driver to a lane that ran behind the tramway houses, to be doubly sure he wasn't noticed.

He stepped over the low wall, stumbling over buckets, a tin bath and an accumulation of rubbish. There was no light in the window. Maybe his mother's habits had changed and she was in bed or, more likely, she was in the dark, not having the price of oil for the lamp or even a candle. Well, that was at an end. She'd never be in the dark again.

The back door was open; the front would be closed, but a key would be hanging from a length of twine easily retrieved by a hand through the letter-box. He opened the back door, heard the mice and maybe rats scattering back to their holes in the skirting. Never before had he thought of his house as having a particular smell. It had just smelt as it always had, of home. But after so long away, living in reasonably clean digs, the odour he inhaled was of dirt, grease, sour milk and dish-rags. He knew the room so well, knew exactly where the fireplace was and made his way towards it, calling quietly so as not to disturb her if she was sleeping, 'It's only me, Ma.'

He stretched out his hand to touch the chair in which she sat and sometimes dozed. It was empty. He noticed that there were no dying embers in the fireplace, no lamp burning before the Sacred Heart statue. He found his way to the dresser and fumbled in the drawer where, among a collection of odds and ends, a candle, half of one, a butt end, was always to be found. He picked out half of one and lit it. Shadows flickered on the walls as he moved about the room. His mother wasn't in it. Neither was his father. He hadn't expected him to be. He could be anywhere – collapsed on the sagging bed, stinking of drink, snoring, semi-conscious, or sleeping in the outside privy, his trousers round his ankles, by the side of the riverbank, in a doorway, anywhere. He climbed the flight of ladder-like stairs leading from the kitchen to the upstairs. His mother wasn't in either of the small bedrooms.

He began to feel apprehensive. Where was she? Maybe she was at an all-night wake, where neighbours collected to watch the dead with their sorrowing relatives, to pray, drink a glass of stout, eat a sandwich, recall the virtues of the departed one.

He went to the bedside table where, when not entwined in her fingers, his mother's rosary lay in one half of a large shell he had brought her from a trip to the seaside. The beads weren't there, confirming his idea that she was at a wake – saying the rosary figured greatly at wakes.

A horrible smell of stale piss came from the tousled bed. He pulled back the covers and saw the stained flour-bag sheets, the brown stains, ring upon ring of them, and he felt alarmed. His mother wasn't the best of house-keepers but she was clean. Such a sheet would never have been left on the bed. She'd have soaked, boiled and bleached it. He felt alarm for the first time since arriving. He moved from the bed to a press where what few clothes she had were kept. They were there, a dark, shabby coat, a dark skirt, two bodices, a couple of summer frocks, patched and much mended, and on a shelf above the hanging rack, a lovely hat, a big black straw with ribbons and flowers, sat next to the battered brown felt hat, which was the only one he had ever seen her wear. She wore it to Mass, to funerals, everywhere.

Where, he wondered, had the other come from? Had she saved some of the money he had sent her and bought it? He doubted it. She'd have had so much else that needed buying. A woman she had done a day's work for had probably given her the pretty hat, one for which she'd have had no use unless to make herself a laughing stock, had she worn it out.

In the room, there was also a chest. The top drawer was empty, the bottom held his mother's prayer book and underneath it a photograph. No underwear – not that she'd have had much but there should have been a few changes, old, torn, some mended stockings, stays. He remembered seeing stays hanging over a line above the fireplace, a pinky flesh colour with pink laces and metal bones inserted here and there in the seams. They didn't look like any bones he had ever seen – well, maybe a little like herring bones. She used to say her stays were good for her back and kept the life in her. Once he had slipped four of the bones from the pockets along the seams in which they were held. He'd developed a knack of using them to catapult small objects. When she found them gone, that he was the culprit and couldn't remember where they were, she half murdered him, then told him not to darken the door again until he found them. He did, eventually, in long grass by the riverbank.

By now he had sensed that something was very wrong. If his mother had gone to a wake she'd have worn her coat and not gone in her bare feet. So where was she? He'd have to go back, waken Jackser. His fancy woman must know something. It was from her his mother collected the money he sent. He came down the stairs and opened the front door. A cold fresh breeze blew in. It wouldn't be light for at least another hour – enough time for him to get out of the village without bumping into anyone. He stood for a little while, breathing in the clean air, clearing his head of the malodorous smells of the house. He was about to leave when he remembered the photograph and prayer book. He went back and retrieved them.

As he passed the row of cottages where Aggie lived, he saw that a light was burning. Aggie, he recalled, had treated his mother with kindness. On an impulse he knocked on her door and called out who he was so as not to alarm her.

'I wouldn't have recognised you,' she said, 'not in a million years.'

She didn't immediately invite him in and wasn't over-welcoming in her greeting. He recalled that though his mother spoke well of her she had never shown him much regard.

'I'm sorry,' he said, 'to disturb you at this hour of the morning.'

'I've been up all night with the toothache. I've only half a dozen left and they do pain me but I can still chaw with them. God knows what I'll do when they're gone. Isn't it well for them that can afford false ones?'

'I was wondering if you knew anything of my mother?'

'Your mother,' she repeated, and the slightly hostile expression that had been on her face left it. 'Come in, son.' She held the door wide. 'Come in, sit down, I'll wet you a sup of tea.' He could tell by her manner that now she was nervous. 'I shouldn't have kept you standing. To tell you the truth you gave me a bit of a fright. Sit down, I'll get the fire going in no time.' She saw him looking at the empty double bed. 'I'm always on edge when Angel's at one of them all-night hooleys.' She was all fingers and thumbs, dropping sticks and sods of turf.

'Would you have any idea where my mother might be? There's no sign of her above in the house.'

She kept her back to him for a few minutes. When she turned round her eyes were full of tears.

'Ah, don't tell me, son, you didn't know? Didn't no one let you have word? Your poor mother died before Christmas, one of the last to go with the flu – the Light of Heaven to her. Isn't that the terrible thing not to know that your mother was dead?'

After seeing her coat and shoes in the press he had half guessed, but hadn't been able to admit it to himself. 'Was she bad long?'

'Three days, that's all.'

'Who minded her?'

'Your father, I suppose, though I'm not sure. Not many went in and out, as you know, because of him. But someone did tell Father Clancy and she was anointed and had a night in the chapel.'

'And a pauper's funeral, I suppose?'

'Sure many a one has that.'

If he didn't leave this minute he'd smash something. He wanted to get back to the hotel, get his hands round Jackser's throat. He must have known and kept it from him. He stood up.

'Don't go without the sup of tea. You look terrible, and no wonder. A shock like that could be the cause of killing you.'

He waved away the proffered cup. 'Just a mouthful,'

she coaxed. 'I put plenty of sugar in it. Have a little sup.' Tears were pouring down her face. His own were ready to shed. He took the cup and drank from it. He noticed her swollen red cheek and wished he had a Baby Power in his pocket to relieve her toothache. He drank some more tea and asked, 'I don't suppose you know where the oul fella is?'

'Now, that I couldn't tell, no more than your poor mother could have done most nights. But at least he didn't run away and desert her.'

She couldn't have been worse off if he had, Johnny thought. He was another one around whose throat he wanted to lock his hands.

He gave her back the cup. 'Thanks very much,' he said, and took from his pocket a pound note. 'I'll not forget your kindness. Buy yourself a Baby Power when the shops open. Whiskey's grand for the toothache. Swill it round the bad tooth. And will you do something for me?'

'I will, but there was no need for the money, though I'm grateful, thanks very much.'

'Don't mention to anyone that you saw me tonight, not even Angel. Will you promise me that? I didn't intend to come here until after the fight.'

'On Monday isn't it? The talk is all round the village. Great excitement altogether. I won't breathe a word to a soul, not even Angel.'

He bade her goodnight, and started walking towards Terenure, not hurriedly, killing time, knowing he wouldn't get a tram until six o'clock. But despite trying to curtail his pace he arrived long before the first tram was due, his speed induced by the urge to confront Jackser, to punish him for not telling him his mother was dead, for fixing the fight. For shattering the dream he had cherished, the return of the victorious hero, plans he had had for his mother, even a possible future with Angel.

Between Terenure and Harold's Cross he hailed a passing cab in which he was driven to his hotel. He bounded up the stairs and into Jackser's unlocked bedroom. The man lay sprawled on his back, snoring. The smell of stale drink was nauseating. Johnny straddled him and put his hands round Jackser's neck.

'You bastard. You cross-born bastard!'

Jackser's eyes opened and regarded Johnny with terror as the fingers tightened on his throat. Unless he did something he was going to die, the life choked out of him. His will to survive eradicated his memory of the Queensberry Rules, replaced by others of his street-fighting days. With what strength he had he kneed Johnny in the groin. Johnny's grip slackened on his windpipe. Jackser kneed him again and Johnny screamed in agony then let go. Jackser wriggled from beneath him and sat on the edge of the bed where Johnny, crucified with pain, lay groaning and clutching his balls.

'You bloody lunatic, you could have killed me, you nearly did,' said Jackser hoarsely, massaging his larynx.

Johnny glared at him like a wild beast. 'Why didn't you tell me my mother was dead?'

'You're a mad fucker. How was *I* supposed to know? You insisted on the secrecy. That's how I didn't know. And, more to the point, why no one let you know. You set the terms. No one was to know where you were, neither in Dublin nor England. You could have told someone – the priest. He'd have kept mum, but not once she died. Some son!'

Still rubbing his groin Johnny sat up. 'Don't give me all that shite. Your fancy woman must have wondered why my mother didn't call for the money. She died before Christmas. She wouldn't have called for the envelopes I've been sending.'

'So your mother missed a few weeks. That didn't mean she was dead.'

'She must have seen it in the paper.'

'Who'd have put it in – your father? She did wonder why she hadn't called, especially for the Christmas money. But there could have been loads of reasons. She could have been laid up.'

'Why didn't she go out to the house?'

'Because you said she wasn't to have the address. Okay, so she knew where the village was. So what was she supposed to do? Go from door to door asking for Mrs Quinn, maybe bump into your oul fella and get a dig in the jaw, let the cat outta the bag about the money you sent?'

Johnny sat on the opposite side of the bed, his face half turned towards Jackser, who wondered if it was yet too soon to offer his sympathy. He judged that it was, stood up and announced that he was going downstairs.

'Not till you've heard the rest of what I have to say.'

Johnny came round and stood towering over Jackser. 'You're to blame – you and her. She could have found the priest, found out the truth from him and let me know. But that wasn't the way you wanted it. You were afraid to break that news to me and then the throwing of the fight.'

The strength drained out of Jackser. He thought, Jaysus, if he goes for me again I'm done for. He looked for something with which to defend himself. There was nothing. Johnny caught hold of him by his shirt collar, a hand on each side, inches only from his throat, and pulled him close. 'I blame you and her, remember that. I'll throw your fight for you on Monday night, you cheating, double-crossing bastard, and that's me finished. I've already made a name for myself, I don't have to depend on you. After the event you'll never lay eyes on me again.' Then Johnny pushed Jackser away, with such force that he bounced off the wall, and went out, banging the door after him.

Aggie spent the remainder of the night putting hot fomentations on her cheek to ease her toothache and thinking about Johnny. He had gone up in her estimation. He had grown from a surly-looking pup into a handsome man and, despite the shock and terrible grief when he learned of his mother's death, he had remembered her pain and given her the price of a Baby Power. Promise or no promise, though, she had to tell Angel. Which she did when her daughter came home early in the morning, looking tired and dispirited.

Aggie could tell by her face that she hadn't enjoyed the hooley. 'It's too much for you, especially during the week,' she said, as she made a pot of tea. 'Losing your sleep and now having to rush up to the presbytery to make the breakfast. You'll run yourself into consumption so you will. What possessed you to go?'

'I was fed up. I miss Mona. It'll never be the same between us again now that she's married. I was broken-hearted when I saw her and Benny leave to go down the country. God knows when I'll see her again.'

Aggie poured out the tea then broke the news. 'You'll

never guess who came here during the night. Frightened the life outta me, he did.'

Angel wasn't in the mood for guessing. On her way to the hooley she had seen numerous posters of Johnny and stopped to look at each one, at his handsome face staring out of them. Her heart soared with hope that she'd get a chance on the night of the fight to speak to him. At least she might catch a glimpse of him. He'd be surrounded by all his crowd, boxing people. She wouldn't have the nerve to approach him. And even if she had, what was to stop him cutting her dead? There'd never been anything between them – not even a conversation.

Mona was right: all he'd ever done was ignore her. If she had any sense she'd go nowhere near where the fight was taking place. If she had any sense she should have saved the money she'd squandered on the clothes and spent it on tickets to England.

'You'll never guess who it was knocking in the middle of the night.'

With little enthusiasm Angel said, 'Go on, tell me then.'

'I couldn't sleep because of the toothache so I was up when I heard the knock. I needn't tell you it put the heart crossways in me.'

'Mother, for God's sake will you tell me or I'll fall asleep?'

'Johnny Quinn, that's who it was. But a Johnny Quinn you wouldn't recognise.'

Angel was now wide awake, her heart singing. Johnny had called to the house looking for her, making arrangements to see her. He did think something of her.

'Poor Johnny, looking for news of his mother, God rest her. I had to tell him she was dead. You should have seen his face. It broke my heart. The poor unfortunate boy. Only he's a man now. A handsome, lovely man, all that surliness gone. He gave me money for a drop of whiskey for the toothache. I never saw such a change in anyone.'

'Did he mention me, ask where I was?'

'Not as far as I can remember. It was all about his poor mother he talked. I said you were at a hooley. He'd have noticed that you weren't in the bed. I take back all I ever said about him. He's grown into a gentleman. The girl who gets him won't be disappointed.'

Angel was revitalised. She washed, changed and set off to make the priests' breakfast. It was to see her he'd come, she thought. Asking for his mother had been an excuse. She'd been dead and buried for months. He was bound to know that. And if he didn't he could have knocked up any of the neighbours, light in the window or not. He had come to see her, she convinced herself.

Chapter Twelve

On the morning of the fight Johnny refused to talk to Jackser and his trainer. He remained in his room considering his future, thinking about his mother and his strategy for the coming fight. Among those in the know, tonight's fight, if lost on points, would be recognised for what it was: a put-up job. Afterwards he'd go back to England, see what was doing there, maybe go to America.

The photograph he had taken from the house lay face

down on the bedside table. He picked it up and studied it, as he had several times during the morning. It had been taken on his parents' wedding day. There they were, two sixteen-year-olds, awkward and stiff, staring into the camera, posed before an imitation balustrade around which garlands were entwined.

His mother's hand lay possessively on his father's arm. She wore a loose frock, which hid Anto in her pregnant belly. He thought how pretty she looked. He had never seen her like that. He remembered her only as his mother, always rushing to the shops, to the pawn, bent over a tin bath washing clothes, cutting up cabbage, peeling potatoes, fine-combing his hair, cracking lice between her nails, her hands always rough and chapped, never showing much tenderness or affection, except during the night if you woke with cramps or earache. Then, if there was enough milk, she'd heat some and bring him a cup, or pour warm oil into the aching ear. She'd talk quietly, telling him to think of something nice, he'd forget his pain and fall asleep.

Mostly he remembered her rushing to make the dinner so that it was on the table when his father came in, saying, 'I hope to Jesus it's to his liking.' If it wasn't, his father often upended the table sending the dinner and the delft crashing to the floor. He only stopped doing that when Johnny and Anto towered over him. 'How did she fare while I've been away?' he asked himself. Not well, he knew.

He thought of all the plans he'd had for her – buying the house, doing it up, though now he realised that that option hadn't been on the cards. The tram company owned the houses: they went with the job. But he'd have found another one.

He dozed and dreamed about his mother and Angel. They became mixed up in his dreams, his mother stroking his face, and the river with Angel and his mother swimming and jeering at him, Angel's voice taunting him with the familiar cry 'raggedy-arsed Quinn'. And he had dragged her out. She was in her skin and he'd punched her in the chest, in the belly. He woke from the nightmare in a cold sweat, shaking all over. 'Food,' he said. 'I haven't eaten since last night.' He got up, splashed his face with cold water and went into town to get a meal.

He ordered a steak, rare. He needed that nourishment for tonight. Trying to lose the fight would be harder than winning it: to lose on points meant going the distance. It galled him that he'd ever agreed to throw it. Hatred welled up in him again for Jackser. To think he'd trusted him, thought of him as a father, a caring father! 'Ah, to hell with him,' he said to himself, paid for his meal, walked down to the quays and along them until he had almost reached the Phoenix Park, then turned and sauntered back to his hotel.

'You'll kill yourself with all the gallivanting you're doing. Dancing on Saturday night, a hooley after it, and out again tonight. I didn't think they had dances of a Monday,' said Aggie, as she poured water into the basin for Angel to have a strip wash.

'What d'ye mean, a hooley? That's all off. I told you about the girl dying suddenly. It's her wake I'm going to.'

'So you did, love – I'm getting very forgetful. You've gone very quiet,' said Aggie. 'The towel's lovely and warm. Are you ready for it?'

'I was just thinking I might give up the work in the presbytery,' Angel lied again.

'Hurry up, now, or you'll get a cold standing there half naked.'

She couldn't look her mother in the face while she told lie after lie. She had confided in the girl from the dance hall, told her about Johnny and the fight and how she would find somewhere near the marquee and watch for him leaving when the match was over. 'I'll congratulate him. He never used to give me the time of day but he might now. There'll probably be a bit of a party to celebrate him winning and maybe he'll invite me. That's what I'm hoping. And that's why I asked you to mind my good clothes and let me stay the night in your place. Are you sure your mother won't mind?'

'No. She's as good as gold. Wouldn't refuse anyone a shelter. I'll tell her about you and Johnny. She loves anything romantic. And I've put your hat safe.'

Angel laughed. 'You should have seen the job I had getting that outta the house. I hid it in the backyard when me ma went for a message. Then I was afraid a young fella would find it and make a football of it.'

When she was ready to leave, Aggie commented on Angel's outfit. 'Why are you wearing that frock? Green never became you and the blue beads are a show with it.'

'Give over, Ma. It's a wake I'm going to not a dance.' More lies, thought Angel. In an hour's time I'll be dressed to kill. All in shades of blue and amethyst and my beads to match. 'If I'm not in before twelve, don't worry and don't wait up. Wakes go on all night. I might decide on staying.'

Aggie kissed her and watched from the door as she went to catch the tram.

In her friend's house Angel changed into her new rig-out, redid her hair and arranged her hat.

'You'll definitely get off with that fella. You look a picture. He's mad if he doesn't ask you to the party. The hall door'll be open and you've got the key of the room. Go on, then, you don't want to be late arriving,' her friend said.

Angel had already reconnoitred the area where the fight was being staged. A big marquee had been set up inside a park, not too far from the entrance gates. Across the road, facing the gates, there was a disused Protestant church. The porch was ideal for Angel's purpose: she'd be hidden from all but the most observant, and had reasoned there'd be few of those about tonight. All eyes would be focused on the marquee. Inside the porch there were three steep steps. On the top one she'd have a grand view of Johnny entering the grounds. She was quivering with excited anticipation of how the night might turn out.

She saw two cabs arrive and Johnny got out of one. It was a great effort for her not to call his name. The posters didn't do him justice; he was tall, very tall, and broad, and he walked as the panther had, long ago, in the zoo. She adored him. She could throw herself before his feet. Please, God, she prayed silently, let him love me too.

The crowds came and some she knew from the village. She guessed the marquee would be packed. A few women were going in but she was surprised to see that some of those who were looked rich; they were beautiful young women, in gorgeous clothes.

Fifteen rounds, she had been told, would be fought, unless one of the contestants was knocked out. She prayed it wouldn't be Johnny. But it couldn't be, not according to Father Clancy and Father Brennan, who had lately been reading all about his namesake, the Bruiser. When Father Brennan had first come across the name she'd overheard him say to Father Clancy, 'Maybe he's a relation, you know, like you and Angel. We could be third cousins.'

Father Clancy had laughed at the young priest. 'He's Johnny Quinn. I've known him all his life. We buried his poor mother just before Christmas, God rest her soul, a pauper's funeral. I only wish I'd had the money for it to be otherwise, the way I wish I could give Aggie a few bob now and then. But it's a poor parish and Mass offerings are few and far between.'

'Don't I know,' said Father Brennan. 'By the time I've bought a stick of shaving soap and a few stamps I'm skint. Ah, well, maybe one day us and the workers will get a fair wage.'

'Maybe,' said Father Clancy, 'but probably not in our lifetime.'

Angel heard the roar of the crowd and a bell ringing, and guessed the fight had started. She wished she could hear what they were shouting but not that she was inside. She couldn't bear to see Johnny touched, never mind hurt.

Almost everyone in the audience, not aware that the fight was to be thrown, had bet on Johnny to win and some, real gamblers, far more than they could afford. Some had borrowed the money. Others had left their wives short in their housekeeping, assuring them they'd pay it back out of their winnings.

Among the audience were keen followers of boxing. They observed the fight critically. It seemed to them that the outcome was a foregone conclusion. 'Five maybe six rounds, then the Bruiser will finish the other bloke off,' one man said to another, who agreed. 'That's been his form to date. A clean fighter.'

Johnny danced round the ring, now and then coming close enough to let his opponent hit him, reminding himself he had to lose, reminding himself that that meant going the full fifteen rounds.

His seconds mollycoddled him. 'You're doing great. It looks real genuine.'

'Fuck off,' he told them as they sponged his face. Then he was sorry, knowing that the fake fight wasn't of their making. After the ninth round, when the crowd became uneasy, Jackser came into the ring and talked in what seemed an earnest manner to Johnny – for the crowd's benefit, appearing to be exhorting him to pull himself together, to get in there and finish the other bloke off. The reality was that he was congratulating him on how convincing he was making each round appear.

Hatred and anger welled up in Johnny. His instinct was to punch Jackser in the face, lay him out on the canvas. During round ten his longing to avenge himself on Jackser grew stronger. For two pins, he thought, I'd knock this bloke out. That'd put Jackser in good stead with his crooked friends. I think I will. The idea grew stronger in his mind. His loathing of Jackser increased. He was a bastard. He had ruined his homecoming, shattered all his dreams. He could never show his face in the village again.

He wouldn't throw the fight. He didn't care about the extra money he stood to gain. He wouldn't be a loser. And, no matter what Jackser said about losing on points, it was bound to be a disadvantage.

The audience became more restless. One of the more knowledgeable ones said to his mate, 'I don't like the look of this. The Bruiser doesn't seem on form.'

His friend replied, 'There's not much in it as it stands. Brennan could lose on points.'

'That's what I'm thinking. Jaysus, I'm destroyed if that's the case. Every penny I could lay my hands on I bet with.'

Johnny's head was whirling. He was tired from lack of sleep and thoughts of his mother's death were in his mind, the disgrace of her pauper's funeral. He was going to finish this fight. He moved in on his opponent who, with a punch to his jaw, knocked him down.

The crowd rose to its feet, booing and hissing. Johnny struggled to get up. The referee continued counting. Half-conscious, Johnny could hear himself being vilified, the taunts, the cursing, the threats to do him in. He staggered and fell again.

In the church porch Angel heard the crowd roar and the names they called Johnny. Tears ran down her face. She wondered if he was badly injured and longed to go to him, comfort him.

She watched the disgruntled crowd trickle out of the marquee, swearing, arguing, their anger directed towards Johnny. She saw cabs draw up and the well-dressed women and their escorts drive away. Then two more cabs arrived. It was a while before anyone else came out, Johnny among them, shrugging off their hands and drinking from a bottle of whiskey. She couldn't see any blood and thanked God for that.

There was a bench near the two cabs. Johnny sat on it and drank from the bottle. The men who'd come out with him were attempting to coax him to his feet. He waved them off. She could hear them praising him, telling him everything was okay, not to worry about a thing. After a long time she heard the oldest man in the group say, in a voice that carried to where she hid, 'Leave him, he'll sleep it off. Come on, lads, we've some celebrating to do. Johnny'll find his way back. Make sure he has a cab fare in his pocket and the address of the kip where we're having the party.'

The lights that had illuminated the outside of the marquee went out. There was a moon, but it kept disappearing behind clouds and Angel had difficulty keeping Johnny in view. She was frightened that he might get up and move so decided to go and sit beside him on the bench. The empty whiskey bottle slipped from his hand, fell and smashed. Johnny didn't stir. She wasn't sure if he was sleeping or unconscious and wondered if she should look for help. He might need hospital treatment. Maybe his head had been damaged – she knew that could be dangerous. But if he was only drunk and went to hospital they might notify the police and he might be arrested. She prayed for God to direct her as she sat holding his hand.

It seemed a long time before anyone passed by. It was a woman or a girl, Angel wasn't sure. 'Excuse me,' she called after the figure, who had passed with only a cursory glance. 'I think my friend is sick and I'm not sure what to do. Could you help me, please?'

The person came back and sat the other side of Johnny. 'He smells drunk to me.'

'He drank a bottle of whiskey but he was in a fight before that.'

'Someone attacked him?'

'No, a real fight, a boxing match. He was knocked out. I knew by the roars of disappointment.'

The young woman leant over and looked into Johnny's face. 'I know him. It's Bruiser Brennan. I had a few bob on him to win.' The moon came out from behind a cloud. 'That's him all right. He's staying in the hotel where I work.'

'What ails him?' asked Angel.

'My guess is that he's stocious, but I'm not sure. The best thing is to get him back to the hotel. You stay with him. There's a hackney stand just down the road – I'll get a cab.'

With the help of the jarvey they got him into the cab. 'I lost five bob on that bastard,' the cab driver said, as he closed the door.

'Are you going with him?' asked the woman, who had introduced herself as Bridie, a chambermaid in the hotel.

'Not really, but I was hoping that after tonight we'd start.'

With the help of a porter they got him into his room and on to the bed. The porter didn't have a word of concern for Johnny. Like the cab driver, he had also bet on him.

In the lighted room Angel saw that Bridie was a woman in her thirties, with a kind face and nice figure.

'Loosen his clothes and take off his shoes. You know, he shouldn't be left alone until he wakes up. He could vomit and choke on it. It often happens.'

'But how could I stay? I mean, it wouldn't be right.'

'It's up to you but if it was someone I was keen on I'd stay all night, if I had to.'

'But what about the hotel? Wouldn't they mind?'

'Listen, love, this place is not much more than a kip.

So long as the room is paid for they don't care what or who is here or what they do.'

'If you're sure?'

'I am,' said Bridie. 'You have to, anyway, because we're not sure if it's the drink or the knock-out punch that has him as he is. We'd better turn him on his side. That's the safest thing in case he vomits. And another thing, give him a shake after about an hour and do it a few times during the night. If he doesn't show signs of wakening we'll have to get him into hospital in case his brain's injured. I have to be up at five so I'll leave you to it in a minute. Otherwise I'll be walking round like a fool tomorrow.'

Not wanting to be left alone in the hotel Angel delayed her by asking questions. 'Is it hard work being a chambermaid?'

'Depends on who's been in the room. Some are dirty bastards – too much trouble to walk to the lav so they piss in whatever's to hand, wipe their arse on a towel. Then you get the decent ones – only an ashtray and the wastepaper basket to be emptied and the bedcovers pulled up. But the wages are chronic – five shillings a week and you don't get many tips here. There's other ways of making a living. You've heard the saying, "all women are sitting on a fortune"?'

'How d'ye mean?' asked Angel.

'Are you really that innocent? Yeah, I can see by your face that you are. A thick, an *amadhaun*.' Bridie gave Angel a brief explanation of what sitting on a fortune meant.

Angel went red to the roots of her hair. 'That's terrible,' she said. 'I could never do that. I'd die first.'

'It depends on who you're doing it with. Some blokes

are okay, gentle, don't want anything out of the ordinary, and some are mad, vicious bastards.'

'D'ye mean you've done it, like?'

'I used to until a fella nearly killed me one night. Now I'm a chambermaid. But I've a friend in Drumconndra. His wife's in the Incurables hospital. I go to his place twice a week. He's a quiet, decent man and he sees me all right. God help her, she's none the wiser and he has his needs seen to. That's where I was coming from this evening when I came across you. I'm on the landing above if you want me during the night. Number ten. I'll make a cup of tea and bring it down to you. But no enticing me in or I'd be here all night.'

After Bridie left Angel took off her shoes, then went and looked down on Johnny in the bed. Now and then he snored. Not being used to drunken men, any men, she wasn't sure if snoring was a bad sign. There was a mark on his cheekbone – from the punch, she guessed, and longed to touch it, but desisted. After Bridie had gone she would try wakening him and would caress it then.

Bridie brought the tea, biscuits and a tin clock. 'Waken him on the hour every hour,' she said again.

'For how long?'

'A couple of hours. If there's nothing wrong with him, by then he'll probably say a few words. The first time he may only open his eyes, grunt or something. If there's no more response the second time round we'll get help. And make sure you keep him on his side.'

'Thanks very much. I don't know what I'd have done without you,' Angel said when she and Bridie parted.

The tea and biscuits were gorgeous. She hadn't

realised how hungry and thirsty she was. It was hours since she'd had anything to eat. The clock ticked loudly. In half an hour she'd try rousing him and, please God, he'd open his eyes. He probably wouldn't recognise her straight away, but then how delighted he'd be seeing a face he knew! The clock ticked and ticked, but the hands didn't seem to move. She forced herself not to keep watching it. Instead she stared at the wall-paper, green with pink roses on it climbing up a trellis. When she next looked at the clock, the hands had moved but not far.

Johnny turned on to his back. She moved him on to his side and marvelled at the fact that she was in the room with him, touching him. 'I love you, d'ye know that? I could kill that fella that knocked you down and hurt you. But in a way I'm glad, because now you'll give up the oul boxing. Don't mind that them in the village'll make a laugh of you. Say it's the price of him. He got what he deserved. It'll only be a nine day's wonder. In any case we'll go to England. England's supposed to be great. No one's poor in England. Thank God no one can hear me talking to myself or they'd think I was mad.' She bent and kissed the side of his face.

Sitting down again she became aware of her hat, that it felt heavy, and thought, No wonder, it's been on my head this long time. She took it off and put it on the bedside table.

When next she looked at the clock the hands had moved almost to the time she should try rousing Johnny. She went to him, placed her hand on his shoulder, bent over him and said his name while she shook him gently. 'Johnny, wake up. It's me, Angel. Wake up, Johnny.' He rolled on to his back, opened his eyes and stared at her. She could tell he didn't recognise her. But he would the

191

next time she roused him. At least he had come to and wouldn't have to go to hospital. After pulling the bedclothes up round him she went back to her chair and fell asleep, then woke with a start: she hadn't turned Johnny on to his side.

The gaslight above the bed flickered. She hoped it wouldn't go out for the want of a penny in the meter, then smiled to herself, thinking even in a hotel Bridie described as a kip the gas light wouldn't depend on a penny in the meter.

She approached the bed again, bent over it and looked into Johnny's wide-awake eyes. This time he recognised her, sat up and asked belligerently, 'What the bloody hell are you doing here and who's with you? The monkey-faced one, I suppose?'

'No, Johnny, only me, as true as God. I hid in the church porch waiting to see you come out, that's all. I've been waiting years to see you.'

She longed to say more, tell him she had loved him for as long as she could remember, but lost her nerve. Something about him frightened her. Maybe it was because he was still drunk – he reeked of whiskey.

'How did you get in here? Who put me on the bed?'

She explained about the cab, Bridie and the hotel porter. 'I've been here for hours, watching you, turning you on your side, making sure you didn't get sick and choke.'

'Wasn't that kind of you?' he sneered. 'And Jackser and the others, those people I was with, what became of them?'

'They went off in a cab.'

Her hair had come undone and lay like a golden shawl round her shoulders. He reached for it and used it to drag her towards him. 'You came to gloat, didn't you? You came so you could go back to the village and tell them? "I saw Johnny Quinn. He looked desperate. Battered to a pulp."'

He was glaring into her face. His fingers wound in her hair, hurting her.

'That's the truth, isn't it? Isn't it?' This time he shouted. 'You came to laugh and jeer. Have you forgotten how you used to jeer me? In the river you'd be screaming after me, "Raggedy-arsed Quinn".'

'That's not true. Never in my life did I jeer you.'

He could smell her scent, violets. It made him want to vomit. Violets the same colour as her eyes. She was so beautiful. But he couldn't trust her. He could never trust anyone again.

'I only ever loved you. For as long as I remember I only ever loved you,' Angel stammered. The smell of his breath was making her feel ill.

Winding his fingers tighter in her hair, dragging her closer so that their faces were almost touching, he hissed, 'No one ever loved me. Not even my mother. Anto was the one she loved.'

He brought her mouth down to his and kissed her. His teeth pressed hard into her lips. She struggled to free herself, and he went berserk. He rolled her over in the bed and began to tear off her clothes while he kept his mouth clamped to hers. His hand tangled in her beads impeding him reaching her breasts. 'Fucking things,' he said, yanking them, snapping the string. They trickled over her now almost naked body.

When he'd torn off everything except her stockings, he pushed her legs apart with a thrust of his knee. And all the time his mouth was still on hers, his tongue choking

193

her. She couldn't move, she couldn't scream, all she could do was pray silently that someone might come, for she was afraid he was going to kill her. And at that moment the kissing stopped and he threatened to do that. Now that his mouth was free, he used every obscenity she had ever heard to describe her. 'If you open your mouth even to talk I'll slit your throat, you rotten little cow. Once I thought I'd come back and marry you but now I know your type. The village bike. The best ride in the fucking village.'

He hit her in the belly. Even though her pain was agonising she became aware that he was fumbling with his trousers – perhaps searching for a knife. She knew now that he intended to kill her and silently said an act of contrition.

With one violent thrust he ruptured her hymen. In her dry vagina the fragile tissue tore and she bled profusely. For seconds at a time he looked at her face and was conscious of who she was, that once he had thought he loved her. Then the rage returned and the face he saw was the sneering, jeering one in the river calling after him, 'Raggedy-arsed Quinn'.

He punched her, pulling the blows so that they hurt but so that the force was not enough to kill her. Her face he didn't touch. Then he fell asleep on top of her.

She waited until he was snoring, then inched from beneath him, raised herself and leant against the cast-iron bedhead. He woke and reached for her. She avoided his grasp and the hand crashed on to the bedside table crushing the crown of her straw hat. He reached for her again. His hate-filled eyes looked into hers. This time she was surely going to die. Futilely she struggled. He dragged her forward then threw her back.

Her head collided with the bedhead and a broken spiky bit tore her scalp. Blood poured from the cut, streamed down the side of her neck on to her shoulder and saturated the pillow. Again he straddled her and again she felt him enter her and begin to move and all the while his crazed eyes looked down on her. She passed out.

When she came to he was so deeply asleep it was easy to move from under him. She looked down at her clothes, her blouse ripped in two, her skirt torn, her legs and belly covered with blood. Only her coat, though creased and stained, wasn't ruined. Her beads were among the bedclothes and spilled on the floor, and her hat, still on the bedside table, was squashed and spoiled. Barely able to move she found two safety-pins, which her mother always advised her to carry, on the inside waistband of her skirt. With one she drew the skirt together and pinned it, then fixed her blouse. She couldn't find her drawers, so she'd have to leave them. She dare not risk wakening him. Her head was spinning and her legs trembling. She wasn't sure if they'd support her, much less carry her. But she had to get out of the room, even if it meant crawling on her hands and knees. She had to get up the next flight of stairs and call Bridie. She desperately needed help – but it was only four o'clock, poor Bridie'd be still asleep. All the same, she had to knock her up. She'd never make the street in her condition, or if she did, the first policeman to lay eyes on her would arrest her. And what excuse could she give him?

On her hands and knees she crawled up the stairs and along the passage to Bridie's room.

Unable to stand she banged on the bottom portion of

the door, not very loudly, because of her aching arms and shoulders. She had to knock several times before she woke Bridie, who opened the door cautiously. On seeing Angel she exclaimed, 'Jesus, Mary and Joseph! What happened to you?' She helped her up from the floor and into the room where she sat her on a chair. 'What happened to you? Who did it? You poor, unfortunate child. Look at the state of you. Tell me, tell what happened,' she asked, kneeling before Angel, holding her hands. For a while Angel couldn't talk, only cry, sobs shaking her body. 'Let me look at your head. It's in gores. You're lucky, it's not deep, but the scalp's terrible for bleeding.'

When eventually Angel told her story, Bridie at first wanted to go for the police, then dismissed that idea. 'They'd do nothing even if he wasn't who he is. They'd do nothing even if he was a labourer, never mind a famous boxer. They'd want to know what you were doing in his room at that hour of the morning. The blame would be all yours. You'd have to be stretched on the floor with your neck broken or slit from ear to ear for the police to pay any attention.'

'Don't tell anyone. I don't want my mother to hear. Could I have a drink, please?'

Bridie brought water and in another glass a small measure of whiskey. 'Like it or not, you have to drink it otherwise you'll collapse. Stay where you are while I boil a kettle and you can have a wash, though God knows it's a bath you need. There isn't one on this floor and you couldn't risk going down to the second. You'll have to strip off.' Bridie picked up the torn clothes. Angel tried to wash herself but couldn't because of the pain and stiffness. 'You'll have to forget about your modesty.

Turn round and let me look at you. The bastard – the rotten, lousy bastard! I could kill him. Tomorrow you'll be like a putrefied liver. I'll just sponge your face and the blood from your thighs and hair. Think of me as your mother washing you as a little girl.'

When the washing was done, Bridie brought an old soft towel and patted Angel dry, then slipped a night-dress over her head and led her back to the chair. 'I'll make you a cup of tea and then we'll have to decide what to do. For one thing you can't go home in them things.' She pointed to the torn clothes. 'Not even your coat. The back's saturated in blood.'

'Oh, God, what'll I do? My mother'll go frantic when I don't come home. And my other clothes are at my friend's. I changed into my good things in her house.' She began to cry again. 'He broke my beads and smashed my hat.'

'You were lucky he didn't break your neck and smash your face, the mad bastard. Where does your friend live?'

'Not far, in Dominick Street.'

'Listen, then, this is what I'll do. I'll spin the manager a yarn, he's not a bad oul stick. Tell him I had word sent in at daybreak that my mother's been taken bad and I have to go home. I'll get the clothes, then I'll take you back. I've a few bob, we'll get a cab. But first I'll rub this stuff called arnica on you. It's miraculous for bruising. Then get into bed and don't open the door for God Almighty's sake.'

Angel was crying again, with pain, exhaustion and gratitude to Bridie. 'What would I have done without you? I'd have died. Thrown myself under a horse and cart.'

'Indeed you wouldn't, you're tougher than that. You

did nothing wrong. You were an innocent victim. Always remember that. But talking about accidents, that's what we'll let on to your mother. You were knocked down by a runaway horse. Does she know the girl from Dominick Street?'

'No,' Angel replied.

'That's great. I'll let on I'm her. I was walking you a bit of the way home when the horse bolted and went up on the path and there wasn't a soul in sight. The driver never appeared. The oul horse had just been standing there not tied up outside an empty shop. Will your ma swallow that?'

For the first time a faint smile appeared on Angel's face. 'My poor ma, she'll believe anything in her relief that I'm home alive.'

'Then it's all settled, apart from your friend's name and address. I'll do you now with the rub then get into bed. I'll put on my things and be off. Don't bother about the door, I'll lock it from the outside.' Angel gave her the girl's name and house number.

The unaccustomed whiskey dulled Angel's pain and she fell asleep. But the effect didn't last long and she woke, her body throbbing, and burning sensations in her belly, breasts and between her legs. She had rarely suffered physical pain but welcomed it for its intensity: it blocked out the memory of the previous night. That, she was certain, would send her out of her mind. For always she must keep it at bay. If her control slipped, she must convince herself it had been a nightmare. No one except Bridie knew her secret and Bridie, she hoped, would keep silent. She'd never see Johnny again. Maybe not because of what he had done to her but because he couldn't face the ridicule of having lost the fight, not in the village, not in Dublin, not in Ireland. No reminders.

In the room below Angel's, Johnny woke when it was light. His head ached and he had a terrible thirst. He sniffed the air like an animal. There was the faint scent of a woman, overlaid by a stronger unpleasant one. It reminded him of something from his childhood. He sat up in the bed and noticed that he was partly dressed, but his trousers were round his ankles. Looking down at the wrinkled trousers he saw the sheet and the blood. That was the smell – blood. He remembered it from the slaughter-house, lying on his belly watching cows being poleaxed, blood everywhere, the metallic smell of it. Then he saw the blood on his thighs, examined himself for sign of injury, but there was none. Where had it come from? He must have had a woman. A prostitute, a dirty cow. They didn't mind having sex and their monthlies at the same time. Believed it was safe then, so he'd been told. He jumped out of the bed, falling in the act because his ankles were imprisoned by his trousers. He kicked them off, then tore the sheet from the bed and threw it into the corner. The mattress was badly stained. He stared at it then said aloud, 'To hell with it, I'm not a chambermaid.'

He had to get washed, change his clothes, and get out of this kip before Jackser and the crowd of leeches woke, congratulated him again on losing the fight. Otherwise he'd break a few skulls. There was a bathroom along the corridor minus a bolt, minus hot water. At this hour of the morning it was unlikely anyone would come in on top of him wanting a piss. He took off the remainder of his clothes, rolled them in a bundle and pushed them into his case, wrapped a towel round his waist and headed for the door.

Before reaching it he trod on something, bent to see what it was. A round blue glass bead. Others were scattered round the room. He picked one up and turned it over in his hand. Like the smell of the blood, there was something familiar about it. He held it to his nose and smelt it. The scent he'd noticed when he first woke up. It, too, reminded him of someone. Someone from a long time ago. And there was a battered straw hat on the chair, its crown caved in as if someone had brought down a fist. Angel, he remembered, had once worn blue beads, though he'd never seen her in the hat. Her face appeared before him. Her angel face, with terrified eyes staring at him. 'Oh, Jesus,' he said aloud, 'not her. Not Angel.' Then common sense asserted itself and he said, 'How the fuck could it have been Angel?' What would she have been doing in his room in the middle of the night? It was a brass nailer. Jackser had brought her up as a consolation prize. Whores wore blue glass beads and big straw hats. It wasn't Angel. Angel wouldn't have let him touch her. She was a decent girl. Decent girls didn't let men touch them when they were bleeding. But supposing she hadn't let him? Supposing he'd forced himself on her? And supposing she hadn't had the others? Supposing she was a virgin and he had raped . . .

There he changed this train of thought. So supposing it had been her. What had she been doing in his room in his bed in the middle of the night? She'd come to gloat for all the times he had ignored her. In which case she had got what she had been asking for. 'Let her go to hell,' he said, and went to the bathroom.

While he dressed he kept his eyes averted from the

bed. Jackser and the others would catch the night boat. He'd get the early one. In case they had a change of plan, he'd go from the North Wall to Liverpool. They'd make their way to Holyhead. From Liverpool he'd make his way to America. He had the loser's purse, and Jackser had paid the bet he'd laid against himself. He put one of the beads in his pocket, got his case and went down the fire escape.

Dressed in the green frock and the coat she'd worn when she left home the evening before, Angel went out of the hotel by way of the fire escape. Bridie went down the front stairs to reassure the manager that she'd be back as soon as possible. She and Angel met up away from the hotel. They got a cab out to the village.

'You look terrible,' Bridie said. 'Your ma'll have no trouble believing you met with an accident.'

And Aggie didn't. 'Someone was praying for you,' she said, throwing her arms round Angel, hugging her so tightly she winced. 'You were lucky it wasn't your head kicked in.'

Bridie agreed and went into the story. 'Standing there munching in his nose-bag when this young fella hit him a terrible blow on his back. The poor oul thing reared on his hind legs, dragged the cart after him on to the pavement, knocked Angel down and trampled her chest and stomach. Show your mother the bruises.' She suggested that a warm bath with a cupful of salt would be a great help.

'It's in the yard. I'll bring it in,' Aggie said, and Bridie helped shift it and put an extra big pot on the fire, got the packet of salt and shook in a liberal amount. 'My poor little child, weren't you unfortunate? But thanks be to God it's no more than bruises.'

When it was time for Bridie to leave, Aggie thanked her profusely, told her she'd always be welcome and called down God's blessing on her for the help she'd been to Angel.

When Angel was comfortably installed in the bed, with every hot jar available, her mother said, 'I'll have to slip up to the presbytery and let Father Clancy know you'll want a week off,' then said of Bridie, 'She's years older than you. I'd have thought her dancing days were over. You never said where she worked.'

Instinct warned Angel that in the future she might need Bridie without her mother knowing so she lied again. 'Jacob's, but she's not keen on it. She's thinking of going to the shirt-making.'

Father Clancy was sympathetic and told Aggie to keep Angel at home for as long as she liked. She called into Danny's for her cheese and a quarter of his best biscuits, and told him about Angel, how she'd escaped death by inches. People in the shop were talking about Johnny Quinn, mostly lamenting the loss of money they'd bet on him, others gloating that he'd been brought down, a few suggesting that it had been a put-up job.

Aggie spoke up for him. 'I felt sorry for him myself. He appeared to have changed.' She told Danny of his visit to her late at night and what had transpired. 'He asked me to keep the visit secret and I did. Of course I told Angel. There's no secrets between us. Now I'm telling you because there's no need for secrets any more.'

When she was leaving, Danny sent a bag of his fanciest biscuits and another of chocolates to Angel, and afterwards pondered on what Aggie had said. There had been a sudden death, and Angel was going to a wake. On a *Monday* night, he mused. *And* on the night of Johnny's fight. Was it possible they had arranged a meeting – which went disastrously wrong? And wasn't it strange that no one except the girl Bridie had witnessed the accident? The streets of Dublin were seldom empty.

He served a few customers and eventually dismissed his suspicions, telling himself they were induced by his obsession with Angel, his love for her and jealousy of any man who looked at her.

Angel recovered physically but there was a change in her – which worried Aggie. She seemed to have gone in on herself, making her mother wonder if, after all, she hadn't suffered a head injury. Something had to account for her long periods of brooding silence. And she didn't go to the dances any more or the all-night hooleys. As for washing herself, as Aggie kept saying, 'Never in all my born days have I known anyone taking a bath every minute. It's just as well we have the fire and not gas or I'd be robbed so I would.'

'Give over, Ma, I have a bath three times a week, that's all.'

'And tell me how many people have you heard tell of who have a bath three times a week? I doubt if even the gentry with all their conveniences do.'

Angel would have bathed every day of the week, every hour of the day, were it possible, for only after bathing did she feel clean. Sometimes for hours she succeeded in banishing from her mind the terrible night, and sometimes, day and night, she relived every minute of it.

She had an aversion to men now that she knew what they were capable of. Many a time Father Clancy had

203

touched her shoulder, held her elbow; now she was careful to avoid any physical contact with him. Walking through the street she steered well clear of other people, crossing to the other side if the path was crowded. Sometimes in bed, if her mother wasn't in, she cried herself to sleep, and before sleep came, blamed herself. I should never have gone anywhere near the boxing match. I should never have gone and sat on the seat and, above all, gone up to the bedroom. I was asking for trouble. Men are like wild beasts, only then I didn't know it.

She wanted to leave the presbytery where she couldn't avoid being civil to the priests or the many men and boys who came knocking on the door. Even the sight of the altar boys made her shudder. And as for Connolly's shop, she never crossed its door. She saw leaving the village and going to England as one solution to her problem, until she realised that in England there were also men. At those moments she thought of doing away with herself.

'Doesn't the time fly? In two months you'll be twenty,' Aggie said one evening in an attempt to start a conversation with her morose daughter. Something was niggling in Angel's brain. Something wasn't right but, in her confused state, she couldn't remember what it was but consoled herself that it would come back to her. It did, in the middle of the night. She'd seen nothing for two months. She who had been as regular as clockwork since her monthlies had started.

She knew, from the confidences Mona had shared with her, that missing could mean you were expecting a baby. A baby! God wouldn't allow such a thing to happen. God would not want a little innocent baby to be born out of such a terrible event. It must be that the blow to her stomach had damaged her insides. Her mother must think the same way – she washed Angel's clothes. If she suspected anything she'd have mentioned it.

Poor Aggie did suspect two things: one, as Angel did, that her insides were damaged, for which Aggie blamed the horse, but worse, that she had consumption. Often that was how it started with young girls. Her beautiful, adored Angel. She'd get the cough and sweat at night and get thin and die, with nothing you could do to save her.

More and more Michael Collins's name was becoming a byword in Dublin. Some attributed magical powers to him for how else was he able to avoid capture – some instances when the place in which he was hiding was surrounded by British troops?

Danny and Father Clancy, who were ardent nationalists though not crediting Collins with magical powers, were filled with admiration for his daring escapades.

'Did you know he rides round Dublin in broad daylight on his bike? As cool as a cucumber, no attempt to disguise himself,' Danny said one morning to the priest, when he'd come into the shop for a chat.

'I did,' replied Father Clancy. 'I read everything I can lay my hands on about him. But what brought me in this morning was to tell you something I heard yesterday. You know the gang that murdered Thomas MacCurtain were supposed to be RIC men beginning to fight back?'

'Poor Thomas, the Lord have mercy on his soul, a grand man, a loyal supporter of the cause and the finest Lord Mayor the city of Cork ever had, shot down like a dog.'

'He was that. Well, this is what's going round. That the gang who murdered him had English accents. What d'ye make of that?'

'That for sure and certain they weren't genuine RIC men.'

'Exactly my thoughts,' said the priest. 'Perfidious Albion up to her tricks again. We're only seeing the beginning of what's going to become a terrible calamity.'

The gang who had murdered the Lord Mayor were ex-soldiers recruited in England at the behest of Lloyd George to stamp out what he saw as terrorism in Ireland. Their role was described officially as support for the Royal Irish Constabulary (RIC) whose numbers were depleted through being shot in raids on the barracks and a fall-off in recruitment. A shortage of uniforms was made good by a mixture of British Army khaki and RIC apparel and earned the new force the nickname of Black and Tans.

Angel went back to work. The priests treated her like a piece of Beleek china. She wasn't to come in until ten o'clock. They'd see to their own breakfast and make their tea in the evening. Even so, she felt exhausted and longed only for sleep. Her sleep was dreamless and her only escape from those times when, despite how hard she tried to keep them at bay, memories of the night in the hotel bedroom filled her mind and sent her to the verge of suicide. She never noticed that she missed a third period. Aggie did, and was now convinced that Angel was in a rapid decline. Morning, noon and night she prayed for her, lit candles and one day walked all the way to an Augustinian church in Dublin's John's Lane to light a lamp before a statue of Our Lady, who was credited with miraculous cures.

Chapter Thirteen

One afternoon, when Angel was dusting Father Brennan's bedroom, she felt hot, then broke out in a cold sweat and fainted, falling across the bed. Father Brennan, who was upstairs at the time, heard her make a strange sound and went to see what had happened. He was used to seeing women, children and sometimes men faint when they'd been fasting overnight before receiving communion but never anyone who looked as Angel did. He thought she had had a heart-attack and then that she was dead. He undid the collar of her blouse, shook holy water on to her face and then ran to seek help. Father Clancy was out on a sick call but in the vestry an altar boy was cleaning a thurible. 'Angel's dead or dying. Quick, go and get help,' he called out.

In the church the boy saw Miss Heffernan and another woman arranging flowers on the altar. 'You've got to come quick! Angel's been taken bad. Father Brennan thinks she's dead.'

The women left what they were doing and hurried after him asking, 'Where is she?'

'In the house, in the priest's bedroom, I'm not sure.'

By the time they arrived Angel had come to. Father Brennan had an arm round her shoulders helping her to sit up. Her hair was tossed, the bed disarranged and she had, when she revived, undone more of her blouse buttons.

Miss Heffernan and her companion exchanged knowing looks. Then, with great solicitude, Miss Heffernan asked, 'How are you now?'

'I'm all right. A bit of a weakness came over me, that's all, but I'm fine now.'

'Don't move too quickly. Stay where you are. Paddy, like a good boy, run and see if John-Joe's at his hackney stand and tell him to come here immediately.'

Paddy had no more liking for Miss Heffernan than most people but he ran to obey her command. Angel protested, 'I don't need a cab. I'm grand now. It's not time for me to go home.' While she spoke she was fastening her blouse, the gimlet eyes of the women on her. They dismissed her protests: she could take another weakness walking home and collapse in the street, and as for the room and the bed, they'd see to that.

Aggie, who was standing outside her door for it was a fine day, watched the cab come down the street and wondered where it was going. When it stopped outside the cottage and John-Joe helped Angel out, Aggie felt her heart turn over. 'What ails you, love?' she asked.

'I fainted above in the house.'

Aggie remembered the day Angel had fainted in the waxworks but took no consolation from the memory. Then her daughter had been at an age when fainting was common with young girls. Now she was nearly twenty. Fainting wasn't usual with women of that age, unless their health wasn't good. If Angel did not pick up in the next few weeks, much though Aggie dreaded having her fears confirmed, she'd have to take her to the doctor, though there was little he could do. A cough bottle, that was all.

It was Miss Heffernan who found the blonde hairs on the priest's pillow. Triumphantly she showed them to her companion, exclaiming, 'Wasn't I right? But would

208

anyone listen? The girl is wanton. You have only to look at her. And did you see her blouse?'

'I did indeed. You were very far-seeing. The rossy putting temptation in poor Father Brennan's way. May God forgive her.'

When he came back from his sick call, Father Clancy heard about Angel's fainting fit. 'That poor child,' he said. 'She's never been right since the accident with the horse. She should have been taken to the hospital at the time.'

Father Brennan agreed, while all the time before his mind was the sight of Angel on his bed, her hair spread on his pillows.

Miss Heffernan had put the golden hairs inside a cambric handkerchief into an envelope which she then locked in a bureau drawer. The woman who'd been with her when they went to Angel's help told her sister-in-law who told her sister. The altar boy came running to his mother with the news that Angel had collapsed on Father Brennan's bed. His mother told her neighbour, and before nightfall almost everyone in the village had heard. Some said, 'Well, thank God if she fainted it was on to the bed and not the floor she fell.'

'But what about her hairs on the pillow?' asked the bad-minded.

And the sensible replied, 'If your head's on a pillow, a few hairs is what you'd expect.'

Father Brennan had his supper, read his office, went to his bedroom, undressed, knelt and said his prayers. In bed, behind his closed eyelids, he kept seeing Angel lying there, his hands loosening the neck of her blouse, his overpowering desire at the time to unbutton it further,

209

to see her breasts, to touch them. Never before had he dwelt on such thoughts. Morning and night he had prayed for the grace of God to help him keep his vows of chastity, poverty and obedience. His prayers had been granted, until the sight of Angel on the bed, his fingers touching her flesh, had put temptation in his way. He prayed fervently again and had banished the thoughts, or so he had believed, until now when they came again to torment him. In the morning he would go to confession. Having decided that, he got out of bed, knelt by the side of it and remained there praying, asking God's forgiveness for succumbing to his impure thoughts.

The next morning Aggie took heart from seeing Angel looking better than she had for weeks, setting out for the presbytery with a spring in her step, more like herself than she had been for many a day, and told herself, 'Maybe I was jumping to conclusions. Maybe she's not going into bad health. It could be missing Mona. Not a line from her since she went off to Athlone and them friends since they were children.' She began to think of Mona's wedding day, the picture Angel had looked in her blue outfit, how the hat had become her. The amethyst scarf had set it off to a T.

She sang as she went about making the bed and tidying up, in between songs talking to herself, 'There's such an improvement in the weather I'll take the heavy quilt off the bed.' She folded it and carried it towards the press where she'd put it on the top. She was reaching to do this when she noticed that the large brown-paper bag in which Angel kept her hat wasn't there. 'Where in the name of God has she put that? There's no room for it anywhere else.' Nevertheless, she looked for it. 'I never missed it before this morning. Maybe she lent it to someone. But sure she hasn't been across the door since the accident. And that girl Bridie's never been back.' She sat down for a few minutes collecting her thoughts. 'Come to think of it, I've not seen the blue costume either. Not laid eyes on it since the day of Mona's wedding.' To convince herself she wasn't imagining things she got up and looked through the few clothes hanging in the press. No suit. She racked her memory as to what had become of it. Had she borrowed it for a pledge and forgotten? She took down her pawn tickets, a pile of them skewered on a bent piece of wire hanging from a nail by the mantelpiece, and went through them, but there was no ticket for the suit. Then she let her mind go back to the last time Angel had gone to a dance. Had Angel worn it that night? No, she was sure about that. She remembered commenting on the green dress she had on and how the colour didn't become her. And the blue necklace, she distinctly recalled Angel wearing that and was surprised because it didn't go with the frock. She became even more puzzled when she looked for the beads and couldn't find them either.

Exhausted from wondering, wandering round the room in a state of confusion and foreboding of something terribly wrong, she felt weak. She sat down and said a decade of her rosary. The praying calmed her nerves and she took herself to task. 'Amn't I the fool? Sure all I have to do is wait for Angel to come home and she'll clear up the mystery.'

The anonymous letter came in the second post as Angel was clearing the table. It was written in block capitals. 'Ask your housekeeper and Father Brennan to explain the long blonde hair on his pillow and the dishevelled state of the bed.'

Just the two lines. Father Clancy passed the sheet of paper to the young priest, who after reading it said, 'The bad-minded oul faggot. I suppose she has it all round the parish.'

'Without a doubt. Poor Angel, I'll have to let her go.'

'But why? She did nothing wrong.'

'I know that, but unwittingly she'll cause scandal. I should have foreseen the outcome of taking her on in the first place.'

'But she's a relation. She's only here for a few hours each day and doesn't sleep in.'

'So what am I supposed to do? Put out placards to that effect? Send you round the village wearing a sandwich board denying the accusation? Already there are them in the village convinced that she never fainted but that the pair of you were in the bed. The talk will keep them going for years to come. Long after you've gone from here to a parish of your own, Angel will have the finger pointed at her. I won't be surprised if the Bishop hasn't had one of these,' Father Clancy said, picking up the letter Father Brennan had put down. 'I'll have to make an appointment to see him. And I'll have to go and see Aggie and explain what's happened.'

'She's probably heard already,' said Father Brennan, 'the unfortunate woman.'

'I hope not. It's better she should hear the vile accusation from me than one of those oul harpies.'

'What about Angel? When will you tell her?'

'When she finishes the delft. I'll break the news then and after walk her home.'

*

'You're back earlier than usual,' said Aggie, when Angel came in. 'But come here. What ails you? You've been crying. You didn't have another bad turn?'

'Oh, Ma, something terrible's happened,' and she went to her mother and began crying loudly. 'Father Clancy's coming down. He stopped to have a word with Danny.'

'Whisht now, love. Stop crying for a minute and tell me,' said Aggie, putting her arms round Angel. 'Whatever it is, you can tell me.'

'I can't, I can't. It's all lies. Every bit of it is lies.' She was inconsolable. Aggie continued holding her, patting her back as if she were a baby, telling her to stop crying, that she'd only make herself sick.

Father Clancy arrived, and for the first time in years Aggie addressed him by his Christian name. 'Sean, what happened to get her in this state? She hasn't been well for months and only today I was thinking she was better. Look at her now. What did she do?'

'Nothing that was her fault, the poor child. She's fallen victim to the bad-minded in the village. I know, Angel, you've had an awful shock but sit down now and stop crying while I explain to your mother.' Gently he took Angel from her mother's arms and led her to a chair. 'You sit down as well, Aggie.' Then he showed Aggie the letter. 'It came at dinner-time. And I've a good idea who's the instigator of it and what the rumour is that'll be all round the village by now. But my hands are tied. There's not a thing I can do about it.'

'Oul Heffernan or the other oul bitch who helped Angel when she took the faint,' said Aggie. 'When I went out for my messages I thought the atmosphere was a bit peculiar, you know, like, but I wasn't sure if I was

213

imagining it. Everywhere I went there were little groups of women gabbing away. Well, that wasn't so unusual. What was, was the way they stopped talking once I was near them. Some of them were women I'd always pass the time of day with but nearly every one of them lost the use of their tongues when I came near. I thought it very peculiar and then I told myself I was just being too sensitive, that it was all in my mind because I've been worrying so much about Angel, thinking she was in consumption. But surely to God, Father,' she had slipped back into giving the priest his title, 'no one will believe a thing like that.'

'Unfortunately, Aggie, some will. And it's all my fault. I never should have taken Angel into the house. And I should have heeded the warning after that meeting was held. They've been waiting for an excuse. I explained to Angel on the way down that I'll have to let her go. But on the way here I had a word with Danny. He'll take her back.'

'What about Father Brennan?' asked Aggie.

'He's young, idealistic,' said Father Clancy. 'He'd be prepared to get up in the pulpit and hammer it out. God help his senses. Much good would his sermon do. Let Angel go back to Danny's and in time it'll blow over.'

'I can't believe it. My Angel to be accused of something like that! A child as pure as the driven snow! May God forgive them.'

After Father Clancy left, Angel remained sitting in the chair. Aggie commiserated with her. 'You were talking of leaving in any case, and there'll be a bit more life in the shop.'

'I'm not going back to the shop for everyone to gawk and point me out.'

214

'But what'll you do, love? We need the few shillings. For a week or two I could manage but not for long.'

'I'll leave. I'll go to England. I'll get a job and send you money. Ma, I couldn't show my face in Danny's. I won't be able to show my face anywhere.'

'Ah, now, come on, love, it'll blow over. A nine days' wonder, that's all it'll be.'

But Angel was adamant and said that as soon as she felt well enough she'd go to England.

'Are you not feeling well? I mean, apart from today's upset. And there was me thinking that whatever ailed you this while back was cured. Is it a pain you have? I still think you could have had a serious injury from that accident.'

'No, not a pain, just out of sorts, tired and sleepy. My stomach feels sick all the time.'

Aggie trembled with fear. Except for lack of a cough, Angel was describing many of the symptoms of consumption, and though she had little faith in doctors, who else could she turn to? Almost everyone she had known with consumption died, but a few did get better. Angel could be one of the lucky ones. She'd give her a few days, then insist she went to the doctor. Not the dispensary one, they'd go privately. She had a few shillings put by.

Danny came to the house. 'Listen, Angel,' he said, 'I'll find you plenty to do in the storeroom. No need to put in an appearance in the shop.' It broke his heart to see her looking the way she did, as if all the life had drained out of her. If only he dared broach the subject of marriage. Aggie, he knew, would be an ally. Even Angel, in her dejected state, might consider it. But that wouldn't be fair. That would be taking advantage of her.

215

He stayed for longer than he had intended, trying to persuade Angel to work for him, but to no avail.

On the night after the fight as Jackser and his entourage were about to leave the hotel, the manager called him to one side. 'Listen,' he said, 'there's something I have to show you.'

'Not now, Larry, I haven't got time.'

'Bejasus, you'd better find time for this or I might have to call the police.'

'Shag off, I'm in a hurry.'

'This is serious, Jackser. I think your ex-champ did someone in last night. The room's like a slaughter-house.'

'What room?'

'The one where your man spent the night.'

Reluctantly Jackser followed the manager up the stairs, effing and blinding as he went.

From the landing above, Bridie watched and reminded herself she had to get rid of Angel's torn, bloodstained clothes. The chambermaid who had gone into the room earlier on had been hysterical when she saw the blood-stained mattress and pillow, screaming that someone had been murdered in it. Had Bridie not known the truth of what had really happened, she'd have thought the same thing herself.

The manager threw open the door. 'Take a look for yourself.'

'Mother of Jaysus!' exclaimed Jackser. 'What d'ye think happened?'

'He could have brought back a prostitute and knocked her about. Used a knife on her.'

'Give over, for Christ's sake. He's a boxer, not fuckin' Jack the Ripper.'

'With one of his punches he could have ruptured her insides.'

'I don't buy that either.'

'All right, then, it was a brass-nailer with her month-lies, dirty bitch. But if I bring a policeman round from Store Street he might consider it a murder and a body stashed somewhere. That'd delay your sailing by a few days, eh?'

'So what are you looking for?'

'The price of a new double mattress and a bit extra, which is what any of the girls will demand to clean the room.'

'You robbin' bastard,' said Jackser, threw him a five-pound note, and went from the room.

Before the manager left, he saw the remains of Angel's beautiful hat and took it with him to the bar where he placed it on a dummy bottle on the top shelf – where it remained for many years and he regaled gullible drunken men with the tale that it had belonged to a girl who was murdered in the hotel, that the police had got nowhere with their investigations because a body was never found. In time he came to believe his own story. The majority to whom he told it were too far gone to listen, never mind remember it, but an occasional one repeated it to his family or friends, and this was how a woman for whom Aggie cleaned came to hear of it.

She was a pleasant, chatty woman confined to her house by arthritis, avid for gossip and to pass it on to the few people who called to see her. Aggie was usually a good listener. 'My cousin told me the room looked like a slaughter-house,' and she repeated in detail what she had heard.

'That was desperate,' said Aggie, not having grasped much of the tale, her mind too preoccupied with thoughts of the visit to the doctor. 'What I can't understand was why the police weren't brought in.'

'Neither could my cousin. Of course, it could have been one of the Black and Tans. I believe they've murdered many a one – women, people who had nothing to do with the fighting. The police won't get involved, afraid of their life. Them Black and Tans wouldn't think twice of shooting them as well! All the same, I'd love to see the hat.'

Aggie, who was polishing a brass fender, put down the rag she was using to bring a good shine to it and asked, 'What hat is that?'

'You weren't listening to me,' the woman complained good-naturedly. 'I told you about it in the beginning. The hat that whoever was done in was wearing. A big blue straw one. In bits now but still with a mauve scarf tied round it. The fella who owns the hotel keeps it as an ornament up on his top shelf. Did you ever hear the like?'

'Where's this hotel?'

'On the north side, but where exactly I couldn't tell you. In any case it's not, according to my cousin, a place you'd want to be seen in.'

'The fella running it probably made the whole thing up,' said Aggie, returning to buff the fender. 'Sure he could have got a hat anywhere.'

'You're right enough. I heard tell Angel had a bad turn above in the presbytery. Is she all right?' Aggie turned to look at the woman's face, wondering if it was a genuine enquiry or a way of letting her know she'd heard the talk about the bed and the blonde hair. She was suspicious of everyone. But the crippled woman was regarding her kindly. Aggie answered, 'She's grand now, thank God, not like she was before the accident, but on the mend.'

'It's a wonder she wasn't trampled to death. I wouldn't like to get a kick from a horse.'

'Nor me neither,' said Aggie, and got up from her knees. 'Well, that's everything done. I'll drop in when I'm passing to see if you want a message.'

'May God bless you. I don't know what I'd do without you.'

Aggie couldn't get the thought of the hat out of her mind. Straw, blue with a mauve scarf tied round it. Angel's hat. How did it finish up in a hotel on the north side? 'Now, stop it,' she told herself, as she neared home. 'In the first place that hotel fella's probably making up the story. Just a yarn. And in the second you don't know how long the hat's been on his top shelf.' But try as she might she couldn't put the thought of it from her mind. The hat, the beads and the suit. She'd have to have it out with Angel. But not before they saw the doctor.

They went the following evening, while Benediction was on to avoid meeting too many people. The nearer they got to the surgery, the more Aggie felt that her heart would choke her, it seemed so far up in her throat, or stop beating altogether. She had very little to do with doctors, for which she always thanked God, telling herself, as her mother had before her, that they came from good stock: not one belonging to them had gone into consumption. She took consolation from this thought as she knocked on the surgery door.

The doctor's wife answered it and told them to come in, then pointed out the waiting room.

'I don't like her,' said Aggie, when they were seated. 'A stuck-up nothing. Lost the run of herself when she married a doctor. He's a gentleman. God knows what he saw in her. A country wan, a farmer's daughter. She probably had a few bob.'

Angel nudged her. 'Ma, keep your voice down, he might hear you.'

'Are you nervous, love?'

'Why would I be nervous? He'll give me a bottle that'll fix me up.'

'I don't think I've seen either of you before,' said the doctor, and invited them to sit down. Then, smiling, he asked, 'Which of you is the patient?'

'Angel, she's my daughter,' replied Aggie.

Then he addressed his questions to Angel but each time, before she opened her mouth, Aggie answered for her. He gave up in the end and let Aggie do the talking.

'But so far, thanks be to God, she has no cough.'

'That's good and now, Angel, I'll have a listen to your chest. Just slip off your coat and blouse.' He moved his stethoscope slowly and carefully over her lung area. Then he percussed her chest. 'That's fine. Turn round and I'll have a listen from the back.' He was silent for a few seconds. 'You can fasten your blouse now. Well, whatever it is that ails you, your lungs are sound as a bell. What about your periods?' he asked, and busied himself sorting papers on his desk so as not to look at her directly. Young women were always embarrassed by that question. Indeed, when he glanced up, her cheeks were flaming.

Again Aggie butted in. 'She's seen nothing this long

time. She had a terrible accident.' And she told him about the runaway horse and the bruising. 'She hasn't been the same since nor seen colour either.'

'And how long ago was that?' asked the doctor.

'March, wasn't it, love? So that's . . .' and Aggie counted on her fingers and said aloud, 'March, April, May, June. Could it be anything to do with the kick from the horse?'

While examining Angel's chest the doctor had seen the prominent blue veins beneath the fair skin of her breast, a sign of pregnancy. Of course, he couldn't be absolutely sure without a further examination. And he'd have been prepared to go into court and swear that the mother had thought of many things that might ail her daughter but not pregnancy. He'd be gentle, if he was right, in breaking the news. 'A kick from a horse could do an awful lot of damage, but there's only one way to be sure. Go behind the screen and take off your skirt.'

Aggie went with her. He could hear her voice reassuring her daughter that it wouldn't take long, that the doctor would be able to tell if her insides had been damaged and make her better. And he smiled and wondered if the girl was as ignorant or innocent as she appeared to be. She wasn't married. That he'd ascertained when he took their names. If she was pregnant, there was a hard road in front of her and her mother, who was obviously devoted to her. Despite the sympathy he felt, he smiled again, thinking of all the reasons he'd heard young unmarried girls give for their pregnancies. The last one had blamed it on having had her ears pierced. But never before had he heard the one about a kick from a horse.

He rubbed his hands together to warm them, hoping

221

that a decent young man might be waiting to marry her. Then, reminding himself that he must remain objective, he asked if the young woman was ready. And Aggie said she was.

He had to move the screen back from the couch to fit himself in. The girl looked at him with trusting eyes as he palpated her belly. Twelve weeks at least.

'Right, then,' he said heartily. 'All over. You can get dressed now.'

They were out in no time.

'Well,' the doctor said, 'it wasn't the horse. What ails you only time will cure. You're expecting a baby. In about six months.' Angel fainted. The doctor came round the desk and bent her head forward. Aggie had burst into tears. She told the doctor he must be mistaken. 'My Angel's a good girl. She wouldn't do anything like that. And sure she isn't going out with a fella. She's never in her life done a line with a fella.'

'There, now, you're grand, hold on and I'll get you a drink of water, Angel.' He gave her the water, which she sipped, and put a hand on Aggie's shoulder. 'Mrs Lucas,' he said, 'I know it must be a terrible shock but isn't a baby better than consumption? This time next year you'll have a grandchild, not a daughter coughing her lungs up.'

'Ah, Doctor,' Aggie said, 'sure couldn't we have done without either.'

Unlike the majority of single girls to whom he had given news of a pregnancy, Angel didn't utter a word, but her face was ashen and her beautiful eyes were angry. 'You were very kind, and we mustn't delay you any longer.' Aggie took from her pocket a shabby black

222

purse, opened it and brought out two half-crowns. 'Five shillings, is that what I owe you?'

'Put it by for the baby, and before you go I'll give you an iron tonic for Angel. Make sure she takes it every day.' Then, to Angel, he said, 'If you can manage to swallow it while holding a piece of bread between your teeth, it stops the iron staining them.'

When they were outside Aggie leant against the garden railings. 'I'm dropping,' she said. 'I can't believe it.'

'Well, don't drop here and cause a commotion. And it's true so you'd better believe it.'

'But how could it be?'

'There's someone coming down the road. Link me and don't talk any more until we get home.'

Aggie did as she was told, vaguely aware that Angel should be the one trembling with fear instead of capably taking charge. When they arrived at the cottage it was she who lit the lamp, put Aggie to sit down, revived the fire and put the kettle on.

'He could have made a mistake, many a doctor does.'

'He made no mistake,' Angel said, while wetting the tea, 'and take off your coat and them shoes. They're crippling your bunions.'

While the tea was drawing she knelt in front of her mother, put her head in her lap and cried, 'Oh, Ma, what'll become of me?'

In charge again, Aggie rose to the challenge. 'You'll be grand,' she said. 'God won't desert us. But we'll have to talk. Put plenty of sugar in the tea and then sit down. First, *did* you know you were in the way?'

'The thought crossed my mind once. I never paid much attention to my periods. Why would I? They came

223

and they went. Not like Mona who knew her dates and dreaded them, but I never had a pain from them. I thought when you never commented on my clothes not being stained that it was the shock of the accident,' she lied.

'I thought you were going into consumption and about the horse as well.'

'I'm sorry, Ma. Never in a million years would I have wanted this to happen.'

'Don't I know that, child? Will he marry you, d'ye think?'

'I don't know where he is. Even if I did, he'd be the last man on earth I'd marry.'

'Who was it?'

'I can't tell you.'

It was seldom that Aggie got angry but now she raised her voice. 'Have you lost your mind? You *have* to tell me. I'm your mother. Whoever he is, he'll have a mother. We could arrange things if you didn't want to marry him, make arrangements for a few bob towards the child's keep.'

Angel didn't answer, and her mother wanted to hit her. Instead, she said something that for years afterwards she regretted and confessed many times when asked to recall past sins. 'Was it anything to do with Father Brennan?'

'May God forgive you,' was Angel's reply. She threw a coat round her shoulders, went out and headed for the river.

It was dark now. There'd be few, except courting couples, along the river, and they'd pay her no attention. In any case she didn't care if they did. She seethed with anger that her mother could have mentioned the poor

224

priest. But her overriding anger was against God, who was supposed to be kind and loving. Where was God when He let a baby be conceived from such an evil deed?

When she came to the deep part of the pool she thought about drowning herself, but she was young and strong, and not yet prepared to die. She could feel resolve hardening in her. She would overcome her trouble. Johnny Quinn would not destroy her life as he had attempted to destroy her body. Then she thought of her poor mother, alone in the cottage, half out of her mind with worry. She'd have to go back and face her, let her keep questioning her. Questions to which Aggie would never get an answer. For to no one in the world could Angel tell what had happened.

When she came back, her mother was still in her chair by the fire, her eyes red and swollen from crying. 'Where did you go? I was worried about you, imagining all sorts of things. I'm so sorry for what I said, I'll have to go to confession tomorrow. And after tonight I'll ask you no more about it.' She thought of all the times when she had congratulated herself on the closeness between her and her daughter. How she would have declared to the world and believed it that there were no secrets between them, that always it would be like that, each opening their heart to the other.

'For a walk down by the river. It's a lovely night. What else did you want to ask me?'

'Something that's been puzzling me. I missed your hat from the top of the press and then I couldn't find the suit you bought for Mona's wedding, nor the beads Mrs Gorman gave you.'

'Oh, them,' said Angel. 'I lent them to Bridie for a

wedding. You remember Bridie? She brought me home the day of the accident. They'll be all right with her.'

'There's another thing I want to say. Why don't you sit down?'

Angel was terrified that her mother was going to delve more into the accident, that her resolve would weaken and she'd tell her about Johnny Quinn. The truth would send her mother out of her mind. Her poor mother, who had never harmed anyone in her life. She sat down and prepared herself for what might come next, praying to the God that a little while ago she had hated to give her the strength to look her mother in the face and tell more lies if it was necessary.

'I don't want you to be thinking that because you're having a baby, please God, I'll want to run you out of your home the way some mothers do. Though half the time I think it's the fathers that can't stand the shame. None of that for you. No being packed off down the country into a home for fallen women, washing and scrubbing. You'll stay here, so you will, have your child, and between us we'll rear it. You're my flesh and blood, and dare anyone look crooked at you.'

'Oh, Mammy.' It was years since Angel had called Aggie that, and it started them both crying. 'Oh, Mammy, what would I do without you?' Angel knelt before Aggie and laid her head in her lap. Aggie stroked her hair, wound it into ringlets round her fingers. 'My little girl. The world hasn't been kind to you, but it will be again. You'll see. Everything will all come right in the end.'

For all that Aggie had assured Angel that she would stay home and have her baby, she knew the reality of the situation would be daunting. There'd be the keeping of them on only her earnings, the disgrace of an illegitimate child, the diminishing prospects of Angel finding a husband, and the slur on the child for the rest of its life.

If only she'd been doing a line with someone. Many girls went to the altar already pregnant and dressed in bridal white. There was nudging and whispering but weddings like that were a nine days' wonder and quickly forgotten. For her unfortunate daughter and grandchild, though, there'd be no forgetting. He or she would be a bastard. Pointed out in school, pitied by the charitable and scorned by the heartless. But, for all that, the child would be reared with the love of his mother and his granny. She'd find a way to keep her family together, even if she died in the attempt – move into the city, if necessary. There would be more work in Dublin. You could lose yourself there.

But why wouldn't Angel tell her who the father was? And where had she met him? It had to have been at one of the all-night hooleys. Where else? Something that had started as a game of Spin the Bottle. Someone had forgotten to call Angel back and the man had taken advantage of her. A stranger it had to be. Otherwise why didn't she name him? She might to Father Clancy. And, for all she knew, he might have been a decent, hard-working lad with a bit too much drink taken, who'd be more than willing to fulfil his duties.

Like herself, Angel had been unfortunate. And, for all her beauty, she hadn't made much headway with the young men in the village, except with that eejit Tommy Maguire, who'd wanted to marry her and she only a child. But wouldn't she be better off married to him in this predicament? Once, years ago, she'd opened her heart about Johnny Quinn until I shut her up, giving her the Quinns' character. But how was I to know the grand man he'd turn into, handsome and prosperous? Aggie couldn't get over the change in him she'd seen the night he called about his mother. When exactly was that? In the last few months since the accident she'd lost track of time. It was all there, tangled in her mind, if only she could unravel it.

Angel hadn't been there the night he came. That was a pity, something might have come of it. It'd been a Saturday night. She'd talked about dancing on the Monday night and maybe a late-night hooley after work, then said it was a wake she was going to. It was all very fishy, thought Aggie. I should have quizzed her a bit more. But, thank God, my mind is clearing. It was the twentieth of March. How could I have forgotten? The night of Johnny's fight. His face was on posters all over the place.

Tomorrow she'd see Father Clancy and tell him the news. And she mustn't forget Angel's medicine. Sleep was beginning to claim her when she remembered the story the arthritic woman had told her about the hat. A hat that might have been Angel's, which she had lent to Bridie with the suit and beads. Round about the time of the accident. After that Angel hadn't gone into town any more. But why hadn't Bridie brought them back? Why, if she was so concerned about her, getting a cab to the door after the horse kicked Angel, had she never even dropped a note asking how she was?

And then a terrible thought occurred to Aggie. Maybe someone *had* been murdered in the hotel. Someone wearing Angel's suit and hat. Bridie. Maybe she'd picked up with a Black and Tan. Some girls did. The Tans were paid over the odds, ten shillings a day. And there were always girls attracted by men who could spend lavishly. And, come to think of it, she was a knowing-looking one. If she had been murdered, and it wouldn't be the first girl the Tans had done in, that would account for no news from her and the clothes not being returned. To herself Aggie said, 'I'll find that hotel, go into the bar, let on I'm lost and see if the hat is there. And then what?' she asked herself, but fell asleep before thinking of an answer.

Chapter Fourteen

The next evening Aggie went to confession and, after telling her sins, receiving absolution and her customary penance of three Hail Marys, asked Father Clancy could she come and see him the next day in the presbytery. 'It's something very important that I need your advice on.'

'I've only one funeral in the morning. Come about eleven. God bless you now.'

It was a beautiful day, warm and sunny, and Aggie thought about Angel cooped up in the cottage, never going out except late at night when the two of them walked along the riverbank. It was no life for a young girl. But she couldn't persuade Angel that not one in a million could tell she was carrying. 'Later on I could understand you feeling awkward, but not so early.'

Angel didn't enlighten her that it was more than being pregnant that kept her in. It was imagining that everyone she passed could see in her face what had happened in the hotel and condemn her for it. Sometimes she wondered if she could ever bring herself to go out again. She longed to be in the sunshine and fresh air, to walk by the river in daylight, watch the children catching pinkeens, pick a bunch of wild flowers.

Staying in was harder now than in the previous weeks when she had felt sick, tired, and her insides still hurt. For the last few days she had felt fit as a fiddle, as her mother would have said. She'd feel like that for hours and convince herself that, even in her head, she was getting better. And then suddenly she was back in the hotel room and waves of nausea coursed through her, her mouth went dry and her heart raced. She'd have to leave whatever it was she was doing, sit down and take deep breaths. And her mother, if she noticed, would say consolingly, 'It often takes you like that in the beginning, but it'll get better in a few weeks.'

Father Clancy had a new housekeeper, a Wicklow woman, stout, friendly without being nosy, who welcomed Aggie, invited her into the parlour and said she'd let the priest know she had arrived. 'Before the pair of you get settled in I'll make a pot of tea and there are scones just out of the oven.' On the verge of tears, Aggie thanked her.

When Father Clancy came in, he said, 'You sounded terribly worried in confession. Angel isn't sick again? You were going to take her to Dr Cassidy. Did you?'

'I did.' She could contain her tears no longer.

'Is it consumption, as you feared?'

For a few minutes she couldn't answer him. Tears spilled from her eyes, a lump formed in her throat. Then she made a great effort and controlled herself. 'It's not consumption but something that never crossed my mind. Angel's expecting a baby.'

Neither had such a thought crossed Father Clancy's. But now, just for a fleeting second, he wondered about Father Brennan, then immediately dismissed the idea and silently said an aspiration, asking that his momentary suspicion would be forgiven. Not that such a thing hadn't happened – priests did make girls pregnant, not often but it happened and was hushed up. Parents, doubly shamed, were easily cowed, persuaded to send the girl away and the guilty priest was moved to another parish. Rarely did the unfortunate girl return home and the subject was closed for ever. In the parish, though, it was remembered for many a long year, and almost always the girl was blamed for putting temptation in the way of one of God's holy anointed. He wished that Angel had chosen somewhere else to faint than on Father Brennan's bed. Or that the curate had had the gumption to let her come round without sending for help. Or that the blonde hairs hadn't been found on his pillow. If word of Angel's pregnancy got out, Miss Heffernan would have a field day. But he was jumping the gun. Angel was probably courting, though he wasn't aware of it. Not that that meant anything – he didn't know everything about his parishioners. She was probably doing a line with someone she'd met in a dance hall, hopefully a nice, decent young man who'd do the right thing by her.

Coming back from his speculations, he apologised to Aggie. 'I couldn't take it in for a minute. I'm sorry. Go on, tell me all about it. Is the doctor definite about a baby?'

'Not a doubt in the world.'

'And Angel, how did she take the news?'

'Fainted, then was as cool as a cucumber.'

'And the father?'

'Ah, Sean, that's the trouble. She won't tell me. Honest to God, I think I'm having a nightmare that I'll wake up from and everything will be all right.'

'Was she doing a line with anyone?'

'Not as far as I know. But there's something very strange about the whole business.'

'May God look down on the pair of you. Maybe she'll change her mind and tell you who the father is. Will I have a word with her?'

'If anyone can get it out of her it'll be you. Though I doubt it. There's such a change come over her. Since she was kicked by the horse. She hit her head when she fell and it could have done damage to her brain.'

'And supposing she doesn't divulge the father's name, what are you going to do?'

'Keep her at home and between us we'll rear the child, please God.'

Aggie rushing to the defence of her cub. Generous, warm-hearted Aggie. Well, this wasn't the time to point out the difficulties, financial or otherwise, of doing what Aggie planned. He'd wait a while. 'You're a great woman, Aggie, and God is good. Have another cup of tea, and you haven't touched your scone.'

'I've no appetite, Father.'

'I'll get the housekeeper to wrap them up and you take them home. Now, about talking to Angel. It'd be better if we were on our own. When's the best time to come?'

'Tomorrow. I've a full day's work then and Angel will be in all day. She doesn't cross the door until it's dark.'

'Then I'll be in, say, about two o'clock.'

'That'll be grand.'

'Finish your tea while I get the scones wrapped up.'

When he came back she was ready to leave. 'My heart's

a bit lighter after talking to you, Father. And maybe tomorrow it'll be lighter still. May God bless you.'

Father Clancy was no more successful in discovering the name of the father of Angel's child than her mother had been. He pointed out that, admirable though Aggie's intentions were, they weren't practicable. 'As it is,' he said, 'Aggie's run off her feet trying to feed the two of you. And I know the saying that God never sends a mouth that he doesn't send the bit to feed it but, more often than not, it means pleading with the relieving officer. Your mother's a great Christian but she's a proud woman too and won't welcome begging for extra money. You owe it to her and the child to name the man. The ideal thing for all concerned would be to marry. For all that we flock to church and chapel, we're not truly Christian and there's still a stigma attached to a child without its father's name. Even if the man or you don't want to marry, he might be willing to help financially. I want you to think it over carefully, for all of your sakes.'

'I know, Father, your advice is good, but I can't tell you. I'll never tell you nor anyone else.'

'I'm very sorry for you. I'm very fond of you and your mother. I'd be sorry for any girl in your condition, but don't forget we're related and blood's thicker than water. I'll leave you now, but if you change your mind, I'll do all in my power to help.'

She took her iron medicine every day, having mastered the knack of keeping the bread between her teeth. Aggie complimented her on how well she looked: 'It's the tonic,' she said. 'A bottle of iron works wonders.'

Angel did all she could to lighten her mother's

burden, having a cup of tea ready when she came in, a basin of warm water for soaking her feet. She even mastered her fear of using the cut-throat razor and pared Aggie's corns. One day while she was doing this, the memory of the scene in the hotel room overcame her. The fear, the pain, the shame. She felt sick, dizzy, and her heart raced. 'I'll have to sit down for a minute, Ma,' she said, rising from her kneeling position. 'Do, child, sure there's no hurry.'

She sat and took long, slow breaths, and gradually the panic subsided. She looked towards her mother, who sat with her feet still in the basin, her eyes closed, her skirt hitched up. Angel saw the exhausted face, the knotted varicose veins, almost black against Aggie's pale skin. Her mother who slaved for any woman who'd employ her, who no longer questioned her about the father of the child. She remembered Father Clancy's words, saw her proud mother pleading with the relieving officer, her mother who had aged ten years since they had been to the doctor.

The razor was still in Angel's hand, its blade gleaming like silver, inviting, its edge honed regularly on the old strop hanging from a nail behind the door. A blade so sharp it sliced the callused skin as if it were butter. It would slice as easily through her throat and put an end to her mother's suffering.

Then Aggie opened her eyes. 'Angel, you're such a comfort to me. I don't know what I'd do without you – the bit on the table when I come in, the bed made, the place tidy and clean. You've done enough for today. Gimme that razor.' Aggie closed it and put it back in its case.

'I'm not a bit tired.'

Aggie wanted to tell her that tiredness, like the sickness, was part of early pregnancy. From now on she'd feel grand, but she didn't. Now, the baby wasn't mentioned: Aggie had decided to let the subject rest for the time being. In a couple of weeks she'd raise it again, when Angel had had time to get over the shock.

Which Angel was doing, since her health had improved. For days she would forget her pregnancy, was delighted to feel strong again. Her only frustration was that she couldn't go out except at night: her body yearned for more exercise than she got doing housework. She scrubbed and washed and ironed and dusted, but the cottage was small and her chores spent little of her abundant energy.

One day after washing sheets, checking that no one was in the yard and pegging them on the line, she made a cup of tea and sat down to drink it. While she was doing so she became aware of a strange sensation in her belly. It was not a pain. In a way it was pleasant, reminding her of years ago when she'd catch a butterfly, hold it in her closed hands and feel its wings flutter against her palms. The sensation lasted only a short time but happened at intervals throughout the afternoon.

When her mother came home from work she told her about it. Aggie's tired face lit with delight and she said, 'Angel, that's the child quickening.'

'What's that?'

'The child beginning to move. Making its presence felt. You'll feel it often from now on. In no time it'll be kicking like a footballer.'

A feeling of loathing engulfed Angel. It was real. Inside her was a baby, his baby, proof of that night, growing every minute. She hated it as she hated him. She

235

wished for the power to reach inside herself and drag it out, destroy it.

'You've gone a bit pale. D'ye feel all right?' Aggie asked concernedly.

'I'm grand, not a bother on me. I'm missing the fresh air, I suppose.'

Aggie believed her, and promised that tonight they'd walk further along the riverbank.

Father Clancy was worried about Aggie's decision to keep Angel at home during her pregnancy and to rear the child. It was admirable, and a decision he would normally have supported. But this case was different. The anonymous letter had proved that. There hadn't been any others so far, but once it became evident that Angel was carrying a child, tongues would wag again.

He went to see Aggie, knowing Angel would be there but it concerned them both. And maybe after she'd heard what he had to say, she might tell them the father's name. As tactfully as possible he questioned her again. And as politely as possible she refused again.

He turned his attention to Aggie. 'If the circumstances were different, I'd never suggest what I'm going to now. Angel has her reasons for refusing to name the child's father and, to a certain extent, that's her own business. But there are things to consider. You are killing yourself working, and even if you work all the hours God sends, in the long run you'll have to look for relief. But, apart from that, doing what you intend doing will be the cause of great scandal.'

'Others have done it before me, Father. Any mother with a bit of nature would do it. I know what I'll have to put up with – what we'll have to put up with. Even the poor unfortunate child. But none of it could be as bad as Angel or the baby being torn away from the only one in the world who'll love them.'

'Ah, Aggie it's hard to go against the tribe.'

'Well, go against it I will, Father.'

'Stop you I can't, but you'll be giving scandal.'

'Because I'm sheltering my own flesh and blood?'

'Because in a short while Angel's condition will be common knowledge. No father named, no marriage to take place. Tongues will begin to wag. Father Brennan's name will be bandied about. But if you follow my advice it can all be avoided.'

The priest looked at Aggie's woebegone face and his heart went out to her.

'D'ye remember Teresa, another cousin, related to me not you?'

'I do,' replied Aggie.

'Well, she's in a convent in Wexford. She's the Reverend Mother. The order takes in a few girls who get into trouble. It's not like the Magdalene places, far from it. The girls are well looked after. So I was thinking that, if you agreed, I'd have a word with Teresa. I'm sure she'd find a place for Angel. And now's the right time, when no one knows how the situation stands. You could put it about that Angel was going to England. A friend she'd met through the dancing had found her a job. Then, when everything was all over, she could come home.'

Aggie appeared to consider what had been said, once or twice looking in Angel's direction, as if expecting a reaction from her. Angel kept her gaze on the floor, where it had been while the priest was talking. Aggie cleared her throat, coughed, took her rag handkerchief from her apron pocket, blew her nose, and gave Father Clancy his answer.

'I've great faith in God's mercy and I'm sure he'll forgive me if I'm giving scandal. But I'll never let Angel go into one of them places. She's my only child. The only thing that made my life worth while. And I'll welcome her baby with open arms. I'm sorry, Father. If it was easy to do, for your sake I'd do it.'

'Don't cry, Aggie, you're truly Christian. Pray to God and His Blessed Mother. And I'll give you all the help I can. May God bless you both. I'll say goodnight now. Don't bother, I'll see myself out,' he said, when Angel began getting up from her chair.

When he was gone, Angel said, 'Ma, don't talk about it, please. I know it's what you want to do but all I want is to forget the whole thing ever happened. It's dark. Let's go for our walk and I'll make a bit of supper when we come back.'

By the following week it was all round the town that Angel Lucas was expecting. Aggie's arthritic woman told her. 'I didn't want you taken unawares by some oul faggot in the street, though knowing how close you and Angel are I'm sure you knew already. Get that bottle of sherry from the sideboard and pour out two glasses. You look in need of one.'

'I knew,' admitted Aggie. 'I went with her to the doctor. And apart from Father Clancy, not another soul was the wiser.'

'The doctor knew.'

'But he's a doctor. Like a priest he wouldn't have said anything.'

'Probably not, but he has a wife and walls have ears.'

'Surely to God she wouldn't have . . .'

'I'm not saying she did, though I've never favoured doctors' surgeries being part of their homes. There's wives and servants. Drink more of that sherry. How are you going to manage?' Aggie told her her plans. 'You're a great woman. It's what I'd do if I'd had a child. But it won't be easy. A big family at a time like this is what you need – aunts, uncles, grandmothers, cousins to back you up. It's only the likes of them generally who keep their girls out of homes and rear the baby among them.'

Aggie told her then how Angel wouldn't name the father, never wanted to mention the child she was carrying, and didn't go out during daylight.

'I'll offer up my communion for the two of you and I think it's time you upped what you charge for your work.'

Aggie didn't know whether or not to tell Angel that word was out about the baby. By the time she was almost home she had decided to leave it for another week at least. But when she arrived Angel handed her a letter that had come in the afternoon post. It was written in capital letters and read, 'You're a hoor. We'll run you and your bastard out of the village.'

It wasn't signed.

The running out began the next night when a brick was put through one of the cottage windows. More anonymous letters were delivered. Aggie's nerves began to give way, but Angel appeared not at all disturbed. After one reading she put aside the letter for her mother to see and afterwards threw them into the fire.

Father Clancy called, and once more entreated Angel to name the child's father, which she again refused to do, even after he told her and Aggie that Father Brennan's name was being mentioned in connection with her and the child. 'Not openly,' he said. 'No one has dared to confront me with it but there's a whispering campaign. They won't rest, our so-called Christian neighbours, until they've run Angel out. Will you not think about my suggestion again?'

'But, Father, the damage is done, everyone knows now.'

'That's true. Even so, once Angel's not here they'll count it a victory and leave you alone.'

'A victory to rob me of my daughter and grandchild! What sort of people are they?'

'We'll always have them with us, Aggie. I've something to see to above in the presbytery but I'll be in again tomorrow. Pray for guidance.'

When it grew dark, Angel asked her mother if she wanted to risk going for a walk. 'And why wouldn't I? Haven't we as much right as anyone in the village to go for a walk?'

'I was just thinking that now everyone knows about me we could be followed.'

'Then let them follow us. If I get my hands on one of them they'll finish up in the water. That'll cool their courage.'

But behind Aggie's brave words Angel heard her uncertainty. And, as she had feared, a gang did follow them, maybe half a dozen – she couldn't be sure in the dark. She thought they were mostly women, and she feared that if her mother tried tackling them, it would be she who would finish in the river. The gang kept a good distance behind them, but near enough for their voices to carry, shouting, 'Hoor, bastard,' and, 'We'll run you out of it.'

Angel held tightly to Aggie's hand and felt it trembling. She decided that turning back would be unwise but feared that her mother was tiring. Nevertheless they walked on. Then the shouting stopped. 'I think they're going back, Ma.'

'Afraid to face us,' said Aggie, the relief in her voice belying her words.

When they got home Angel insisted that Aggie get into bed, helped her to undress, told her how brave she was. She sat on the edge of the bed and they drank some hot, sweet tea.

'What's that?' asked Aggie, looking towards the door. 'I thought I heard the letter-box.'

The smell of paraffin filled the room and there was smoke. Angel went to look, and on the floor found smouldering rags and paper.

'Jesus, Mary and Joseph!' exclaimed Aggie, who'd got out of bed. 'They're trying to burn us out.'

Little flames were licking the edges of the bundle. Angel stamped them out. 'Probably some young fellas did it. I don't think it would have caught. The floor's stone.'

'But the bedclothes aren't. Supposing they'd fired it through the broken window – the bit of cardboard would have taken no knocking out. It'd have landed on top of us and we'd have been roasted alive.'

'Ma, we won't be able to sleep for a while. Let's sit down and talk.'

Going to her chair, looking haggard and years beyond her age, Aggie said, 'That's after frightening the life out of me. Name-callin's one thing but, Sacred Heart of Jesus, to try and set fire to your house!'

'It frightened me too. I couldn't go through this for

241

months, maybe years. It's me they're after, not you. Tomorrow I'm going to the presbytery to tell Father Clancy I'll go into the home.'

'Oh, no, love, you'll be playing into their hands. Don't, we'll get through it,' Aggie pleaded, but Angel who knew her mother so well, every nuance of her voice, was aware that though her leaving would break Aggie's heart, she was beyond coping with any more of the appalling things that had happened in the previous weeks.

'God forgive them,' Father Clancy said, when Angel told him about the attempt at setting the house on fire, the jeering crowd who had followed them along the river-bank.

'So, Father, I'll go to the home.'

Chapter Fifteen

The arrangements were made for Angel's leaving. Mother Teresa had written to her, explaining the rules. She would be expected to help with light housework in the sewing room, and attend lectures on child care. There was a library and a piano. Unless there were complications the baby would be delivered in the home, and the choice as to whether it was adopted was entirely up to its mother.

Angel read the letter aloud to Father Clancy and her mother. Aggie said, 'It sounds a grand place, like as if it's private.'

'It is,' the priest replied.

'You mean, girls have to pay to go there?'

'They do, but that won't apply to Angel. Teresa has taken her as a favour for me.'

'Well, aren't you the lucky girl?' said Aggie, fighting back the tears that had been ready to spill over since the decision had been reached.

'Oh, indeed I am,' said Angel, and her mother's heart broke a bit more.

Aggie cried inconsolably, castigating herself for letting her daughter down, for reneging on a mother's duty. Angel and the priest did their best to convince her that she had been left with no choice. How long Aggie would have continued crying would never be known, for someone knocked at the door. With a great effort she controlled herself.

It was Mrs Gorman. 'I heard tell you were off tomorrow and I couldn't let you go without saying goodbye.' She embraced Angel and kissed her cheek. Aggie left her chair and moved the kettle from the hob over the fire. 'I'll wet a sup of tea. Take my chair. I'll sit on the bed.'

Mrs Gorman told them that her husband was now completely paralysed and not able to utter a word. 'With the best will in the world, I'm not able to nurse him any more. It's the lifting. But he'll be well looked after in the Incurables.'

Aggie served the tea and Mrs Gorman went on, 'All the changes. It's like only yesterday you came to work for us, Angel. I know that if Jim was able to understand your plight he'd be heartfelt sorry. Like myself, he was very fond of you.'

'He was that,' agreed Angel, and shuddered remembering her experience with Dr Gorman.

When they bade each other goodnight, Mrs Gorman slipped two pound notes into Angel's hand and kissed her cheek. Fifty-four pounds, a small fortune, thought Angel. The woman with arthritis had also given her two pounds, and Danny had sent fifty pounds by Father Clancy, with just a few lines wishing her well.

'You're lucky you got it safe,' the priest had said, when he brought her Danny's gift. 'I caught him just before he posted it. I don't know what made me ask was it for you. When he said it was, I told him what you do with letters nowadays – straight into the fire they go without being opened, I said. Are the anonymous ones still arriving?'

'On both posts now,' replied Angel. 'When I'm settled in I'll drop a note and thank Danny.'

Father Clancy took his watch from his breast pocket and exclaimed, 'Eleven o'clock! We've an early start in the morning so I'll let the two of you go to bed. The cab will be here at half six and the train leaves at half eight. It's a lovely run along the coast most of the way to Wexford.'

Aggie and Angel saw him to the door. When he was gone, Angel made more tea and sat down to talk with her mother, both of them aware that their minds weren't easy enough to sleep yet awhile.

Aggie repeated the priest's advice, given earlier in the evening. 'He thinks we should make a fresh start in England or down the country. If we stay in Ireland he said we could let on your husband had been shot by a Black and Tan. No one would doubt that and be very sympathetic to you. If it's to England we go it'll have to be a different story. Your husband was caught in the cross-fire between the Tans and the Republicans. Where would you rather go?'

'England, I think. Though I don't really mind.'

'Me, you and the baby. We'll have a grand life, please God. I'd say there's plenty of work in England.'

'I'd say so too,' agreed Angel, covering her mouth with her hand and pretending to yawn. 'All of a sudden the sleep has overtaken me,' she lied.

'Get into the bed, then, love. I'll rinse the few cups, sweep in the hearth and say my beads. By then I'll be ready for bed myself.'

In bed, Angel turned her face to the wall, shut her eyes and continued making her plans for the next day. Before the gifts of the money she had only the thirty shillings her mother had given her, enough to get her a night's shelter, maybe two, while she looked for Bridie, and enough to buy a ticket back to Westland Row, a station further down the line from Harcourt Street. Of one thing she was certain: she wasn't going to the home. Of another she was even more certain: she wasn't going to have this baby. Not his baby. Not a baby conceived the way this one had been. She'd loathe it, smother it rather than rear it.

In the dance halls she had heard how girls, sometimes married women, got rid of babies. There were other women who'd do it for you. Who or where they were she didn't know but she was sure that Bridie would. The women charged for what they did. It was very dear, someone had mentioned. But she wasn't short of money.

Used all her life to praying every night, for fine weather, for her mother's health, for Johnny not to be hurt or killed in the ring, for him to notice her, to love her, she longed for the comfort of praying. But since the night in the hotel she had never prayed. She wasn't sure if she believed in God now, not any more. God wouldn't let someone do to you what had been done to her. Well, maybe he might, but not let you have a baby as well. But if there was a God, then all that the nuns had taught her was true: hell was real, a burning pit into which she'd be thrown to roast for ever and ever. For what she was planning to do to the baby was murder. And murder was a mortal sin. It was for mortal sins you went to hell. Then, remembering the night in the hotel, she made up her mind. The baby had to go, even if it meant she went to hell. And, for all she knew, if there was a God he might understand and forgive her. Then she'd only have to go to purgatory. There was always someone praying for the souls in purgatory: if enough prayers were said for your soul you were let out and went up to heaven. Before she went to sleep she remembered that tomorrow was 1 July, her birthday. She'd be twenty.

Aggie stood by the door waving to Angel and Father Clancy as the cab drove away, and Angel wondered when, if ever, she would see her mother again. But soon her thoughts were concentrated on what lay ahead: leaving the Wexford-bound train and catching another to Westland Row. As far as she remembered, it wasn't too far from the north side. She could remember the name of the street where the hotel was. In the midst of all her distress and pain on the morning after Johnny had attacked her she had spotted it. North Great George's Street. She didn't know the name of the hotel but she'd ask for Bridie in every one.

The cab bowled along. Soon they were in the outskirts of Dublin. Many people were about, mostly women. The priest said, 'They're weavers going to work. We'll be over Harold's Cross Bridge in a minute, then turn on to the South Circular Road at Leonard's Corner, and Harcourt Street'll be the next stop.'

Harcourt Street, she remembered it. Her mother had pointed it out on her birthday on their way to the waxworks, and she had mentioned a seaside place called Bray, supposed to be a beautiful place, how she'd never seen the sea. And Angel recalled promising to take Aggie there one day when she grew up.

For the first time since leaving home that morning, tears pricked her eyes. She brushed them away. No more crying, no more looking back. From now on she was on her own. She had to find Bridie. She had to get rid of the baby, and after that she would find a way to earn her living.

'Well, here we are and in plenty of time.' She'd never been in a railway station before and was surprised at how much noise there was, how many people moving about, the shouting, the laughter. She wondered where they were all going.

Father Clancy bought her a single ticket, the *Irish Independent* and, from a machine fixed to the wall, two penny bars of Urney's chocolate. As they walked to the platform from which the Wexford train would leave, he reminded her, 'Two of the sisters will be waiting for you. I won't promise, but if I can, I'll come down to see you and bring your mother.'

She smiled, said that would be great, and thanked him for all his help.

'You'll be off in a minute. There's a good head of steam up and your man's there with his flag. Get into this carriage, there's a woman in it. A chat would pass the

247

time or you can read the paper. And don't worry, you're doing the right thing.' He squeezed her shoulder. 'Get in now, and may God bless you.'

She sat by the window nearest the platform, and wished he would go.

'Are you going far?' the woman asked.

'Westland Row,' replied Angel.

'We won't have time for a chat, then.'

A guard came along, checking that the doors were shut, and the train began to move out of the station. Again Angel counted in her head how much money she had, and thought how generous people had been. But also how, if she had intended keeping the baby and had wanted to stay at home, everyone had let her down. It was just luck that Father Clancy's cousin was a nun in charge of a private home. She had been driven out of her own home by the mob. So much for the priest and the power he was supposed to have over his parishioners. She didn't blame him or her mother. They had done what they could. In any case it didn't matter now. But she had learned a lesson from it: you couldn't depend on anyone.

When she came out of Westland Row station, she turned right and began walking down the street. As she continued she saw, from the view ahead, that she was walking away from town. She turned, stopped, and asked directions from a passer-by. She recognised Sackville Street, and stopped to look into Clery's window at the display of women's outfits. She didn't like what she was wearing – it was a navy jacket and skirt of such a dark shade in certain lights that it appeared black – but her mother had thought it suitable for her arrival at the convent. And even Angel was glad of the semi-fitting three-quarter-length jacket, which hid the bump, slight though it was, of her pregnancy. Her blouse was pale pink, quite becoming, but her hat she thought, desperate-looking. A black felt, unadorned.

In the window there was a rose pink straw hat, not too widely brimmed, but that wouldn't matter now that she wasn't going to a convent, and she needed cheering up. It was priced at nine and eleven. She felt she could afford it, went in, tried it on and smiled at her reflection. It was her first genuine smile for a long time. She bought it. Further down the street she went into a café where she had coffee and two scones. A woman at the table said, 'Isn't it a grand day?'

'Beautiful,' said Angel.

'If only it wasn't for the shooting.'

'What shooting is that?' asked Angel.

'Are you not from the city?'

Angel said she wasn't and the woman told her how lucky she was. 'Nowadays you never know when you'll get a bullet in the head. I've never had a bad word to say about British soldiers but the Black and Tans are murderers. Stocious morning, noon and night, and swaggering through the city as if they owned it. Look there, quick, out through the window. There's a couple of them.'

Angel saw two men dressed in black and green, drunk and swaggering.

'Still,' said the woman, buttering a scone, 'they won't stop me from going out. Where d'ye live?'

Angel told her and went on to say she was looking for a hotel in North Great George's Street, but she couldn't remember its name.

'Whereabouts in the street was it?'

'It sort of went round the corner.'

'That's the Grand. It's only a stone's throw from here. I'm going the other way or I'd show you, but when I finish my tea I'll point you in the right direction,' which she did.

In no time Angel stood before the door of the hotel. It took her a few minutes to pluck up her courage and go in. Immediately she felt sick as the smell of stale porter and tobacco wafted out of the open bar doors. A young man came out of the room, looked at her and asked, 'D'ye want something, Miss?'

'I'm looking for a friend of mine who used to work here. Bridie.'

'She left just after I started. Herself and the boss had a row over a hat, so I believe.'

'Oh,' said Angel. 'I wanted to see her about something important.'

'I know where she lives – Buckingham Street, not that far from here. Over the North Strand, facing Amiens Street station. I think she's a wardsmaid in the Mater.'

The young man's eyes were fixed on Angel's face. He had never seen anyone so beautiful and wished he wasn't on duty so that he could have walked her to Buckingham Street.

It was a wide street. She walked down it, noticing the houses, that some were well kept and others dilapidated. Outside one of the run-down ones, an old woman was standing nursing a baby in a shawl. Angel avoided looking at the baby and asked the woman if she knew anyone called Bridie. 'Half a dozen. What's her other name?'

I'm an eejit, thought Angel. I never asked the fella in the hotel, and admitted to the old woman that she didn't know.

'D'ye know anything about her?'

'She used to work in a hotel as a chambermaid. Now I've heard tell she's a wardsmaid in the Mater.'

'Bridie Breen, that's who you want. She lives in the next house up. You're in luck, it's her day off.'

Angel knew it wasn't the custom to ignore a baby. People said, 'Isn't he or she lovely? God bless and spare him or her.' But she never glanced at the child, just thanked the woman and went. Behind her she heard, 'Frosty-faced bitch.'

The door was open and there was a terrible smell in the hall, like the smell in the backyard privy at home. The walls were pockmarked; in places lumps of the plaster had fallen out exposing the cowhair that bound the mortar. A beautiful flight of stairs curved to the upper landings but the steps were filthy and the mahogany banister chipped in places. Where in the house, she wondered, did Bridie live? A woman came down the stairs carrying a zinc bucket.

'Excuse me, ma'am, I'm looking for Bridie.'

'The back parlour,' she jerked her head back, then to the left.

'That door there. Knock hard – she'll still be in the scratcher.'

Angel had to knock several times before an irate voice asked, 'Who is it?'

'Me, Angel. You probably don't remember me. You helped me a few months ago in the hotel.'

A bolt was drawn back and the door opened a few inches, was then flung wide. Bridie was there in her shift. 'God Almighty, it's you! I never thought I'd lay eyes on you again. Come in, come in. How are you? Sit down.

251

Don't mind the state of the place. How did you find me?'

Angel's sense of relief was overwhelming. While Bridie went round the room, picking up clothes from the floor, filling the kettle and putting a frock on, she told her about going to the hotel, talking to the young man who had given her the information she wanted. 'He said you'd left after a row over a hat.'

'You wouldn't want to mind him, he's not right in the head. I left because I was working for nothing. A hat indeed! I wonder what put that idea into his head,' she lied. To tell Angel that her hat was on display was a cruelty she wouldn't practise.

When the tea and bread and butter were ready and the two of them seated at the table, Bridie remarked on Angel's appearance. 'You're looking great. Not like the girl I first met. But how are you in yourself?'

'Pregnant. This minute I should be on my way to Wexford to a home for girls like me. Won't they get an awful suck-in when I don't arrive?' she said light-heartedly, then broke down, cried, and told Bridie about the last few weeks. 'There was no one else I could turn to except you, even though I wasn't sure if you'd remember me.'

'I never forgot you. I was always meaning to drop you a line but kept putting it on the long finger and anyhow though I'd been to your house I never knew your address. What are you going to do?'

'For a start I want to get rid of the baby.'

'I can't say I blame you. If I was in your shoes I'd do the same.'

'But I don't know how to go about it.'

'Don't worry about that, I do. But it's not cheap. How are you fixed for money?'

Angel told her about the fifty pounds and the other gifts of money. 'Will that be enough?'

'Ten times over. And you can doss here for the time being. When it's all over, I'll get you a bit of work and find you a room. I don't suppose you heard any more about your man? That bastard deserved hanging. Will you let your mother know where you are?'

'No, I'll send a card telling her I'm all right so she won't think I was done in. Then maybe later on, when it's all over, I might write and tell her I had a miscarriage, meet her in town, but I'll never set foot in the village again.'

'You've grown up since we last met, become your own woman. The world does that to you, love. We'll do nothing for today. Talk and eat, that's all. Tomorrow I'm back in work. I'll find out from the girls who's the best to go to. The sooner you have it done the better.'

In the afternoon Father Clancy's cousin phoned him from the convent to tell him Angel hadn't been on the Dublin train when it arrived in Wexford. The sisters had met the two following trains and she wasn't on either of those. 'But, Teresa, I put her on the train myself and saw it leave the station.'

'The poor child. I hope nothing untoward has happened to her. Make enquiries and let me know, Sean.'

He phoned Harcourt Street and asked to speak to the stationmaster, who promised to telephone other stations on the way to Wexford and ring back with any news.

Father Clancy called Father Brennan, and together

they talked about what might have happened. 'If there'd been an accident on the line they'd have known at Harcourt Street,' Father Clancy said, and Father Brennan suggested that Angel might have left the train at the wrong station.

'But surely to God she would have realised her mistake and telephoned me or the convent. She's not a child.'

'Neither is she used to the telephone, nor approaching strangers.'

'You're right enough. Maybe she's huddled in a waiting room somewhere.'

'How am I going to tell—' Before he could finish the sentence the telephone rang. It was the stationmaster, confirming that there had been no accidents, no reports of anyone being taken ill, but a ticket collector remembered a girl fitting Angel's description getting off a train at Westland Row. Putting down the receiver Father Clancy asked, 'What could have possessed her to do that?'

'Nerves, possibly. It must have been a daunting prospect, going off to a strange place in her circumstances.'

'How am I going to tell her mother?'

'Maybe you won't have to. Maybe she went home,' Father Brennan said.

'Wouldn't that be grand?' said Father Clancy, his face full of hope. 'She could go next week, Teresa would understand. I'll see Aggie now and find out if you're right. Say a prayer that you are.'

When he discovered that Angel wasn't at home and told Aggie, as gently as he could, that she hadn't arrived at the convent, Aggie at first looked bewildered then became hysterical. 'They've killed her, followed her, that's what they did, on to the train, killed my lovely child and threw her out the door. And it's all my fault. I let her go. God forgive me, I let her go and was relieved she went and now the tormenting won't stop.'

'Aggie, Aggie, she wasn't harmed. She's all right. She got off the train at Westland Row. Don't keep screaming – you'll bring a crowd round the door.'

'Then where is she now? Why didn't she come back? If it was not them from here, the ones who tried to burn us out, then the Black and Tans shot her. Took her in a hurry up the mountains and riddled her with bullets. My child, my little child, and to think I sent her to her death.'

Never in his life had Father Clancy felt so helpless. He couldn't leave Aggie alone while he went for help. The neighbours on either side had been hostile towards her once they knew of Angel's pregnancy. He offered to make her tea. She looked at him as if he had lost his mind. 'Tea?' she said. 'Drink tea and my child lying murdered? Why did I listen to you? Why did I let you persuade me?'

If only, he thought, there was a drop of whiskey, that might calm her. If only he could leave her for a minute to go and get some. But he was afraid of what she might do if he did. All he could do was keep telling her Angel was alive and try to convince her that it wasn't her fault, that no one could have been a better mother. Father Brennan was above in the chapel praying for Angel's safe return, the nuns in the convent were praying for her. On and on he talked, until gradually Aggie's voice became quieter until she sat crying dejectedly.

He made tea and persuaded her to drink it, assuring

her that everything would be all right. 'Angel will be somewhere safe. You'll see her soon. I can't tell you why she got off the train or where she went but trust in God and you'll see how everything will come right.'

'I'm sorry, Father. I know what you did was all for the best. It was the shock. And she will be all right, won't she?'

'Of course she will,' Father Clancy assured her. And Aggie accepted it, as she had accepted his assurance throughout most of her life. Looking at her woebegone face, he knew that once he left she might easily lapse again into despair. She couldn't be left to spend the night alone in the cottage. He'd take her to stay with Mrs Gorman. Aggie liked and trusted her, and Mrs Gorman was a good, kind woman. Maybe by tomorrow word would come that Angel was safe, wherever she was.

He put his plan to Aggie. 'But, Father, supposing she comes and I'm not here?'

'Is the key still on the string behind the door?'

'We took it off once the trouble began and blocked up the letter-box.'

'I don't think there'll be any more of that trouble,' and he thought, Not unless Angel intends returning here to live. 'Put the string and the key back. I'll tear the cardboard off the letter-box. And leave a note on the kitchen table telling her you're in Mrs Gorman's for the time being.'

When the key, the letter-box and the note had been seen to, he got Aggie's coat. 'Don't bother about the shoes, sure your slippers will do fine,' he said, watching Aggie dithering, knowing she was reluctant to leave. He'd have to be patient with her. She took ages collecting together a pathetic few possessions to take with her – a nightie, her rosary and a prayer-book, underclothes. Then, as they were about to leave, she remembered something else and went back to a drawer. Angel's likeness.

'She had it taken for that fella in India and a copy for me. I couldn't go without that.' She looked at the photograph, kissed it. 'God bless and protect you, my little child, wherever you are,' she said, then let Father Clancy lead her through the door.

The gossip was rife in the village. Congratulatory. 'We ran her out of it. We won.'

'We want no hoors here giving a bad example to our innocent children.'

'England, so I believe.'

'I heard it was down the country.'

'I don't care if it's to Timbuktu so long as she doesn't show her face here.'

'Wonder who the father is?'

'Draw your own conclusions. Everyone knows where the blonde hair was found.'

'That I'll never believe. That's a sin to even suggest such a thing. You need to go to confession so you do.'

A woman who'd just joined the gaggle of gossips added her twopenn'orth. 'She left at the crack of dawn in a cab. I'd swear there was a man with her but it was too dark to see who he or the jarvey was. If he was known to me, I'd have found out where he dropped her. And did you hear the latest? Aggie's sleeping in the Gormans' place. I wonder what's behind that?'

'Nothing to write home about. She's turning out the doctor's room. You know he's gone into the Incurables? And I overheard Mrs Gorman say it'll take Aggie a few days. So to save dragging her to and fro she's sleeping in.'

Only Aggie, the two priests, Mrs Gorman and Danny knew that Angel had left the Wexford train at Westland Row station. After the shop closed, Danny went there, found the guard who'd identified Angel and asked him to describe again what she looked like. 'The best-lookin' mot I ever laid eyes on. She was a beauty, all right. That's how I came to notice her.'

Danny tipped him a shilling and thanked him, then toured the city looking for Angel, stopping to ask paper-sellers, men lounging on corners outside public-houses. He went as far as the GPO, crossed the wide street and retraced his steps back towards the bridge and College Green, telling himself Angel would have avoided the north side for, like most from the south side, to cross the bridge was as far into it as they'd venture. He saw the swaggering Black and Tans and the auxiliaries, their supposed officers, whom everyone knew had no control over them – any more than anyone controlled the auxiliaries. He wondered and wondered where could Angel have gone. He longed to find and rescue her. If he ever did, he'd ask her to marry him. He'd sell up, move from the village and rear her child as if it was his own. Love it as if it was his own, because he loved its mother.

Chapter Sixteen

The day after arriving at Bridie's, Angel ventured out and walked along the North Strand. The weather was glorious. She should have worn a light frock, the suit was too warm. People looked at her but she knew it was because she was a stranger in a neighbourhood where most knew each other, where they weren't well-off and, on a day like today, the women went for their messages wearing shabby, dirty frocks under pinnies, clutching their purses in their hands, calling greetings to each other. If they assumed anything about her it was that she was killing time while she waited for a train. In a news-agent's she bought a pencil, notepaper and envelopes, and asked the way to the nearest post office.

In the post office she wrote a short letter to her mother: 'Dear Ma, Just a line to let you know I'm all right, staying with Bridie for the time being. Remember she brought me home after the accident. She'll get me work. I'll send you a few bob when I can. And we'll meet soon. Mind yourself. Love, Angel.'

To Father Clancy she wrote that she was sorry but couldn't face the convent and she thanked him for all he had done. She hoped he wouldn't mind if she sent letters for her mother to the presbytery but addressed to him, just in case they were stolen. There was no telling what the villagers might do to find out what was going on. She wouldn't trust any of those who had hounded her and her mother.

'There, now, didn't I tell you she was all right?' said Father Clancy, when he came to the Gormans' with the letters. Eagerly Aggie took and read the note. Then she looked crestfallen when she realised that Angel had given no address.

'Well, at least you know she's safe and well. I'd say she wrote in a hurry and forgot to put it on.'

'All the same, it's terrible not knowing where she is.'

'This time yesterday, Aggie, you were convinced she'd been murdered,' Mrs Gorman reminded her. 'Leaving out the address was an oversight. Father's right, she'll put it on the next letter.'

'I don't know,' said Aggie. 'There's something fishy about the whole business. I didn't warm to that Bridie, even though she did bring Angel home on the morning of the accident. Isn't it terrible for mothers, thinking they know all that goes on in their child's mind, then realising they don't? This couldn't have been a spur-of-the-moment thing. She must have had it planned all along. Sitting there making eejits out of me and you, Father. Listening to you talking about your cousin Teresa and how kind she'd be.'

'Don't jump to conclusions, Aggie. Don't forget the state she was in. I'd say she'd every intention of going to Wexford and took fright at the last minute. Anyway, let's give her the benefit of the doubt. It'll all be explained when you see her.'

'I suppose you're right,' Aggie admitted resignedly. 'I'll just have to be patient.'

'I fixed it up for next Wednesday night,' Bridie informed Angel.

'What'll she charge?'

'Five quid, but she's the best. Spotlessly clean, and I've never heard of anyone taken bad after.'

'Do some women?' asked Angel.

'If it's a botched job you could die.'

'I always knew it was a sin but never that it was dangerous. But, to tell you the truth, apart from it being a sin I knew nothing about it. Never gave it a thought in my life. How can it be dangerous?'

'Well, for one thing you're reefing a child out before its time. And for another, if the woman is dirty or not experienced you can get fever or she'll make a hole in your womb.'

'I wish you hadn't told me them things. Now I'm afraid of my life.'

'I had to tell you – to be sure you knew the risk you'd be running so that you could make up your own mind. But, as I said, you'll be as safe in her hands as you would in the Rotunda, not that I imagine the Rotunda gets rid of babies.'

'What's her name?'

'Smith she goes by, but that's not her real one. I don't know what is. Everything has to be kept secret. She could go to gaol for what she does.'

'Where will I have to go?'

'She has a room in Gardiner Street but I don't think it's where she lives. I've heard tell she just rents it for her business. Anyway, think about it. I asked for Wednesday night because Thursday is my day off and I'll be here to keep an eye on you.'

'Why will you have to keep an eye on me? I thought once the woman had done whatever it is she does, that was an end to it.'

'It's not that simple,' said Bridie. 'Sometimes you lose it in an hour or two. Sometimes it takes longer. I didn't want to give you too much time to think of the pros and cons, your nerves still being in a state. You mightn't feel all that great after it, but only for a little while.'

'I'm petrified with fear but I'll go through with it. Would you if you were me?'

'I would. I couldn't look on the face of a child I got that way. I think I'd remember whoever did it to me and know that if the child looked like him I'd kill it myself. Yeah, I'd definitely get rid of it.'

'That's the same as me. That's how I think.'

'It'll only take a day or two before you're on your feet. And there's two jobs going the following week, one in the hospital and another as a chambermaid in a hotel in Abbey Street. You'd live in in that one, but not as a wardsmaid. If you take the hotel job, you could doss here on your night off. One night a week on the sofa won't kill me. We could take turns. But if it's the hospital you go for, you'll have to find a room. This is too small for both of us. After a while we'd get on each other's nerves. So money-wise, the chambermaid's the best bet.'

'I think I'll be a chambermaid. I'd be frightened working in a hospital.'

Bridie and Angel walked to Gardiner Street, then climbed four flights of stairs to the top of the house. Mrs Smith, a stern-faced woman, no longer young, opened the door when they knocked. The room was very clean and smelt of Jeyes Fluid and furniture polish. There was a table, two kitchen chairs, single bed, a small table beside the bed and, on a shelf in an alcove, a spirit lamp, a teapot and a saucepan. Beneath the shelf was a built-in press. The grate was blackleaded and had a fan of crêpe paper in its well. There were no ornaments on the mantelpiece, or pictures on the walls, no religious statues. Angel had never seen a room so bare.

Mrs Smith told them to sit down, then questioned Angel. 'When did you last see colour?'

'I think it was March.'

'And you're sure you want to go through with this?'

'Definitely,' replied Angel, in a shaky voice, for now that the moment was near she was frightened.

'You're far on if your dates are right. Could be dangerous, but I'll know when I have a look at you. Take off your things.'

'Everything?'

'Your coat and hat, your petticoat, stays, knickers, shoes, and roll down your stockings.'

While Angel undressed the woman was spreading an oil sheet on the bed, a thick brown rubber one, and on top of it a sheet folded in two. 'I'd rather keep on my petticoat,' Angel said, amazed she had the courage to speak.

'Suit yourself,' Mrs Smith said, 'but if I decide to go ahead roll it well up. I don't want it getting in the way of what I'm doing. Come on, then, up you get.'

Angel lay on the bed as tense as a coiled spring. The woman's hands moved over her belly. Then she snapped, 'For Jesus' sake, let yourself go. It's like trying to feel through a sheet of tin.'

Angel looked uncomprehendingly at her.

'Take a few slow, deep breaths, go all floppy. That's better. That'll do.'

Her hands moved as the doctor's had, Angel recalled.

'You're not too far gone. I'll do it. You can sit up for a few minutes while I boil the water.'

Angel leaned against the bedhead. Bridie winked at her.

When the woman had the spirit lamp going and the saucepan on it, she returned to the bed. 'I'll have the money before I start,' she said, holding out her hand.

'Bridie, it's in my purse, will you give it to her?' said

Angel, and watched Mrs Smith put the five-pound note in the pocket of the white apron she was wearing, then bend and take something from the press beneath the shelf. Angel couldn't see what it was but heard the sound of metal on metal as something was dropped into the pot.

After a few minutes the woman told Angel to lie down, which she did, and watched Mrs Smith turn off the spirit lamp, remove the saucepan and come to the bedside table where she laid down the pot.

'You'll be all right, love. It'll only take a few minutes,' Bridie said, speaking for the first time since she'd introduced Angel to Mrs Smith. But her voice was quivering and frightened. For the first time, Angel wondered how exactly the woman was going to get rid of the baby. Was it a knife she'd dropped into the pot? Was she going to cut her open? Was that how it was done? Why didn't I ask Bridie? she wondered. Oh, God, I'm quaking.

'Pull your petticoat well up,' said the woman, 'then raise your knees and open your legs as wide as you can.' As she spoke, Mrs Smith was fishing in the saucepan with a pair of scissors. She caught and lifted from it what looked like the longest crochet hook Angel had ever seen. 'I told you to lift your knees and open your legs.'

Angel raised her knees. 'Come on, higher than that, I haven't got all night.' Then, losing patience, Mrs Smith laid the crochet hook on the bed, shoved up Angel's legs and pushed them apart.

Immediately Angel was back in the hotel room, in the position into which Johnny had forced her, and she screamed.

The woman clamped her hand across her mouth and hissed, 'Don't you make a sound.'

Bridie hurried to the bed and looked down into Angel's terror-filled eyes. She grabbed Mrs Smith by the shoulder. 'You bloody oul cow,' she said, turning the woman to face her. 'You've been talking to her as if she was a dog. I explained to you how she got in the way. You could have been kinder.'

'I'm not interested in how they got in the way. I'm here to get rid of what they got. You tell her that if she wants me, her and you arrested she can scream again.'

'I'm sorry. I couldn't help myself. It all came back to me. It was as if I was in the hotel room again. I'm sorry, ma'am. I won't make another sound,' Angel said.

Bridie squeezed her hand. 'You'll be all right, love, but she's right, you can't scream. Here, stick this hanky in your mouth, but no more screaming. We don't want to finish up in the Mountjoy. I'll stay beside her if you've no objection,' she added to Mrs Smith.

'Stay where you like as long as you don't get in my way,' the woman replied curtly.

Angel felt the instrument being inserted, the sensation of it moving inside her, not painful but peculiar as if something was scraping a tender part of her flesh. She heaved once or twice as if she wanted to be sick. Then she felt the instrument being withdrawn.

'Stay lying down for a few minutes. I'll make you a cup of tea,' the woman said, as she dropped the hooked instrument into the pot, then relit the spirit lamp and put a kettle on to boil.

Bridie sat beside Angel, wiped the sweat from her forehead and assured her it was all over, that soon they'd be on the way back to her place.

'You can dress yourself,' Mrs Smith said, while the tea was drawing. She gave Angel a thick pad of wadding. 'Wear it,' she said, 'though you probably won't need it for a good few hours, maybe not until during the night. It differs with everyone.' While the three of them drank the tea, Mrs Smith gave further advice. 'You'll have pains, worse than your monthlies, but that's nothing to worry about and you'll bleed, all normal. If the pain becomes unbearable or you haemorrhage, get yourself to the hospital as quick as you can, the same thing if in a week or so you get a fever. But on no account mention you came here. What I do helps many a one like you. There's a need for it. But that wouldn't stop me being arrested. Don't look so worried – no one I've ever handled had anything go wrong. If I was a bit brusque with you, I'm sorry, it's my manner.'

During the night Angel woke with pain worse than any she had experienced before. She called Bridie from her bed on the sofa. Bridie assured her it was normal. 'It's like being in labour but it won't last as long.' She rubbed Angel's back and spoke words of sympathy and consolation. By early morning the baby and the detritus were expelled, Angel had been made comfortable, given tea and encouraged by Bridie to sleep, which she did.

When she woke, feeling a bit dizzy but free of pain, Bridie made her porridge, toast and tea, and told her to stay in bed. By the afternoon she felt better except for her legs, which were groggy.

'There y'are now, it's all over, thanks be to God. This time next week you'll be working.'

'What would I have done without you?'

'Ah,' said Bridie dismissively, 'you'd have managed. There's many a one would have done the same for you.'

266

When Angel was well enough to go out, she sent Aggie another letter, just a few lines and a ten-shilling note, told her she was grand and would keep in touch.

The letter had been sent care of Father Clancy. He saw the disappointment on Aggie's face that Angel had still given no address, and tried to think of something appropriate to say when, with imploring eyes, she looked at him and asked beseechingly, 'Father, how am I ever going to find her? Why doesn't she want me to? I'm her mother. Never in our lives have we been separated.'

'Give her time, Aggie. She'll come round. God look down on her, she'll be confused and troubled, carrying a child, finding a place to live, a bit of work, wanting desperately to come back here but knowing that, for both your sakes, she can't.' He felt hypocritical, aware that Angel's failure to return was a relief to him. He had a duty to all of his flock, he couldn't single out one for special treatment.

Aggie had left Mrs Gorman's house and was back in the cottage. At night she lay awake for hours, wondering where Angel was, what arrangements she was making for when the baby was born, wondering how the villagers would react if after the birth she brought the baby home. There'd be more trouble, but maybe the heat would have gone out of it. But supposing it didn't? Night after night she told herself they'd have to go to England, her, Angel and the child. Towards that end she was saving every penny.

Remembering that Angel had missed her first period in March she calculated roughly when the birth would be. Sometime in December, she thought, or January maybe. Bad, damp, foggy weather. She hoped the child would be healthy, for it was a bad time of the year to give birth, and, with the winter stretching in front, bad for its rearing.

She'd fall asleep when it was nearly morning and wake tired and bleary-eyed, and as it had been before she slept, so it was during the day: Angel always on her mind. Who was the father of the child? Why hadn't Angel told her? Surely it couldn't have been someone she didn't know, someone she had met casually at a dance or hooley. These things happened, she knew. But not to her daughter, not to a girl as good-living and pure as Angel. And where did Bridie fit into the picture? What had become of Angel's suit and the beads? Was there any truth in the story about the hat in the hotel? One day, she told herself, when she wasn't so tired, so lifeless, she'd search the north side for a hotel with a battered straw hat on its top shelf.

Chapter Seventeen

After her abortion Angel made a complete recovery. She caused a great stir in the hotel where she went to work as a chambermaid. At first among the women staff there was jealousy, because of her beauty and what appeared to be standoffish ways. The men, old and young, customers and staff, lusted after her. But in a short while the women discovered that in fact Angel was shy, and the men that, though she was friendly, she was not free-making. In no time she was as popular with them as with the women.

She was generous and obliging, would lend sixpences and shillings, listen attentively to stories of sick wives, husbands and children, laugh at jokes that weren't too smutty, and she worked hard without complaining. But they never learned anything about her, where she came from, if she had a family, not a thing. Many of the staff knew Bridie and that Angel slept at her place on her one night off. Whenever Bridie dropped into the hotel they quizzed her. 'Ah, for Jaysus' sake, Bridie, you didn't pick her out of the air. You must know where she comes from,' one or other of the men or women in the staffroom would say. 'We're just curious, that's all.'

'I know that, and I'd tell you if I could but, honest to God, I don't know. I met her at a dance, we got talking. She said she wanted to leave home, live in the city. I took a liking to her, that's all there is to it.'

Angel made beds, changed the sheets, emptied chamber-pots, rinsed and wiped them dry and replaced them under the beds, swept the floors, rubbed a duster over the sparse furniture and occasionally across the bottom window-panes. Like all windows in hotels that had once been private Georgian houses, they stretched almost to the ceiling and were impossible to reach without a long ladder. And in any case, as the manager had said when she started and he was explaining her duties, 'The fellas that stay here are mostly commercial travellers. They wouldn't give the windows a second glance. The oul fellas are exhausted after walking the streets dragging their attaché cases after them. A pint or two and they collapse into bed. Another thing, go easy on the sheets and towels. If the top one isn't stained or too creased then it's top to bottom. Same with the towels – if they look clean, leave them. You could spend a fortune on laundry otherwise.'

She considered herself lucky not having to share a room, even though the one she had was very small. Once she'd finished her work and had her bread, butter, cocoa and a bit of cheese for supper, she'd go to bed. Sometimes the travellers checking out in the mornings would leave the previous day's paper. These she'd collect to read by candlelight in her room.

As the days and weeks passed she'd go for long periods without ever reliving the dreadful night in the hotel. Then sometimes she would waken, soaked in sweat, feeling the hand landing punches on her body, the fingers wound in her hair, the tremendous weight pressing her into the bed, the pain. She could smell blood, drink, and she would scream as she had in Mrs Smith's room. She was at the top of the house, no one else slept up there, so no one ever heard her distress, for which she was grateful. She'd relate the nightmares to Bridie, who'd console her by pointing out that the gaps between them were getting longer and longer, and one day they would stop altogether.

If her day off coincided with Bridie's, they'd take a chance on the fighting in the streets. At the sound of the first shot, they'd run into a doorway or shop until the firing stopped. If the battle was likely to be prolonged, streets would be cordoned off and she and Bridie would go by way of alleys and lanes to reach the shops they wanted to look at.

Angel paid Bridie a small amount for the night she spent in her house and the food she ate. Bridie had only agreed to accept the money after Angel said that if she didn't she'd spend her time off somewhere else. They took it in turns to buy the coffee and cakes to which they treated themselves in Bewley's.

From time to time Bridie asked when, if ever, she intended letting her mother know where she was. 'She must be nearly out of her mind with worry,' Bridie said.

'I know, Bridie, but how can I? She'll see that I'm not pregnant. What will I tell her when she asks?'

'That you had a miss.'

'I'd break down, I know I would. I'd tell her everything, maybe even the truth about how I got the baby in the first place. That'd kill her altogether. Between that and knowing that I was in a state of mortal sin, she'd drop stone dead.' Always Angel gave the same replies to Bridie.

And Bridie would say, 'Well, you know best.'

Danny enquired regularly of Father Clancy if he'd heard anything of Angel. The priest hadn't, and they would wonder what had become of her. How was she managing for money? He longed to have an address, or be able to arrange for her to pick up money that he'd send *poste restante*. Often he couldn't sleep at night from worrying if for lack of money she was hungry or had nowhere to sleep.

Apart from the five pounds to pay for the abortion, Angel had not broken into Danny's money. In fact, she had added to it from her earnings. She had a plan going in her mind: so long as she was able to keep her job and not go mad buying new clothes, she hoped that in another six months she'd have enough saved to take herself and her mother to live in England.

She'd go there first, find work and a room, then let her mother know where she was and ask her to come and live with her. Bridie was delighted when she heard Angel's intentions. 'I only met her once but I warmed to her. You won't live to regret it. And from next week you pay me nothing. Put that towards your fares.' Angel protested, but Bridie was firm. 'Take the offer or you're out of here. I'm serious.'

'Why don't you come with us?'

'Amn't I doing a serious line? Remember I told you the first time we met? I'm very fond of him and I know he feels the same about me. It'd have a terrible effect on him if I walked out on him.'

'How's his wife keeping?'

'The same as usual, God help her.'

'If she died, would he marry you?'

'He's never mentioned it. In any case she could live for years.'

Only for her belief in God, Aggie often told herself as the months passed and no word came from Angel, did she desist from doing herself in. But God wouldn't forgive her for taking her own life. It was a mortal sin for which she'd go to hell. And, although she might never again see the face of her beautiful Angel on earth, one day they'd meet again in heaven.

As winter set in she'd wonder if Angel was warm enough, wherever she was, if she had enough to eat, were the soles of her shoes broken and letting in the wet. Her poor child who wouldn't have the sense to make cardboard insoles. And if she was badly off now, how much worse she'd be when the child arrived.

Once she'd walked to Kevin Street police station, a long distance from the village, and told a policeman her troubles. He listened to her patiently and was sympathetic, but told her there was nothing the police could do. 'As you say, ma'am, she's going on twenty-one. She'd be twenty-one by the time we'd get going, and free to go where she liked. All you can do is pray and walk round the city. You might be lucky and bump into her one day.'

In November, in newspapers left behind by the commercial travellers, Angel read of Kevin Barry's execution for shooting a British soldier outside a bakery where he'd come to collect bread. Kevin Barry was eighteen, a medical student. He had a nice face and Angel felt very sorry for him and learned the words of the song everyone was singing, supposed to be his own words spoken in the dock.

> Shoot me like a soldier,
> Do not hang me like a dog,
> For I died to free old Ireland,
> For a good and faithful cause.

On the morning of his execution, everyone in the hotel stopped work for a few minutes before and after the hanging to say a prayer for him.

In another newspaper Angel read and saw a picture of Terence McSwiney, another Republican, Lord Mayor of Cork, who had died on hunger strike. Now that her health was fully recovered she couldn't imagine how anyone could refuse food for so long. She was sorry that he and Kevin Barry had died. She admitted that the Tans were murderers but she wasn't really interested in politics.

Each week she banked her small savings, and looked forward to the day when she'd have enough money to take herself and Aggie to England. She went without coffee and cakes so she could save and still send her mother money. Sometimes, when her stockings had gone beyond mending, she missed a week but she always sent a short letter.

Aggie took the policeman's advice and when she felt well she searched the streets of Dublin for Angel. It was November and soon her grandchild would be born. Then what would become of Angel and the baby? But she had a plan. Danny was the only one in the village who could lend her money. Once she found Angel she'd borrow enough from him to set herself up in a room. So long as you didn't mind the locality, rooms were ten a penny. She'd pick up a bed for next to nothing – not a mattress, they could be stinking flea- and bug-ridden. No, she'd buy a tick and clean straw – there were shops that sold straw all over the city. When it got soiled she could throw it out and replace it.

It was usually in the afternoon when she set out on her search, after she had finished her cleaning work, and also on Sundays. To start with she concentrated looking on the south side, in Grafton Street, Westmoreland Street, Nassau Street and Stephen's Green. As she became more used to the city she ventured into side-streets, into Clarendon Street where she found a lovely chapel in which to kneel and pray and light candles. There was a beautiful statue of our Lady of Dublin in another chapel in Whitefriars Street. A woman she got into talk with as they both shared the same holy water font told her, 'D'ye know, she was lost for hundreds of years, I think from the time of that oul bastard Cromwell, may he roast in hell. And then didn't she turn up in a shop on the quays and we got her back. She looks after women who are expecting. I always prayed to her when I was carrying and every one of my children was born alive and kicking.'

They finished blessing themselves with the holy water and walked together out of the church. 'You're not from round here?'

'No,' replied Aggie, and told the woman where she came from. 'You could say I'm on a fool's errand, looking for a hotel in a street and I don't know where it is or what it's called. I think it's over on the north side.'

'There I couldn't help you,' said the woman. 'I've never been further than Henry Street and that only round about Christmas. The dealers do have great bargains.'

'The same as myself,' Aggie told the woman, and they said goodbye.

Then she went back into the chapel and knelt before Our Lady of Dublin, praying for Angel to have a safe confinement.

The lie she had told the woman about searching for a hotel brought back into her mind the story of the hat that might, from its description, have belonged to Angel. She made up her mind that the following Sunday she'd go to the north side, find the hotel and, if the story was true, satisfy herself about the hat.

In the meantime she pursued her search on the south side. One day she climbed the steps to the Coombe lying-in hospital. There was a porter in a little cubicle who, on seeing Aggie, came out and informed her it wasn't visiting time.

A little monkey man, thought Aggie, full of his own

importance. 'I'm not visiting. I'm enquiring after a patient, a close relation.'

'You still wouldn't be able to see her, not at this time of the day.'

She was tired, her bunion was crucifying her, she felt like giving him a dig in the jaw. But she controlled the impulse: she was interested in getting information not putting him on his arse.

'I know, I know. What I want to find out is if you've a girl by the name of Angel, a Mrs Lucas, as a patient.'

Grudgingly he went back into his cubicle and looked through a ledger, came out and almost as if glad said, 'No one of that name.'

'What about last week, or the week before?'

'We only give information for the current week.'

She left without thanking him. Walking back towards Patrick Street she was thinking, Sure God only knows what name she's using, she could be calling herself anything.

In Patrick Street there was a little park by the cathedral, with benches in it. She went in to rest for a while. Flocks of pigeons pecked round her feet, searching among the plethora of cigarette butts for something to eat. A man joined her on the bench, ragged, dirty, unshaven, and lit a Woodbine, inhaled deeply, had a fit of coughing, then said, 'Not a bad oul day if the rain keeps off.'

'I hope to God it does, I've to go to the north side.'

'Not today, ma'am, you won't. Everywhere in town's cordoned off. Have you not heard what's happened? Slaughter all over the place. British officers shot in their beds beside their wives. Spies, so I've heard tell. Then after dinner at the match in Croke Park the Tans arrived and opened fire on the crowd, killing dozens.'

Aggie made the sign of the Cross. 'Lord have mercy on them all.'

'It's terrible times we're livin' in. But all the same you have to hand it to the Big Fella. If anyone'll ever run the British out it'll be Mick Collins. Have you relations over the north side?'

'Not a soul. It's a hotel and a street I'm looking for. And I know nothing about them. All the same, I have to find them.'

'Not today you won't. Next week chance your arm again. But if you don't know the names you can't even ask the way. Have you nerra a clue?'

'Nerra a one.'

'Then how d'ye know in the first place they exist?'

'A woman I do a day's work for told me a story about the hotel. Her brother or a relation stayed in it. A terrible story, if you could believe him.'

'What was the story?'

She stood up. 'I couldn't repeat it, it was too terrible, but for all that I'm curious about it.' She opened her purse and took out a couple of coppers which she gave to the man.

'May God bless you,' he said. Before she left he added to his thanks, 'If I was you I'd ask the woman to find out the name.'

'D'ye know,' replied Aggie, 'I must be losing my mind that I didn't think of that. Thanks very much, and mind yourself.'

She cleaned for the arthritic woman on Mondays and mid-morning, when they were having a cup of tea, the woman asked if there was any news of Angel. Aggie told her there wasn't, but that she was still searching the city. Then she brought the talk round to the relation who'd told the story about the hat.

'Didn't I see him yesterday? He was up for the match in Croke Park. I made him a bit of dinner and then his stomach got bad and he didn't go. Someone must have been praying for him. If he'd gone he could have been shot like some of the other unfortunates, Lord have mercy on them. We settled down for a great oul chat about all the good times when we were young. He related again the story about that hotel and the hat on the shelf. If I could walk any distance I'd ramble over there and have a dekko at it.'

'I didn't think you knew where it was,' said Aggie, silently praying that now she did.

'No more I did until yesterday. I suppose it was the relief of having escaped the shooting made himself more talkative than usual. It's a hotel called the Grand, though from his description there's nothing grand about it and it's in North Great George's Street.'

Right there and then Aggie wanted to rush out and make her way to the north side, for the more she thought about the hotel and the hat, the more she was convinced they would throw light on where Angel was and whether Bridie was alive or dead. She felt sure that Bridie was mixed up in Angel's disappearance.

She finished the cup of tea and the rest of the housework while planning that she'd visit the hotel on Wednesday. The crippled woman said she'd pray that before she came next week there'd be news.

On the following Wednesday Aggie found North Great George's Street and the hotel. Outside it she lost her nerve. It was such a big place. She thought it grand with its brightly polished bell and knocker. She had never set foot in a place so big. But big and swanky though it seemed, she had to find an excuse for going in. She'd let on she'd taken a weakness and ask for a drink of water.

Holding the railings she climbed the outside steps and pushed open the doors, paused, confused-looking, and made her way to the bar. There was no one about but before she reached the counter a man appeared. 'Are you looking for someone, ma'am?'

'Could I sit down for a minute? I'm after taken a terrible weakness. I thought I'd collapse.'

'Of course you can. Bend your head down to your knees and I'll get you a drink of water.'

While he was filling the tumbler she looked up at the shelves. The colour drained from her face. For the hat, despite its smashed crown, was unmistakably Angel's. Any doubt would have been dismissed by the now bedraggled, dusty amethyst scarf trailing from its brim.

'You look terrible,' said the barman, holding the glass to her lips. 'Have you had anything to eat?'

Aggie shook her head. 'Not since morning. I had a cup of tea then.'

'Listen,' said the man, 'and I'll tell you what I'll do. I can't serve women in here, but we've a snug. It's round the corner. I'll take you there. Grand and comfortable. I'll make you a few sandwiches, and a glass of whiskey'll put you right. The snug's warm and there's always a few of the local women in there.'

He helped her stand, for her legs were shaking, threatening to give way. She kept her eyes averted from the hat crowning the large bottle. The barman took her arm and, as if she was an old woman, helped her down the steps and walked her round the corner to the snug. It was a small room, half-length curtains at the windows ensuring privacy from outsiders.

It smelt of stout and snuff, was warm and welcoming. Ushering her in, he said, to the half-dozen women seated on the red plush benches, 'Here y'are, girls, I've brought you a newcomer.' The women looked at Aggie and nodded. 'She had a bad turn outside the hotel. Sit down there near the fire, you're perishing with the cold.' A woman shifted her chair to make room. 'I'll get the whiskey and the sandwiches. You'll be grand in no time.'

The women regarded her with curious, hostile glances. Aggie didn't know where to look and didn't have the nerve to speak. After a few minutes they began talking as she guessed they would have been doing before she came in. Glancing furtively at them she saw that half were about her age and the others elderly. They laughed a lot, drank from their glasses of stout and some took snuff, reaching into small Colman's mustard tins for a pinch, which they put into their nostrils, sniffed deeply, then sneezed loudly.

The woman who sat by the fire offered her the tin. 'Have a pinch, daughter, it'll clear your head.'

She didn't want to offend by refusing and took a pinch but couldn't get the knack of putting it up her nostrils. It fell on to her lips. All of the women laughed, and the barman brought in a tray with a glass of whiskey, a pot of tea and a plate of sandwiches. The women ribbed him. 'Jaysus, Billy, she must have taken a very bad turn or else there's something between you. You wouldn't give your piss to the dogs.'

Despite her nervousness in the midst of strangers and the picture of Angel's hat in her mind, Aggie couldn't help laughing at the banter. The ice was broken and the women began to talk to her. 'I've never seen you round the neighbourhood before,' one said.

'I'm from the south side,' and Aggie told them the name of her village.

'Up the mountains,' another said.

'Not far from them,' Aggie replied.

'Did you faint or what?'

'Not right out, just come all over queer. I haven't been well lately. Internal trouble.' They nodded wisely and sympathetically.

'I'd come over to the Rotunda, I'd heard tell there's a great man there, a Dr Fischer, and that he sits in the out-patients today.'

'So did you see him?'

'I lost my nerve as soon as I set foot inside the door. It was the smell, disinfectant, it turned my stomach, and the place was packed so I ran out of it.'

One of the younger women said, 'Dr Fischer delivered every one of my childer. He's the master. Grand man, it's the effin' students I can't stand. A crowd of thicks pullin' and haulin' you about.'

'They have to learn on someone, Mag,' another woman said.

'I'm not sayin' they don't, only I wish to Christ it wasn't on me,' Mag retorted. Then she turned to Aggie and asked, 'How did you finish up in here from the Rotunda? You must have got lost.'

'I did,' lied Aggie, 'though I've always been meaning to drop into the Grand. There's a woman I do a bit of work for and she told me this story about a hat. I've been dying to see it. She said it was to do with a murder.'

'She's right enough about the hat. But it was no murder although your man who owns the place spins a

281

yarn that one was committed in the room where the hat was found.'

'And there wasn't?' Aggie asked.

'Not at all. But whoever the unfortunate girl was, she was lucky to get away with her life. My niece was working there at the time and she said you never saw anything like it, the blood everywhere. Bucketfuls. The bastard raped her. I know what I'd have done with him if I'd ever got my hands on him. It's his mickey and his balls that'd be on the top shelf, I'm tellin' you.'

Aggie's heart was banging against her chest, she could hear it in her head. If it didn't slow its beating she felt sure she would die. But there was a question she had to ask. 'Did they ever find out who did it?'

'Course they did. That boxer, the Bruiser Brennan. That was the room he stayed in. Not that anyone would have done anything anyway. He must have gone in the middle of the night. No one ever laid eyes on him since.'

Then Aggie fainted.

'This woman's not well,' Mag said, as she loosened Aggie's clothes and brought her round. 'Get her another cup of hot, sweet tea. You're all right, love. You fainted, but sure you're grand now. We'll get a cab to take you home.'

'But it's an awful long way. It'll cost a fortune,' Aggie protested.

'Don't you worry about the money. Drink the tea and eat a bit of the sandwich. You must be wall falling with the hunger.'

When the women considered her well enough they got a cab, said they'd say a prayer for her health and told her to mind herself.

At home she sat in the dark. The fire was out, even the

light was gone from the Sacred Heart lamp, and her mind was filled with the vision of Angel, battered and bleeding. Her Angel, her beautiful baby. And to think she had received that brute in her home, had thought what a lovely man he had grown into. And then he'd destroyed her daughter. Tears ran down her face. 'My little love,' she said aloud to the empty room, 'was it any wonder you didn't want to talk about the baby or name its father? You poor, unfortunate child. Oh, God, where are you tonight? I have to find you. I'll borrow the money from Danny. I'll take you away to England. We'll make a fresh start. And we'll never tell anyone, not even Father Clancy. Not a soul. And me thinking badly of Bridie and she shielding you, telling the lies about the runaway horse. God bless her, wherever she is. I wish I could thank her. I was a terrible mother, filling your head with rubbish. Telling you about the "wiles and ways". But I'll make it up to you. And I hope that bastard gets his just deserts and I hope his child was born dead. I could never look on its face without remembering how you got it.'

She cried and talked to herself all night. The next day and the next she didn't go out. On the third, a neighbour noticed that the cottage was unusually silent, that she hadn't seen Aggie go to the privy, and thought she must be sick. She looked through the window and saw the slumped figure in the chair. Knowing that the door would be either unlocked or the key hanging on a piece of twine from a nail above the letter-box, she tried the door. Dreading what she might find, she turned the handle. It was unlocked and she went in. Aggie's eyes were open, she was breathing but her hands were icy cold. The neighbour dragged the quilt from the bed,

covered her and told her she'd be back in a minute. In no
time she had made a cup of tea, round which she
wrapped Aggie's trembling hands. Then she got a good
fire going before questioning Aggie. She got no
response. She debated whether to call the doctor or the
priest then decided on the priest, whom she'd get Danny
to telephone. The presbytery was too far and she didn't
want to leave Aggie on her own for long.

Father Clancy came and asked questions. Aggie's only
response was a sobbing that shook her body, but she
never uttered a word. He sent for the doctor, who
diagnosed Aggie as being in a state of shock. 'Unless I
send her to hospital she'll need minding for a few days.'

'We'll mind her. She's my own flesh and blood. The
hospital might be too much of a shock for her. I'll send
my housekeeper down to stay with her and I know Mrs
Gorman will lend a hand.'

'I would as well, Father,' the neighbour said, 'only we
were never that close, but I'll cook a bite for her.'

And so the looking after Aggie was organised.

Angel still sent letters to her mother, slightly longer
nowadays as she outlined her plans for them to move to
England. She could only manage to send five shillings
now because, she explained, she was saving for the fares
to England.

Being young and healthy, her body had recovered
from the ordeals of rape and abortion. Her hair had
recovered its golden gloss, her eyes their sparkle, her step
its spring, and whether she was in the hotel or walking
through the streets admiring glances followed her.

But at night when she slept the nightmares came to
terrorise her, and she'd waken sweating and struggling to

escape the terrible weight pinning her to the bed. Day and night, she carried with her a fear and revulsion towards all men.

Father Clancy passed on her letters to Danny. Now that Aggie was no longer capable of reading them, Danny visited her regularly, read them to her, put the postal orders in his safe for the day Angel would include an address, and supplied free of charge what little food Aggie ate. The women washed and dressed her, changed her underwear, sang familiar songs as they moved about the cottage always hoping to strike a chord in her mind, which daily receded far from reality.

'She's living in a world of her own. Never utters a word except to call out again and again, "Angel, my poor little child",' Mrs Gorman said one day.

The priest's housekeeper replied, 'And 'tis my belief that if Angel walked through the door, poor Aggie wouldn't know who she was.'

They prayed for her return to normality, but felt that unless a miracle occurred there was little hope of it. And they had their own duties to attend to. They weren't young women; the caring for Aggie was wearing them out.

Reading Angel's letters kept Danny informed of her determination to settle in England. Once again he considered proposing – if ever he could find her. But he consoled himself that when the time came for her to leave Ireland she would have to show herself if only to collect her mother. And as usual from her letters he would have knowledge of where and when. She might accept him, if only for the sake of the child and the expense of supporting her mother. He would sell the business and set up again in England. He'd make it clear that he didn't expect anything in return. He only wanted to mind her.

No one in the village, no one in the world except Johnny Quinn and Bridie knew what had happened to Angel on the night he had thrown the fight. And his memories were confused and vague. No one knew who was the father of the child she had conceived that night, except Bridie. That was until Mona came on a visit from Athlone. The story of the hat had got out, told innocently as a bit of gossip to a neighbour, and retold by her after her relative's lucky escape from the Tans in Croke Park. Now she was able to name the hotel and the street it was in. A few people out rambling on a Sunday after dinner went to see the hat, the men going into the bar, the women looking in through the door.

Mona went with her sister and their husbands. She immediately recognised it as Angel's and, putting two and two together, recalled that the date when the hat and the bloodsoaked bed were discovered was the night Johnny Quinn had lost the big fight. She realised that Angel must have made contact with him. She knew her friend hadn't been murdered as her sister had lost no time letting Mona know that Angel was pregnant, and that bad-minded people were saying the child could be Father Brennan's, 'Not,' she added, 'that I'd ever think such a thing myself, and may God forgive anyone who would. But all the same it's queer that she never mentioned who owned the child.'

Mona now deduced that Johnny, along with raping Angel, was responsible for her pregnancy. She lost no time in spreading the word. Not many were interested:

Angel was gone and good riddance, they said, to bad rubbish. Nevertheless the names of the two suspected men were in their minds, sometimes recalled, and sometimes repeated.

'The poor, unfortunate child,' Father Clancy said, when the news reached him. 'Was it any wonder she wouldn't talk about it? Was it any wonder she chose to disappear? The only consolation is that Aggie never came to hear about it.'

When Danny heard what had happened to Angel he cried openly and again on the night he and the priest talked about it. 'Father,' he said, 'I loved her. I adored her from the time she was a little child, and still do. There's never a night or day passes that I don't think of her, wonder where she and the child are and how they're faring.'

'I've known it all along, Danny, and what a wonderful husband you'd have made. It ruined your life, your love for Angel. Not that it was her doing. But if you hadn't been obsessed with her, you'd have looked somewhere else. You'd have found another good woman for a wife. You'd have had a fine family by now, sons to take over your business. And, you know, it's not too late. You're still in your prime. And you have to face facts. There's little likelihood of you ever finding Angel. I can't see her showing her face in the village again, and who could blame her?'

'I agree with you. But don't you see? If she's planning to take Aggie to England, I'll know when and where. You and I handle her letters. And if that doesn't come off, I'll stay a bachelor till the end of my days.'

'For your sake I'd love to see your wish granted. But Aggie is deteriorating. I had a word with the doctor the other day. He can't foresee any improvement. A few of my relations, far out, went the same way, finished up in the asylum, and I think the same will happen to Aggie.'

'But how will Angel know? Don't you see that all hope isn't lost? If Angel doesn't know, the letters will keep coming, and one of these days, in one will be her plans for England.'

'Ah, Danny, that's a bit dishonest. Like tricking Angel. I think we owe it to her to let her know what's in front of Aggie.'

'But how, Father?'

'I've been giving it a lot of thought. Dublin's a small city. Couldn't we put an advertisement in a newspaper? In several? The morning and evening ones. Someone's bound to see it. She must know people. Even if Angel never read it, one of them might and tell her. That might rob you of the chance to meet her again, but at least you wouldn't have got it through reading letters never meant for your eyes.'

'You're right. Angel should know about poor Aggie. I'll go along with you on the advertisement. In fact, I'll foot the bill.'

'You're a good man and who's to say things couldn't work out in your favour?'

Chapter Eighteen

In the Punjab Tommy lay on his bunk. Despite the efforts of the punkah-wallah, the room was stifling and the men were sweltering. It had been one of the hottest days they could remember, but worse than the heat was the scene many of them had witnessed at eight o'clock that morning when one of their Regiment, an Irishman, Jim Daly, had been executed by firing squad for his part in what was named a mutiny, and what the majority of the men considered a legitimate protest against the atrocities of the Black and Tans in Ireland.

It had been a peaceful protest: no one was injured, not a shot fired. News had come from Ireland in letters written by parents, wives, brothers and sisters relating the happenings at homes. The torturing, raping, murdering of men and women. The ransacking and burning of homes. How the British soldiers were horrified by the Tans' behaviour. How leading English newspapers had condemned the turning loose of a brutal force in Ireland with virtually no one to control them. The men who received letters read them aloud to their comrades in the Connaught Rangers, many of whom had served in France during the war. Now in India, when the occasion arose, they defended the interests of the Empire. They were brave, loyal men, and all they desired was that as the Regiment was made up of Irishmen, they should let their voices be heard, that their commanding officer should contact the British government on their behalf and ask for pressure to be applied that would take the Black and Tans out of Ireland. Until this was done they refused to soldier. There were about thirty protestors. Jim Daly, their appointed leader, was charged, court-martialled and sentenced to death. Tommy Maguire was one of the attending party at the execution.

Now, on the November evening, he lay on his bed tormented by prickly heat, insects and the picture of Jim blindfolded, a white disc stitched on his tunic above his heart where the marksmen would aim. He heard voices saying the rosary as the sun shone from the brazen sky. His pith helmet seemed to shrink, pressing into his skull, and he could barely believe that Jim was going to be shot, would fall back into the armchair placed conveniently behind him.

India had aged Tommy prematurely. The sun had bronzed his skin, wrinkled it, given it a leathery appearance, and although he was surrounded by men, he was desperately lonely.

Since his mother had died and Angel no longer wrote, he dreaded wakening each morning. In rational moments he told himself that Angel would have long since married, but otherwise he hoped for a miracle. So he still played brag, saved his winnings, seldom visited the 'wet canteen' to slake his thirst and never went after a 'bint'.

His mates said the heat had got to him, that he was doolally-tap. He never took offence at their ribbing him and sometimes he thought they were right. That he should put thoughts of Angel from his mind, go to the wet canteen, go into the bazaar and find a woman, dig into the money Angel had returned to him, make the best of India. And he'd imagine what it would be like to return after a night's carousing and see pink elephants. Then he'd see Angel's glorious face, her shining hair, her violet eyes, and ask God, 'Please don't let her be married. Let her be there for me. I'll mind her. My time will be served. I'll get a job. Her mother can come and live with us. Please, God, if it be welcome to Thy holy will, let it be so.'

Danny put the advertisement in two of the evening papers, the *Herald* and the *Mail*, and a morning one, the *Independent*. 'I didn't think she or her friends would be likely to buy the *Irish Times*,' he said to Father Clancy.

'I wouldn't have thought so either. It must have cost you a pretty penny.'

'Sure won't it be worth it if we get a response?'

'Indeed it will. How did you word it?'

'Will Angel Lucas, if she reads this, contact the following box number.'

'And how long are you running them for?'

'A month. That'll take us over the Christmas.'

'I'll say a Mass for our intention.'

'What'll happen to Aggie over the holiday?'

'She'll come to the presbytery for her dinner.'

'I suppose if Angel doesn't come forward we'll have to act after Christmas?'

'We will. Those two poor women are worn out looking after her. I know they're earning their beds in heaven but, all the same, an undisturbed night's rest on earth is a grand thing.'

Angel was wearying of making beds and washing chamberpots and having only one day off a week. This seldom coincided with Bridie's so they saw little of each other. Often Angel was aware of how little she knew about Bridie, only that she had a lover, that his wife was an incurable invalid in a home, that Bridie was fond of the man. But she knew nothing about her parents, not even where they lived, what sort of a childhood she had had. It wasn't, she knew, that Bridie was secretive, just that they spent so little time together.

She found herself longing for the intimacy of her village, to walk along a street where you knew everyone, not necessarily liking them but able to put a name to a face, going to Mass, working in the presbytery, answering the door and finding someone there who smiled or was crying, always someone you could exchange a word with. She missed going home to her mother at the end of the day, and working in Danny's, the smell of familiar food cooking, the cosiness of an evening spent before the fire, her mother repeating the gossip she'd heard during the day. When this humour was on her she'd wonder what her mother made of her disappearance. Did she cry about her? Think about the baby? It would have been born about now. Or maybe as late as at Christmas. Everyone said it was lucky to have a baby at Christmas. Her baby hadn't been lucky. Only just beginning to move inside her when its life was snuffed out. And she had deliberately committed a mortal sin in getting rid of it. It wasn't easy to commit a mortal sin. You had to be in no doubt about the action you were taking, understand fully what you were doing and know that it was a grievous sin. But even so I'd do it again, she thought. I couldn't ever have loved a child who'd been fathered by such a man and in such a manner.

In her depression and loneliness she toyed with the idea of going home, imagined the joy that would light up her mother's face, how Danny would greet her, and those of the neighbours who had been kind, Father Clancy and Father Brennan. Then she'd remember her last weeks in the village: the anonymous hate-filled letters, the women who had followed her and her mother along the towpath, the curses they'd shouted and the paraffin rag pushed through the letter-box. She could never endure that again, so she could not go home.

One day shortly before Christmas, when she and

Bridie were off duty, a bad day with freezing rain lashing down, she confided her thoughts to her friend. 'I'm fed up making beds and emptying pos.'

'I don't blame you. At least I've someone to gasbag with. The women are a howl, even them that are in for serious operations. I didn't tell you about the woman who had her breast off and what she said when she came round.'

'No, you never.'

'The night before, her husband came to see her, but she was still sleepy after the operation. And didn't he leave this paper on her locker. It was the first thing that caught her eye in the morning. "*Tit-Bits*," she roared, "the bloody oul get, he did that on purpose. His idea of a joke. But wait'll I'm on my feet. I'll give him *Tit-Bits*. If I could get my hands on them I'd make them into a coddle. My tit-bits, and watch him smack his lips over them. Then I'd tell him what was in the coddle." By this time everyone in the ward was in stitches, even the nurses when they heard the story.'

'You're lucky. I seldom lay eyes on them whose rooms I clean. Usually they only stay the one night and leave nothing behind except their smell. I hate it.'

'Maybe you should look for another job.'

'But where?'

'A shop – a draper's, a cake shop, any sort of a shop.'

'I think I'd like that, but then I'd have to find a room and feed myself, and I'm still trying to get a bit put by to take my ma and me to England.'

'You'll have to let her know where you are as soon as you've got the money together. Like, you can't just arrive at the cottage one night and say, "Ma, put on your coat we're going on the night boat to England."'

Angel sighed deeply. 'Honest to God,' she said, 'I think I'm going mad. One minute I'm scrimping and saving and the next I'm tempted to go into town, take out the money and buy a new rig-out. And I find myself dying to go to a dance or an all-night hooley.'

'That's a sure sign you're getting over it. I went through it all myself, don't forget. I know what I'm talking about.'

'But I never thought I would,' said Angel.

'Listen, love, you never forget it, but you do get over it. In time you get over everything. Otherwise you might as well lie down and die.'

'I suppose you're right. Listen, I'm starving. I'll slip out to the pork shop and get the makings of a fry. You lay the table and have the kettle boiling.'

Angel brought back a pork steak, sausages, onions and a flaky-pastry apple tart. While she fried the meat, the apple tart was put to warm in the oven at the side of the fire. They gorged themselves on the succulent pork steak, then finished with the tart and strong sweet tea.

'We'll leave the delft till later,' Bridie said, getting up from the table, building up the fire, then sitting down again. 'Were you serious about going to a dance?' she asked Angel, when she was seated facing her.

'I was and I wasn't. It's just that I'd love an excuse to get dolled up again. I haven't since you-know-when.'

'Well, I'll tell you what. Leave it for another little while and I'll come with you. I can't, for the time being. My fella's not in the best of health.' And, to Angel's amazement, Bridie began to cry.

'But you never said a word.'

'No point in upsetting you. In any case it may be nothing.'

'All the same, you should have told me. What way is he complaining?'

'He's lost his appetite and gone to look like a skeleton. And his nerves are bad. He wants me to move in with him. I sleep over there every night except when you're off.'

'Ah, Bridie, I wouldn't mind sleeping here on my own.'

'I know you wouldn't. It's not only you I'm considering. If I left the room altogether you couldn't afford to take it on while you're trying to save. Think of the waste of money just to sleep here for the one night. And, d'ye see, I don't really know where I stand with him. I think he owns his house. If he dies, God forbidding all harm, I suppose it'd go to her or her relations. They'd probably sell it and I'd be out on my arse. So I have to keep on the room. I'd never get another like it for the price.'

'That's terrible, and there's me always moaning and complaining to you. Could you not go back to your mother's to live if you moved in with him and then he died?'

'Not unless God struck her oul bastard of a husband down dead.'

'But, Bridie, he's your father!' Angel exclaimed, aghast at what she'd just heard.

'No, he isn't. My father was killed years ago. Three months later my mother married that oul bastard. I don't think she was in her right mind. While my father was away she'd buried my two brothers within a week of each other with diphtheria. One was ten and the other twelve. In between them and me she'd buried my three sisters with consumption. Anyway, she married him. I was eighteen then. Me ma was thirty-nine and in no time

295

she was carrying. She was taken bad one night and rushed into the Rotunda with a threatened miss. That's the night he raped me. When I tried defending myself he knocked me about, nearly strangled me. I hid the marks on my neck by letting on I had a sore throat, and the rest of my injuries to a fall down the stairs. I told no one but I think Mother Mary Angela suspected the truth. The nuns are wise women. In the hospital they see a lot of terrible things. She didn't probe but put me on light duties. My ma lost the baby and I found out I was having one. You know what happened to that. I moved in here afterwards. I seldom see my mother. I sometimes wonder if she smelt a rat. But she's still with him.'

No one who knew Angel read the message in the newspapers. Bridie's lover didn't improve. She said to Angel, 'I'll have to spend Christmas Day with him. It's a bloody shame and you off as well. I'd ask you over to his place but he doesn't take to strangers. What'll you do with yourself?'

'Change my duty – anyone will jump at the chance. I'd be better off in the hotel than on my own. There won't be many staying the night but I can help out in the bar and I'll get a Christmas dinner. It'll probably be lively in there in the evening.'

In her bedroom that night she thought about her mother, wondering what sort of a Christmas she'd have. They could never afford a turkey. Sometimes Aggie managed the price of an old hen, simmered it for a few hours, then pot-roasted it for the final cooking. Danny always gave them a half of ham, a bottle of sweet sherry and an Oxford Lunch. Weeks beforehand Aggie would have made a plum pudding. On Christmas morning, neighbours would call in to sample the pudding and a small glass of sherry. She and Aggie would return the visit while the hen was browning, surrounded in the pot by roasting potatoes. The fat red candle that had been lit on Christmas Eve would still be burning on the window-sill and behind the few pictures there would be well-berried holly. Sitting in her narrow cold bedroom, Angel could almost smell the gorgeous smells, see the blazing fire, the little cardboard crib and her mother's smiling face. She loved an occasion, any excuse to celebrate. Tears ran down Angel's face, thinking of Aggie all alone in the cottage on Christmas Day. And she made up her mind there and then that early in the New Year she and her mother would be in England. Never again would they spend Christmas Day apart. And this week she'd send a pound. She had scrimped and saved, only buying stockings and a new vest and knickers. She had most of Danny's money and what she had put by since. It was plenty to pay their fares and find a room – in Liverpool, she supposed. That's where the boat from the North Wall docked. If they settled for Liverpool there'd be no extra needed for train fares. And from all she'd heard, Liverpool was a grand, friendly place, hundreds of Irish there.

On her day off before Christmas week she went into town, bought the one-pound postal order and scribbled a few lines on a sheet of cheap notepaper she'd brought with her.

Dear Ma,
Not much longer now I promise you. In 1921 we'll be together in England. Then I'll tell you all. I'm grand

so don't be worrying about me. Say a prayer for me at Midnight Mass.

And have a happy and a Holy Christmas.

Love,

Angel.

She posted the letter then, before leaving the building, decided to draw out all of her savings on the off-chance that she might make the move to England in the first week of January. Christmas week wasn't a good time to go into town – she might meet someone from the village. Once or twice a year they would venture across the bridge to the north side and the week before Christmas was the most likely time.

She put the eight five-pound notes into her handbag and went for a cup of coffee to a café where she sat making plans for going to Liverpool. She would have to arrange for her mother to meet her in town on the night they would take the boat, send her extra money to pay for a cab. She would tell her to bring a bag with just a change of clothes, to leave everything in the cottage, the statue of the Blessed Virgin, the Sacred Heart lamp. Just to walk out of the cottage. After a couple of weeks without his rent the landlord would repossess the place. But would it all go as smoothly as that? Until this moment she had taken it for granted that it would.

But supposing Aggie wouldn't go to Liverpool, or at least not without discussing the ins and outs of the move? She didn't own much but what little she did was precious to her. The statue, for instance. That had belonged to her grandmother, as had the Sacred Heart lamp. And the big iron kettle, the three-legged pot in which she boiled the Christmas pudding. Aggie's few treasures. She'd need some persuading to leave them behind. No good telling her you could pick up the same articles for a few shillings in Liverpool. She would react the same way about just walking out of the cottage. 'Angel,' she could hear her protest, 'the landlord knows I wouldn't just walk out of my home. He'd have the police out looking for me. They'd think I'd been murdered. And what about Father Clancy, Danny and Father Brennan? Wouldn't I want to say goodbye to them?'

Angel held her head in her hands and depression settled round her. Her plan wouldn't work. Certainly not in a hurry. Certainly not in the first week of January. Little by little, she'd have to introduce the idea to her mother, write longer letters, maybe even tell her about Johnny Quinn and that terrible night. Confess about the abortion and plead with her mother to understand why she had to leave Ireland, why she needed to make a fresh start but couldn't face the prospect without her by her side.

In the long run she would agree. And they'd find a way to bring Our Lady's statue and the lamp with them and whatever else her mother wanted to take – but not the kettle and the pot. She'd have to start writing the long letters soon. As soon as Christmas was over she'd begin. They'd wait to leave until the weather improved. She'd been mad thinking you could rush at things.

A young girl came to clear the table and Angel ordered another cup of coffee. 'I'll have a cream bun as well.' The girl gave her a lovely smile. When Angel was leaving she left her sixpence. 'Excuse me,' the girl said, following her to the door holding out the silver coin, 'you forgot this.'

'I left it for you.'

'But, sure, Miss,' the girl said. 'That's as much as the cake and coffee cost.'

'Well, it's nearly Christmas,' Angel said, and went out into Sackville Street. She felt happy and excited. It was the crowds in the street, the sound of a barrel organ playing on the bridge. I love it all, she thought. I love Dublin. I feel like I used to before it all happened. Maybe I'll go to confession on Christmas Eve and receive communion on Christmas Day. Maybe, like Bridie said, you never forget it but you do get better.

She crossed the bridge where the organ grinder was playing 'After The Ball Was Over'. A cold wind blew off the Liffey. It and the music invigorated her. She felt like dancing there and then on the pavement, and for an instant imagined how people would stop and stare if she did. They'd think she was mad, not realising that for the first time in months she was feeling glad to be alive, to feel young and whole again. She took a penny from her purse and dropped it in the organ-grinder's cap on the path.

In Westmoreland Street, gusts of warm, coffee-laden air wafted from Bewley's each time their doors were opened. At the furrier's next door she stopped to look in the window at fox furs, the silver skins, one snowy white, draped around the shoulders of life-like mannequins. She had never seen a live fox, only one in a story-book with a rough red pelt. The furs on display were complete with head, paws and claws. She imagined one draped round her shoulders. She crossed to the other side of the street, pushing her way through crowds of men and women, tall students coming out of Trinity, and was aware for the first time in many months of admiring glances.

In Grafton Street she stopped to look into the

windows of Brown Thomas, where the latest fashions were always on display, and longed to have the courage and the money to enter the store – the money mostly, knowing that if she had the money, the courage would not be so hard to find. She noticed, as she had before, an elegant though not young woman being handed down from a carriage, the driver listening attentively to whatever it was she was saying, the nodding and touching his hat before remounting the carriage and driving away. She wasn't sure if she was imagining it but thought the woman smiled at her before going into the store.

One outfit in particular caught Angel's eye. It was a dusty pink, the semi-fitting dress a shade paler than the three-quarter-length coat. The shoes, with straps across the ankles, were the colour of chamois, the large-brimmed hat the same colour with a scarf round its brim that matched the coat exactly. The mannequin's wax legs were encased in sheer silk stockings, the ankles and legs visible as far as the calves. She could visualise herself in such an ensemble. During the last months she had lost interest in clothes, but now, as once before, she craved beautiful, expensive things.

She lingered a little longer gazing at the pink outfit, aware that she could never afford it but that in the cheaper shops she might find something that looked like it. On her way back she turned into Talbot Street where there were several dress shops and went into one.

There, staring her in the eyes, was an almost exact replica of the outfit she had seen in Brown Thomas, including the hat and shoes. She knew that the cut, the stuff wouldn't be the same, but she also knew it would be a quarter the price, even less. And she knew too that in her handbag there were pound notes – notes that now she had seen what she desired were fighting to get out.

An assistant who had been watching her finger the material, stroke it, came to her side. 'Gorgeous, isn't it? The only one in stock. And the colour would be very becoming on you. Would you like to try it on?'

For a few seconds Angel's conscience took charge. That money, it told her, is to take you and your mother to England. 'I'll think about it and come back.'

'It's the only one in stock. A model. It'll be snapped up.'

Angel capitulated, telling herself, as the assistant led her to the cubicle, 'We're not going until the fine weather. I'll get the money together again.' Once adorned in the clothes, any remaining doubts fled. Not giving them a chance to return, she said, 'I'll take it and the shoes and gloves to match.'

'You look beautiful in it. It couldn't fit you better if it was made to measure. But then, and this isn't sales talk, you're very lucky. Not many have a face and figure like yours.'

Proudly Angel carried her parcels back to Bridie's room. On the way she had bought cooked ham, crusty bread, cheese and a currant loaf, telling herself, as the savings were broken into, that a few more shillings spent wouldn't be missed.

She got a good fire going, laid the table and watched the clock impatiently for when it was time for Bridie to arrive. She had so much to tell her: her change of plans about going to England; her intention to break the news gently to her mother; that she'd probably go to confession on Christmas Eve. And she wanted to show her the new clothes. She knew exactly what Bridie would say. 'Didn't I tell you you'd get better?' And Bridie would give her a hug saying, 'I'm delighted for you.' She would tell Bridie that if it hadn't been for her she'd be dead and buried by now. 'Without your help I'd never have pulled through.' And dismissively Bridie would assure her, 'Indeed you would. You're tougher than you think.'

She heard Bridie's footsteps on the landing and hurried to open the door, then exclaimed, 'Oh, my God, what ails you?' and stood back to let Bridie in.

'I'm droppin'. She died during the night and he's got cancer.'

Angel shut the door and led her friend to a chair. 'Sit down, there's a drain of whiskey – I'll get it.'

'Her death wasn't unexpected, lord have mercy on her. You could say it was a happy release, but I never thought he was that bad.' In all the time Angel had known her, Bridie had never mentioned her lover's name. She always referred to him as 'my fella', 'him', or 'your man'. Bridie continued, 'Like, I knew that whatever he had was serious but not as bad as it is. They've given him three months. It's all through with him.'

'When did you find out?'

'In work, as soon as I went in. He took bad during the night. He has a telephone and called the doctor and was rushed in. A massive haemorrhage.'

'Into the Mater?'

'One of the nurses who knew about us told me. But it wasn't until after the ward round that I heard the truth. This nurse was going round with Mr Donavan – he's the top man there – and he was explaining to the students what ailed my fella. All medical terms. But she knew what he was talking about. And after they'd left the bed she heard Mr Donavan say, "Three months at the outside."'

'Oh, Bridie, I'm so sorry. Has he found out about his wife being dead yet?'

'Yeah, the matron broke that news to him. But, as I said, he was expecting it. And I think he knows he's finished.'

'How d'ye say that?'

Bridie shrugged. 'I had a feeling when I went to see him after dinner. And when he asked me to marry him I was in no doubt.'

'And will you?'

'I think so. I'm very fond of him. He's been kind and understanding about what my stepfather did. Never too demanding.'

'When will you get married?'

'It'll have to be soon. St Stephen's Day, after Advent.'

'And you'll be moving in with him?'

'I'll have to, won't I?'

'I was just wondering about the room.'

'Don't. I'll keep paying the rent. And you come any time. You've got a key and can sleep here on your night off.'

'But can you afford it?'

'I'll be a married woman, won't I? He's bound to give me a few bob.'

'You'll have to give up your work.'

'In fairness to him I will. But it's no good pretending this thought hasn't crossed my mind that maybe he'll leave me the house. If he does, you can move in with me. We'll take in a couple of lodgers and be on the pig's back.'

304

Angel took time off to go to the funeral of the wife of Bridie's lover. He wasn't well enough to attend. At the requiem before the burial she and Bridie heard for the first time the woman's name, and on the coffin Angel read, 'Kathleen Hughes, aged fifty-three'. She was still no wiser about his name but at least now she could think of him as Mr Hughes.

It was a sad, lonely funeral, only herself, Bridie and the priest at the graveside in the lashing rain. When it was over she and Bridie had to hurry back to work. The hospital, although they could do nothing for Mr Hughes, had agreed to keep him in until Christmas Eve. Bridie was leaving her job and would marry him the day after Christmas, then look after him until he died.

Before parting Bridie told Angel that if he was well enough they'd get married in his parish church, and if he wasn't the priest had agreed to marry them in the house.

'Wherever it is, the priest says not to worry about witnesses. He'll supply them.'

'I was going to say I doubt if I'd be able to get the time off. I'll be helping in the bar and St Stephen's Day is busy anywhere drink is being served.'

'I'll be in and out of town so I'll drop in to see you whenever I can,' Bridie assured her as they parted.

Angel lost her nerve about going to confession, but went to an early Mass on Christmas Day in the cathedral in Marlborough Street not far from the hotel. She sat at the back of the church so as not to stick out like a sore thumb as the surrounding pews emptied when the congregation went to receive the Blessed Sacrament. She prayed for her mother, for Bridie, for Mr and Mrs Hughes, and for the child she had aborted. Not sure

305

when the soul entered the body, she wondered where the baby was. It hadn't been baptised so it couldn't be in heaven. Maybe it was in limbo. She hoped so. Limbo wasn't a cruel place, not like hell.

She enjoyed her turkey dinner, plum pudding and glasses of red lemonade. There were no guests, only two middle-aged men who lodged permanently in the hotel. They were clerks in a nearby office. One of the other chambermaids had told her the hotel gave them a good price, cheaper than renting a room and feeding themselves. For the dinner, as it was Christmas, everyone ate in the dining room. One of the permanent guests sat next to Angel. She tried to get him talking but to most of her questions his replies were brief. When she asked where he came from, he said, 'Monaghan,' and didn't enlarge on it.

After the meal she went on duty behind the bar. Christmas Day was a bad time for business: the majority of men did their drinking at home on this day of days. Another girl relieved Angel when she went to have her tea, a lavish one of cold meats, trifle, biscuits and cakes. She thought of Bridie and her husband-to-be, toyed with the idea of telephoning her to wish her a happy Christmas but decided against it. How could it be a happy occasion sitting by a man so sick that Bridie had told her he couldn't keep water down? And Angel knew now that the wedding ceremony would be performed in the house. Early on Christmas Eve morning, Bridie had telephoned to say he was ten times worse than when he had left hospital and she didn't think he'd last three weeks, never mind the three months the doctor had given him. Angel supposed it was just as well, if he was in terrible suffering.

Knowing that there was no urgency about returning to the bar she dawdled over her meal, thinking thoughts and remembering things – that Bridie had never seen the new clothes she had bought. She'd forgotten all about them when Bridie came to the room so upset. If it had been an ordinary wedding she could have worn them to that. Though if there'd been a wedding breakfast and hooley later she couldn't have stayed. Like New Year's Eve, St Stephen's Day was, the barman had told her, one of the busiest days of the year. Not being experienced in bar work, she hoped she could manage – all the money that changed hands, all the counting to be done. One of the other chambermaids had told her it was desperate, everyone roaring for their orders, oul fellas trying to put their hands up your skirts, others accusing you of overcharging them.

Then her thoughts turned to Aggie. Throughout the day, on and off, she had been thinking about her, composing in her head the first long letter she would write, beginning her persuasion of a move to England. Then she thought, There's no time like the present. I doubt if more than half a dozen customers will come in during the evening. I'll go up to my room, get a pencil and paper and write the letter in the bar.

When she began it was seven o'clock. The two permanent clients came in. Both saluted her. The one she had sat next to at dinner asked her if she would like a lemonade. She had drunk so much she felt as if her stomach was ready to burst but she accepted the offer. The man smiled, and she was surprised at what a lovely smile he had. It lit up his eyes and showed his nice white teeth. She was tempted to try again to engage him in conversation but after paying for the drinks he left the

307

bar quickly and sat quite a distance from the other lodger.

She began her letter to her mother. Except for an occasional cough, as one or other of the lodgers cleared his throat, and the ticking of the wall clock, there wasn't a sound. Her pencil flew over the sheets of paper. And then there was a most unusual noise: a lorry was pulling up outside the hotel. Even on a weekday, lorries were few and far between. The barman, who had been upstairs resting, came running in through the door. He looked terrified. 'The Tans are outside,' he said, as he went behind the bar. 'I think they're coming in. Don't look crooked at them.'

The lodgers left their unfinished drinks and hurried out of the bar. Moments later the door was pushed open and in came the men, in their uniforms of black and khaki. Angel counted six. Soon they were followed by another three. They had already been drinking – you could see it in their flushed faces, hear it in their loud laughter, smell it on their breath as they clustered round the bar.

It was the closest Angel had ever been to them. She had heard of their indiscriminate killings, rapes and looting. But now, seeing them at first hand, except for the rifles slung on their shoulders and the uniforms, they looked like any crowd of drunken men. Some, she noticed, were handsome.

The barman asked, 'What are ye drinking, lads? Have the first on the house as a Christmas box.' Angel detected the quiver in his voice. 'Jameson's,' answered one, then turned his attention to her. 'Well, aren't you the loveliest colleen I've ever seen?' She smiled nervously before turning away to help pour whiskey into tumblers. Her hands were shaking and she felt sick with fear.

After several whiskeys apiece the Tans left the bar, pushed two tables together and sat round them where they drank, smoked, laughed uproariously and shouted when their glasses needed refilling.

'Don't you move from behind the counter, I'll see to their wants,' the barman warned her in a whisper.

The men went in and out at regular intervals to relieve themselves. Then one, wearing sergeant's stripes, shouted across the room, 'The funds are running low, Paddy. We'll have another round on the house.'

'Certainly, sir, the same again, will it be?'

'The same again,' replied the NCO. Angel helped pour the drinks in clean tumblers. Then one of the group, pointing to a large picture hanging at the end of the room, said, 'That's one of their fucking heroes, him that fucked the Major's wife, Parnell. Let's make a cock shot of him.'

The table was laden with used tumblers with which the Tans began pelting the picture. They were so drunk their aim was unsteady and most of the glasses fell short of the target. Then the sergeant took a revolver from its holster, aimed at the picture and fired.

'Sacred Heart of Jesus protect us,' the barman said, not needing to whisper as one after the other the men followed their sergeant's example and fired at the picture.

At any minute Angel expected the guns to be turned in their direction and silently said an act of contrition. 'Well done, lads.' The sergeant guffawed. The bullets had smashed the picture glass and shredded the print. Parnell's face was riddled with holes. Only his beard and the frame were intact. The force of the bullets had altered the position of the picture – it now hung crookedly on the wall.

'Let's give him a close shave,' one of the men shouted, then straightened the picture. 'You're the marksman, Waller, bring him down cleanshaven.' Waller was sitting next to the wall. He moved out on to the floor, a young, good-looking man, took aim and fired three shots in rapid succession. Parnell's hirsute chin disappeared, the cord snapped and the picture frame crashed to the floor. The Tans cheered, the sergeant called for more whiskey.

The barman's hands shook as he filled glasses and murmured aspirations. 'Sacred Heart of Jesus, protect us. Holy Mary Mother of God, save us.' The glasses rattled on the tray as he carried it to the table.

'Irish hospitality,' said the sergeant. 'Everywhere we go we find it.'

Back behind the counter, the barman wiped his sweating hands, and Angel, in a low voice, asked, 'How long d'ye think they'll stay?'

'Till they feel like going. Maybe all night.'

'Could you not get the police?'

'They wouldn't come within a mile of them.'

More Irish hospitality was demanded and delivered. 'We could be here all night. It's my first experience of them, please God that it'll be my last. Oh, Jaysus, that fella the sergeant's on his feet again. He's heading this way.' Angel kept her back turned, busying herself rinsing tumblers that didn't need it, terrified to look round and draw attention to herself. She listened to what the NCO was asking the barman.

'Is this one of his hidey-holes?'

'I don't understand what you mean, sir.'

'Oh, yes, you fucking do. Is this one of Collins's places from where he does his disappearing tricks?'

'No, sir. Honest to God, sir. I've never laid eyes on him in my life. That's as true as God.'

'Is it now? I believe you. All the same, I wouldn't trust one of you fucking Micks.' And he shouted to his carousing men, 'Up the stairs, down the stairs, attics, cellars, every room, every inch of the place. At the double.' Yahooing, they went and he after them. Angel made the sign of the Cross.

'Listen to that. They'll destroy the place.' The barman poured whiskey into a tumbler and drank it in one gulp. 'I'm afraid of my life. Collins isn't here. I wish to Christ he was. They'd be so delighted they'd forget about me and you, and our lives might be spared.'

'They wouldn't shoot us!' said Angel, and began to cry.

'Maybe they won't. But you never know with the mad bastards what they'll do. Listen to them, will you? That's them putting in the doors above with their rifle butts. If I were you I'd go home. I've a good mind to do the same myself. Only you'd never know how them above have fared. They might be in need of assistance when those curs leave.'

Angel was sorely tempted to flee. There was nothing of value in her bedroom – just the old coat she wore to work. Her handbag with the money in it was under the counter. 'Go on,' urged the barman. 'Make a run for it.'

She collected her bag and the partly written letter to her mother, as terrified of leaving as she was of staying. Slowly she put one foot in front of the other. Her legs were shaking, her heart racing. Then she heard the pounding of boots on the stairs. It was too late. She'd missed her chance. The Tans were coming back. But not coming in.

'Thanks be to Jesus, we've been spared,' the barman said. The words were hardly out of his mouth when the sergeant pushed open the door and stood partly in it with a grenade in his hand.

'Get down on the floor, quick,' the barman shouted, shoving her and falling to lie beside her. The sergeant pulled the pin from the grenade and, just before lobbing it at the wall where Parnell's picture had hung, shouted, 'Happy Christmas,' and ran.

'Holy Mary Mother of God, pray for us sinners now and at the hour of our death. Amen.'

Angel and the barman prayed as the grenade exploded.

They lay without moving. A couple of bottles fell from a shelf, and glasses danced on the bar top. After a while the barman rose to his knees and then a little higher until his chin was above the counter. 'You want to see the hole that's blown in the wall. You stay where you are for a minute till I see if they've gone.' He went to the window and peeped through a chink in the curtains, calling back to Angel, 'Thank Christ they have. Only I never heard the engine. Must have been drownded out by the sound of the explosion.'

Angel stood up and smoothed down her dress, ran her fingers through her tossed hair and said, 'I suppose we got off lightly.'

'Yeah, it could have been worse. D'ye smell burning?'

She sniffed the air. 'There's something on fire.' Smoke curled under the bar door, and up in the house women were screaming and feet running down the stairs. One after another the staff who had been working on Christmas Day came stumbling into the bar, the women

312

in their shifts with sheets, shawls or coats draped round them followed by the two lodgers in their long drawers and vests.

'It's blazing up there,' the man who'd sat next to Angel at dinner told them. His face was white and, embarrassed to be in his underwear, he kept his hands over his crotch.

The women and girls were crying or all talking at the same time.

'They ransacked the rooms.'

'Threw the bedclothes on the floor.'

'You've never heard anything like their language.'

'One of them kicked over my lamp, that's what started the fire. I tried to beat it out but sure it took hold too quick. It's blazing up there.'

'Are youse all here?' the barman asked. The women dithered, naming this one and that one, frightened and confused, not sure if anyone was still in the upstairs rooms. 'What d'ye think, Angel?' She was now more composed, took stock of the women and assured the barman that everyone was accounted for.

'Right, then,' he said, 'everyone outside. The fire will race through this kip. You'll have ceilings collapsing, falling down in flames. So out you go, quick. I'll call the fire brigade.'

'Jesus, Mary and Joseph, we'll freeze out there and me in my shift.'

'My handbag's above in my room with the few shillings in it.'

'You can freeze or roast, now move your arses.' The roar of the flames was now audible and so was the crashing of plaster, wood, no one was sure what. But, terrified, they protested no more and went out into the street.

A crowd had gathered. People living nearby ran back to their homes and returned with old coats, quilts, all sorts of coverings and draped them over the women from the hotel to protect them from the bitterly cold night. Every one of them, including the lodgers, had come barefoot from their rooms and hopped and skipped, trying to keep their circulation going.

'Maybe the fire brigade can master it,' said one of the lodgers. 'All my belongings are above in the room. If they could damp it down I'd risk going in to get them.' They were all dazed, couldn't believe what they were witnessing: the devouring of the hotel by gigantic tongues of flame.

'You'd be better off going home,' the hotel manager, who'd arrived in the wake of the fire brigade, advised his staff. 'I'll get cabs to take you.'

They agreed, and the two lodgers were accommodated in another cheap hotel across the road. 'Well, that's our bit of work up an apple tree, but sure God never shuts one door but He opens another,' a woman said.

The one standing beside her laughed and retorted, 'I only hope to Jesus he doesn't take long about it or it's not only a job I'll be out of but my home and habitation. I'm already in arrears with the rent.'

The manager went into a huddle with the chief fireman and they talked for a few minutes. Then he came back to his shivering staff and broke the bad news. 'Your man says the fire's out of control.' He spread his hands in a hopeless gesture. 'No point in you turning up in the morning, the place will be gutted.'

There were protests from the crowd. 'What about the money you owe us? How are we supposed to live?'

'I know, I know. I'll tell you what I'll do. Tomorrow evening meet me in Flanagan's, I'll be in the pub from six o'clock with the money. I can't say fairer than that. All right?'

'Not much shaggin' choice,' one of the women snapped.

'Upstairs in the private room, so there'll be no bother about the women getting in. Come on, get organised, here's the cabs.'

There was confusion among them as they sorted out who would share, argued as to who lived nearer to whom, with the jarveys getting impatient, telling them, for Jaysus' sake, to make up their minds, adding, 'It's cold enough to freeze the balls off of a brass monkey.'

Angel sat disconsolate, leaning against the musty-smelling leather, the smell of smoke still in her nose, the taste in her mouth, listening to the horses clip-clopping through the cobbled streets, the sounds seeming to echo her thoughts, I've lost my job and I've nowhere to live. Sacred Heart of Jesus, what am I going to do?

At the end of January, when Angel hadn't responded to the newspaper advertisements, Father Clancy decided that the time had come for Aggie to be committed to the asylum. There was no one to look after her and, though not violent, she was a danger to herself. Left alone just for a short while she had caused a fire, scalded her legs, and was confused all the time.

Danny and he were reluctant to make the decision. 'I think when she spilled the boiling water and when she caused the fire she was back in the days when Angel was

315

still at home and was trying to make a meal for her,' Danny said.

'The poor creature. Isn't it the terrible thing to lose your senses? But not being violent, she'll be in the open ward, and when the weather's fine, they'll let her walk in the grounds. We can visit her and a few of the neighbours will as well,' Father Clancy said.

The following week Aggie was committed to Grange Gorman. Danny was still hoping and praying that Angel would return and decided to continue paying the rent of the cottage a while longer. As he said to Father Clancy, 'Wouldn't it be the desperate thing if she came back, found her mother gone, and another renting the place?'

Angel was still living in Bridie's room. She hadn't found work, and was into the last of her savings. Bridie called in now and then while a neighbour sat with Mr Hughes, who was nearing his end. 'I pray for a miracle that he'll get better, or for a happy release from his suffering, whichever is God's will,' she said. Forcing a shilling into Angel's hand, she went on, 'I'm not flush but don't you refuse it. You look perished with the cold. Buy a stone of coal for the fire. If God chooses to take him, our worries are over.'

Chapter Nineteen

To eke out the remains of her savings, Angel boiled the kettle over twists of paper and a few sticks, leaving the lighting of the fire until she returned from wandering the city looking for work. Her stomach ached and rumbled from lack of food. The February cold found its way through her threadbare coat and into her bones so she was seldom without pain in her joints. On her sojourns through the streets she searched for the cheapest food, yesterday's bread, flaccid cabbages, stewing pieces, more gristle and fat than lean and tinged a sickening green at their edges.

She felt permanently light-headed and confused, as she knocked at doors of houses and went into shops, hospitals and hotels asking for work. One day, in desperation, she rang the bell on a convent door. An old nun answered the ring. It was a day when the rain fell in stinging arrows that bounced off the path and Angel was soaked. 'Well, you poor child, come in out of that before you get your end,' the little fat sister said.

The kindness overwhelmed Angel, made her want to fall at the nun's feet, bury her face in her habit, as she had so often done in her mother's lap, and be comforted. The nun took her into a small parlour, sat her down before a good fire and told her to wait. In a little while she came bustling back, her rosy, wrinkled face wreathed in smiles, and she set down on a low table a pot of tea and a plate of bread and butter. 'Take off that coat and throw it over the fireguard,' the sister said, as she poured the tea. Angel luxuriated in the heat and the food. She longed to confess her troubles – her worry and guilt for leaving her mother, her terrible sin, to throw herself on the nun's mercy, to listen and take her advice.

Instead she spoke of the hotel fire, the loss of her job, the temporary loss of contact with Bridie. 'Her husband's dying. She used to drop in now and then but I haven't seen her for ages.'

'The poor man, I'll say a prayer for him. What about your own family?'

'My mother died years ago, and my father left us before I was born.'

'And where are you living now?'

Knowing that nuns often followed up people in distressing circumstances, Angel gave a wrong address. 'D'ye know the people in the house?' the nun enquired.

'One or two to pass the time of day with. When I was working I only slept there once a week. It was Bridie's room until she married Mr Hughes. That was only lately. He must be on his last and she not able to leave him. But she'll be back again – Bridie's a true friend – and then I'll be all right.' She didn't mention that when Bridie's husband died all her worries would be at an end. 'In the meantime, if I could find a bit of work I'd be grand.'

'God look down on you, I only wish I had it to offer you. But whenever you're in the vicinity knock on the door. You'd never know the minute something might turn up. Finish up that bread like a good girl.'

When she had, the nun took away the tray. The food and heat had made Angel drowsy. She looked round the little parlour. It reminded her of her schooldays, and times in the presbytery: the same smell of cleanliness, of holiness; the picture of the Sacred Heart and another of Our Lady. The crucifix over the fireplace.

The nun came back with a brown-paper parcel. 'Here's a few things – a couple of vests to keep the life in you, a loaf, a bit of cheese, odds and ends. And don't forget, any time you're passing drop in.' She pressed a sixpence into Angel's hand. 'That coat's still damp,' she said, as she helped her on with it. 'Take it off the minute you get in.'

The next day, as she was getting ready to walk the streets again looking for a job, she recognised the sound of Bridie's feet running up the stairs and had the door open by the time she arrived on the landing. 'I couldn't face you,' Bridie said, and began to cry. 'After building up your hopes I couldn't dash them. Wait'll you hear what happened.'

'Come in, take off your coat. You're frozen. I'll get the fire going. Sit down, sit down. How is he?'

'Dead this three weeks.'

'Lord have mercy on him. Why didn't you let me know?'

'Because I didn't know how to face you.'

The paper caught and the sticks snapped and crackled, the sparks flew up the chimney like golden stars against the sooty blackness.

'The house wasn't his. To give him his due, he never said it was. I jumped to that conclusion. There was just enough society money for a matchwood coffin and the hearse. I had to go to Glasnevin in a cab, not enough for a mourning coach, or to open a new grave. He was buried with her, so we'll be three in a bed. Apart from his pension, he was penniless and the pension died with him. The landlord's been to see me. I can keep on the house and between the two of us, if we had work and a few lodgers, we could manage it. Otherwise I'm out on my arse in two weeks. Wasn't I the foolish woman to marry him?'

'Don't blame yourself. It's not as if you married him only for the house. You were fond of him and sorry for him,' said Angel, wanting to comfort her friend.

'I was, but always at the back of my mind was the thought of the house. And look where it got me. There's no one belonging to him so I suppose the few sticks of furniture are mine – not that I'd get twopence for them. What are we going to do?'

'Unless there's a miracle we'll have to let the room go,' replied Angel, and shuddered inwardly at the prospect of being without shelter.

'I'll try for the job back in the hospital, but I don't hold out much hope – and I don't suppose anything's turned up for you?'

Angel told how every day she walked the feet off herself looking for work.

'I suppose if all else fails I could go back to my mother. So could you. She'd make a shake-down on the floor.'

'No, you couldn't. For one thing she'd want to know what happened to the child and for another you'd have to contend with your good Christian neighbours. The rent is paid up to the end of next week, I'll get something for the furniture and move back in here. And maybe God'll open a door. We can do nothing for the time being but live in hopes. Then, if nothing turns up, I'll go over the other side. Both of us. There's bound to be more work in England. I'll go down to the pork shop and get the makings of a fry. I suppose, as usual, you've got nothing in your stomach. You've gone to look like a rake.'

Angel admitted she was starving, and Bridie went to buy a quarter of sausages, two rashers, a kidney and an onion.

When she'd left the room Angel cried heartbrokenly, with sorrow for Bridie and pity for herself, faced as she was with what might lie ahead for them. She had only one thing on which she might be able to raise a few shillings – the pink outfit. She could pawn that. It would keep a roof over their heads for a few more weeks.

The IRA and the Black and Tans continued to wage war on each other. But rumours began to percolate that a truce was being negotiated. They dribbled down through all layers of society. For Bridie, Angel and the majority of the working class they made little impression. Truce or no truce, their lot wouldn't improve much. Bridie and Angel would still be trudging the streets looking for work, as would most of those living in the tenement houses.

'Still and all,' Bridie said one evening, after returning from another fruitless search, 'I suppose we'd be able to walk the streets without fear of being blown to smithereens.'

And Angel agreed, while thinking that being blown to smithereens would be one sort of solution: no more begging for a job, no more painful searching her mind if she should go home, throw herself on her mother's mercy and face the tormentors in the village.

Bridie got two pounds for the contents of the house, and the following day found two days' work cleaning a house in Wilton Place. 'It's only for a few weeks, scrubbing the steps and polishing the knocker and handles on the door while the permanent girl's out sick. Still and all, it'll pay the rent here for another couple of weeks.'

Angel was down to her last five shillings and guilt-ridden living off Bridie, who told her that while she had it they'd share. But Angel knew that, in another couple of weeks, the pink suit would have to be pawned.

Johnny Quinn was climbing the ladder in the boxing world of Chicago. He seldom gave Ireland a thought and had blotted from his mind the rape of Angel, convincing himself that it had happened with her willing consent. She had followed him to the room in the hotel, made overtures to him and they had had sex. He had given her five pounds and she had given him a blue glass bead as a keepsake; a lucky charm, she had said. When he had woken the next morning she was gone. So far the bead had been his talisman and he carried it always on his person. Next year or the one after he'd fight his big fight in Carnegie Hall. He'd win and go back to Dublin a champion, as he had always intended.

Once a month Father Clancy and Danny went to see Aggie. If the weather was fine, she would be walking in the grounds with the other harmless lunatics. One man believed he was Napoleon and strutted round with his hand holding an imaginary lapel, another proclaimed, in a loud voice, Robert Emmett's speech from the dock. Pathetic old women acted coquettishly, smiling and preening, shaking imaginary fans, dressed in their institutional uniforms. One young girl believed she was Mary Queen of Scots, knelt down now and then and lifted her thin lank hair from the nape of her neck.

'May God look down on them,' Father Clancy would say. 'If it wasn't so tragic it'd make you laugh.'

The attendants told Danny and the priest that Aggie was very biddable, enjoyed her food, slept well, would cry from time to time for hours, but never spoke. They left their gifts of fruit and sweets, kissed her cheek and told her they'd come again. On the way home they'd talk about Angel, wonder where she was, would she ever show up, and hope she was safe if not happy.

Every night Danny prayed for her and prayed for a miracle that would one day enable him to help her. He hoped that she had found someone who cherished her, had married her. He changed his will, leaving the shop and his considerable amount of money to her as beneficiary. Like everyone else in the village, he had heard the story put about by Mona that Johnny Quinn was the father of Angel's child. And from time to time Danny fantasised that he had Johnny Quinn's neck in his hands and was squeezing the life out of him, a fantasy that he would confess monthly to Father Clancy, who absolved him and gave him a light penance. And who later on would think that it was better that Johnny Quinn was blamed rather than Father Brennan. Johnny had the bad drop in him. Wherever he was, Father Clancy prayed he would never come back to the village. His father was still driving the trams. How he kept down the job Father Clancy never understood, for he was more often drunk than sober.

He also wondered if Angel had got word that her mother was in the asylum, for the letters that used to come care of the presbytery had stopped coming this while back, though he didn't see how Angel could have found out. But, then again, you'd never know for sure. The most likely answer was that she had gone to England or America.

The girl whose job Bridie was doing had a relapse and would be off work for several more weeks. 'It means we'll be secure for a while longer,' Bridie told Angel.

'They're very considerate holding the job open for her. You don't hear of that happening very often.'

'Indeed you don't. But they're one of these good-living Protestant families, very honourable. I was telling the cook about you losing the bit of work when the hotel burned down and she's promised to keep an eye out for you. Not that I'd wish bad health on anyone else, but all the same wouldn't it be grand if another scullerymaid got sick? Nothing serious, God forbidding all harm. Just a touch of something, so you could earn a few bob.'

And, as if God heard her wish and granted it, a maid in a house not far from where Bridie worked got a touch of something and Angel stepped into her place. The house was near the Grand Canal. After finishing work Angel would walk along the banks looking at the water, remembering the river at home, playing there in the summer, catching pinkeens, picking wild flowers, chasing butterflies. But always back in her mind would come the terrible memory of the night the crowd had followed her and her mother along the riverbank, screaming and cursing after them. Tears would fill her eyes and confirm her decision that she could never return to the village, but at the same time strengthen her resolve to get in touch with her mother. Her poor mother, who by now must be demented at not knowing where she was. And it was ages since she had sent her any money. Once she got on her feet, she'd send letters again, care of Father Clancy.

After walking for a while along the canal's banks she'd turn back and begin the walk to the north side, down Baggot Street, past Stephen's Green, the Shelbourne Hotel, where beautiful women in gorgeous clothes, usually escorted by handsome men, went in and out and where smells of delicious food drifted up from the kitchens to make her mouth water. She would turn into Grafton Street and saunter down its right-hand side, gazing into shop windows at exquisite clothes, jewellery, oil paintings, confectionary, inhaling the scents of perfumes, chocolate and always the tantalising aroma of roasting coffee beans.

One day, while standing before Brown Thomas's window, she saw the woman she had once imagined smiled at her. Out of the corner of her eye she looked at the woman, who turned, smiled and spoke. 'I haven't seen you this long time. I've often thought about you, wondered if I'd see you again.'

Angel was astounded. She blushed and couldn't think of anything to say but nevertheless managed a smile.

'You don't look very well. Have you been ill? You've lost weight.'

'A touch of a cold,' Angel stammered.

'You poor child, and me keeping you standing out in the wind. Let's go and have some coffee.' The woman took her by the elbow and they walked away from Brown Thomas and past Mitchell's where Mrs McEvoy, for that was her name, usually went for coffee. Now, though, she decided against it, knowing that it would overawe Angel in her shabby clothes. 'There's a nice little café in Wicklow Street. We'll go there.' Still holding Angel's elbow, she guided her across the road and into a narrow street. It was a small café, smelling of coffee and cakes, its clientele humbler than those who frequented Mitchell's, Angel, unaware of this, was impressed.

After ordering, Mrs McEvoy asked Angel's name. 'Katherine,' replied Angel, then went on to explain that she was better known by her nickname.

'And am I at liberty to ask what that might be?'

Angel told her and Mrs McEvoy exclaimed, 'How becoming. How apt. You have the face of an angel.'

Angel blushed, and was again rendered speechless but soon began to feel more at ease. As she replied to Mrs McEvoy's questions she couldn't take her eyes off the woman's face. It was a lovely face, old but the skin was soft, powdered and slightly rouged. Her eyes were vividly blue, shadowed and pencilled, Angel guessed, and her lips painted a delicate shade of pink. In all her life she had never seen a woman who was old and still pretty.

By the time they had finished their first cup of coffee Mrs McEvoy knew about the hotel fire, loss of job, difficulty in finding another permanent one and that Angel had run away from home because her mother hadn't approved of the boy she had fallen in love with. A boy who not long afterwards had gone to England and from whom Angel never heard again.

'Why didn't you go home?'

Having told lies already Angel told another. 'My mother is very strict. I don't think she would have wanted me.'

Mrs McEvoy sighed. 'Poor mothers, we are often misjudged. I had a daughter who did as you did and fell in love with a boy I didn't approve of. She ran off to Paris with him. I never heard from her again. Perhaps, like you, she's afraid to come home. Little does she know how I'd welcome her with open arms. I pray that she's alive and well, and that she still loves the young man and he her.'

Angel was fascinated by the number of rings Mrs McEvoy wore, one on every long, slender finger, diamonds, emeralds, a ruby one and a sapphire, which reminded her of Tommy Maguire and the ring from the penny bazaar.

'Well, I suppose I'd better let you go home but, please, you'd be doing me a great favour if you'd have coffee with me again.'

'I'd love to,' said Angel.

'Then shall we say a week today, same time, same place? And let me send you home in a cab.'

Eagerly Angel agreed.

The coffee afternoons continued. As they did, each woman confided more to the other. Angel rectified her version of her story, though still didn't tell the whole truth. She confessed to loving someone her mother considered unsuitable but that she hadn't run away with him. At the time of her leaving home he was already in England. He had promised to send for her but never did.

Mrs McEvoy was a shrewd woman, well up in the ways of the world, and deduced that there was more to Angel's story than she had told but knew that, in time, she would hear it all.

She told Angel that once she had been a wealthy woman but that lately business hadn't gone so well. 'Once,' she said, 'I had the biggest house in the street. What a time that was – the parties, the dances, the music and the lovely young men and women who used to attend them. But, like everything else, nothing lasts for ever. Times change. Mind you, I still have a beautiful house and home, but it's smaller and the street is becoming somewhat run-down. You must visit some time.'

Angel said she'd be delighted, and felt emboldened enough to ask what sort of business Mrs McEvoy had. 'I run a salon. I invite special people to my soirées – aristocrats, artists, writers, officers from prestigious regiments and, of course, beautiful girls. I'll invite you to one. You'd enjoy it so much.'

'You are so kind and good to me. I feel as if I've known you all my life.'

Mrs McEvoy reached across the table and clasped Angel's hands. 'And so do I. I think of you as a daughter. Promise that when I invite you you'll come.'

'On my word of honour,' replied Angel.

'Are you still seeing that oul wan?' Bridie enquired one night, when she and Angel were sitting by the fire.

'You know I am, every Thursday. Why?'

'I was just wondering, that's all. She's very generous, always slipping you a few bob.'

'She says I remind her of her daughter.'

'The money's handy – keeps the roof over our heads. I heard a rumour going round that the scullerymaid from your house is in the way so she won't be coming back. Mine is on the mend, though. We have to face up to it that without permanent work I'll have to go to England. And one half day a week, even with what the oul wan gives you won't keep you going for very long. What'll you do?'

'In the long run, I suppose, I'll have to go over as well. It's my mother who's holding me back. God, I feel terrible about it all. It's been so long now since I left home, and months since I sent her the few bob. I should write to Father Clancy – only if I want news of me ma I'd have to give him my address and I don't want anyone knowing where I am, not yet anyway, not even him. But he'd lend us the fares. I'd have to meet him in town.'

'Put it on the long finger for the time being. Things have a way of working out.'

Bridie returned to skimming through the *Evening Herald*. 'Eh!' she said, laying it on her lap. 'Wasn't that fella, that Tommy Maguire, in the Connaught Rangers?'

'I don't know who you're talking about.'

'Ah, you do, the soldier in India, the one who wanted to marry you. You mentioned him a few times, the gas about the ring from the penny bazaar.'

'Oh, him. I don't know what he was in, except it was in India. Poor Tommy, he was mad about me. Wanted us to get married. I was only fourteen. I didn't know how to refuse him. Father Clancy put him right, though. I let on I'd wait for him. He used to send me money, our savings to get married. I stopped writing to him ages ago. Anyway, what about him?'

'You might be seeing him sooner than you thought. His regiment's being disbanded. They had a so-called mutiny. You could still finish up with him.'

They both laughed at the idea. And, looking at Bridie, Angel thought how much she'd miss her. She was talking of leaving for England the following week. Bridie with her good-natured face, always ready to look on the bright side. She was not interested in her appearance but always scrupulously clean and had not an ounce of vanity in her – a comb pulled through her rough gingery hair, spit on a finger to smooth her unruly eyebrows, and she was ready to face the world.

They continued talking about this and that. Angel said she was going to Mrs McEvoy's home the following week. She was holding a soirée.

'What I've been meaning to ask you is, how does she

make her money? You can't very well ask people to a party and then expect them to pay.'

'Maybe they're like our hooleys where everyone gives two shillings or half a crown.'

'Maybe,' said Bridie, 'but a florin or half a crown wouldn't keep her in the style you say she has.'

'I never gave it much thought.'

'Where did you say she lived?'

'She calls it Mecklenburgh Street, but she says that's the old name. It's had two new ones since – Tyrone Street, and what it's called now, Railway Street – but she still uses the old one. Everyone knows it by that.'

'Sacred Heart of Jesus!' Bridie exclaimed. 'That's Monto, the kips, the digs.'

Angel looked uncomprehendingly at her. 'What are they? I never heard tell of them.'

'Ah, come on now, don't act the innocent, you must have. That's where the brothels are, the bad houses. Your woman is a brothel-keeper.'

'She is not,' retorted Angel indignantly. 'She's a kind, decent woman.'

'She saw you coming. Saw you were a beauty, found out you were destitute, a great asset. The bloody oul bitch! Well, you're not going next nor near it, not if I have to drag you to England by the hair of the head. For two pins I'd be round there and smather her. If I have to pawn every stitch I own, my wedding ring, myself – you're not going there.'

'You've got it all wrong, Bridie. Maybe it's true what you say, but that'd been years ago. Mrs McEvoy is a weekly communicant, never misses Mass in Marlborough Street. She wouldn't lead me astray. In any case, it would be a waste of time. I could never let a man touch me

330

again. And, for another thing, I'm going to see her at home. You can't stop me doing that. I'll be twenty-one this year and I have to stand on my own feet some time.'

'But I'll be worried sick about you. I'm sure that oul bitch will inveigle you into something. Promise me one thing, if she does try that let me know somehow.'

Angel promised, then asked Bridie to tell her more about Monto. Why, for instance, was it called that?

'There's a lot of streets in the brothel area. It's as big as Stephen's Green. One is Montgomery Street and that's where the name Monto is supposed to have come from. They were all different. In some streets only toffs were allowed in the houses. Then there were the middle ones, clerks and that could go to them, and the last lot were for the gurriers and sailors off the ships. In the low-class ones there were fellas to keep the girls in order – beat them and their clients up if they looked crooked. The police were afraid to go in – get their heads kicked off them. Along with doing the other thing with the fellas, the prostitutes robbed them and I believe the price of a drink was scandalous.'

'And you expect me to believe Mrs McEvoy took part in such things? I'm telling you, she's a lady.'

'Lots of the madams appeared ladylike. My mother told me some of them would drive down Grafton Street in their own carriages, send their daughters to posh schools, and the girls, dressed to the nines, would be sent to the Park, to the races and polo matches, luring the men for later that night. The poor unfortunates! In the long run, most would die in the Lock Hospital from the bad disease.'

'I still don't believe any of that about Mrs McEvoy.'

'Suit yourself, then, but remember I warned you.'

Mrs McEvoy's house was a storey shorter than the one in Wilton Place where Angel had her temporary job. That one had been built in 1831 but Mrs McEvoy's was the genuine article – eighteenth century. It was early afternoon when she arrived for her first visit. The cabby who drove her was inquisitive. 'Don't get many callers here so early in the day. You a friend of Mrs Mac's, then?' Angel said she was, and didn't encourage any more conversation though the cabby didn't give up. 'Trade's slackened off in the last few years. You should have seen the street in them days, especially the lower end. Beauties they were then, the girls. Sit out on the steps with hardly a screed on them and their petticoats, all colours of the rainbow, hanging on the railings to dry. Drinking their red biddy, smoking, laughing, calling out to passers-by, "Are you doing business, sir?" I knew most of them. Not a bad lot, so long as you didn't get on the wrong side of them. Could have had it for nothing, me. But I resisted the temptation, afraid of the bad disease. You'd never know who they'd been with before you. All sorts, sailors off the foreign ships, niggers. Now, Mrs Mac never kept a house like that. Them in the top end of the street didn't. More like hotels, they were, reserved for the toffs.'

He was corroborating all that Bridie had told her, and Angel was quaking as she paid him and left the cab half in a mind to say, 'Stop, take me back.' But back to what? Bridie had already left for England, her own temporary work was finishing next week – the girl she was replacing had come back. Only the pink suit stood between her and eviction. She had to risk going through with the visit. After all, Mrs McEvoy wasn't going to imprison her, couldn't make her do anything against her will.

She went up the granite steps and pressed the gleaming brass bell, noticing the immaculately white-painted door with its brass furnishings. A maid, in black and white with a little cap perched on her head, answered the ring.

'You'll be Miss Lucas. Come in, Mrs McEvoy's expecting you,' she said, opening the parlour door. 'I'll tell her you're here.'

Angel noticed that along the right-hand side of the hall there was a thick brass rod, several inches from the wall and its red flock wall-paper. There was a similar one in the house where she worked. She had asked another servant what it was for. 'Some say,' the girl had replied, 'that's it's to protect the paper from people brushing against it, marking and scuffing it. Then again there's them who say it was for the gentlemen years ago to fling their cloaks over. As far as I'm concerned, it's only another lot of brass for me to polish.'

The parlour was papered in a deep shade of blue with matching swag curtains, and the thick carpet was patterned in shades of pink and blue. A gilt-framed mirror stood on the white marble mantelpiece. On the mantelshelf there was a photograph of a young girl. There were several occasional tables on which lay books, newspapers and on one an open workbox with skeins of coloured wool spilling out. This, she thought, must be where Mrs McEvoy spent much of her time.

Before she had time to take in any more Mrs McEvoy came into the room, kissed her on both cheeks and invited her to sit down. 'Rose will bring in the tea presently. How well you're looking, and your suit is gorgeous, the colour becomes you. So at last,' she said, when the maid had brought the silver tray laden with china, tiny sandwiches and pastries and left them, 'you've come to see my home. A hundred thousand welcomes. May it be the first of many visits.'

Angel admired everything. 'That is my daughter,' Mrs McEvoy told her, pointing to the photograph, 'my only child. I wonder where she is today. If you knew the tears I shed for her, the prayers, morning and night, I pray for her.'

While murmuring words of comfort Angel thought of her own mother and all the suffering she had caused her.

Mrs McEvoy dabbed at her eyes with a lace-edged wisp of cambric. 'I'm just a silly old woman. Let's have a cup of tea before it cools. And let me confess that you bring me great consolation.'

'Me!' exclaimed Angel.

'Yes. You and my daughter are not unalike, though I have to say Alice isn't quite as beautiful as you. I've never seen such an exquisite face. You were rightly named Angel – you have an ethereal quality about you. An innocence shines out of your eyes. Your face is like that of a beautiful child.'

Angel blushed and, as usual, didn't know what to say. In her mind, though, she was convinced that this was a sweet, good woman who, no matter what Bridie said, intended her no harm.

They talked of other things, the weather, how soon it would be May, the beginning of summer. How rumours were growing stronger that a truce was at hand. Eventually Mrs McEvoy asked Angel if she would like to see over the house. 'The back parlour's behind this room and downstairs are the kitchens and storerooms. But today we won't bother with those. I'll show you the front and back drawing rooms.' She led the way up the shallow flight of wide steps, carpeted in a red that matched the wall-paper. Angel had never seen such a vast room and said so when the drawing room door was opened. 'That's not all. Come, I'll show you the rest' and, leading the way, Mrs McEvoy went to a cream-panelled section of wood that ran the width of the room, undid the brass fitting and folded back the panels to reveal the next drawing room, which was as large as the one in which they stood.

Angel gasped. 'It's as big as a ballroom.'

'Exactly. And, as you can see, the floor isn't carpeted.' Angel looked down at the honey-coloured parquet boards. 'For the dancing. You'll enjoy that.'

There was a grand piano, an Irish harp and music stands. Chaises-longues, comfortable sofas and easy chairs were arranged around the walls. The plasterwork on the ceilings and friezes was breathtaking. Angel stared, fascinated, at the flowers and puttis, at the two great chandeliers, the enormous white marble mantel-pieces, the four sash windows reaching from floor to just below the frieze. 'I could die in these rooms,' she said.

'Please God you won't, but dance and be merry many, many times. Now we'll move on. I want you to see the room that'll be yours if you agree to come and keep a lonely old woman company. Another flight of stairs.'

It was sumptuously furnished, the enormous bed covered by a quilted ivory spread and matching pillows. There were mirrors everywhere, which gave back a reflection of the bed, of every object of interest and beauty in the lovely room.

'This would be mine? I'd sleep here?'

'Well, of course you would.'

'But how would I pay for it?'

'For the time being don't worry about that. Didn't we agree that you weren't to be rushed into anything? By next week you'll have decided. Time enough then to talk about such mundane things as payment.'

Angel went back to the tenement in a daze, longing for someone with whom to share her good fortune. Mrs McEvoy must be taking her in to replace her lost daughter. What other reason could there be? she asked herself when, after lying awake for hours seeing again the fabulous house, she fell asleep.

On Angel's next visit, the pleasant, softly spoken maid told her Mrs McEvoy was waiting for her upstairs. 'In the room that's to be yours, Miss. You're to go on up and I'll not be a minute after you with the tea.'

'Come in, dear. Do sit down. We have so much to talk about that I thought this was the best place. Comfortable, soothing, a lovely bedroom has that effect. Sit down, facing me, by the fire . . .' Angel sat and looked again at the sumptuous room, imagined herself in that bed propped on those pillows, gazed at the silver-backed brushes on the dressing-table.

After the maid had brought the tea Mrs McEvoy said, 'I'm sure there's a hundred and one things you want to know. Don't be bashful, do ask.'

'Mostly I'm wondering why? Why me? And how could I afford such a room?'

'Because you're so beautiful. Because I took a liking to you. And because you'll be doing me an enormous favour if you accept my offer. Now you must listen while I explain.'

Angel nodded.

'You might say my house is like a hotel. A very high-class hotel. There are five other bedrooms, all occupied. The girls usually rest in the afternoons. Yours, of course, is the best, the most expensive. The girls have friends, special gentlemen friends, who hire the rooms for them – as Lord Brightwell will for you, if you come to live here. Some of the girls have been here for several years. We are like a very happy family.'

'What do the girls do?'

'They entertain the gentlemen. Dance with them at the soirées or when we have a ball. They sing, play the harp or piano. They are all talented. Many of them marry their gentlemen friends. The men make gifts to the girls of jewellery, money, clothes. It's all very straightforward, really.'

Angel's mind was addled. Hotel rooms, money, jewellery, marriages, and Lord Brightwell renting a room for her. But why? She didn't sing, play an instrument, wasn't even much of a dancer.

'I don't really understand. I don't understand any of it. Haven't the gentlemen got homes to go to? Will I see much of the other girls?'

'Of course they have. Lord Brightwell has four. He's Anglo-Irish so he has a townhouse in Dublin, an estate in West Meath – an enormous place with thousands of acres – a London house and another estate in Shropshire. Then, of course, there's his club in Kildare Street. As for the girls, I doubt you'll see much of them. As I told you, they rest in the afternoon, or they entertain their guests or go shopping. In any case, they aren't talkative types. Some come from very good families, families who, like yours, may not know their whereabouts. They are all beautiful, but none as beautiful as you. Many will marry well. We've had a few marry into the upper classes so it pays them to be discreet. They'll all do well, one way or the other. If a man they'd hope to marry from choice or pressure from his parents reneges on them they usually make provision for them. He sets them up in business, that sort of thing, because sadly, like all of us, they will grow older and lose their looks. Now to come back to your first question as to where the gentlemen sleep. The officers go back to barracks, the men to their clubs or townhouses. Those who stay the night usually use the dressing rooms. Come, I'll show you.'

Angel followed her to one of the two closed doors in the bedroom. Mrs McEvoy opened it and stood back. By comparison with the bedroom it was minute, but spacious and well furnished by Angel's standards. She felt her first qualms of fear. Had Bridie been right? Had she landed up in a brothel?

Noticing that her colour had changed, Mrs McEvoy closed the door and led her back to the fire. She poured a small measure of brandy from a decanter and said, 'Drink that, it'll steady your nerves.'

The taste was horrible, but after a few seconds Angel felt less frightened, better able to ask her question. 'Lord Brightwell, who is he? And why would he rent this room for me?'

'He's a friend of mine from years ago. He has four sons. Patrick is the youngest, a junior subaltern stationed in Dublin. His father's worried about him.'

'What ails him?'

'Nothing, probably. Immaturity, crippling shyness. But, of course, fathers want sons to prove their manliness. You know, they're always terrified that they've produced an Oscar Wilde character. You've heard of Oscar Wilde?'

'A bit. I didn't understand what it was all about. I don't think I was born when he died. Maybe I saw him in the waxworks. Maybe my mother mentioned him. What did he do?'

'He was a lovely, gentle creature, married with children. But he had a flaw in his nature. He was in love with another young man, which is considered to be a sin against God and man. It's my belief that men like Oscar cannot help themselves. It's in their nature.'

'But what happened to him?'

'He was brought to trial, disgraced and imprisoned.'

'Just for loving a man?' Angel asked.

'Ah, my dear, you are so innocent. You are thinking along the lines of your love for Bridie. Oscar, and many men like him, take their loving of a man a step further. They have a physical relationship with these men, a relationship such as a man and woman would have.'

'But how could that be? It isn't possible,' Angel said, as the colour drained from her face.

'It is, but there's no need for me to go into details. All you need know is that the stigma carries not only disgrace for the man and his family but the unfortunate man can be gaoled, cashiered from the Army, ruined.'

Still not fully understanding what Mrs McEvoy was telling her or how it concerned her, Angel asked, 'But what has any of this to do with me?'

'It's just an idea of Lord Brightwell. He doesn't want to admit that Patrick may not be as most other men. It's possible that Patrick's first encounter with a woman may have been disastrous. Perhaps she was greedy, insensitive, wanting the job over quickly. That could be enough to turn a young man of Patrick's gentle, reticent nature away from women. My girls are not like that. They'd look after him. No scorn, no humiliation.'

Angel had difficulty in believing what she was hearing. Mrs McEvoy was admitting that her girls were prostitutes. She began to sweat profusely. The tea turned to acid in her stomach and came up her gullet in a scalding rush. She began to retch. Scenes from the night with Johnny Quinn appeared before her eyes.

'Take deep breaths,' Mrs McEvoy advised, coming to her side holding a bottle of sal-volatile under her nostrils. Angel pushed away the bottle, stood up and made her way to the door. She was sobbing. 'You tricked me into coming. You want me as a prostitute. Bridie said you did and I wouldn't believe her. Oh, God, if you only knew what you've done. I was getting over it. It was hard but I was. Only once in my life did a man ever touch me. He raped me, nearly killed me. What helped me recover was the thought that never again in all my life would I let a man touch me. And you brought me here.'

She was on the verge of hysteria. Everything was closing in on her. Her clothes felt too tight, her stays were like a band of steel around her waist. She began to tear at the constraining clothes. Then she blacked out.

Mrs McEvoy rang for the maid. 'She's taken a fit or a weakness. Help me lift her legs on to the bed and get her undressed.' They stripped her down to her chemise and manoeuvred her under the covers, by which time Angel had come round and stared, out of terror-filled eyes, at Mrs McEvoy, who was bathing her head with cologne. Tea was brought and the maid dismissed. Angel waved away the cup and began crying again, quietly, heartbrokenly.

'I'm so sorry, child. I was clumsy in how I related my

idea of what happened to Patrick. It was never my intention to turn you into a common prostitute. You're like a daughter to me. I had much higher hopes for you – you must believe that. But first you must sleep. That's the great cure-all. Later, when you waken, we'll talk. There's a lot you have to tell me. The first time I spoke to you I guessed something terrible had befallen you. I promise you, no harm will come to you in my home. Now, close your eyes and sleep for a while. I'll stay with you.'

When Angel woke she didn't know at first where she was. Only one small lamp burned in the room, but gradually, as her eyes became accustomed to the shaded light, she recognised her surroundings and panicked, believing that she was being held prisoner, fearing that at any moment a man would come into the room and pounce on her.

Then Mrs McEvoy was bending over her, speaking soothingly, 'You slept for hours. I have been with you all the time. You were very restless, tossing and turning, talking in your sleep.' She placed a cool hand on Angel's forehead and asked if she was thirsty. Angel said she was and sipped water from the cut-glass tumbler that Mrs McEvoy held to her lips.

'I'm so sorry I alarmed you. You must believe that you are as safe here as my own daughter.' She turned up the dimmed lamp. 'I'll run a bath for you, bring you a robe and nightdress. Perhaps later you may fancy a light supper. But first I'd advise a cup of my herbal tea. It has a calming effect on the nerves. And I think you should tell me more about your dreadful experience. That's the reason you left home. The reason you've never been back.'

Angel shook her head and said, 'No. First of all you must tell me what you expect of me and Lord Brightwell's son.' She amazed herself that she could put such a question, that by asking it she was making an admission that she was considering the proposition instead of running like a wild thing out of the house. But common sense, or desperation, was forcing her into the situation. Where could she run to? Back to the tenement room which she would have to leave in a few days? And what then? She'd be destitute. She'd finish up on the streets or throw herself into the Liffey. Yet with Mrs McEvoy as her friend, it was possible she might find respectable employment.

'It depends on whether you and he take a liking to each other. He's a charming young man, nothing brash or swaggering about him. Good-looking. You could become friends, sweethearts, even.'

'Sleep with him, you mean?'

'I was thinking of marriage.'

'Marriage to me? The son of a lord?'

'It has been known.'

A memory surfaced in Angel's mind. Aggie's 'wiles and ways'. Aggie's belief that if you had them you could marry anyone. Mona had accused Angel of having them – not in so many words, but she had said that she set out to allure men. And much success I had when I thought I had charmed one. He raped and nearly killed me.

'I've known of many such marriages, especially where a son is the youngest in the family, the girl like you is exceptionally beautiful, and the succession is ensured. Lord Brightwell has three sons married with a stableful of boys between them.'

'And if we didn't marry, were sweethearts, would he expect me to sleep with him?'

'He is an honourable young man. He would never force you against your will, no more than his father did me.'

'You were Lord Brightwell's sweetheart?'

'For many, many years. Alice is his daughter.'

'Then why didn't he marry you? You're still a pretty woman, you must have been beautiful.'

'I suppose I was, but he was the eldest son, the title would come to him, and a suitable match had already been arranged.'

'But you went on seeing him after he was married?'

'Yes, for many years we were lovers. I believe his wife, once she had given him sons, had a similar arrangement.'

'But that's a sin.'

'I know, but I loved him very much and it was beyond our control. Now we are old, passion gone, but we remain good friends. I suppose he trusts me more than any other woman in the world. That's why he has entrusted me to find out about Patrick.'

'I still don't understand my part in it,' confessed Angel.

'It's very simple, really. I'll introduce you to Patrick. You'll converse. He's bound to be smitten, if he's a normal young man. You'll dance together, dine together. And if he's normal he'll begin to desire you.'

Angel raised her hands in alarm. 'Oh, no. Never. You've no idea what that was like. I'd rather scrub steps for the rest of my life than have a man near me.' She began to cry.

'I think you'd better tell me the whole story. Have you told anyone else?'

'Only Bridie.'

'Not your mother?'

'It would have been the cause of killing her.'

'That I can well believe. Now, you must tell me everything.'

Angel did, stopping now and then in an attempt to control her crying. She described her terror, the fear for her life, her injuries. Her pregnancy. Her refusal to name the father. Her decision not to go to the nuns. Her abortion. The belief, only recently beginning to leave her, that what had taken place was her fault. 'I'm sorry I can't help you and Lord Brightwell. If you let me stay the night I'll leave in the morning.'

'You poor, sweet child. How you've suffered! Men who do such things should be whipped through the streets then publicly executed. But it's behind you now. You've made a good recovery. The damage that's left is in your mind, in that you're still blaming yourself. You have to be strong, convince yourself that in no way were you to blame. Start by having courage in yourself and faith in what I have told you about Patrick. He would never lay a finger on you without you being willing. After spending time in his company, I promise that you will begin to feel a great affection for him and he for you. When two people feel like that about each other, everything else follows naturally. At least meet him. Tomorrow evening come to the soirée. He's expecting to see you there. Will you do that for me?' Mrs McEvoy wheedled. 'Later you'll have supper in your room to give you a chance to be alone. If you should get frightened ring the bell. Or tell Patrick – he's a gentleman and would leave you immediately. I give you my word of

344

honour. Please, as a great favour for me and his poor, worried father.'

It seemed to Angel that to refuse one meeting would be ungrateful, after all Mrs McEvoy had done for her and she agreed, though many doubts and fears still lingered in her mind. 'Tomorrow I'll take you to Brown Thomas. You need some more clothes,' Mrs McEvoy said.

In the lovely shop, handling silks and satins, trying on frocks and wraps, Angel temporarily forgot her worries and entered whole heartedly into the moment. But once back in the apartment where Mrs McEvoy insisted on helping her to unpack, they returned tenfold as Angel received her first instructions about how not to become pregnant.

'There's something I have to advise you about, dear. It's very personal, but don't be embarrassed or frightened. After all, you and Patrick may not fall in love. Though I doubt that. But this is something every young woman should know anyway.'

Angel had no idea what it was she should know. She only hoped Mrs McEvoy wouldn't call her dear again. She was used to pet, love, dote, and a few Gaelic terms of endearment, and liked being so-called, but the word 'dear' she hated.

Mrs McEvoy carefully hung a pale blue satin dress on a well-padded hanger and asked, 'Do you know how to avoid getting pregnant?'

Angel shook her head and her worst fears were confirmed. This was a brothel. And this Patrick would do what Johnny Quinn had done to her. Cold shivers ran up her spine and at the same time, she was overcome by a wave of heat. She left the unpacking, sat down and drank some water.

'Now, dear, pull yourself together and listen. You know from bitter experience how women get pregnant. Now I'll tell you how, nine times out of ten, you can avoid it. The men who come here are very responsible and want to protect their partners from unwanted children while at the same time protecting themselves from any infections. Not,' she added quickly, 'that any of my girls have the bad disease. They have regular medical examinations. I'll arrange for you to be looked over too. But to come back to what I was saying, the men use French letters, known also as condoms.'

'What are they? I've never heard of such things.'

'But surely the men in your village must use them.'

'If they do it's not something I'd have known about,' retorted Angel, her fear being replaced by anger, which lent her a little courage.

'I do forget that married women don't talk about such things to those who aren't married. Ireland's so backward. And, of course, judging by the arrival of babies with barely ten months between them, the men probably don't use them.'

'I don't see what any of this has to do with me.'

'You will, if you and Patrick fall in love and in that rapturous heat of the moment you yield to temptation. You may shake your head all you like but these things do happen. And a girl mustn't rely entirely on a man to take care of these matters. She has to look after herself. I do wish you'd stop looking so terrified. No one, absolutely no one, will touch you without your consent, Angel. Don't you believe me?'

Angel didn't know what to believe. She felt sick to the

pit of her stomach. She wished Mrs McEvoy would stop smiling. It was a horrible insincere smile. She no longer looked like an older woman who had once been pretty. Now Angel saw her as evil.

'I won't be a moment,' said Mrs McEvoy, still smiling her hyena's smile. 'There's something I have to fetch, something for you.' She returned soon afterwards, carrying a small white box on the lid of which was painted a red cross. 'Your first-aid kit. And now I must fly, I'm late for an appointment. Have a look at the different items, and when I come back I'll explain what they are and how you use them.'

Patrick was already in the salon when Angel came down. Mrs McEvoy introduced them and Angel immediately warmed to him. He was charming, there was nothing brash about him and his eyes twinkled like those of a mischievous little boy. Several other couples were there, of various ages. All the women had partners but many of the men, who were, on the whole, elderly, were unaccompanied but appeared contented to sip drinks, watch the dancing and play cards.

As he waltzed her round the floor Patrick said, 'All past it, but it's a great place to come. They can drink all night, if they want to. My father's relegated to that lot now. Angel ... What a glorious name and how it becomes you. But Mrs Mac's warned me it's special and only to be used by those close to you.'

'Her idea, not mine,' replied Angel. 'She has been introducing me as Katherine, my real name.'

'She's a wily old bird, our Mrs Mac.'

'She's been very kind to me,' Angel replied, defensively.

347

'You can be sure she'll be well rewarded. She's a great businesswoman. Let's sit down. I'm thirsty.'

He ordered champagne. She had never tasted it before and wasn't sure if she liked it, but nevertheless finished the glass. He finished the bottle, and qualms of fear gathered round her heart. He ordered a second bottle and lemonade for her. 'Never eat or drink what you don't enjoy. What about supper? I'm ravenous. My God, you are gorgeous.'

His fingers stroked her bare arm and the qualms multiplied. Mrs McEvoy had promised that Patrick wouldn't lay a finger on her without her permission. Already his fingers were sliding up and down her arm. And he was persuading her to go upstairs. On quaking legs she rose and they began to climb the stairs – but not before she had decided that if he attempted any liberties she would scream, put one of the fire irons through the sash window and cause such a commotion that Mrs McEvoy would be glad to have her removed from the premises.

She needn't have worried. As soon as they entered the bedroom he made his way to the bed, collapsed on it and fell asleep. A maid brought supper, a cold selection of chicken, goose and salads, with a dessert of raspberries and cream.

Angel was afraid to get undressed and sat as far from the bed as possible. Shortly after midnight Patrick woke. 'Why aren't you in bed?' he asked. He looked at his watch. 'God!' he exclaimed. 'I've got to dash. I should have changed the guard at midnight. Just as well I'm not in mufti. I'll tell a fib about trouble on the street.' He got up, came to her and dropped a kiss on the top of her head. 'See you tomorrow, my darling Angel. My saviour.' And he was gone.

She woke the next morning in her silken bed and stretched sinuously, feeling as happy and secure as when she had shared a bed with her mother. She sat up, looked round the room and again marvelled at its opulence. Then her eye fell upon the untouched supper tray. She remembered the previous night, Patrick sleeping off his champagne, waking with a start, making a dash back to barracks, and doubts assailed her. Supposing, she asked herself, had he not fallen asleep, had not to hurry away, what then would have been the outcome of the night? She had Mrs McEvoy's word that, without her permission, Patrick would never lay a finger on her. Had that been the truth? Tonight he was visiting her again. 'Oh, God,' she prayed aloud, 'let it be the truth. Don't let him attack me. He's enormous. Against him I could no more defend myself than I could against Johnny Quinn. Please, dear Jesus, don't let me suffer such an ordeal again.'

She attempted to get up, and suddenly the well-being she had felt on waking deserted her: her legs shook and her heart beat faster than normal – so fast she heard its sound in her ears, felt it pulsing in her throat, and clammy sweat was on her face and hands. Supporting herself with her hands on the edge of the high bed, her feet were inching towards the floor when, after a knock, Mrs McEvoy came into the room, hurried over and embraced her. 'You clever, clever girl, Patrick left here like a victorious king. What did you do to him? No, no, don't tell me. His appearance told it all and, in any case, what lovers do is secret and sacred. He's coming in again this evening.'

Her eyes moved round the room. 'Ah,' she said, spying the untouched tray, 'not even time to eat your supper. But you look so tired. Back into bed with you, my beauty.'

'We were too excited, then too tired to eat,' Angel said.

Mrs McEvoy arranged the silken pillows behind her back. 'In two shakes of a lamb's tail you shall have the most delicious breakfast sent up. Then, later on, we'll go into town. You need more lingerie. Lingerie fit for a princess. You can borrow some of my jewellery, for the time being. Simple pieces are becoming on one so young. Patrick will soon be buying you more elaborate items.'

Still feeling anxious and overwhelmed by Mrs Mc-Evoy's effusiveness, Angel said nothing.

When Patrick arrived that evening he came straight to Angel's room. 'I don't feel like dancing tonight. How about you? You look a bit – I don't know – not on top of your form. Last night, you resembled a scared rabbit. Is it me? Are you frightened that I'm going to roger you, is that it, eh?'

Angel looked uncomprehendingly at him.

'I don't suppose you've ever heard the word before,' Patrick said, grinning at her. 'Shag's the usual one in Dublin, the politest anyway. Rogering's another, especially among my lot. It's what I'm supposed to do to you. Or, rather, what Papa and Mrs Mac hope you'll help me to do.' He laughed heartily. 'Well, let me tell you a secret. Sit beside me on the bed, stretch out – let's make ourselves comfortable. Eh, but wait a minute.' He got off the bed, went to the door and locked it. Returning, he said, 'We don't want any polite knocks followed by entry from our host.'

Angel lay like a corpse, a statue beside him. 'Turn round,' he said, and gently moved her to face him. 'My God,' he said, unpinning her hair, 'you are so beautiful.' He stroked it and then her face, lifted one of her hands and kissed it. 'Now, listen,' he said, 'you've been imprisoned here like a decoy duck. I don't suppose you know what that means either. You are a naïve little thing. So simple language, OK? My father thinks I may have homosexual tendencies. He's scared stiff. A dreadful disgrace for the family, never mind the possibility of being imprisoned if found out. My brothers were introduced to the ways of the flesh at sixteen, or thereabouts, here, with Mrs Mac's girls. Then I was brought for my initiation rights and failed the test. No bloody wonder. The woman was a vicious slut. Even if I'd been interested she soon put me off. You see, the thing is, my sweet girl, I *am* a homosexual. Hush,' he said, and put his hand gently over Angel's lips to stop her gasp. 'I love women, revere them, but never have and never will desire them. So you've nothing to fear. You and I could sleep in the same bed and you'd be as safe as if it was your mother beside you.'

'As true as God?' Angel asked, when he took his hand from her mouth.

'As true as God,' Patrick repeated.

'I don't really understand what it means.'

'Of course you don't, my sweet, innocent darling. Nor do you need to. It's enough for you to know that I will never want carnal knowledge of you. I'll kiss and cuddle

351

you, tickle you, wine and dine you with adoration and affection, and you'll keep *my* secret – for my father's sake, more than mine. I love him. But not only for his sake. The Army doesn't look too kindly on its deviant members.'

The weeks slipped by. Patrick took Angel to the races, polo matches, the theatre, to dine and dance at other establishments. He bought her valuable presents and others that cost pennies – a tin monkey playing a drum, a woolly lamb, peacock and ostrich feathers, paper fans and an ivory one carved with exquisite filigree. And they tumbled about the bed like two puppies, laughing and giggling, sometimes falling asleep with arms thrown across each other. Angel, feeling more secure than she had since she was a little girl, slept long, dreamless sleeps, and grew ever more beautiful.

As Mrs McEvoy had warned Angel seldom saw much of the other girls. She was curious about them, and one afternoon got into talk with a chambermaid who hadn't come to her room before. The girl was friendly and willing to chat but kept a wary eye on the door. 'I'm only working up here today because Hetty, the regular one, is sick. I'm in the kitchen most of the time.'

Angel took the opportunity to quiz her about the other girls and how she came to be in the house.

'I used to work in the one further down the street. My mother and father died when I was only twelve and left me destitute. Oul Mac took me in. The men like us young and I was glad of the shelter. About the girls, Bella's the one with the fair hair. She looks a bit like you but not as gorgeous. Before you came she was considered the greatest beauty. That oul fella she does be with is a lord, a widower. She's waiting to marry him. She's been waiting a long time now. I think he's stringing her along. And the price of her – she's a stuck-up cow, never raises her eyes to look at me. And I wouldn't mind, only I remember her when she worked down the street in the other houses. Sailors, dockers, anyone then she took.'

'How d'ye know all this?' Angel asked.

'Wasn't I one of them myself? I just told you. But it was brutal. Dirty, drunken fellas. I couldn't take to it. I didn't know what to do. Mrs Mac had all these fellas working for her. No good complaining to them. Sure they were hand in glove with the bowsies. Didn't care if they murdered, never mind raped, you.'

'So how did you get out of it?'

'Only because one night I *was* nearly murdered. I was raped back and front, pouring blood, and oul Mac got the wind up, afraid I'd die on the premises. She had to get the doctor, didn't she? A bloody quack, but he was petrified and said I should go into the Rotunda, that I needed surgery. I'd have told them in there the truth. Mrs Mac could have been charged. But she managed to get round him and he cobbled me up. I couldn't walk for weeks and now I've got trouble passing anything. I think she'd have thrown me out only it was when she was trying to land Lord Brightwell. Well, she had landed him but the transaction about this house was going through. I don't know for sure but I don't think she wanted to risk me being away from here and talking. Anyhow, she let me stay on as a chambermaid and I moved here with her. She watches me like a hawk. I wouldn't put it past

353

her to have me done in some night when I'm away from the house. Don't ever let on I told you any of this.'

'Oh, I wouldn't, as true as God.'

The girl was preparing to leave. 'Don't go for a minute. You never told me your name nor what the other girls are called,' Angel said.

'I'm Teesha, there's Bella, the French one's Nicole, and Lottie. She's the best of the bunch. You'll like Lottie. When I'm passing, if there's no one about, I'll drop in again.'

Chapter Twenty

Patrick and Angel's halcyon days continued. When they danced together in the evenings all eyes in the salon were on them, the other women's envious and the men's admiring, lust-filled or adoring. Later in the bedroom they rolled on the bed, hysterical with laughter.

'If they only knew the truth,' Patrick would say, when they had calmed down.

'You don't think anyone suspects it?' Angel asked him once.

'The only one who might is Mrs Mac. That woman knows more about men than anyone on earth. She's a fly old bird. But I don't believe so. And she's not likely to blow the gaff.'

'But wouldn't that be deceiving your father, taking money under false pretences?'

'Yes, if she was absolutely sure and an honourable person. But you don't think she's about to lose the rent for this room, and the board and all the extras she'll be charging him? It's more than the best suite in the Shelbourne. He bought her this house.'

'Your father did?'

'Oh, yes. It was her pay-off, you could say, though he did love her.'

They were dining in their room, and while they sat in bed gorging themselves on delicious titbits he told her the story of his father and Mrs McEvoy.

'She was one of the girls in a bigger house – the girls who serviced the toffs of whom my father was the king pin, heir to a title and a vast fortune. There's no doubt she was very beautiful, but whether she loved him or not is another story. More likely she had her eye to the main chance. And it did sometimes happen that prostitutes and chorus girls married into the aristocracy, if they were sufficiently attractive. But my father had a great sense of duty and a marriage to a suitable girl was already being arranged. So marrying her was out of the question. I suppose you know about Alice, my half-sister?'

'Yes, I do, Mrs McEvoy told me. She went to Paris and never came back.'

'I suppose,' Patrick continued, 'it was the least he could do, in the circumstances. He loved her and couldn't relish the thought that once he was married she'd become one of the girls again. So he set her up in business.'

'Then that's very mean of her, isn't it, charging him money for a house he gave her?' said Angel.

'No, I don't think so. He did it so she could make money and her rooms are always sought after. Think how much she'd be losing if he didn't pay up.'

'How long,' asked Angel, 'can we go on like this? You know, fooling them.'

'Fooling them? What do you mean?'

'Pretending everything is normal.'

'Are you objecting? Feeling guilty?'

'Neither. I could live the rest of my life like this. I've never been so happy, felt so secure.' She ran her fingers through his bright golden curls and kissed his cheek. 'You're so handsome. Sometimes I feel like biting lumps out of you.'

'Ah, my darling girl.' Patrick sighed. 'If only, but what's the use of wishing? I am as I am, and that's all there is to it.'

'How long have you known?'

'Always – well, since I was about eleven. Nothing startling happened then, it was just a knowledge inside me.'

'Did it frighten you?'

'Not then. At that age it didn't matter. But when I understood that it could make me an outcast, that it was considered a criminal offence, yes, it did then. I didn't want to bring shame on my family. I suppose I was angry more than anything at the injustice of it.'

'Are there many men like you?'

'Thousands and thousands, all over the world, in all walks of life.'

'And what will become of us?'

Patrick stretched, got up from the bed and paced about the room. 'I've been thinking about just that. There are several options. We could get married. My parents wouldn't object – not my father anyway. After a while you'd be referred to as barren. We could lead a double life, as some do, both take lovers.'

'But that would be a terrible thing.'

'It would. I think for that to work it takes a woman who is immoral, and that you're not. And I don't intend staying here or in England. As soon as things settle down in Ireland I'll leave the Army and go abroad, somewhere more civilised than England. I have friends in France. I dabble a bit in painting.'

'My poor love,' Angel said. 'Let's go out for a walk, a bit of fresh air. I don't want to talk about your leaving.'

'That's not such a good idea. Rumour in the mess has it that the IRA are planning something big. They've recently suffered heavy losses. I believe talks are going on behind the scenes for a truce. This gesture may be the big bang before the whimper. And anyway I have a lot more to say to you.'

'Will I order dinner up here? I don't feel like dressing for the salon.'

'Do,' said Patrick. 'I'll have a quick bath, then we'll get into our dressing-gowns and relax.'

During dinner he told her of the plan he had in mind. 'How would you like to get engaged?' he asked.

'Engaged, but why?' asked Angel, as she sucked a chicken bone.

'Firstly, because I want to buy you a valuable present, and secondly, because it's a convincing strategy. Then, when this charade we're playing ends, I want you out of this house, far away from Mrs McEvoy. You can sell the ring, buy a flat, set yourself up in business, whatever, but you must get out of this place. She can choose to call it what she likes but in fact it's a high-class whorehouse. And she has no scruples. She'd sell you like that,' he snapped his fingers, 'to the highest bidder and that would break my heart.'

'Oh, Patrick, you're talking as if you were planning on leaving at any minute.' Angel began to cry. 'I thought we'd be together for a long while.'

'And I hope we will, but who's to say how this trouble with the IRA will turn out? Don't forget I'm a soldier and have to go where I'm told.' He took hold of both her hands, raised them to his lips and kissed them. She looked at his handsome face, into his mischievous eyes, their expression grave for once, and wished he was an ordinary man and that they were in love, that they could marry, have children, and she imagined what beautiful children he would give her. How their sons would be tall and strong like him yet kind and gentle, and if all that was said about her was true, she'd have girls, too, who resembled her, beautiful girls.

'There is another promise you must make me, Angel. A very important one. I know you seldom meet other men, for we aren't often separated. But that could change. If there is a crisis I may not be able to see you so often. You go to town shopping, to cafés, to drink coffee, you may attend the soirées. You could meet another man, one who would be smitten by your beauty, have serious intentions towards you, honourable ones. You and he could fall in love. You must promise that you wouldn't let our arrangement stand in your way. We would put it around that we'd fallen out of love and called off our engagement. Will you promise me that?'

'But I won't, I don't want to fall in love. I only love you. I never want to love anyone else.'

'You don't know what it's like to fall in love. We love each other like a brother and sister. Falling in love is different. It won't spoil what we feel for each other. So promise me.'

And as he held her close in his arms, patting her back as her mother used to do, she promised.

The Customs House, probably Dublin's most beautiful Georgian building, was burned down by the IRA in the latter end of May 1920. It was the centre of British administration in Ireland and during the raid petrol was poured over documents deliberately spilled out of filing cabinets, destroying not only papers concerned with British administration but thousands of birth, death and marriage certificates of ordinary Irish people. Badly informed supporters of the IRA greeted the destruction as a great victory for the rebel forces, but the more astute, whatever their leanings, saw it as a desperate move.

Michael Collins was doing badly in Dublin, short of men and ammunition, though in rural Ireland he still had great support. But the attack on the Customs House ended disastrously for the IRA. They were quickly surrounded, several of their members shot dead and more than a hundred surrendered.

The truce that had been rumoured for so many months came into effect on 11 July 1921. Once again the people of Dublin could walk their streets without fear of being shot. Talks began between the two sides that at the end of the year would result in a treaty being signed.

Walking in the summer sunshine in the grounds of Grange Gorman Aggie tripped on a carelessly discarded mineral-water bottle, fell and broke her hip. She developed pneumonia and died peacefully in her sleep. With parish funds and a donation from Danny, she was saved from a pauper's funeral. Danny also put notice of her death in the evening papers, hoping that though it might not flush Angel out, she would know at least that her mother was dead.

Angel seldom read newspapers and never the death notices. At present, she had thoughts of nothing but her magnificent diamond solitaire engagement ring. She spent hours admiring it, fascinated by its gleaming blue flashing lights. Mrs McEvoy congratulated her gushingly. Teesha, on a secret visit, was mesmerised by the sight of the magnificent stone. The other girls, whose names she now knew, offered their congratulations. The only regret she had was that only once had she heard from Bridie, from an address in Formby, Liverpool, to which she wrote again and again without ever receiving a reply.

Patrick and Angel decided to gloss over her parents when she met his father. He knew her origins were humble. What he didn't know was that she wouldn't take him to the village. She still couldn't face her mother. 'I'll say she was sick, dose of pneumonia, and give him the impression I've met her. And your father, will we tell the truth about him?'

'No, let on he's dead. He might be, for all I care. We'll say he died in an accident.'

Lord Brightwell arranged a small dinner party to celebrate the engagement. Angel was nervous about meeting him, but immediately warmed to him. He was a tall, elegant man, who looked as she imagined Patrick would when he was older.

'At last,' he said, when he was introduced to her in Mrs McEvoy's sitting room. 'The great beauty of whom Patrick has told me so much. Young men tend to exaggerate when describing the women they love, but if anything Patrick hasn't done full justice to you, my dear.' He embraced her and kissed her cheek. 'I'm delighted to welcome you into the family.'

When he sat down Mrs McEvoy hovered round him, plumping a cushion to place behind his back and dropping a kiss on his head. When he spoke to her he called her Queenie. 'I try so hard to stop him using that ridiculous name.' She simpered.

'But you are my little queen.' He took one of her hands, turned it over, kissed its palm and closed it. Patrick looked away, and Angel thought of Lady Brightwell and the illegitimate Alice who had run away to Paris. At the same time she tried to think of something to say, for so far she hadn't uttered a word. Lord Brightwell came to her rescue. 'Angel,' he said, 'I've booked a table at the Russell. Do you know it?'

'Only to see and admire. I've been dying to go inside.'

'So why haven't you taken her, Patrick?'

'Too busy, Papa. Food's not top of our list.'

'Well, tonight you'll see for yourself. It knocks the Shelbourne into a cocked hat. And now isn't it time we had a toast?'

Patrick opened the champagne that had been waiting in its silver ice-bucket. Glasses were filled and Lord Brightwell proposed the toast to Angel and Patrick. The bubbles went up Angel's nose and she still didn't like the taste. After a few more sips, and a nod from Patrick, she put the glass down.

'I was in two minds as to what sort of a party to throw – perhaps a big shindig in Dublin, at home, but Margaret's attack of arthritis put an end to that. When it's bad she finds walking difficult – a sea journey would have been impossible. And the boys and their families are holidaying in Tuscany so for the time being I've postponed the big affair.'

'I'm very sorry about Lady Brightwell, arthritis is terrible painful. My mother has a friend who suffers from it. But sure we'll all meet again,' said Angel.

'Of course we will. Perhaps we'll have the party in London and announce the engagement in *The Times*. And by then your mother, I hope, will have recovered from her pneumonia. How is she?'

'On the mend, but the doctor says it'll take a while,' replied Angel, and went on to enlarge on the story she had concocted about her mother's illness.

'I'm looking forward to meeting her. Patrick tells me she's a brick. She did a grand job of rearing you.'

'And on her own,' said Angel, and told more lies about a father who had died tragically young. 'I've only vague memories of him. He used to take me fishing.'

'You'll get plenty of fishing in Shropshire.'

Angel laughed aloud for the first time that evening. 'It was only for pinkeens.'

'Tiddlers, Papa.'

'I know what pinkeens are. Don't forget I spent most of my childhood in Ireland. I bet you carried them home in jam-jars.'

Angel laughed again. 'How did you know?'

'Did the same thing myself.' Lord Brightwell looked at his watch. 'Well,' he said, 'I suppose we'd better make a move. I'm feeling quite peckish.'

He had booked a small private dining room on the first floor overlooking the Green. Attentive waiters served delicious simple food and Angel enjoyed the wine. She drank several glasses and was completely relaxed. She described the village, talked at length about her mother and Father Clancy, but didn't monopolise the conversation. Mrs McEvoy, Patrick and Lord Brightwell all had anecdotes to recount. And so the dinner proceeded until the last course was served. Then more champagne was served and a waiter brought in an enormous bouquet of white lilies, which Lord Brightwell presented to Angel.

'They are so beautiful, lilies are my favourite flowers,' she said, staring at them in delight. 'Thank you, thank you so much. How did you guess?'

'What else but lilies for an angel?' And then he handed her an oblong red velvet box and told her to open it. Inside, on a crumpled bed of satin, lay a string of pearls. She gasped. 'Can I take them out?'

'They're for wearing, not looking at. Of course you can. Patrick, fasten them round her neck.'

She blushed with pleasure and shame as she looked at his delighted expression and remembered the lies she had told him, the deception she and Patrick were practising on him.

His face was flushed also, with too much wine and pleasure. He leant towards Angel and kissed her cheek. 'The pearls become you,' he said. 'Your skin has the same glow. They're a private gift from me and Margaret. Nearer the time of the wedding you'll be showered with more jewellery, some to keep and family heirlooms to be passed on to your daughters.' He raised his glass. 'That your girls may be many and as beautiful as their mama.'

Angel wept.

Back in their bedroom Patrick told her that arthritis hadn't been what had kept his mother from the party.

'What was it, then?' asked Angel, who was sitting in front of her mirror, admiring her pearls.

'Having to be in Mrs Mac's company.'

'She could have been left out, surely,' Angel said, turning to face him.

'I suppose so, but there was another reason. Mama isn't exactly ecstatic about our engagement.'

Angel fingered her pearls and laughed. 'We could always send her a letter telling her not to worry, that it's all a cod. Don't look so worried, I'm only joking. Your father is such a gorgeous, kind man, I'd lie until I was blue in the face to have him believe what makes him happy. Tell me more about your ma's objections.'

'She's a snob. Can't help it. Her mother was a Gaiety Girl. A Cockney beauty. Gaiety Girls and actresses often married into our lot, younger sons as a rule. My grandfather was a younger son. Two in front of him for the title, only one was killed in a Zulu war and the other eaten by a lion.'

'Honest to God! A lion ate him?'

'So the story goes. His body was never found and Harry, my grandfather, inherited the title. The Gaiety Girl became her ladyship and lost the run of herself. As the saying goes, "Put a beggar on horseback". And Mama's a chip off the old block. Nothing but top drawer is good enough for her.' Then he laughed heartily. 'I'm so carried away by our charade. Don't worry, darling, she'll come round.'

Sometimes, when alone, Angel thought about the time when Patrick would no longer be with her. She worried about selling the ring, buying a flat, setting up in business or finding a job. How would she cope, living on her own? Not only had she become used to Patrick's almost constant company, but she loved her new lifestyle – her bedroom, all the comfort and luxury. Ring a bell and food was brought, whatever she fancied. Her clothes were laundered to perfection, ribbons rethreaded through camisoles, snagged hems repaired, shoes cleaned. How could she ever go back to looking after herself? But, most of all, she dreaded Patrick's departure. He had become part of her, a mother, sister, brother, an adored friend.

When she voiced these thoughts to Patrick, he reassured her, reminding her of how valuable the ring was and of the reputable jeweller who would buy it back at a fair price. Once she had bought a flat she'd engage a personal maid and a char for the rough work.

Once, during one of these discussions, she said, 'Wouldn't it be easier if we sold the ring and you helped me find a flat before you left?'

But he didn't agree. 'I'll prepare the way. I'll let it be known you no longer love me but that I'm still hoping you'll have a change of heart. Otherwise, it would seem I'm giving up too easily – not putting up a fight for you.' And he would tell her this over and over again, concluding with, 'Darling, you'll be fine. You're a very capable girl.'

'But I'll be lonely,' she would protest.

'For a little while, perhaps, but it'll work out. You're young, beautiful, have a lovely manner and you'll still be in Dublin,' he would say.

And she would agree that he was probably right. And he'd go on, 'In no time you'll meet a man and fall in love. You'll marry, settle down, have gorgeous babies and send me pictures of them – so chin up, no more gloomy thoughts, eh?'

One evening, when Patrick was attending a mess function, there was a knock on Angel's door. She opened it and saw Teesha and one of the girls, Lottie, standing there. Teesha said, 'I knew your man wouldn't be here, so I brought Lottie to meet you.' She introduced them to each other.

Angel invited them in, but Teesha said, 'I've things to do downstairs. I'll see you again.'

Lottie came in, sat down and looked round the room. 'God,' she said, 'you're living in style. All the rooms are lovely but not a patch on this.'

Angel gave her lemonade and biscuits and they began to chat. Angel liked her vivaciousness, how her brown eyes sparkled and dimples appeared and went in her cheeks. 'I was awful sorry to hear you'd thrown Patrick over. Is it definite, like, for keeps, I mean?'

'To tell you the truth I'm not really sure. One minute being married is the last thing I want and the next I'm regretting being so hasty.'

'You must be mad. I think he's the bee's knees and what a catch.'

'He is lovely-looking – maybe I'll change my mind. He's prepared to wait while I think it over. What about you? Is your fella serious?'

Lottie shrugged. 'He says he is, but no talk of a ring or setting a date.'

'Would you marry him?'

'Jump at the chance. Anything to get out of here.'

'D'ye not like it here?' Angel asked.

'While you've got a permanent fella it's all right. He's

your guarantee of an easy life and a protection against Mrs Mac. You're being wined and dined, and he's giving you money and presents.'

'D'ye have to give her a share of the money?' asked Angel.

'No, but it's a different story in the lower-class house. There, you pay for your room, the madam takes a cut of your earnings and the pimp who's supposed to be your protector gets a cut too. You might as well be doing it for nothing. But in a way you're always running a risk. If the bloke paying for your room here reneges, you'd be out on your arse, unless oul Mac found a replacement immediately. Ten days' grace she gives you. You're hoping and praying, prepared to take on an oul fella in his dotage. Anyone to save you going down the street.'

Angel said a silent prayer for the provision Patrick had made for her. Lottie stood up. 'I'd better make a move. That oul cow'd foal an elephant if she knew I was here. But I'll come again when your man's on duty.'

'It was great talking to you. You won't let me down about calling another time?'

'On my word of honour. Have a dekko to make sure the coast is clear.' Angel did, and Lottie hurried away.

Lottie visited again when Patrick was on duty. Her first question was, had Angel decided about her engagement? Angel made excuses that she was still dithering and wished Lottie could be taken into her confidence. 'Better not,' she would tell herself, and questioned Lottie about her affair and about the other girls in the house. 'Apart from Bella, they're not a bad crowd. Of course, Nicole's not really French. Well, she was born there, in a place called Marseilles. Her father was a sailor and her mother Irish, on the game. She brought Nicole back to Dublin and the nuns reared her. She never laid eyes on her mother again and ran away from the orphanage. Mrs Mac picked her up in Grafton Street and brought her here. There's where she got the others, except me.'

'I keep wondering,' said Angel, 'how Bella finished up here after working in the other houses?'

'Mrs Mac was desperate to get started in her new house. And though I don't like Bella you have to give credit where credit's due – she is beautiful. And the gents that come here wouldn't have ever been in the other kips.'

'Why doesn't she like us mixing with each other?'

'Because she gives us flash backgrounds to our gentlemen. According to her, we've all fallen on hard times but our families were highly respectable. None of us was raped or interfered with by our fathers or brothers or had abortions. Though, like myself, we all were one way or another. I'm not including you, of course – after all, I know nothing about you.'

If you only did, thought Angel, but you never will.

'Though I'm not complaining. It's not such a bad life. And I can live in hopes that your man will come up trumps,' Lottie said. 'And if not, pray that I have my health. For once that goes, so do your looks, and if you get the bad disease you're out – finish up in Townsend Street in the Lock Hospital dying in agony. But God's good and it might never happen. And the men are generous. Buying you jewellery and giving you money. Say a prayer my oul fella gets a move on. I have my work cut out with him. He's going soft in the head, never mind in other places where he shouldn't be. Listen, I'd better be going but I'll drop in again.'

One night while talking to Patrick about their future, Angel asked, 'How soon will you be going away?'

'Not until this treaty is signed.'

'What'll happen when it is?' asked Angel.

Patrick shrugged. 'Depends on what's in it. I can't see it operating smoothly but it should mean that we pull out – no more British soldiers in Ireland, that sort of thing. But don't look so downcast. I'll be one of the last to go. Before I do, we'll let it be bandied about that you wouldn't change your mind, and have fallen out of love with me, and that I'm devastated. I'll resign my commission and go abroad, but to ease your position I'll take over paying for this room for a few months – can't expect Papa to continue as you've jilted me. I'll make it clear to Mrs McEvoy you'll be living here as a private individual. There'll be absolutely no pressure on you to take part in anything you might find objectionable. Mrs McEvoy, the greedy old cow, will jump at the chance. In the new set-up after the treaty, there won't be as many men like me and my father about.'

'As you say, it'll ease me into my new life. Oh, Patrick, Patrick, what a wonderful husband you would have made.'

'Maybe not. Ours is a unique relationship. Marriage is different. Now, my little darling, you've nothing to worry about. This time next year you'll be as free as a bird, with your very own nest, well-feathered, new friends, new interests, maybe even a man you've fallen in love with. So no more worrying, eh?'

'No more worrying,' she promised, then laughed.

'Let me in on the joke.'

'It's so funny. The day before we met, Mrs Mac told

me about contraception. It wasn't funny then – I was petrified.'

'Tell me, I can't wait to hear.'

'Well, first of all she put on the twang. Awfully lah-di-dah. "My gentlemen use French letters. For their own protection, of course. But the precaution works both ways. They're protected from the bad disease and the girl from pregnancy. Not that my girls are unhealthy – I have a doctor who looks them over. I'll arrange for him to examine you. But about precautions, I like my girls to take their own. Not difficult or unpleasant to use." Well, between her accent and my nerves I didn't know whether to laugh or cry. I was nearer crying. She offered to demonstrate. Imagine that! Of course I refused. Later on I told her you showed me how to douche and use the sponge. She made an appointment for me to see the doctor but I let on I was having my period.'

Patrick laughed throughout the telling of the tale. 'You've got her voice off to a T and you've become an accomplished liar. You'd make a damn fine actress. Maybe it's the stage you should try for when you leave here.'

The thought of their inevitable separation saddened her, as did the realisation that for the first time in her life she had used the word period to a man. And from that she saw that now she wasn't thinking of him as a man.

Brian Nolan, Danny's old friend, had come through the conflict unscathed and was now a full colonel. He was stationed in Dublin and had again renewed his visits to Monto. Mrs McEvoy had a vacant room, not as expensive as Patrick's and Angel's, and suggested on his first time back that he should rent it. 'Cheaper than a hotel or casual dropping in and out. Always sure of the same girl. Think about it.' She gave him a glass of champagne on the house.

Brian promised he would, then concentrated on looking at the girls, those who appeared unattached. It had always been difficult to choose from so many beauties. But if he was to rent a room and wanted a permanent mistress, he must be extra careful in his choice. He ordered more champagne, and thought about his future. With hostilities about to end, he would look up Danny again. Brian was fond of him, even if he was a rabid Nationalist. But soon, once he had finished in the Army, their different opinions wouldn't matter. He wondered what employment he would seek. Perhaps he would join the Irish Army – they'd be wanting experienced officers. But he knew he mustn't plan too far ahead: the treaty could collapse before it was half-way off the ground. As he looked round the salon, half listening to the piano being played by a stunning-looking girl, he caught sight of another, about to leave the room. She was the most exquisite creature he had ever seen. There and then he made his decision. If he could have her for his mistress he'd take the room. She waved to Mrs McEvoy, smiled ravishingly and left.

Brian beckoned Mrs McEvoy, who came to where he was sitting. 'That girl,' he said. 'The one who just left. She's the one I want. My God, she's gorgeous. I'll rent the room if she comes with it.'

'I'd love to oblige but she's engaged to be married. Pulled off one of the big bugs, Billy Brightwell's youngest son, Patrick. They're crazy about each other.'

'Just my rotten luck. I've never seen anyone like her. And yet I have the craziest feeling I have.'

'Not here you haven't. You haven't been in for years and she's only come lately.'

'I'm definitely sure I saw her somewhere. What's her name?'

'Katherine, with a K – mean anything to you?'

Brian shook his head, 'No, but it'll come to me. Just when I'm not thinking about it, it'll come to me.'

Father Clancy had left the parish and gone down the country to spend his last years in a home for retired priests. He hated it but resigned himself to the knowledge that he was seventy-five, not as agile as he once was and going deaf. His sight was beginning to fail, too, and sometimes his memory.

The funny thing was, though, that he could remember his childhood as clearly as if it was only yesterday.

Father Brennan was now the parish priest. On his good days Father Clancy pitied him, recalling that running a parish was no easy matter. A priest's first duty was the spiritual health of his parishioners, the saving of their souls. You had your work cut out doing that. But there was all else besides. You had to act as referee between the committee members of the various societies, the little empire-builders, the Miss Heffernans and her cronies. They were good women, in their own way, willing to do anything for the church, forgetting that it was more than a building. The church was the people, the poor, the sinners along with the comfortable and righteous. It wasn't for the Miss Heffernans of the parish to be judgemental.

When his mind followed this train of thought, he would remember Angel and Aggie, the suffering they had endured at the hands of the holier-than-thou brigade, and castigate himself for not having had the courage to stand up for them. Had he done so, Angel might still be in the village and poor Aggie wouldn't have died in the madhouse.

He spent many hours praying for his dead parishioners, for Mrs Quinn, Mrs Maguire, Maggie Dignum and her family, who were scattered God alone knew where, except the oldest lad, whose name he couldn't remember although he had christened the poor unfortunate, who turned up now and then in the village. He was a vagrant now, had taken to the drink and wandered the little streets. He prayed for Tommy Maguire, a decent young man. And for the sinners, too – for Johnny Quinn, who had been Angel's ruination. And he prayed for Father Brennan who had inherited his legacy.

Patrick took Angel to the Royal Dublin Horse Show in Ballsbridge, to a seat in the members' enclosure where he introduced her as his fiancée to his many friends. Later in the month he took her to the Galway races. He could have stayed in a dozen or more houses throughout the county but chose the Great Southern Hotel in the centre. She fell in love with the city and thought she might settle in Galway when Patrick was gone. In a city smaller than Dublin, she believed, it would be easier to make friends.

During the week he hired a car and took her to see Connemara. The weather was glorious and Angel was enchanted with the scenery, the hues of blue and mauve, the immense stretches of bog and the white bog cotton growing on them, the Twelve Bens soaring to the sky, the little whitewashed thatched cottages in their minuscule fields, smoke from fragrant turf fires rising from chimneys.

There were other landscapes too bleak for her liking: whole fields strewn with boulders, flat slabs of granite reminding her of a graveyard where all the tombstones had fallen down. From almost anywhere along the coast the Arran Islands were visible, and Patrick promised that if the weather held they would visit them. She thought that perhaps she would buy a cottage in Connemara, keep chickens, a cow, have turf stacked against the gable wall. She'd learn how to speak Irish so that she could converse with her neighbours, learn country skills, breathe in the health-giving air, wash in the soft brown water, even learn to fish. She would be self-sufficient and write long letters to Patrick, put all thoughts of falling in love far from her mind. She would grow old there in her little cottage and be buried in a graveyard they had passed high on a headland where wild flowers grew in profusion.

When she woke the next morning, a gale was lashing the city. The water in the bay boiled, bubbled and battered the quays. Perhaps having guessed what had gone through her mind the following day, Patrick insisted they drive out again into the country. They progressed only slowly as sheets of rain cascaded down the windscreen and the wind found its way into the car and keened like a soul in torment. The weather remained like that for the rest of the week, banishing Angel's ideas of settling either in Galway or Connemara.

Chapter Twenty-One

In December 1921 Eamon de Valera and Arthur Griffiths were the first two delegates to attend the talks in London. Thereafter de Valera absented himself. As the titular head of the Republican government in Ireland, he knew that compromise on the Irish demands would be necessary, and therefore it was up to him, using his political skills, to make it acceptable to his government. The negotiations became the responsibility of Michael Collins and the delegates who went with him to Downing Street.

Collins was under instruction from de Valera on no account to sign the final agreement without consulting him. But under pressure from Lloyd George the treaty was concluded on 6 December 1921. Ireland was granted Dominion status and henceforth would be known as the Irish Free State.

After the signing Michael Collins was reputed to have said, 'I have just signed my own death warrant.' But the majority of the Irish people sighed with relief that their streets would be free from danger for the first time in years.

Among the IRA, though, it was a different story. Half its adherents felt a sense of betrayal: an Irish nation was what they had fought for; a country robbed of six of its northern counties was what they had got. And a demand to sign a declaration of allegiance to King George V.

De Valera came out on the side of the discontented and Irishmen who had served in the war flocked to join the newly formed army of the Free State, their experience and skills welcomed. Michael Collins was commander-in-chief. Brian Nolan, one of the Irishmen to join up, was promoted to major-general and posted to Cork. Patrick was staying on in Dublin to assist with the handover.

By the summer of 1922, civil war had broken out between those who supported the treaty and those who did not. Men who had fought side by side during the Easter Rebellion, who had been imprisoned together, now faced each other in terrible conflict on opposing sides, members of the same families, fathers against sons, brother against brother. Friends who had been best man at each other's weddings, godfathers to their sons, shot and murdered each other. There were summary executions and merciless ambushes, more atrocities than those perpetrated by the Black and Tans.

The government forces were known as Free Staters, and the rebel IRA as Irregulars. Hundreds of the latter were on the run. Some, with a price on their heads, made it out of the country to England and America, but many more found safe-houses in Dublin. Up and down the country at Sunday Mass parish priests exhorted their parishioners in the name of God to lay down their arms. Some threatened excommunication. Among the latter was Father Brennan, who used it as a last resort to bring to an end the appalling bloodshed.

Tommy Maguire was counting the days until he returned to Ireland and had to rely on newspapers and letters sent to his mates for information on what was happening at home. He didn't care who won the civil war, only that it should end before Angel's life might be endangered. He couldn't wait to get back to Dublin to find and protect her. He still hoped he would be her husband. They'd marry and live in the village in his mother's house. He had always meant to let it, but when he considered how he'd go about it, too many complications arose: who'd attend to the business of finding a tenant, of collecting and banking or sending on the rent to him? And supposing, when he came home, the people wouldn't leave it? If he'd had a relation in the village it would have made things easier, but he had no one.

'Bloody awful kip of a country you live in, Pad,' the man who slept in the next bed said to him one evening. 'What you need is a gun. That way you'd stand a chance of defending yourself against that lot of bleeders.'

Tommy thought about it. He could protect Angel if he had a gun. Supposing when they were married and he was working nights a fella on the run came to the door? She could shoot him in self-defence. He'd teach her how. 'I suppose you have a point, but where would I get one?'

'Listen, cock, don't forget I was in the war. I brought home more than myself. I nicked a Luger off a dead Gerry. Never meant to flog it. A keepsake it was, like. But since the so-called bloody mutiny, a wog in the bazaar's been hiding it for me. You can have it for a quid, bullets as well. What d'ye say?'

Tommy was carried away by the idea of Angel being able to protect herself. And a quid was nothing – he'd win that at brag before he sailed for home. He had eighty pounds already, his savings, winnings and the money Angel had sent back to him. They'd be very comfortable. His mother's house was furnished, no outlay there except for a lick of paint and wall-paper, maybe. And he had been collecting presents for Angel over the years. That lovely Kashmiri shawl, all the swirls of colour on it, two gold bracelets to wear on her ankles and lots of other knick-knacks that women liked. 'Right,' he said to his mate. 'I'll buy the gun. A quid – don't you go changing your mind and upping the price.'

'As if I would.'

'I know you bloody well would. Only, if we had a fight over it and it came out what we was fighting over, you'd be in the shit, wouldn't you?'

'No flies on you, Pad. Bloody blackmailer. A quid it is, on my mother's life.'

Patrick and Angel kept up the pretence she was falling out of love with him, but Angel was crestfallen at the prospect of their wonderful relationship ending.

'Oh, my little love, you knew it had to come. But you'll be secure. I'll go off one day after a supposed bitter quarrel. But, as I told you, I'll make arrangements to keep your room on in the hope that we'll be reconciled. We'll eventually break off the engagement. I'll be so devastated I'll resign my commission and go abroad to heal my broken heart.'

'And the ring – what happens to that?'

'You little goose, I've explained all that. You'll put it about that I wouldn't take it back, hard though you tried to persuade me. You'll sell it and get to hell out of here. You put the money in a bank, buy an apartment and set up in business.'

'I'll be terrified. What do I know about business?'

He put his arms round her. 'You're a very brave girl. A survivor. Just think of all you went through before I came on the scene. You'll have no trouble starting a business. Open a luxury lingerie shop – men will flock in to buy presents for their wives and mistresses just to have a look at you. You'll see, I promise you.'

He kissed her forehead, then suggested they went out for a drive.

In August 1922 Michael Collins, returning from a funeral in Cork, was shot dead. Those still loyal to him were devastated and thronged the Dublin streets watching the state funeral, lamenting the death of their hero and saviour. Others who, before the signing of the treaty, had been equally loyal, now vilified him.

The Irregulars' position was weakening. They could no longer continue the war on a large scale. Now they set out to kill individuals, rob banks and blow up buildings. New leaders took over the running of the Free State, with William Cosgrave as prime minister. Kevin O'Higgins had been elected to the Dáil in 1918, and Ernest Blyth and Collins's chief of staff were now in charge of the Free State Army. These men set out to restore peace.

An Emergency Powers Bill was introduced and went through the Dáil. Its draconian measures equalled anything the British had ever introduced. Any armed Irregular who didn't immediately surrender his weapon was shot and seventy-seven executions were carried out in seven months. Four men who had taken part in the capture of the Four Courts earlier in the year, once active supporters of Collins before the treaty, were taken from their cells in the middle of the night and shot without trial. Another, Erskine Childers, was shot at dawn for having in his possession a pistol given to him by Michael Collins when they were still on the same side.

Cold feet or a lovers' tiff was how the teetering of Angel and Patrick's engagement was treated in the house. Some of the girls were sympathetic towards Angel and voiced their opinions. 'You can't blame her. I'm not sure I would want to marry into the aristocracy. She's bound to be resented or made little of.' Others thought she'd be a fool to let go such a catch. 'She's gorgeous and a nice person, she'd charm them in no time and anyone can see he's wild about her.' Mrs McEvoy dismissed it as a young girl's skittishness. The room was booked, the rent paid for a further six months. But in any case Mrs McEvoy had more to worry about now than Patrick and Angel. She knew, as did the other brothel-keepers and girls, that Irregulars on the run were sheltering in the houses. Many were relatives, others had forced their way in at gunpoint. The majority made their escape but the one hiding in her house was likely to stay indefinitely.

One night she woke to find a hand clamped over her mouth and a man's figure bending above her. She thought she was having a nightmare until she heard the voice whisper, 'Aunt Stasia, it's me, Sean, I'm on the run. I'll be shot out of hand if I'm caught. Can I stay for a while?'

Sean, her sister's son. Her godson. A child she had worshipped from the minute he was born in the little cottage in County Clare. She'd held the Tilley lamp so the doctor could see what he was doing and watched Sean born – a big lump of a baby with a pair of lungs like a jackass. He took his hand from over her mouth and spoke. 'I'll only stay the week. I climbed in over the roofs and got into the attics. There's a grand hidey-hole in one of them. No one saw me. If you bring me the bit of food and water every day, no one will be any the wiser.'

She had no choice but to agree, not only because he was her sister's son but because these men on the run were ruthless. He was bound to have a gun. If she informed the police, he'd go out fighting, killing God only knew how many – and maybe her – before he was shot. One way or the other, her business would be ruined. It would soon leak out that they were related. She could be imprisoned, even executed for harbouring him.

Each night, long after everyone else was in bed, she crept up to the attic, bringing food and jugs of tea, cigarettes, a torch, blankets and a pillow. At the end of the first week he had an excuse for not leaving, but promised to be gone by the following one. The weight fell from her and she now looked what she was – a haggard old woman.

An abject Patrick came to see Angel. 'Darling,' he said, 'I'm so sorry, I wanted to give you a lot more notice but I'm leaving. I've put in my papers. My friends have found a lovely place – we're meeting up next month. I won't see you again for a long time. Now, don't cry. You knew it had to happen. Be a brave girl.' He wiped away her tears. 'We'll put it about that I'm going away to give you time to think things over. Then you'll decide to break off the engagement and I, being heartbroken, won't return. You'll sell the ring and start your new life.'

'When are you going?'

'In a few days. You know it has to be.'

'I know, I know, but somehow I always fooled myself it never would come to this.'

'Oh, my little love, you would have grown tired of me, of the charade we live. You're young and beautiful. You deserve a real life, a real man. I'll always remember you, come to see you when I can, be godfather to your children – well, maybe not that. I don't suppose the Catholic church would allow it. We'll spend the next few days having a good time and then you'll be very brave . . . promise.'

'Tell me more about your friends – the ones in France. Are they all French?'

Angel and Patrick were lying on the bed. She had been crying and he dried her tears and kissed the tip of her nose. 'No, three are English and one American. I was at school with Simon. Didn't see him for years then met up after the war in London. He'd been a conscientious objector, drove an ambulance at the front. He's a painter – a really good one. The other three dabble. I'll be a dabbler too. I've been on holidays with them. We're five of a kind. You'll meet them. You'll come and see us.'

'Won't your father get suspicious, with you resigning then going off to France to live with four men?' asked Angel.

'I shouldn't think so. He was totally convinced you and I were in love. And I did always dabble a bit with painting. No, I don't think he will for a minute. I was never an Army wallah, and I'm not the eldest son. Stop worrying. I love you. And you *will* get in touch with me if anything goes wrong?'

'I will, I will. How many more times d'ye want me to promise you that?'

'I do pray. I think there *is* someone up there and I'll remember you in my prayers. I don't know about you but I'm peckish. Let's go out for a bite. How about Jammet's?'

Angel clapped her hands like a little girl. 'Oh, yes, Jammet's. I'm mad about Jammet's.'

Mrs McEvoy was livid when Angel told her the engagement was off, that Patrick was resigning his commission and planning to live abroad. 'He can't do that. He had a posting coming up.'

Angel loathed her: she knew the old woman was angry because she would have had a big pay-off once she and Patrick were married. But secured by the money she would have from her ring, Angel was no longer obligated to her or in awe of her.

'You can have postings cancelled and resignations rushed through if you're the son of Lord Brightwell. You should know all about the influence of men like him.'

She knew by the expression on Mrs McEvoy's face that the woman longed to strike her; her fists were clenched, too, and her face puce. However, she controlled her rage and used her tongue instead. She lapsed into her Mayo brogue: 'The boy's mad about you. Anyone could see that. It's all your doing, you little cow. Is it a bigger catch you're hoping for? Well, I hope it keeps fine for you – and after all I did for you! Took you off the street, you bitch.'

'You wouldn't have cared if I had married him – prostituted myself for money and title. Well, I may be living in your brothel but I'm not one of the girls. I fell out of love with Patrick. I didn't choose to – he's the loveliest man I've ever known. I only wish it could have been different. But you can tell his father he's a normal full-blooded man. And don't you forget these rooms are paid for in advance. Remember and respect that. Patrick has told me that if you suggest anything not above board I should contact his father who, though he may be in love with you, is a gentleman and wouldn't allow such a thing.'

'It's easy to see that you were dragged up,' Mrs McEvoy said, but the wind had gone out of her sails and she left the room.

After Patrick went back to England Angel slept badly. The slightest noise woke her, little noises of which she had taken no notice before, like creaking wood, the rustling of trees when a wind was blowing, the sound of her heart thumping, any scampering in the rafters, which she thought might be rats or mice. Then, one night or early one morning, she distinctly heard someone climbing the stairs stealthily. Up and up they went. She was sure it was a ghost and buried her head under the blankets.

At the same time the following night she listened again, praying for the spirit to find rest. Eventually she heard the same steps returning. A courage she didn't know she had possessed her and she got up, went to the door, opened it and cautiously stepped out onto the landing. She looked over the banisters and saw Mrs McEvoy, in her dressing-gown, descend the last flight of stairs.

No wonder she'd been looking ill recently, Angel

thought, as she got back into bed. It could be something serious, something that made her walk in her sleep. She wished Patrick was here. What fun they'd have trying to guess what took Mrs Mac to the top of the house every night. He'd suggest that maybe his half-sister was being kept a prisoner up there, that she had never run away to Paris, then dismiss that theory because it was only lately that the trips up the stairs had started. And she'd say, 'But we don't know, we've always been asleep before.'

Angel didn't attempt to sleep until after Mrs McEvoy had returned from her visits upstairs. She was consumed by curiosity as to why she went. One night after she'd heard her return and allowed enough time for her to be back in her room, she decided to investigate, taking with her a candle and matches. Quietly she began her climb, up the stairs past the other girls' bedrooms. These passages had a light burning to allow for latecomers, but once she reached the narrow stairs leading to the servants' quarters and the even narrower ones to the attics, she needed the candle, which she stopped to light. There were four attics. She tried each door. The first three opened and she looked inside each one. The candle cast dancing shadows on trunks, picture frames, discarded chairs, jugs, basins, all sorts of things stacked against walls and filling the centre.

The fourth door was locked. Was that the one Mrs Mac visited, she wondered, and turned away. Before she had gone more than a foot, the door was opened and she was grasped roughly by an arm round her throat. The candle fell and went out. A voice whispered, 'Don't make a sound and I won't hurt you.' She was dragged into the room and let go. A candle burned on a tin trunk and the room smelt of cigarette smoke. 'Not a sound,' the man towering over her warned again but Angel was so frightened she knew she wasn't capable of making a sound. She nodded to indicate that she would remain silent. The man drew her further into the room, nearer to the trunk and the lighted candle. 'Who are you?' he asked, speaking very quietly. 'How did you know I was here? Who else knows?'

When she didn't answer, he closed and locked the door. 'You can speak but keep your voice down.'

'I didn't know you were here. I don't think anyone else does, except Mrs McEvoy. I heard her going up and down the stairs. I was just curious.'

'Curiosity killed the cat.' He brought the candle closer to her moving it up to her face. 'My God,' he said, 'you're so beautiful. Are you one of the girls?'

Angel shook her head vigorously. 'No, I am not. I just live here.' She was looking at his face now, at his black curly hair and his eyes. He smiled, and his teeth were lovely. 'You don't know who or what I am. I'm Sean, her nephew. I'm on the run. D'ye know what that means?'

'That you're wanted. That you could be shot if they find you.'

'Right, and if anyone informed on me my friends would shoot them. D'ye understand what I'm telling you?'

'I do.'

'No matter where they went, no matter how far, my friends would find and shoot them.'

'I won't breathe a word.'

'Sit down,' he said, pointing to another trunk. 'Make yourself comfortable. I'm sorry if I frightened you. I'd

386

have shot you except for the noise. So, tell me, if you're not one of her girls what are you?'

'I'm engaged to be married. I've no people of my own and my fiancé rented a room here for me. He's an old friend of Mrs McEvoy's.'

'Begod, he must be worth a few bob to afford her prices. What does he do?'

'He's in business. He imports whiskey from Scotland.' She was amazed at how her brain was working.

'I thought you said you were engaged. Where's your ring?'

'I take it off at night. I've a ring tree and I hang it on a branch.' She was no longer frightened: he fascinated her, his face, his tall, powerful body. She found herself wanting to reach out and touch him.

'I'll let you go back in a minute, if you promise to come and see me again. It gets very lonely. And bring me a paper so I know what's going on out there. Will you do that? And say nothing to anyone, that's the important thing. Let me get your candle and see if the coast is clear. When will you come again?'

'Tomorrow night,' she promised

Before falling asleep, she usually thought about Patrick or sometimes her mother filled her mind, or lovely kind Bridie. Where *was* she? Would Angel ever hear from her again? Wouldn't it be grand to have money to share with her? To tell her about Patrick. Bridie had compassion. She'd understand, pass no judgement on Patrick. And then Angel would cry, tears running down her cheeks for the lonely years ahead. Patrick had been wrong: she would never fall in love again, never marry, never allow a man to touch her.

But after meeting the man in the attic, her thoughts,

to her amazement, centred on him. A dangerous man. A man on the run. A man who wouldn't hesitate to shoot her. A gorgeous man in dirty, creased clothes that looked as if he had slept in them – which he probably had. Dark stubble on his face, black rims under his fingernails. And eyes the colour of the little blue bag her mother put with white clothes she was washing. The loveliest blue in the world. He smelt of tobacco and sweat, and the musty odour of the attic.

Was this what Patrick had meant about falling in love? But she had sworn never to do that, never to let another man touch her. Never, never, never. Not after Johnny Quinn. Yet here she was, recalling everything she could about the man in the attic and longing for the following night when she would again climb the attic stairs. She wanted to touch him, sit close to him, very close to him, run her fingers through his dark curly hair. And she ached to feel his arms around her. In parts of her body she felt sensations she had sometimes experienced long ago when she was in love with Johnny. Lovely, lovely feelings but which she had believed to be sinful. Since the rape she had hated the same parts and avoided touching them, except when she washed. Now she felt an urge to do so, while imagining that Sean's fingers were moving over her flesh.

Sean. Even his name was beautiful. She lay watching daylight come into the room, longing for night to come again, longing to hear Mrs McEvoy's footsteps come down from the attic so that she could go to him.

She had lunch served in her room and wrapped slices of chicken breast, bread roll and an apple in a hand towel to take to him. She asked the maid to bring the evening papers, the *Herald* and the *Mail*, along with her dinner.

Later she had a deep perfumed bath, and afterwards rubbed scented oils over herself. She waited impatiently for night to come and then the small hours when Mrs McEvoy would be back in bed.

She thought of the lies she had told Sean, that Patrick was an importer of whiskey. She must not forget that and guard her tongue from both men. She must never forget that Patrick, kind and wonderful though he was, was a British soldier who wouldn't hesitate to turn Sean in, or that Sean wouldn't hesitate to kill Patrick.

He had made an attempt to tidy the attic, had brushed the cigarette butts out of sight, folded his two grey blankets and placed his pillow on top. His face and hands had been thoroughly washed. When she arrived, he was cleaning his nails with a penknife. He smelt of carbolic soap.

They sat on the trunk while he wolfed down the chicken and bread. She watched his strong white teeth bite into the apple, and saw the juice run down his chin. She trembled. She wanted to lick the juice, wanted to taste his mouth.

'I'll read the papers when you've gone down,' he told her. 'A mug of tea would be grand to wash that down or, better still, a pint of stout. Or maybe a kiss. I haven't kissed a girl for a long time.'

'I'm sure you've kissed plenty in your time,' she said.

'I was a divil for the kissing, all right. Would you let me kiss you?'

'I wouldn't mind,' she replied, 'but only the one. Don't forget I'm an engaged woman.'

His lips were soft and his mouth had a lovely taste.

She closed her eyes while the kiss lasted. It was the first time she had ever been properly kissed and she marvelled at how delightful it was.

They talked a lot that night. He asked more questions about Patrick. Where was he from?

West Meath, she told him. He wanted to know if he was a Catholic, and again she lied telling him he was. For, although Patrick had left and probably for good, you never knew. He could come back. Sean could be still in the attic. She wanted to protect both of the men she loved in such different ways.

Sean was interested in her ring, made her promise that when next she came to see him she would wear it. 'I'd love to see a yoke like that, a real valuable thing. It's few valuables I've seen.'

By nature he wasn't a thief, but to save his skin he was prepared to kill, never mind steal. And the ring, if it was worth anything, might oil his way of escape and give him a start in America. He kissed her again before she left.

She went back to her room in a state of ecstasy. She was sure she was in love. How pleased Patrick would be. If she knew where to reach him she'd write and tell him. He had sent her a short letter, telling her he was heading for Antibes where his friends were. He promised that he would write again with an address when he was settled in and reminded her to sell the ring as soon as possible.

She would, too. And if things worked out as she hoped, there'd be no need to start a business. The civil war couldn't last for ever. Sean wouldn't always be on the run. Of course, it was early days to be making plans but she felt that he loved her as much as she loved him.

Well, he must feel something for her: he wouldn't kiss her and hold her as he did if she meant nothing to him.

Sitting in the attic chain-smoking, Sean was thinking about her too. She was a grand girl, and a beautiful one. If he could write poetry he would write a poem about her. How she had skin the colour of a wild dog-rose, pale with a hint of pink in the cheeks, and her eyes were like the violets that grew on the banks of the hedges. A grand girl, all right, with a ring worth more than the dowry a strong farmer would give with his daughter. She was innocent too: it wasn't hard to tell she wasn't experienced. There was nothing forward about her – but she was red hot for all that. With a few more kisses and a little persuasion he could have had her tonight. He wouldn't let the grass grow under his feet. He'd have her and soon, before this Patrick fella came back from buying his whiskey.

Danny was pleased and delighted to hear again from Brian Nolan, to know that he was in the Free State Army, and glad that he hadn't turned against Collins after the treaty had been signed. He looked forward to his visit and wrote telling him so. They'd have plenty to talk about. The same day he heard from Brian, he was told by a customer in the shop that Johnny Quinn was also coming to the village. 'The cur,' he said to himself: coming back to do the big blow after winning his fight in New York. For a minute he indulged in his favourite fantasy of squeezing the life out of Quinn, but there was enough violence in the country without him adding to it. And, as he admitted, he'd be lucky to get within spitting distance of Johnny, never mind put his hands round the man's throat. Though he'd cry no tears for him if he fell over the side of the *Mauritania*, on which his oul fella was saying he was coming and first class at that.

A grand high tea was set out for Danny and Brian – and, as was their custom, the Jameson's would be to hand. They greeted each other affectionately and Danny asked after the girl to whom Brian had been engaged. 'I never hear a word about her – nor give her a thought, for that matter, which is all for the best. Since going to Cork I've found a grand woman, a widow with two grown-up children and not short of a few bob. D'ye remember the song, "A Bachelor Gay Am I"? Well, I've put all that behind me. God forgive me, I was a terrible sinner. There was a place I used to go to here in Dublin to satisfy my lustful needs. But that's a thing of the past.'

Danny poured more whiskey. He knew that Brian was fishing for information, wanting to know how he satisfied his own needs, but he didn't rise to his bait. Brian wouldn't ridicule him if he admitted that he had never had a woman: he was too decent a skin to do that. Nor would he pour scorn on him if he was to admit that the only woman he had loved was Angel, but she was for his private thoughts. She was part of his dreams.

It was long past midnight before they went to bed pleasantly tipsy, singing a verse of 'A Bachelor Gay Am I' as they went up the stairs, Brian assuring Danny that he was top of his wedding-invitation list.

Mrs McEvoy was fuming that her nephew showed no signs of leaving the attic. She was weary from trudging up and down the stairs in the middle of the night, carrying water and food and returning with a slop-bucket. But, most of all, she was terrified that the Free Staters would get word of Sean's whereabouts. Her premises would be raided, her business ruined, and if she wasn't executed for harbouring a man on the run she would be imprisoned. All this she told her nephew, who kept making promises. Only another few days and he'd be gone, as true as God. And he'd make it up to her, see her all right in her old age.

There was nothing she could do. She might convince the Free Staters that he had broken in without her knowledge, that someone, she didn't know who, had kept him in food, smokes and drinks unknown to her. But she would be followed to the ends of the earth, no matter how long it took, and get a bullet in the head. Every Irish man and woman knew that that was the punishment meted out to informers.

All she could do was pray that the civil war would end. Business wasn't as good as usual, few of the rooms were let. It was common knowledge that men on the run were hiding in the lower-class houses, and this was enough to discourage her wealthy clients from keeping on their rooms. There was discontent among the girls too, now forced to take any man able to afford the price demanded of them.

In another couple of months, Patrick would stop paying Angel's rent. She had never got to the bottom of which of them had broken off the engagement – it was such a pity: they had seemed meant for each other. It was terrible how times changed. Lord Brightwell appeared to be going senile – either that or he had lost interest in her, not that they'd had a proper physical relationship for years although she was skilful in the arts of love and had ways of arousing and satisfying him. Nowadays, though, he just wasn't interested. Nor was he as generous with his gifts as he had been in the past.

Her only hope was that when Angel's tenancy expired she could find a wealthy lover for her. After all, somewhere among the Free Staters there was bound to be a man who would be enchanted by Angel's beauty. She'd find a smaller house and install her there, with another beauty perhaps. That way she'd ensure for herself a comfortable old age.

Sean played Angel for another week before he seduced her. He kissed her lips and eyes. His tongue probed her mouth, he licked her earlobes, then nibbled them. He squeezed her buttocks, spanned her breasts, lingering over them. Her erect nipples strained against her bodice and waves of heat lapped her body. A pulse she had never known existed throbbed between her legs. Her nails dug into his back and she pressed close to him, wanting to melt into him. He stroked her hair and, taking his mouth from hers, told her how much he loved her. He would die for her. He would kill for her. He wanted her for his wife. 'Kiss me again,' she pleaded, reaching for his lips.

Then he let go of her, took her hand and led her to sit on the trunk, murmuring endearments. He wet a piece of rag and wiped her face until her flushed cheeks cooled and her breathing slowed.

'Darling, we'll leave it there for the time being. I don't want you doing anything you'd regret. I don't want you committing a mortal sin. We'll wait. It won't be long now till our wedding day.'

She sighed and leant against him.

And for the next six nights he raised her passion to unbearable heights until she wanted to reef off every stitch, then cooled her face and talked of when they would marry. The little farm he would buy. How she'd love Ballyvaughan. The Burren, where flowers grew that grew nowhere else in Ireland or England, where the air was sweet and the friendliest people in the world lived.

Each night he soothed her with sweet talk while his hands took liberties with her body, and he knew that the time had come. She was begging for it. And he was desperate for sight of the ring.

On the night he decided to take her, he rearranged the attic. The blankets were laid on the floor, the pillows arranged. He kissed and caressed her before they lay down. Then he lit a cigarette and called her a *ghoille mo croide* – '"The love of my heart", that's what it means in English.'

She repeated the Gaelic words. 'They're beautiful, softer than English. Always call me that.'

'They are,' he said, 'but sure aren't you engaged? And in the long run isn't all we've been doing and saying only a lot of cod? You're going to be married. It's not the sky over Ballyvaughan you'll be wanting to look at, nor a little cottage with a turf fire. It's in a fine house in Limerick city you'll be living and never a thought for poor Sean. And I never even saw the ring. But sure that doesn't matter. I saw you, and I'll always see you – till the day I die I'll see you.'

'Oh, my love, don't look so sad. I broke off the engagement after I met you,' she lied.

His heart dropped, like a stone falling down a well, as he said, 'And I suppose you sent it back.' And with it, he thought, my chance of getting to America. He felt like crashing his fist into her adoring face.

'I did not. This morning I sold it back to the jeweller it was bought from. That's how Patrick wanted it. The money was mine to keep. We can have our little farm and live happily ever after.'

'Well, aren't you the darlin' little girl? And weren't we meant for each other, our marriage made in heaven? How much did you get for it?'

'Eight hundred pounds.'

'Eight hundred pounds! He must have been mad about you. That's a fortune. You banked it, I hope.'

'I was going to, until I remembered all the bank raids and thought, supposing I was just paying it in when the robbers came.'

'Well, isn't it the grand head you have on you?' He lit another cigarette, took a few puffs then said, 'I hope to God you've put it somewhere safe.'

'Oh, I have.'

'You'd want to be certain, with them maids in and out of your room.'

'No one could ever find it unless they knew where to look.'

He wanted to see the money, handle it. For all he knew she could be having him on. Wasn't that what he was doing to her? Though, God knows, she looked innocent enough.

'That's grand then, so long as you're sure,' he said.

Angel detected a note of doubt in his voice. 'To put your mind at ease you can come down now and I'll show you.'

'Not at all. There's no flies on you. I'm sure you did a great job of hiding it.'

He needed another week in the attic to think out his plan of escape. Then he'd be down like a shot to see the pot of gold.

He led her to the blanket, stopping to kiss as they walked the few feet. For any passable woman he could always oblige.

'Lie down,' he said, and lowered himself beside her. He began his routine, the kissing and caressing the murmuring of endearments as he undid her bodice. 'Why you come to me still dressed I don't know. All the buttons.'

'I'll undo them,' she said. He licked her nipples, he sucked them, she bucked beneath him. He put a hand on her lips. 'You mustn't make a sound.' She moved this way and that to accommodate him undressing her. He used the skills he'd been learning since he was thirteen, from farmer's wives, prostitutes, all the women he'd had. He kissed Angel's naked body from head to foot. She writhed and moaned.

For a brief moment, as he straddled her, she remembered the rape and was afraid. Then, when Sean was inside her, she relaxed and surrendered.

Afterwards she lay beneath him, gazing at his face while he, still playing the part of the devoted lover, fought off the overpowering urge to sleep, showered her with compliments, gentle kisses, and wondered who had had her before him. Not that he cared. She was beautiful and passionate. In different circumstances he would have hung on to her for a while. Not now, though. Just the week, while he perfected his plan of escape. But for that week he'd keep her sweet. Neither say nor do anything to make her have second thoughts about showing him where the money was.

Chapter Twenty-Two

Johnny Quinn arrived in Dublin the day before Tommy Maguire. He was dressed in the height of fashion with a camel's hair overcoat, unbuttoned to show off his well-tailored worsted suit, a snap brim trilby to match and several gold rings on his fingers.

He had spent the day in town, looking up acquaintances from his boxing days. Being fawned on and splashing his money about. When the drink was beginning to tell on him, he ordered a cab and travelled out to the village. Cutting a dash, he told himself. Delighted when doors opened and children gathered round the cab to see 'the Yank'. His father was all over him. Johnny thought of him as a drunken oul bastard, who had been the cause of his mother's death and wouldn't have come near him, except that he wanted the villagers to witness his return. Tomorrow he'd swagger through the streets and let them see how raggedy-arsed Johnny Quinn had prospered. While he was about it he might find out where Angel was. Was she married? Not that he cared. He had a woman in America. A woman who knew what it was all about. The drink had made him sleepy. He took off his coat, hung it behind the door and dozed in an armchair. 'Ah, Johnny, don't go to sleep,' said his father. 'I wanted to be seen with you in the pub.'

He waved him away, 'Maybe I'll pay a visit later.' He wouldn't be seen dead with him, the bastard, he thought, and pretended to sleep.

Tommy Maguire wore the shabby coat and trousers he had worn eight years previously when he joined the

Army. His uniform had been handed in at the depot. He carried his few possessions, the presents for Angel, the Luger pistol and bullets, wrapped in a shawl in a small haversack. His money to get married on and set up house was secured in an inside pocket.

A mile from the village he got off the tram. Now that he was almost home, his nerves were getting the better of him. Doubts crowded into his mind. Eight years was an awful long time to be away. Angel would never have waited this long. God knows, he wasn't much of a catch and she such a beauty. He'd been codding himself. But, all the same, he had to find out one way or the other.

By the time he reached the village his hopes had risen again. He had to pass her cottage to reach his house. His heart leaped with joy when he saw a light burning in the room. He was sorely tempted to knock. Then he realised he was dressed in the clothes he'd worn eight years ago – not that they were that dilapidated, for he'd seldom worn them since he had enlisted, but they'd lain in his barrack box all that time. Even Ahmed, the kind, courteous dhobi-wallah, had commented sorrowfully when Tommy had taken the jacket and trousers to be pressed, 'Ah, sahib,' he'd said, 'very, very old. Why you no go to bazaar? Nice jacket, nice trousers. Good tailor sewing all time. Good price. Tell him you friend of Ahmed's.' He couldn't let Angel see him like this, not in his rags, and he needed to spruce himself up, wash and shave. He'd have to curb his impatience, go into town first thing in the morning and get a shirt, trousers and jacket.

He walked on to his own house and had a struggle to unlock the door. Eventually the key turned, then he had to push and shove: over the years the wood must have swollen.

He should have bought a candle. He couldn't see his hand in front of his face. He heard the scurrying of rats and mice. That he had expected. All the houses had rats and mice. He used to set traps for them. What he hadn't expected was the terrible smell, of damp and dirt, decay too, dead birds down the chimney, dead rats and mice. He thanked God Angel wasn't with him. It would have put her off the house for good. He remembered where the stone sink was and inched his way towards it. A douche of cold water on his hands and face would liven him up. Then he'd go to the public-house to see if anyone he knew was about, buy a couple of candles from the huckster's and fish and chips from next door. He'd eat them on the way home, out in the fresh air away from that smell. Whatever else might have rotted in eight years, the metal spring on his bed wouldn't have and he could sleep on anything. The Army taught you that. The tap wouldn't budge. Ah, well, he thought, my hands will have to do.

I can't believe it, he kept telling himself, I'm home. Angel's only a few yards from me, please God. I'll see her tomorrow. I'll see Aggie. I liked Aggie. I'm glad now I bought her the slippers. Tomorrow will be a great day.

It was a fine night, yet on his way to the pub he didn't see another passer-by. The civil war, perhaps, made people wary after dark. In any case, he thought, after all this time who would know me, or me them? The barman might, not that I was a great customer, but he knew my father and mother, and lived not far from us. There must be a great age on him now. My mother and father, Lord have mercy on them, would be over eighty now and he'd be the same age.

As he neared the pub, doubts again assailed his mind. Angel was bound to be married or, if she wasn't, courting. What could she see in someone like him? India wasn't kind to man, woman or child. His face was the colour of leather, looked like it, and was as wrinkled as a belly of tripe. If he was right in the head he'd carry on walking, get a tram into the city, find a lodging-house and take a boat to England in the morning.

Then hope came again to him. He'd nothing to lose by going into the pub. It wasn't as if Angel would be there, telling him to leave her alone. He wouldn't see her until the next day.

The pub was empty, the barman a surly stranger who barely glanced at him as he poured whiskey, took the money and went back to reading a newspaper. Tommy felt the whiskey warm his throat, then his belly. He wasn't used to drink, but the spirit was making him less jittery. He ordered another and tossed it back.

'I don't suppose . . .' he began hesitantly but, when he heard the door open, didn't finish the question as he turned to see who was coming in. He knew the face but couldn't put a name to it. The newcomer recognised him, though, and greeted him enthusiastically. 'Jaysus, you're a sight for sore eyes. You've been gone for years. Ten, isn't it?'

'Eight,' replied Tommy, as the man shook his hand and his face slid back in time, to when they were in school. It was the bully, the sneering, jeering young fella who terrorised younger or smaller boys, who had terrorised Tommy, until at eleven he'd shot up and could defend himself. He reminded Tommy of a weasel, with his narrow pointed face and skittery movements, his small sharp teeth green near the gums. The weasel Bolger, he remembered now that that had been his nickname. He never grew very tall or broad, and answered to his nickname. In fact, his name was Willie, and this was how Tommy addressed him when he offered him a drink.

'I won't say, no. A Jameson's. God, it's great to see you again. There's not many of us left. They all went off to the war, few came back.'

'Did you join up yourself?'

'Wouldn't have me. Heart trouble. Said I could drop like that.' He snapped his fingers. 'Must have been bad, sure they were taking shaggin' cripples. Never gave me any bother. I'm as fit as ever I was.'

Tommy bought him two more whiskeys. They moved away from the bar and sat down.

'Is business always this slack?'

'Since that fucker bought the pub it is. Wouldn't throw a word to a dog and no slate. Them that have the price of a drink go down the road to the Red Cow. I only dropped in tonight because the leg is playing me up. Got a bullet in me knee doing a bit of poaching. Them gamekeepers are all Protestant bastards. It's only the Protestants have any money round here. I'd love to see every one of their houses burned to the ground. See them run out of the country. It was never theirs in the first place.'

This was the Weasel on form, Tommy thought. Never utter a good word if a bad one could be said.

'And you take that Danny Connolly, coining it, he is. Made pucks during the war.'

'Are you working?' asked Tommy.

'When I can get it, a bit here and there when the leg's not playing me up. Then it's parish relief. Father Clancy's gone. Out in a retirement home for priests – he won't go short of anything. When did you ever know a priest that did? And as for Father Brennan, well, he's asking to have his head blown off. Sunday after Sunday preaching against "the boys", threatening them with excommunication. The only ones lifting a hand for Ireland! That other lot, the Free Staters, are hand in glove with the British. I'll tell you something else. Johnny Quinn's back from America. You want to see the style of him. A real Yank. Another fucking bastard. D'ye know, he passed me by yesterday? Raggedy-arsed Johnny let on not to know me. A champion boxer.'

The Weasel continued in the same vein, denigrating the character of everyone he could think of. Tommy decided he'd heard enough. The Weasel wasn't the one to ask about Angel. He'd buy him another drink then head for his bed.

He brought back the two whiskeys and sat down. His head ached. He hadn't eaten for hours. There was a tight band pressing on his skull and bile rising in his gullet. He could feel its burning, scalding sensation. After he left the Weasel he'd stick his finger down his throat and make himself sick. He smoked a Woodbine and lit one for the Weasel. 'Will we be making a move, then?' he asked. 'I'm jaded.'

'Aye, in a minute, but first you have to hear this. D'ye remember that Angel? Stuck-up bitch. Well, she was run out of here.'

The vice tightened round Tommy's temples. 'She had a child. Quinn's or Father Brennan's. She was working above in the presbytery at the time. Brennan should have been run out of it as well. Quinn had already scarpered. Dirty bitch – do it with anyone. Anyway, the women ran her out. No one knows where, but hide nor sight of her has never been seen since. Her oul wan went mad and finished up in the Gorman. A den of iniquity, that's what she was turning the place into. Eh, don't forget your haversack.'

Tommy picked it up and together they left the pub. The landlord never raised his eyes to see them go.

They walked along by the canal bank. The night was dark, an owl hooted and from the hedge came the sound of small animals. Tommy's head was pounding. Willie kept on talking, venting his spleen on anyone who came into his mind, his voice like a rusty hacksaw, the sound competing with the throbbing in Tommy's brain.

He remembered that there had always been a grain of truth beneath Willie's vilification of people. Priests, in or out of retirement, lived better than the poor for all their vows of poverty. Protestants had ruled the land for centuries. Johnny Quinn had been an unpleasant character. It wasn't unknown for priests to make girls pregnant, though seldom. But his Angel. His shining star. That was the exception. There was no grain of truth in what Willie had said about her. Angel was as pure as the driven snow. But Willie wasn't fool enough to say she'd been driven out of the village if she hadn't. That was too easy to disprove. He only had to turn back, knock on Aggie's door. But Angel wasn't in the village. Someone had destroyed her. Someone had given her a child, against her will, and then absconded. His beautiful Angel, with her flower-like child's face. The pressure inside his skull was unbearable.

Willie stopped by the riverbank. 'I won't be a minute,' he said, fumbling with the buttons on his fly. 'A queer oul world, isn't it? Angel that looked as if butter wouldn't melt in her mouth. I'd say she'd have been hard put to say who owned the child. But Quinn and Father Brennan's the favourites.'

Down the years Tommy could hear Willie's squeaky voice, repeating the same words wherever he had a listener. Tommy reached into his haversack, shook the pistol from the shawl and withdrew it. 'That's better out than in,' said Willie, turning round, doing up his fly buttons. Tommy shot him through the forehead.

Then he made his way back to the presbytery and rang the night bell.

Father Brennan opened the door. Tommy shot him in the chest and walked away.

There was a light still burning in the Quinns' and through the window Tommy saw Johnny dozing in a chair. He knocked. Johnny yawned and stretched, then stood up and came across to the door. He pulled it wide. Tommy raised the pistol and shot him in the face, just above his nose.

A neighbour of the Quinns was woken by the shot. She shook her sleeping husband awake, asking, 'Did you hear that? A gun going off?'

He got up and went to the window. The curtains didn't meet in the centre, so he peered through the gap. 'You must have been dreaming,' he said, going back to bed. 'There's not a soul about.'

'I'm telling you I heard something.'

'For the love of Jaysus, will you go back to sleep? I've to be up in an hour.'

405

Tommy went back along the riverbank. Birds were stirring, it would soon be daylight. The thumping in his head had stopped. He felt grand. In a few hours he'd see Angel. That Willie was an awful liar. Jealousy, that's what had ailed him. He had been jealous that Tommy was going to marry Angel, that he had a house to take her to and money to do it up. He wouldn't ask Willie to the wedding for sure. And this time when he went to see Father Clancy there'd be no fobbing him off about Angel only being a child, nor India not suitable for her, no talk about the Army and him not being on the strength.

He came to a place where the ground began to rise. Gorse was growing on the little hill. He remembered that at the top it grew in plenty, that there was a hollow before the hill dipped again. He remembered playing there as a child. You could have a kip in the hollow. He needed to sleep now, for his head was bad again and he had a lot to do still before he brought Angel to see the house. He lay down in the hollow, closed his eyes and slept for a few minutes. Something woke him, a noise. He listened. It was the birds. They were singing. But, thank God, his head had cleared.

He sat up, and then he remembered the shootings. They'd catch him. They'd stitch a white patch on his breast and kill him. They might make Angel watch the execution. He wouldn't let that happen. He wouldn't let her witness such a thing.

He rooted in his haversack, took out the Kashmiri shawl and spread it on the ground. On it he laid the presents he had brought home, his black leatherette wallet, in which were his money and discharge papers. With the stub of a pencil he wrote across the papers. 'For

Angel. I love you. Say a prayer for my soul.' Then he took the gun, put it inside his mouth and shot himself.

Maggie Dignum's son had been following Tommy from when he had killed Willie on the riverbank, had hidden in the trees opposite the presbytery, in a doorway near the Quinns. He waited and watched until the man on the ground had lain still for a long time. Then he approached him and bundled everything into the haversack. Last, he searched his pockets, took everything from them and finally the gun. He gathered armfuls of brush, covered up the dead man, picked up the haversack and went on his way.

'I can understand them getting poor Father Brennan, Lord have mercy on him. He was going too far lately, with his threats of excommunication,' the police sergeant said to the village constable. 'But why Quinn? Sure he'd been in America for years.'

'They have their connections in America, don't forget. How do we know what spouting he'd have done there? Whether he favoured the Free Staters or the Irregulars, he'd have had plenty to say,' replied the constable.

'You may be right – but what about the Weasel?'

'That fella would have sold his mother for a glass of whiskey.'

'All the same, aren't we living in terrible times? D'ye know? Before the Troubles the only violent deaths in the village were a few accidents in the slate quarry – and now we've had three in one night. Thanks be to God, we won't have to break our necks trying to find the culprit.'

'Not a bit of it. Life's the cheap thing nowadays. But we'll have to show willing and make a few enquiries.'

'Oh, that we will.'

No one had seen or heard anything. The barman in the public-house thought Willy might have been in. He seemed to remember another bloke buying him whiskey, but he couldn't be sure. Neither could he describe him. 'To tell you the truth, Sergeant, I was more interested in my paper.' The woman who thought she'd heard a shot had been warned by her husband to say nothing.

'And that's an end to that, thank Christ,' said the sergeant, when they got back to the station. 'They'll get a few lines in the paper, but only because of Father Brennan and the boxer. All over the city and the country dead bodies are being found, murdered, shot. People are so used to it they don't give a shite any more.'

The three bodies were brought to the chapel at the same time. Father Clancy was one of the celebrants of the Requiem Mass. He tried to keep his mind concentrated on what he was doing but could not help thinking now and then what a strange trio it was to finish up dead together in the aisle of the chapel. Or that, in some way, the deaths of Johnny Quinn and Father Brennan were connected with Angel. What else had those two in common? For one crazy moment he suspected Danny of avenging her. The thought had no sooner entered his mind than he dismissed it. In any case, he told himself, the Weasel had never been a suspect in the Angel affair. But, whoever it was, he would never be convinced it was an IRA killing. He'd probably go to his grave never knowing who the culprit was.

As the sergeant had forecast, the incident merited only a few lines in the paper. Angel no longer read the newspapers and so was never aware of what had taken place in her village.

Mona, in Athlone, was always avidly eager for news of Dublin and read the item. Like Father Clancy, she thought it had something to do with Angel but could not fathom where the Weasel had come into it. Lonely as she was, down in the country, she painted scenarios of Angel, or some new fella of hers, as the avenger but came up against a blank wall when she remembered the Weasel. But when she became pregnant she seldom gave the murders any more thought.

Eventually Johnny's father inherited his son's money and drank himself to death in no time. Maggie Dignum's son gave the village a wide berth for a long time. There was no one to miss him so no one to remark on his absence.

Chapter Twenty-Three

Angel had hidden the money in a small trunk left behind by Patrick. It had his initials on it. He had told her it was one he had had at boarding-school and had shown her its false bottom. She thought it was a safe place for her bundles of banknotes. She spread them out evenly, replaced the false bottom and on top of it packed her glamorous dresses. She'd never wear them again – in Ballyvaughan you'd look a sight in them.

She was happier than she had ever been in her life. God had come back into her life. For the first time in years she prayed morning and night, asking forgiveness for all her sins and, after attending a mission in Francis

Street, made up her mind that the time had come to confess all of her sins, including her abortion. Only then would she be in a true state of grace. Then she could get married with a clear conscience.

In confession, she had told the priest about her love for Sean, how they were marrying soon, and that she had sinned with him. Before granting her absolution the priest made her promise that she would lie with him no more until they were married. Then she knelt before the high altar and prayed for the strength to refuse Sean. He was very persuasive so it wouldn't be easy, loving him as much as she did. He only needed to touch her and her will deserted her. But he was a Catholic, too, and would understand. Anyway, it was only three weeks, which wasn't such a long time to wait. And Sean was convinced that, before then, the civil war would be over.

'How can you be so sure?' she had asked him, on the night he told her this.

'I can read between the lines. Night after night in the papers you bring me there's clues, if you know how to interpret them.' She believed him as she believed everything he told her.

When his aunt broached the subject of him leaving the attic he told her a different story. She mentioned her belief that the end of the war was in sight.

'You don't want to believe what you read in the papers,' he said. 'It could go on for months yet. And even if it ended, where's the guarantee that we'd be let off scot-free? Sure them bastards are just as likely to execute everyone like me who stood out against them. You'll just have to be patient. As soon as things are settled, I'll be off to America and you can have your attic back.'

'Every night you stay here you're endangering my life.

I'm an old woman. I can't sleep any more. I'm in dread and fear for my life that one night the Free Staters will come knocking down the door, find you and arrest me. It's happened in other houses not a stone's throw from here. You should show me a little pity. After all, I am your own flesh and blood.'

'And doesn't the same apply to me? Amn't I your sister's child? You might get slung in prison but I'd be slung into a lime-pit.'

He didn't care what became of her. He wanted out of the place as much as she wanted him gone, but first he had to have the money. And Angel was dragging her feet in showing him where it was. She had gone all religious on him too, insisting he had to wait until after they were married. Well, he hoped it kept fine for her. Once he knew where the money was and got his hands on it, he'd be gone over the rooftops and making a run for Boston. He'd miss her, but only for a while. She was beautiful, the most beautiful girl he'd ever seen, but he'd lose no sleep over her. The world was full of beautiful girls.

Angel sat in her bedroom, waiting for when she'd hear Mrs McEvoy return from the attic. While she waited, she sorted out the presents Patrick had given her. Those she knew to be valuable she'd sell to the same jeweller who'd bought the ring and put that money aside for Aggie. She could visit her now that she was getting married, bring Sean with her. On his arm, she'd face the villagers, and once they were settled in Ballyvaughan Aggie could come and live with them. They'd have a grand life. She might even hear from Bridie.

Maybe she'd keep on her mother's cottage; that would be great to have if she and Aggie fancied a trip to the city. The funny little valueless gifts from Patrick she'd always keep – the tin monkey, the feathers and paper fans. She always said a prayer for God to spare him and keep him well and happy. She owed Patrick so much, her golden, handsome man, who had restored her sanity. Her lovely man who, because he was different, had had to go away or maybe some day face disgrace and imprisonment. The world could be a cruel place. But he was safe now, away in Antibes. She wished she knew his address. She'd write and tell him of her good fortune in falling in love.

She had finished sorting her possessions. When it was time for her to go away with Sean, she'd take the fine dresses from Patrick's box and give them to the girls, hand the money to Sean and pack her ordinary clothes in the box. She'd never part with that. She dozed fitfully, one ear open for Mrs McEvoy's step. When she heard it, she waited the usual few moments before going to the attic.

Sean enfolded her in his arms and kissed her passionately, then tried to persuade her to let him make love to her. Held in his arms, dizzy from his kisses, feeling his body pressed close to hers, it was hard to refuse him but she remembered her promise in confession. 'And, in any case, there isn't time. I want to show you where the money's hidden.'

At the mention of the money his ardour cooled, though he pretended disappointment. Feet bare, he followed her down the stairs to her bedroom, where he watched as she lifted out the dresses, then the false bottom of the box and displayed the money. 'Where could be safer than that?' she asked triumphantly.

'In the ordinary way I'd agree with you. But sure the wans who live here and the maids are up to every trick in the book. They'll be suspicious the minute they see all this stuff in the chest,' he pointed to the finery, 'wonder why, all of a sudden, it's there and not in the wardrobe.'

'I never thought of that. But where else can I hide it?'

He looked round the room as if searching for a secure place. 'To tell you the truth I can't see anywhere. You could carry it round with you, sleep with it under your pillow. But you'd never want to leave your bag out of your hand for a minute. That could cause suspicion.'

She thought for a while, then suggested what he had been leading her to.

'You could mind it. No one goes into the attic.'

'It's an awful lot of money – would you trust me with it?'

She laughed. 'Trust you with it? Amn't I going to trust you with my life? In a few weeks won't we be man and wife? Of course I trust you with it. And you might as well take these as well.' She gave him her other valuables, including the pearls.

Concealing his excitement he said, 'God, you're putting a terrible responsibility on me.'

'Well, isn't that one of the things about being married? Won't you have a great responsibility from now on? Take them and go, then I'll sleep with an easy mind.' She reached up on tiptoe and kissed him. 'Away you go now, before you drag me into the state of sin again. I love you. I'll see you tomorrow night, please God.'

Pretending reluctance, he went. Once outside the door he took the steps two at a time to the attic. He opened the attic window and looked out, studying the sky. It wouldn't be light for a good while; plenty of time for him to make his getaway. He looked around the room. There was nothing in it to show that he had

413

stayed here. The newspapers, anyone could have put them there, the same with the blankets and pillows. Not a letter, a scrap of paper with a name or address. He chainsmoked, treading butt after butt beneath the boots he had put on. He packed the money and jewellery into a pouch, which he belted round his waist. His gun went into his pocket. He smoked a last cigarette, trod it out carelessly and went back to the window. He did not notice that his foot knocked the still smouldering cigarette end nearer the blankets. He hoisted himself up to the window-ledge, pushed the window wider and left by the way he had first entered. As sure-footed as a goat, he climbed over the roofs.

It was a long street, straight as a ruler, two roofs to each house, a valley between them, skylights galore into which he could slip, drainpipes to slide down, protruding flat roofs of out-buildings. He was away.

Angel slept the sleep of a contented baby. When she woke she blessed herself, thanked God for bringing her safely through the night, for sending Sean into her life. She prayed for her mother and that soon they would be reunited. Then a little frown creased her brow. Sean had given her the impression that they would soon marry, but hadn't mentioned how or when he would leave the attic. He'd have to do that if he wanted their banns called. Ah, well, she thought, maybe he had learned from his newspaper reading that the end of the civil war was really imminent. Sean was the clever one. He knew what he was about.

She wasn't sure exactly how many months rent in advance Patrick had paid for her room. She hadn't asked him. Several, she thought he had said. But how many was several? It wouldn't be wise to ask Mrs McEvoy, she thought. Lately she had changed so much: she looked ill; ill and old. Of course, that could be the strain of knowing Sean was in the house, although there was probably some truth in Patrick's description of her. Maybe it *was* the making of money that motivated her. That had made her pick me up in Grafton Street even if I *do* remind her of her daughter.

Angel got up, went to the bathroom and stood in front of the long mirror. She took off her nightgown. Her golden hair was disarranged, making her face more childlike than ever. Vanity, she knew, was a sin but even so she couldn't deny that she was beautiful, her hair, her face and her body. Sean had never seen her naked. Cupping her breasts in her hands, she longed for the time when he would. Then, remembering that she was trying to be a better-living person, she put on her nightgown and went back into the bedroom. Crossing the floor, she smelt smoke. The maids, she thought, starting the fires – only it didn't smell like turf. Perhaps today they were burning coal.

She got back into bed. The smell grew stronger, of scorching wool. She got up again, opened the door. Smoke was curling down the stairs and Angel's heart almost stopped when she realised it was coming from the attic. 'Oh, Jesus, Mary and Joseph!' she exclaimed. She raced up the remaining stairs, calling Sean's name. He had fallen asleep smoking and the cigarette had dropped on the blanket. 'Sean!' she screamed, and pushed open the door. The cross-current of air between it and the open attic window fanned the smouldering blanket into flames that jumped the distance between them and the yellowed tinder-dry newspapers. She moved into the room searching for Sean, calling his name, blinded by the smoke. Discarded paintings, picture frames, lifetimes of rubbish were soon engulfed by the fire. She tripped and fell, lay on one side temporarily concussed. Flames licked up the side of her lawn nightdress, her face, and devoured her hair. She came to and began screaming again.

The screams woke Mrs McEvoy. Then she, too, smelt smoke. The house is on fire, she thought. Sacred Heart of Jesus, they'll find Sean, I'm done for. From her landing she saw the smoke billowing down the stairs. From one of the maid's rooms, she assumed. Or the attic. Don't let it be the attic, not the attic. Please, God, don't let Sean, alive or dead, be found in the attic. Terrified, she climbed the stairs. So far there was no sound from the servant's rooms but the attic door was open, flames dancing in the room. A figure crawled across the floor. It was Angel, her hair on fire, repeating over and over, 'He's gone. Sean is gone. He's safe, thank God.'

'You bitch. You bloody cow. You've been coming up here! I'll kill you.'

Angel reached the open door. 'Help me,' she pleaded, stretching out a hand to Mrs McEvoy, who dragged her to her feet, then to the landing edge and pushed her down the stairs.

The noise of her fall brought out the servants, who gathered round her screaming and crying.

Mrs McEvoy's mind worked frantically. Sean was gone. From what she'd seen of the fire, there'd be nothing to connect him with the attic. Nothing except Angel. She mustn't be found where she was. She glanced down the stairs to where the servants, like a flock of demented hens, had gathered around her.

'You, Tessha, and Peg, carry her down to the hall then strip her room. Empty the drawers. Don't leave a trace of her. Wrap her clothes in the sheets. Everything else in the pillowcases. Don't forget the waste-paper basket.'

'But, ma'am,' said Peg, 'she needs attention first. And we'll have to get an ambulance or she'll die. Look at her! Look at the burns! Her nightdress is stuck to her skin in charred bits. And she's unconscious. If we don't help her she'll die.'

'Pray that she does. Who'd want to live looking the way she will? Hurry up.'

The fire brigade would come of its own accord for by now the attic roof would be alight, blazing like a beacon, and the police would not be far behind them. She anticipated their questions and had ready her answers. 'No, Sergeant, I never laid eyes on her before tonight. I heard screams, then smelt smoke, heard someone running down the stairs, then falling. She must have been homeless, hiding in the attic. Probably drunk. Knocked over a candle.'

A few of the girls had now come up the stairs. She screamed at them: 'Get her down into the hall and strip the room now, this minute. And you know nothing! You never saw her before in your life!'

'But, ma'am, if she lives, she'll answer for herself!'

'*If* she does. It'll be many a long day before she'll be able to talk. Move her now.' And she thought, By that time I'll be gone, bag and baggage. 'And don't one of you get loose-tongued to the police. None of you knew her. Never saw her before tonight. Unless you want your faces disfigured too.'

They knew it wasn't an idle threat. The house was full of men who, for a few quid, would slash the face of their own mother. They'd keep silent tongues in their heads.

And they did, except for Teesha, who broke her heart crying as Angel was carried out. As the ambulance started on its way to Jervis Street Hospital, she answered a man's question: 'Katherine, I think, sir. I saw her in the street a few times and someone once called her Katherine.' The reporter wrote the name in his notebook.

'The poor child,' one of the nursing nuns said to another. 'I never thought she'd pull through.'

'No more did I. She must have a grand constitution. If only she had someone belonging to her. From the one side of her face you can tell she must have been a beauty.'

'A raving one. I'm dreading the time when she'll ask for a looking-glass.'

'I think that'll be a while yet. All she does is sleep.'

'The best thing for her. God knows there's nothing else to do, change her dressings, keep her clean and pray she doesn't get blood poisoning.'

The older nun lifted one of Angel's hands. The burns on it had lost their angry hue, and it lay brown and shrivelled. 'I'd say the nerves in that have been damaged. And her poor face looks like a piece of raw meat. I noticed today her hair is showing signs of growing. Little curly wisps.'

'The gossip that's going round! I try to discourage it, but sure you know what the maids are like and, God forgive me, I'm as curious as the next,' the young nun said.

'Aren't we all. So what's the latest?'

'That she lived in Railway Street in one of the houses,

418

but wasn't a prostitute. She was engaged to an English officer, but they broke it off. And that she was never known by any name except Katherine.'

'That oul faggot Mrs McEvoy! She'll know the truth, not that anyone will ever get it out of her.'

'I wonder what'll become of poor Katherine when it's time for her to be discharged?'

'Kilbride was telling me on his rounds this morning that that won't be for weeks, maybe months. We don't even know if she'll be able to walk. She injured her head in the fall, and along with the burns she could be brain damaged.'

'So she could finish up in the Incurables?'

'She could indeed, the poor child.'

A letter came for Danny from Brian. It was full of apologies for what a terrible letter writer he was.

> It isn't that I don't give you a thought. Many's the time I do, and in my mind write reams that never get put on paper. Mind you, after all we've gone through in the last few years, it's a wonder we've stayed sane. And the papers always full of one atrocity or another – so many that often you skip them. D'ye think that's a callous way of protecting our sanity? I'm dying to have a long chat with you. Our minds work alike to a certain extent.

Brian wrote about his hopes for the future, about beginning to feel the years catching up on him. 'Get the odd twinge now and then, a reminder of how time flies.'

In the last paragraph he went off on a different tangent.

D'ye remember I used to tell you about a place I went to before I turned over a new leaf? Well, I was in there one night debating whether to rent a room or not, and the oul wan who ran the place doing her best to talk me into it. I decided to leave the girls alone and settle for a few drinks, when the most beautiful girl I'd ever seen came into the salon. Or, rather, passed through, for she was on her way out. I can't begin to describe her. 'I'll rent a room if she goes with it,' I said to your woman.

The oul wan pretended to look indignant. 'Katherine is engaged to be married,' she said. 'She isn't one of the girls. She has a suite of rooms here and her fiancé is the son of a lord.'

So that put paid to my temptation to commit a mortal sin. And, like the virtuous man I was trying to be, I went and booked into a respectable hotel. But I couldn't get the girl's face out of my mind. I was sure I'd seen her somewhere before, but, for the life of me, I couldn't remember where.

Then one day, while reading *The Cork Examiner*, I read about a girl suffering terrible injuries in the house I used to frequent. All they knew about her was that her name was Katherine, and I wondered if she was the girl I'd admired. Then one evening I was talking to my intended. We were reminiscing about our pasts, me telling her about visiting you in Dublin, and all of a sudden I remembered going out on the tram to you and seeing this little girl. She had a face like an exquisite flower. So did Katherine, but she must have been nineteen or twenty and the child about twelve or thirteen. Flashes of memory are tantalising, I find. You

420

never know if they're imaginings or real. In any case I've only included this to fill out the letter.

Your next communication from me will be the wedding invitation.

All the best.

Brian

Danny's hand was shaking as he laid down the letter. He remembered the christening. There had been few at it. Lizzie, the midwife, and a couple of the women Aggie cleaned for.

She had no relation in the village except Father Clancy who baptised the child. He supposed there must have been godparents but he couldn't remember who they were. What he did remember was Aggie whispering to him, 'Katherine after her grannie, but to me she'll always be Angel'.

The shop was always busy on Saturday so he put the letter in his pocket and sliced bacon assuring his customers it wasn't salty. He packed brown-paper bags with fancy biscuits and, between times, listened to the latest news of the body that had been found in a hollow up in the hills.

'The poor unfortunate,' a woman said. 'I believe the face was ate off of him by rats and foxes and the crows had had his eyes.'

'Go way,' said another customer. And another wondered who he was.

'Some poor mother's son,' replied the woman who had described the devouring vermin. 'They say there wasn't an iota of anything to identify him,' she continued.

A man waiting for cigarettes wondered aloud if the dead man was connected with the other three killings.

Danny's mind was in a ferment. Was it possible that Angel and Katherine could be one and the same? It felt as if his brain was bubbling inside his head as question after question rose in it. If it was her, how had she finished up in Monto? Had she been driven on to the streets? If it *was* her, would she want to see him? Want him to see her?

He longed for closing time, to go upstairs and sit in his room. He toyed with the idea of ordering everyone out of the shop, getting in a cab and going to Jervis Street Hospital where Brian's article had said Katherine was.

When, eventually, he did go upstairs he drank so much whiskey on an empty stomach that he fell asleep and woke up several times during the night to be sick. Towards morning he woke again with a splitting head-ache and a deep feeling of despair, thinking of all the Katherines there must be in Dublin. Brian's letter had filled him full of false hopes: his friend had only ever seen Angel once and this Katherine had been found in Railway Street. In Monto. What would Angel be doing in such a place? But if he knew for sure that the tragic Katherine was Angel, he wouldn't care where she'd been or what she'd done if he could find her, rescue, mind and cherish her.

After several cups of tea he felt better, went to Mass and prayed for guidance. And knew he had to go and see Father Clancy. He went home, made a bit of toast, had several more cups of tea and felt more like himself. From the shop he took a bottle of Jameson's went out and got a cab to the retirement home.

The old priest was delighted to see him, and delighted

with the bottle of whiskey. Danny told him about Brian's letter and the newspaper article and the hopes it had raised in him. 'D'ye think it could be her, Father? Railway Street, and all that?'

He expected Father Clancy to dismiss his suggestions out of hand. But after pondering the questions for a while the priest said, 'Well, she was christened Katherine, and she was exceptionally beautiful. And it's possible that, even after such a long time, Brian never forgot her face. And, as for Monto, well, it might very well be where she finished up. She didn't have many choices, the poor child. Don't forget, we all failed her in her greatest need. I hope God will forgive me for the part I played in it. He may very well judge us more harshly than the unfortunate women in Monto. In any case, Danny, you'll have to go to Jervis Street and satisfy yourself. Otherwise you'll spend the rest of your life wondering if it was Angel, whereas if it's not it'll only be one more disappointment in your life.'

Danny took the priest's advice and the next afternoon went to the hospital, where he asked the porter if he could see the Reverend Mother. She wore the white robes of a nursing nun, and a black rosary suspended from her waist. The beads rattled as she came down the stairs.

'I read, Mother, that you have a patient who was badly burned, a girl who goes by the name of Katherine. I wondered if you would let me see her?'

She quizzed him thoroughly. Often with a severely injured patient, who appeared to have no family, voyeurs came wanting to gawp. When he had satisfied her of his genuine concern, she told him that, although Katherine was greatly improved, it wouldn't be advisable for her to

423

receive visitors yet. She suggested he come back towards the end of the week. Before they parted she said that, if Katherine was who he thought she was, he must be prepared for a shock. One side of her, from head to foot, was severely burned. 'I'll bear that in mind, Mother, and thank you very much.'

Never in his life had his emotions been in such turmoil as on the afternoon later that week when he approached the hospital. He desperately wanted the girl to be Angel, and yet another part of him hoped she wasn't. It was all very well to tell himself that no matter what she looked like he could accept it. But supposing his first reaction was one of revulsion? And, worse still, supposing Angel noticed it? That would be the cruellest blow. As he entered the hospital porch he was regretting having come. He toyed with the idea of turning away, telling himself that in time he could convince himself that the girl wasn't Angel. He would go on for the rest of his life believing that he was never meant to have Angel to cherish. But the gist of Father Clancy's words was forged in his brain. 'If you don't look on her and satisfy yourself, you'll spend the rest of your life wondering if it was.'

He would look on her. He had to. And, in any case, hadn't he loved her for years? A poor sort of love if he couldn't bear the pain of witnessing hers.

The Reverend Mother met him on the landing outside the ward. 'I was watching out for you. The terrible pain she's been suffering has diminished a little so we've cut down on the morphia. That means she's not in a constant state of drowsiness. She may be awake now. She must have been beautiful.'

'Oh, she was, Mother, the most beautiful girl in the world.'

Her eyes were closed. She was lying on her back. At first glance she reminded Danny of a baby in a closely knitted bonnet and one side of her face was perfect. A fringe of dark eyelashes rested on her pink and white skin, the tips curling. Then he saw that the bonnet was arranged in such a way that it reached down over her other cheek covering it completely.

'I told her you were coming. I didn't want to give her a shock. I told her your name, but she made no response.' The nun paused. Then she whispered, 'Is it her?'

Danny was so overcome he could only nod.

'Sit down, but don't stay too long and come into my office before you go.'

He sat at Angel's good side and softly spoke her name. 'Angel, it's me Danny.' His voice was hoarse with the effort he was making not to cry.

She opened the one eye and looked at him. 'How did you find me?'

'A bit in the paper, only I wasn't sure. They were calling you Katherine.'

'Don't cry, Danny. You'll make me cry and the bandages will be soaking wet. I'm that tired I want to sleep all the time.'

'Can I come to see you again?'

'If you like.' Then she shut her good eye. He waited for a while, then left to see the Reverend Mother.

'How did she receive you?'

'Hard to tell. We exchanged only a few words.'

'Will you visit again?'

'If she doesn't object, as often as I can. I love her. I've

425

loved her since she was a child. But only from a distance. I don't think she was aware of my existence, except as the man she worked for.'

'Don't forget, you've seen her today at her best. One side of her face is so severely burned it will be grotesque to look at.'

'Always?'

'The angry red will pale in time but the puckered skin will never improve. We hope the sight of the eye won't be affected but the eyelid was burned. At one time we thought she had brain damage, that it might affect her walking. But we've had her out of bed and, thank God, it hasn't.'

'How long will she be in hospital?'

'At least another six weeks.'

'And then what?'

'She'll be discharged. If she's nowhere to go we'll find a place for her for the time being.'

'This is a private room?'

'It is. We have a few. We thought she'd die soon after admission. And when she didn't, thanks be to God, we decided to leave her here for her privacy and the sake of the other patients – she was in terrible agony and made a lot of noise despite the drugs.'

'Who's paying for it?'

'In an emergency our funds can cover a deserving case.'

'I'll pay, and for the previous weeks. And, if things go the way I hope, maybe I could engage it for longer than the six weeks?'

'Danny,' the nun said. 'I think I know what you're planning. But, remember, you haven't seen Angel without her bandages. For a lay person it's a horrendous sight. You'll feel revulsion and then an overwhelming sense of pity. Pity doesn't often last the course.'

'Well, of course I'll feel pity. Wouldn't you pity any maimed creature? But I've loved Angel for years and years. Whatever arrangement we reach, or she accepts, will have nothing to do with pity.'

'I only wanted to warn you. You're a great man. I'll pray that God will grant Angel the wisdom to recognise that.'

Each day Angel slept less, grew stronger and thought more. On the next of Danny's visits she asked about her mother. He was sitting at her bad side. He lifted the brown, wrinkled, claw-like hand, stroked it, and told her that Aggie was dead – but not that she had died in the asylum or had lost her mind for months beforehand. 'Pneumonia, very peaceful. We gave her a grand funeral.'

Angel didn't cry. When she spoke it was to say, 'I think I knew. I think I may have dreamed she was dead. In a way I was glad. I knew she was at peace. Now I know for sure and I'm still glad.'

After he left she thought that now her mother would never need to know about Johnny Quinn and the rape, or the abortion, need never blame herself for not being able to keep her daughter at home in the village. Neither would she see her disfigured face. For the first time since the accident Angel smiled then winced with pain as the burnt side of her face contracted. The wiles and ways, my poor mother. A world of woe was all I ever had. Thinking about the misfortunes that had befallen her, she was consumed with a great anger for those who had inflicted them on her. Johnny Quinn, who had raped and nearly killed her, who had left her carrying his child – an innocent child, who hadn't asked to be got, or scraped

427

out of her. Once she had likened Johnny to a beautiful creature, the black panther. Now she knew that no animal would cause such deliberate suffering: only human beings were capable of that.

Then there was Mrs McEvoy, all sweetness, who had inveigled her into the brothel to please Lord Brightwell and make money. And Patrick, gorgeous Patrick, who had lavished her with gifts – gifts that, in his position, had cost him not a thought. But no, she corrected herself, she mustn't include Patrick among those who had harmed her. He had been sweet and kind, had cared about her welfare, her future. And there had been Sean, to whom she had given herself. Sean, whom she had adored. Sean, who had painted the picture of their life in Ballyvaughan. And then robbed her. She knew that now because why else had he cleared out. The villagers who had run her out, the hatred Miss Heffernan had felt towards her. And Mrs McEvoy: she remembered the woman's hand between her shoulders, pushing her down the stairs. She'd been robbed, raped and finally disfigured for life. And why? She couldn't remember committing a cruel act in her life.

Except for the abortion. And look how easy life was for other people. Mona, for instance. All the other girls in the dance halls who had got engaged, married. She hated God, she hated Danny, visiting her as if he was one of the St Vincent de Paul. She cried herself to sleep.

The next day she sat in a chair for a couple of hours, her anger gone. She remembered Bridie and all her kindness. And she remembered Tommy Maguire, the poor eejit, wanting to take her to India, writing to her for years, sending the money for her to save. He was a good man. He loved her and asked for nothing in return.

Again she made her face ache remembering the night they'd got engaged with the ring from the penny bazaar.

My life, she told herself, wasn't all woe. I saw the other days, too, and even when I was pregnant there were those who tried to help – Father Clancy's cousin, prepared to take her into the private home, Mrs Gorman, who had given her money, and the woman with the arthritis. Danny had given her fifty pounds. The nuns and staff in here had nursed her, put up with her tantrums. She had a lot to be grateful for. There were those she'd never forgive, Sean most of all, but in time she'd put them out of her mind.

During the many weeks he visited, Danny told her of the happenings in the village, but never all at once so as not to burden her with too much sorrow. In time she learned about the shooting of Father Brennan, of Johnny Quinn and the Weasel. At another visit he told her of the unidentified man who had been found in the hollow grave. She knew without a doubt who he was – she remembered Bridie telling her that Tommy's regiment was being disbanded.

Tommy had got to hear of how she had been mistreated and had avenged her – wrongly in the case of poor Father Brennan. That had been the result of Miss Heffernan's malicious gossip, which the Weasel had probably whispered in Tommy's ear. She hoped Johnny Quinn had had time to feel the paralysis of fear she had felt when he almost strangled her.

She said nothing of this to Danny. Neither did she tell him of her past. But as the days went by she began to look forward to his visits, enjoyed being with someone she had known for so long, who could talk about her mother and make both of them laugh, remembering Aggie's idiosyncrasies.

Recently Danny had spoken of when she would be discharged. He had asked what plans, if any, she had. She had shaken her head, unable to speak for fear of breaking down. She lived in dread of the day when she'd have to face the world without her mask of bandages.

'You ought to give it some thought. I could help if it was money that was worrying you.'

'I'll manage,' she said.

Day after day Angel worried about what was ahead of her. Who would employ her with the face she'd be showing them? Who'd let her a room with a face that would frighten the crows? She had an idea what it would look like. The nuns had been preparing her: they had showed her the healed flesh on her breast, part of her belly and her arm. It was red, like uncooked meat, but creased and crumpled, like an overdone rasher. Tactfully they'd explained that one side of her face would be the same, although, 'In time,' the senior sister had said, 'the redness will fade slightly but not the bunched scarring.'

Danny had been given the same information. On the off-chance that she might accept his proposal of marriage, he had made enquiries about selling the shop.

On the night before the bandages were to come off she decided that she would borrow money from Danny and go to England. She was too young and felt too well in herself to be buried alive in an institution. In England, so she'd been led to believe, people were more distant than in Ireland. She'd be less likely to have there what she'd get here: 'God help you, love, were you in a fire? I had a friend the same thing happened to.' And in England, she guessed that there must be hundreds, thousands, though mostly men, who'd been badly burned in the war. She wouldn't seem such a freak. Even so, she dreaded being in a country where she knew no one. Here, Danny would always be her friend. She'd grown so used to him in the last weeks. Danny, the boss whom she and Mona used to make a jeer of, imagining him in his big boot and underclothes. Now she never noticed his gammy leg. It was his kind eyes, his lovely smile and ways that she noticed.

Danny got the time wrong of when the bandages were supposed to come off. He had planned to be there when it happened to comfort Angel. Instead he arrived just after they had been removed by the consultant on his ward round. Angel was sitting up in bed. When she saw him she called, in a voice hoarse with anger, 'Well, now that you're here you might as well come in and gawk.'

He walked slowly towards her, his eyes never leaving her face and her eyes watching the expression in his. As he came closer she saw the terror, the revulsion in them. Then they were just Danny's brown eyes. He bent and, with a finger, traced the scars all over her cheek, over her damaged eyelid, leaned down and kissed the crumpled, flaming red skin. She caught hold of his hand, held it tightly and cried.

'Will you marry me?' he asked. 'I'd never take you near the village. We can go anywhere you like to live. Angel, I've loved you for years. I always will. We'll be happy together, I know we will. I've already made plans to sell up. We can live anywhere you like, anywhere. We don't have to stay in Ireland. I love you, Angel.'

He loves me, Angel thought. He's always loved me and I never gave him a thought. I'm not in love with him, I probably never will love him. But he makes me

431

feel happy and secure. She whispered, 'Do you really mean it, Danny?'

'I've wanted to marry you for years.'

'Oh, Danny, Danny.' She leaned her head against his chest and cried with gratitude, relief and happiness. 'Oh I will, I will. I'll marry you, Danny.'

He touched her scarred face, kissed its rough creases, and cried with her. 'We'll be grand, Angel. You'll see, we'll be grand.'

His fingers moved to her scalp and he touched the newly grown tendrils of golden hair. 'I'll love you for the rest of my life.'

Afterword

Danny was visiting Angel in the nursing home where she had gone to convalesce. It was in a remote part of Ireland, a large house once owned by a wealthy family. The gardens were beautiful. Flowers grew in profusion; there were rose-draped pergolas, wide curved beds of perennials, a blaze of colour, mature trees, stretches of lawn, ornamental lakes, a maze and a gazebo. There was also a view of a mountain range that changed colour according to the weather and time of day.

Expert medical staff came from Dublin regularly to check their patient's progress. The rooms were spacious, the bedrooms well appointed, there was an excellent library and delicious food. In such surroundings Angel recovered her physical health. Gradually she was becoming reconciled to her disfigurement, her morale boosted by Danny's devotion and by her skin specialist, who told her that although the scarred side of her face would never recover its smoothness or suppleness, the colour would become less lurid. He recommended a theatrical makeup and told her to buy hats with veils.

On the day Danny came to tell her that the shop was sold she watched him approach the house, and decided against a veil. She told him, 'I think those hats and fecky veils draw more attention rather than less. People can like me or lump me. When I'm out in the street again, sure they'll all be strangers anyway. You love me as I am, and isn't that enough?'

That was the day he had been later than usual arriving and a terrible thought had entered her mind. Maybe he had tired of her; regretted having asked her to marry him. And suddenly it came to her that she had fallen in love with him. It wasn't because he offered her security. Or that she had been able to confide in him all that had happened to her.

She watched him limping the last few yards to the door, and her heart beat faster. When he came into the room she hurried to him, put her arms round him, crushing the flowers he had brought her, and kissed his lips for the first time. 'Danny, I love you. Really and truly. I suppose I've known it for a while. It was only today, though, because you were later than usual and my heart went all flippity-flop when I saw you that I knew for sure that I'm head over heels in love with you.' She kissed him again. He dropped the bouquet and kissed her back until she thought that if he didn't let her up for air she'd suffocate.

Then he let her go and asked, 'Are you sure?'

'Certain.'

'I hope you don't, but if you changed your mind I wouldn't hold it against you. I'd mind and cherish you. Take you to the ends of the earth. I'd—'

'Ah, for God's sake, Danny, will ye shut up? I'm a woman, not a child, not a pet. I'm a woman, and I want you for my man. D'ye understand what I'm saying? I want to be your wife, lie with you. My face is disfigured and you've a lame leg, but the rest of us is whole and healthy. We could have a family.'

Tears ran down his face and, half-blinded by them, he gazed at her with adoration.

'I can see,' she said, 'that sometimes I'll have to be the boss, so where and when will we get married?'

'That's up to you,' he said, drying his eyes.

'Then why not here? There's a chapel. Father Clancy's not too frail or doddery to perform the ceremony. Sister Quinlan can be bridesmaid and Brian Nolan your best man. Last week the doctor said I'd be well enough to leave in a month. You can come down every weekend. We'll stay in the local hotel. Get me used to the outside world again. What d'ye say to that?'

'You're the boss.'

Angel rejected all the faraway places. 'One day I'll want to see Ireland again, put flowers on my mother's grave, walk down Grafton Street, drink coffee in Bewley's. And I don't want thousands of miles to travel before I can.'

They settled for Wales. Danny bought a high-class provision shop in Cardiff, very similar to the one in the village. A sign-writer came to replace the previous owner's name with Danny's. He and Angel lived over the shop. She took to Cardiff and the Welsh people, who were warm and friendly. There were theatres and picture-houses, and high-class drapers like Brown Thomas where she bought clothes and hats.

Father Clancy wrote regularly. Brian Nolan and his wife visited. They were part of the parish and made many friends. She often thought about her mother and the pity it was that Aggie hadn't lived to see her married to Danny. But she consoled herself that in heaven where she surely was she'd know. She had Masses said for Aggie and also for Bridie, wherever she was. Occasionally she had one said for Patrick, remembering his kindness.

Five years after their marriage Angel gave birth to a son. Danny was delirious with joy, and sometimes got on Angel's nerves with his fussing over her. As was the custom then, the baby was baptised, Daniel Brian Patrick, before Angel's ten days in bed ended. Brian and his wife were godparents.

Once Angel was up and about the christening party was held. A lot of their Welsh friends were Murphys, O'Briens, Crowleys, McCarthys and O'Sullivans, descendants of the Irish who had come to Wales at the time of the Famine. They had brought with them their music, songs and dances, and passed them down the generations.

'It's like being at home,' said Danny, listening to the music and singing, watching the reels, jigs and sets.

'A bloody sight better,' said Brian. 'At home, nowadays, nothing will stick on their chests, only what's coming out of America. If we're not careful we'll lose all our traditions.'

Daniel Brian Patrick was at the party, being passed around and admired, the blessings of God being called down on him. Some likened him to Angel, some to his father. The very old women dismissed both descriptions and declared, 'The child, God bless and spare him, is like himself.'

When the guests had left, and Danny and Angel were getting ready for bed, he thanked her for the baby and kissed her. She pushed him away and said, playfully, 'It wasn't an Immaculate Conception.'

'No,' he said in his shy way, 'it was not.'

'I'm surprised at you,' said Angel, watching him from

the bed as he emptied his pockets on to the bedside locker. 'I thought it was the first thing you'd have done after the baby was born.'

'What did I not do?'

'You forgot the sign-writer.'

'The sign-writer?' He looked puzzled.

'I think you're drunk.'

'I am a bit,' he admitted.

'The name,' Angel said. 'The name over the shop, it'll have to be changed.'

'The name. Of course. Imagine me forgetting that. But first thing in the morning I'll have it put right. Daniel Connolly and Son. My father'll be dancing a jig in heaven this minute. Daniel Connolly and Son.' He fell asleep repeating it.

All Orion/Phoenix titles are available at your local bookshop or from the following address:

Mail Order Department
Littlehampton Book Services
FREEPOST BR535
Worthing, West Sussex, BN13 3BR
telephone 01903 828503, *facsimile* 01903 828802
e-mail MailOrders@lbsltd.co.uk
(Please ensure that you include full postal address details)

Payment can be made either by credit/debit card (Visa, Mastercard, Access and Switch accepted) or by sending a £ Sterling cheque or postal order made payable to *Littlehampton Book Services*.
DO NOT SEND CASH OR CURRENCY.

Please add the following to cover postage and packing

UK and BFPO:
£1.50 for the first book, and 50p for each additional book to a maximum of £3.50

Overseas and Eire:
£2.50 for the first book plus £1.00 for the second book and 50p for each additional book ordered

---

BLOCK CAPITALS PLEASE

name of cardholder ....

address of cardholder ....

postcode ....

delivery address
(if different from cardholder)
....
....
....
....

postcode ....

☐ I enclose my remittance for £............................

☐ please debit my Mastercard/Visa/Access/Switch (delete as appropriate)

card number ☐☐☐☐☐☐☐☐☐☐☐☐☐☐☐☐

expiry date ☐☐☐☐ Switch issue no. ☐☐

signature ....

prices and availability are subject to change without notice